D0899003

The Boggart

A free, open access companion volume, *The Boggart Sourcebook: Texts and Memories for the Study of the British Supernatural*, curated and edited by Simon Young is also available from University of Exeter Press:

https://doi.org/10.47788/QXUA4856

In three corpora, it contains the raw materials that have informed the writing of *The Boggart*.

Exeter New Approaches to Legend, Folklore and Popular Belief

Series Editors:
Simon Young, University of Virginia (CET, Siena) and
Davide Ermacora, University of Turin

Exeter New Approaches to Legend, Folklore and Popular Belief provides a venue for growing scholarly interest in folklore narratives, supernatural belief systems and the communities that sustain them. Global in scope, the series encompasses milieus ranging from ancient to contemporary times and encourages empirically grounded, source-rich studies. The editors favour the broad multidisciplinary approach that has characterized the study of folklore and the supernatural, and which brings together insights from historians, folklorists, anthropologists and many other branches of the humanities and social sciences.

The Boggart

Folklore, History, Place-names and Dialect

SIMON YOUNG

UNIVERSITY
of
EXETER
PRESS

First published in 2022 by
University of Exeter Press
Reed Hall, Streatham Drive
Exeter EX4 4QR, UK

www.exeterpress.co.uk

A CIP catalogue record for this book is available from the British Library.

ISBN: 978-1-905816-90-3 (Hbk)
ISBN: 978-1-905816-91-0 (ePub)
ISBN: 978-1-905816-92-7 (PDF)

https://doi.org/10.47788/KZLH9484

Front cover: a boggart throws its head after
an escaping pedestrian (Bowker, *Goblin Tales*, 136).

Typeset in Perpetua 11½ point on 14 point by
Palimpsest Book Production Ltd, Falkirk, Stirlingshire

'Boggarts!' the antiquary sneer't. '... When shall we hear the end of these foolish superstitions?'

'When fancy's dyead, an' imagination buried undher t' brass yeps we keepen pilin up o through England ... Th' end o' superstition 'll be th' beginnin o' summat a dyel wur.'

John Trafford Clegg, Works

Nineteenth-Century Boggartdom

Contents

Abbreviations

BC: Boggart Census (online PDF, see Preface)
BN: Boggart Names (online PDF, see Preface)
Ch: Cheshire
De: Derbyshire
ERY: East Riding of Yorkshire
La: Lancashire
Li: Lincolnshire
OCR: Optical character recognition
OED: *Oxford English Dictionary*
OSK: Six-inch Ordnance Survey Map of Kent
OSLa: Six-inch Ordnance Survey Map of Lancashire
OSMi: Six-inch Ordnance Survey Map of Middlesex
OSSur: Six-inch Ordnance Survey Map of Surrey
OSWe: Six-inch Ordnance Survey Map of Westmorland
OSY: Six-inch Ordnance Survey Map of Yorkshire
WRY: West Riding of Yorkshire

Illustrations and Maps

Acknowledgements

In two cases, passages in this book have been published before. About two thirds of Chapter 2 appeared in the *Transactions of the Yorkshire Dialect Society*, 2018: the principal map shown there and some of the findings have been revised for this volume. About half of the 'Boggart A–Z' (the Appendix) appeared in *Folk Life* in 2018. I am extremely grateful to the editors of these two journals for permission to republish, not least as relatively little time has passed since the articles in question first came out. I am also grateful to Forteana Exchange, the Lancashire Place Name Survey, Helmshore History Society, Minorvictorianwriters.org.uk, and the Talking Folklore group for many different references. A number of editors and writers helped me with the Boggart Census. I would like to thank David Sutton at *Fortean Times*, Dee Dee Chainey and Willow Winsham at *Folklore Thursday*, and journalists on the *Huddersfield Examiner*, the *Lancashire Post*, the *Lancashire Telegraph*, the *Manchester Evening News*, and the *Saddleworth Independent*. It goes without saying that my greatest debt here is to the 1,100 people, mostly from the Northwest, who sent boggart emails, boggart letters, boggart Facebook comments, or who allowed themselves to be interviewed by a complete stranger.

I have relied on a large network of colleagues, academic and otherwise, who have helped me by obtaining scans and by advising me on individual points. These include Joan Beal, Valentina Bettin, Francesca Bihet, John Billingsley, David Britain, Paul Cavill, David Clarke, Alan Cleaver, Mike Dash, Gerry Desmond (Cork Library), John Duff, Holly Elsdon, Richard Green, David Hawkins, Katja Hrobat, Richard G. Jefferson, Richard Green, Peter Harding, David Haslam, David Hawkins, Ceri Houlbrook, Melanie James, Najla Kay (map-maker), Michael Kennedy, Roberto Labanti, Katherine Langrish, Nigel Massen, Silvia Meggiolaro, Alan McEwen, Stephen Miller, Lee Nicholson, Zach Nowak, Niall O'Donnell, Caroline Oates, Georgina Ormrod, Cristina Paravano, David Pattern, Sofia Adele Frances Polcri, Louise Sylvester, Ray Sutcliffe, Roy Vickery, Steven Waterhouse, Carol Yoon, Emily Young (relation), Lea Young (relation), and Francis Young (no relation). I am especially in the debt of Simon Baker, Davide Ermacora, Lucy Evans, Jeremy Harte, Jessica Hemming, Ron James, Lynda Taylor, John Widdowson, and Chris Woodyard who commented on earlier drafts of this book; in some cases, several earlier drafts ... I am much obliged, too, to my father, who introduced me to boggarts by taking my brother and me to the Boggart Stones at Widdop in around 1980 (and failing to tell us what a boggart was!) and who has sent, in the last years, scores of boggart volumes to me in Italy. I dedicate this book to my eldest daughter, Lisi, 'the midnight boggart', one of the sunlit joys of my life.

Preface

In this book I attempt to recreate the boggart-lore of Victorian and Edwardian times. What was a boggart (Chapter 1)? When and why did the word 'boggart' start to be used (Chapter 2)? In what parts of Britain did boggart beliefs feature in the 1800s (Chapter 3)? Where were boggarts to be found in the landscape (Chapter 4)? How were boggart tales passed on (Chapter 5)? How did nineteenth- and early twentieth-century communities react to boggart hauntings (Chapter 6)? How did boggart beliefs die away (Chapter 7)? And how have folklorists and fiction writers misreported popular beliefs about boggarts (Chapter 8)? The chapters are clearly about local and regional themes but the questions behind them are found much more widely. Here, after all, are matters of etymology, of distribution, of classification, of imagination and the environment, of the transmission of tradition, of the psychology and sociology of haunting, and of language and folklore. Here are topics that recur again and again in the study of the supernatural.

Conventions

The word 'boggart' is spelled in many different ways in our sources: Joseph Wright alone has in his *Dialect Dictionary* 'boggard', 'boggat', 'bogard', 'boggerd', 'bugart', and 'buggard',[1] to which I can add 'baggard', 'bogerd', 'boggert', and 'buggart'.[2] I have consistently used 'boggart', save in quotations. 'Boggart' is the preferred form in Lancashire, and, in as much as the boggart had a country-wide profile, nationally, its only literary rival, particularly in some older and some Yorkshire sources, was 'boggard'.[3] I have, for similar

---

1. Wright, *Dialect Dictionary*, I, 326.
2. Elder (ed.), *Word Books*, 68 for 'baggard'; Heathcote, 'History', 17 for 'bogerd'; Sweeney, 'Dumber' for 'boggert'; and Lahee, *Betty*, 6, for 'buggart'.
3. See, e.g., Smith, *Old Yorkshire*, 11; Carr, *The Dialect*, 40. Note the *OED* uses the form 'boggard' instead of 'boggart' perhaps because 'boggard' is more common in older sources, see further, Chapter 2.

reasons, preferred 'bogie' (not 'bogey'), 'boggle' (not 'bogle', the usual Scots spelling), and 'dobbie' (not 'dobey'). There are many quotations in the following pages from the dialects of Cheshire, Cumberland, Derbyshire, Lancashire, Lincolnshire, Westmorland, Yorkshire, and from Scots. In cases with difficult dialect words, translations are given in square brackets—'for the benefit', as Charlotte Burne had it, 'of the unlearned!'.[4]

Throughout the book I use the pre-1974 English counties (including the three Ridings of Yorkshire). This makes sense because these are the counties described in our sources; because place-name studies (an important part of the present volume) refer to these boundaries; and because the pre-1974 counties correspond much better to supernatural terminology and belief than the authorities that replaced them in 1975. I have used the phrase 'Boggartdom' to refer to the lands where the boggart was known, feared, and sometimes celebrated.[5] I also refer frequently to 'the Northwest' of England for what might be called—as a Yorkshireman I write this with distaste—'a greater Lancashire': Lancashire (including what is today south Cumbria, or 'Lancashire beyond the Sands'),[6] northern Derbyshire, northern Cheshire, and much of the West Riding.

In writing this book I created three corpora and I offer two of these and part of a third in a single free online PDF which can also be bought as a physical book: *The Boggart Sourcebook*. The three corpora are (i) 'Boggart Ephemera' (approx. 40,000 words): a selection of boggart comments from newspapers, and boggart broadsides and rare nineteenth-century books and articles; (ii) 'Boggart Names' (abbreviation BN) runs to some 15,000 words and includes a list of boggart place-names and boggart personal names (a term explained pp. 17–18); and (iii) The 'Boggart Census' (abbreviation BC) is, meanwhile, some 80,000 words of folklore memories (collected in 2019) and is broken down by county. The *Sourcebook* may be accessed here: https://doi.org/10.47788/QXUA4856

In references, I have followed a version of the Oxford style, providing a full bibliography, and giving abbreviations in footnotes. However, many of the sources come from anonymous newspaper articles and this has created a number of problems. In these cases, rather than have tens of articles written by 'Anon.' with all the attendant confusion that this would cause, I have used the title of the article as the author: e.g. 'A Ghost Story', *Sheffield Independent* (26 Jan 1839), 6, is filed under 'A Ghost Story' in the Bibliography rather

4. *Shropshire*, I, 47.
5. Inspired by Widdowson, 'Bogeyman', 111; and 'bogydom' in the *OED*.
6. Evans, *Lost Lancashire*.

than under 'Anon., "A Ghost Story'". In the footnotes I have, naturally, given just abbreviated titles. However, as many of the newspaper titles are similar—eight titles, for instance, begin with the words 'A Ghost'—I have often included the year in brackets in the notes. In a very few cases I have also had to include the day and month. The notes are slightly longer than they would otherwise be, but there is at least no ambiguity in referring back to the Bibliography.

Controversies (Folklore and Otherwise)

Other writing conventions depend more on folklore theory, or rather my interpretation of the same. There is, firstly, the question of belief. Anyone working on the supernatural will frequently encounter scholarly protestations that there is no supernatural reality. Indeed, at the back of much academic writing on the supernatural (particularly historical writing) is the 'Whiggish' assumption that 'superstition' evaporates in the face of Reformation, reason, and education.[7] The same erroneous assumption is found in many Victorian writers on the subject.[8] Not only is this point of view misguided, it is not even applied uniformly. Some types of supernatural belief are judged indulgently by academic writers (e.g. the Dalai Lama or Sufisim); some politely (most major world religions); and some are treated with undisguised hostility (e.g. evangelical Christianity or modern fairy belief).[9] No scholar when writing about, say, the sociology of Islam would take time out to deny the revelations given by Mohammad. Yet the traditional supernatural beliefs of European populations seem to be deserving of infinite derision. Throughout this work I have, while taking account of the many nineteenth-century sceptics, followed Minor White Latham's advice and treated the boggart and its kin 'according to the popular belief of the period, as real and living characters'.[10] This is not only a historically sound position; it also extends a basic courtesy to those who believed, or to those who *sometimes* believed, in boggarts.

---

7. An influential example of this is Thomas, *Religion and the Decline of Magic*; useful counter arguments in Walsham, 'The Reformation'; Josephson-Storm, *The Myth*; and Landy and Saler, *The Re-Enchantment*. See also Hunter, *The Decline*.

8. See, e.g., Kerr, 'Marriage and Morals' (1892): 'the advent of railways and the spread of education, now free, has put an effectual spoke in the "boggart's" wheel'.

9. These different gradations of approval depend not on the shared properties of similar belief systems, but on the shared prejudices of academics.

10. Latham, *Fairies*, 111, was applying this to fairies.

There is too the question of general methodology. Folklorists have often been criticized for partaking in a search for origins. The attempt to regain a pristine folklore past characterized many early studies of the supernatural in Britain, particularly in the nineteenth century: 'Not every scrap of folklore could be traced back to its murky origins in nature-worship and sacrificial cults and pagan pantheons, but where the evidence looked promising the collectors happily supplied the missing connections.'[11] A characteristic of folklore studies more generally, and one that has had more staying power, has been the determination to look at questions comparatively, examining one facet of folk life in apparently unconnected settings. Alan Dundes went so far as to claim that 'folklore has steadfastly continued to consider [comparativism] as its *sine qua non* among competing methodologies'.[12] Comparative work remains an ideal for many, although one that demands extreme rigour to be done well.[13]

I will investigate, in what follows, the origins of the boggart, by way of background for a study of the mid to late 1800s and the early 1900s. I will also include references to different belief systems (from Britain and abroad) when they can give us insights into supernatural life in nineteenth-century England; or, more typically, an insight into how we can best study these matters. However, the aim of this book is neither comparative nor 'retrospective'.[14] I want, rather, to reconstitute beliefs for one place (Boggartdom) and for one period (1838–1914) using contemporary or near-contemporary documents. The history and any wider 'meaning' of these beliefs are peripheral matters compared to the central task of writing a supernatural ethnography. That supernatural world has been forgotten. It can, with diligence, be reclaimed, at least in outline.

A final point relevant to the study of the boggart is that since the 1990s, a profound and often sensible pessimism has grown about the very notion of supernatural categories. Supporters of this position would argue that it makes no sense to look at the supernatural through vague and liquid terms like 'boggart'.[15] This is a huge subject. I would just make here a modest observation. Supernatural creatures primarily exist as ideas in the brain, and ideas—despite their potential flexibility—have a consistency of their own and can be classified. Take three supernatural creatures common in British legend,

---

11. Dorson, *Folklorists*, 326.

12. Dundes, *Folklore Matters*, 57.

13. Lincoln, *Apples*, 1–33.

14. Heide and Bek-Pedersen, *New Focus*, for temporally long studies of folklore continuity.

15. Jakobsson, 'The Taxonomy'; Löfstedt, 'Define'; Ostling and Forest, 'Goblins', 547: 'the study of such preternatural beings is properly the study of rhetorical patterns'.

all of which appear in British memorates, British place-names and British legends: angels, demons, and mermaids. These are heavily codified 'ideas' and there is little risk of confusion between them. The three entities remind us that ideas are flexible, but not to the point where terms become useless. Demons do not bring in the harvest for farmers, mermaids do not play tricks on country roads, angels do not change babies in the cot … The supernatural *was* loosely classified in folk taxonomies. We have, though, 'tendencies' rather than categories.

I: Situating the Boggart

'The Boggart!' whispered Mr. Clement, hoarsely, casting an appre-
hensive glance about him for an instant … 'what is the Boggart?'

Payne, *Clyffards*, I, 17.

Figure 1: 'The Pillion Lady' (Bowker, *Goblin Tales*, 79).

CHAPTER ONE

Boggart Definitions and Sources

Sam and the Boggart

The story takes place some two hundred years ago on the wild edges of a tiny Lancashire village. A young boy, Sam, has been compelled to attend a Methodist service. Bored, he and other children sneak out into the night-time fields, and there run around, trying to escape the hum of prayers. In this thrilling dash, Sam sees one of his friends, Bill, tearing ahead of him in the dark. Sam trots up shouting, but strangely, Bill does not react. Sam pushes forwards and overtakes his friend, looking back in triumph. It is, however, not Bill. The 'boy' has a dreadful, decayed face. Terrified, Sam sprints away. 'I now ran in earnest to get rid of him; but on looking back, saw he was within a few yards of my heels.' Through the dark fields the pursuit continued between this fragment of nightmare and the child.

The boggart, for so monsters like this were known in Lancashire in the nineteenth century, was now almost upon Sam, its feet sweeping effortlessly over the ground: 'I know not how, but at an incredibly swift pace'. The hunt ended only when Sam came within sight of the chapel and heard the sound of prayer. Perhaps, like many supernatural beings, Sam's pursuer could not abide Christian words and symbols; or perhaps the boggart had come to the edge of its territory—such beings were often said to have their own 'patches'. The terrified boy had, in any case, escaped. Chastened by his ordeal, Sam sneaked into the building—breathing, we might imagine, rather heavily—and found himself kneeling in prayer next to the real Bill. Indeed, the adult Sam, writing some twenty years after his brush with the impossible, recalled that, having knelt in chapel, he had 'prayed more really in earnest' than 'during a long time before'.[1]

The present monograph is a study of boggarts in the nineteenth and early twentieth centuries. The word 'boggart' turns up in sources dating back to

---

1. This chase was an early episode in the life of Samuel Bamford, Lancashire radical and author, *Passages*, I, 114–17.

the 1500s, but the vast bulk of material for boggarts emerged in the mid to late 1800s and the early 1900s in Lancashire, Sam's encounter among them. In fact, looking at how much material relates to boggarts from that period— hundreds of thousands of words—and how little secondary literature has been written, it would be fair to call the boggart Britain's most understudied supernatural being. I have attempted, in this volume, to cover all boggart sources from Tudor asides to modern boggart memories. But I am primarily interested in the mid-nineteenth century to the early 1900s; from approxi- mately the coronation of Queen Victoria (1838) to the outbreak of the First World War (1914). This is, after all, the period for which we have the most evidence and it was a time when beliefs in or about boggarts were demon- strably strong in places.

But What Is a Boggart?

Boggart stories often begin or end with someone racing through the dark, much as Sam ran to the chapel. Rather than kneeling in prayer, the terrified man or woman crashes through the door to announce to a tavern full of friends or to their family that they have encountered 'a boggart': 'do let me in, I've sin a boggart!'[2] What did those listening envisage when they heard these two syllables? Did those sitting around the fire imagine something whose likeness was well established? The lineaments of a demon or an angel, for instance, were known to all living in nineteenth-century Britain. These beings appeared in images, in story books, on stained-glassed windows and, often, in copies of the Bible. A ghost, on the other hand, was vaguer. Typically, in the 1800s the ghost wore a death shroud and carried a clinking chain, but these accou- trements were optional and descriptions varied greatly. There are then more general words like 'spirit' or 'apparition'. These would be imagined freely, according to the fears and prejudices of the listener—the supernatural à la carte. How precise was the word 'boggart'?

The simplest way to understand the meaning of 'boggart' in Victorian and Edwardian times is to list all early definitions from glossaries and dialect lists from the areas where the word was used. With this approach there is the great advantage that writers knew local usage. These were not metropolitan authors, hundreds of miles away, making assumptions based on, say, philology or their latest readings in German folklore. I know of twenty-seven such texts (which give the word 'boggart' with a supernatural sense), dating from 1790 to 1940,

---

2. BC, Milnrow 6 (La).

with twenty-three of the twenty-seven clustering in the period 1860–1900.[3] Twenty-five are from the Northwest of England; one is from Cleveland and another from Lincolnshire.[4] Of course, often these glossaries and lists have more than one definition and in these cases all definitions have been counted.

What then is the boggart according to regional writers who were familiar with the word? The definitions can be fully examined in note 3. However, there is no question that the most popular in these works was 'ghosts'—with thirteen occurrences. 'Ghost' referred, in the period in which these glossaries were written, as it does in the 2020s, to the undead. After that we have 'hobgoblin' with six—it should perhaps be taken together with 'goblin' (three occurrences). There are four 'bugbears' and 'spectres'. There are also 'apparitions' and 'spirits', both of which appear three times. There is one 'sprite'. There are then a number of more elaborate definitions that are used just once, such as 'Old Bogy', 'a subject for a scare', 'something hideous', 'evil spirits

3. A.W., *The Westmorland Dialect* (1790), unnumbered final glossary, 'BOGGART: a spirit, a spectre'; Wilbraham, *An Attempt*, 17 'a bug-bear or scarecrow', for Cheshire; Carr, *Horae* (1824), 60 for Craven, 'Boggard, A goblin'; Bamford, *The Dialect*, 159, for south Lancashire, 'Boggart, a spirit, an apparition' (see also Bobbin, *Lancashire Dialect*, from which this draws); Robinson, *The Dialect* (1862), 254: 'BOGGARD. A goblin, generally supposed to be of a sable complexion'; Bamford, *Homely Rhymes* (glossary from) (1864), for Lancashire, 246, 'boggart, a ghost'; Linton, *Lake* (1864), 297, for 'Lancashire beyond the Sands': 'Boggart, and Bogie, and Bogle, ghosts, and spectres, and evil spirits made visible'; Atkinson, *A Glossary* (1868), 56 for Cleveland: 'Boggart, sb. A hobgoblin, a sprite'; Morris, *Glossary* (1869), 11 for Furness, 'Boggert – a ghost'; Peacock and Atkinson, *A Glossary* (1869), 10 for Lonsdale, 'BOGGART, n. an apparition, a hobgoblin'; Wilkinson, 'Dialect', 56 (1874–1881), for Burnley 'Boggart ... a ghost'; Nodal and Milner, *A Glossary*, 1875 for Lancashire 'BOGGART/BUGGART, sb. a spirit, a ghost'; Robinson, *A Glossary* (1876), 12, for mid-Yorkshire 'a hobgoblin'; Peacock, *A Glossary* (1877), 31 for Manley 'BOGGART, BOGGLE, BOGIE. Something of an unearthly nature that is terrible to come in contact with; a bugbear'; 'Staffordshire Dialect and Folk-lore' (1877), 'Boggart. A Hobgoblin. Something hideous'; Easther and Lees, *A Glossary* (1883), 13 for Almondbury 'Boggard, a ghost'; Holland, *A Glossary* (1886), 35 BOGGART, s. 'a ghost or a hobgoblin' for Cheshire (1886); Cudworth, *Rambles* (1886), 232 for Horton, in the glossary 'boggard, a subject for scare'; 'Buggart: a ghost, spectre, hobgoblin', Darlington, *The Folk-speech*, 132 for southern Cheshire (1887); 'Yorkshire Dialects' (1888), 15 for Yorkshire, 'Boggard, ghost'; Addy, *A Glossary* (1888), 21, for Sheffield 'BOGGARD, sb. a ghost, apparition'; 'Dictionary of the Lancashire Dialect' (1891) for Manchester, 'Boggart (ghost)'; Dyer, *Dialect* (1891), 70 for West Riding 'Boggard (Yorkshire word), for what is called in London Old Bogy'; Wright, *A Grammar* (1892), 218 for Windhill 'Bogəd, ghost'; Pegge, 'Derbicisms' (1896), 90, for Derbyshire, 'Boggard, s. a spectre, a bugbear'; Haigh, *Huddersfield Dialect* (1928), 13 'boggerd, a boggart, bugbear; ghost'; Wrigley, *Old Lancashire Words* for Saddleworth (1940), 7 'a goblin'. I have not included Hunter, *The Hallamshire Glossary*, 9–10 and 13 where boggart is assimilated with Barghast, 10, 'I know not that he is discriminated by any attributes from his equally terrific brother the Boggard'; nor have I included adjectival use in Malham-Dembleby, *Original Tales*, 157: 'eerie, ghostly, devilish'.

4. Atkinson, *A Glossary*; Peacock and Atkinson, *A Glossary* (1869).

made visible', and, winningly, 'something of an unearthly nature that is terrible to come in contact with'.

A jarring note, for someone who knows only folklore writing on boggarts[5]—where household spirits of the brownie type are pre-eminent—is how often boggarts are identified as ghosts. References to ghosts are found again and again in nineteenth-century publications on boggarts. They dominate those publications just as they dominate this list. Take James McKay's comment in his 1888 article on east Lancashire boggarts, the most sustained writing on boggart-lore from the later nineteenth century: 'a boggart is a ghost, a spirit, a soul of either man or brute'.[6] There are also frequent references to departed members of the community returning as boggarts. We know, for instance, that a boggart was seen after the death of a villager at Worsthorne in 1883. One woman who ran into the boggart in human form said 'she knew perfectly well that it was the ghost of the deceased person'; in other words, she had recognized him.[7] In a similar vein, an old woman at Godley Green in Cheshire told a researcher in the early twentieth century: 'Many a time ... I have seen "Old Nanny"—the boggart—wandering about after dark ... I can remember the old woman during her lifetime, and the boggart is just like her.'[8] There are also instances where a man or woman threatens to come back as a boggart to haunt someone: 'she told him that her "boggart" would haunt him unless he complied with her wishes to the letter.'[9]

---

5. Briggs, *Dictionary of Fairies*, 29–30 for the most important version of what might be called 'the folklorist's boggart', as opposed to the boggart of tradition: she offers a house spirit. A different and equally unhelpful version of the boggart is the extremely atypical 'squat hairy man', reported in Peacock, *Tales*, 67–71 at 69–70 (for the unclear origins of this tale see pp. 65–66). This has been picked up by various scholars including Eberly, 'Fairies', 81, who uses it to diagnose a form of infant disability! For still another version of the folklorist's boggart, although one that is perhaps closer to the traditional entity Bronner, *Practice*, 94.

6. *East Lancashire*, 17. A unique counter point is made by Joseph Baron, 'Lancashire Boggarts' (1894): boggarts are 'altogether distinct from ghosts, fortunately; for when all is said and done ghosts are rather monotonous by reason of the sameness of their appearance, and their limited programme'. Baron goes on to describe boggarts as shape-changers.

7. A Villager, 'A Boggart at Worsthorne'.

8. Middleton, *Legends*, 117.

9. Channon, 'Legends'. See also BC, Ashton-in-Makerfield (La) 1: 'My grandmother—born 1903 in Ashton-in-Makerfield used to threaten to turn into a boggart and go up through the hessoil (the gap under the fireplace) and come back to haunt us!' Or consider this letter from a failed suicide and the journalist's comments, 'Romantic Suicide': "O Ellen, how could you do this I am dieing and you have been the cause of My [sic] death Cruel Woman as you ar [sic] you have as false as the open sea, O Ellen you will be sorry when it is too late when my Spirit is always before your eyes and I hope that I may be able to aunt [sic] you both nite and day, for you have killed me."' (At this picture of a 'boggart' the Coroner and jury could not refrain from smiling, and the witness, Ellen Berry, seemed quite tickled at the prospect).'

But the real key to understanding the nineteenth-century boggart is the generic words in the list: 'apparitions', 'spirits', 'spectres', 'a subject for scare', 'something of an unearthly nature'. Even 'goblin' and 'hobgoblin' have a similar generic sense prior to the 1900s.[10] These generic words correspond to our four pre-nineteenth-century definitions for the word 'boggart'. In 1570, in a rhyming dictionary, Peter Levins defined a boggart as a 'spectrum' (i.e. an apparition).[11] In 1678, John Ray in a proverb collection, wrote that a 'boggard' was 'a bugbear or a phantasm'.[12] In 1697, in a religious controversy, Zachariah Taylor defined 'boggart' as 'a Bug-bear, or Spirit that Frights one'.[13] Then in 1764 a magazine editor glossed 'boggart' with 'apparition'.[14] Such generic definitions correspond to the generic sense of most words in the 'bug' family of words, from which 'boggart' comes (of which more in Chapter 2). The high number of 'ghosts' in the list, meanwhile, does not contradict this general sense. It is just that, as we shall see, the spirits of the undead were, in nineteenth-century Britain, as they are in most supernatural systems, by far the most common type of entity.[15]

The best definition known to me for the traditional boggart was given by the dialectologist Elizabeth Wright. A boggart was, Wright stated in 1913, 'a generic name for an apparition'.[16] Kai Roberts, a Calderdale folklorist put this in more concrete terms in 2018: the word 'boggart' 'might have been used to refer to anything from a hilltop hobgoblin to a household faerie, from a headless apparition to a proto-typical poltergeist'.[17] My own definition is that a boggart is *any* ambivalent or evil solitary supernatural spirit: a ghost, a hob, a shape-changer, a demon, a will o' the wisp, a Jenny Greenteeth ... Indeed, it is a challenge to find a supernatural creature that could not have been called a boggart in, say, the 1850s. I can, as it happens, only think of two: an angel (too good); and, for reasons I cannot confidently explain, a fairy (that is the 'trooping fairies' not the 'household faerie'

---

10. For example, Samuel Johnson, in his mid eighteenth-century dictionary, unnumbered, defined 'goblin' as: 'an evil spirit; a walking spirit; a frightful phantom'. His second definition was closer to the modern sense of the word, 'a fairy, an elf'. For an eighteenth-century instance of generic goblin, see Forster, 'Dear Sir', quoted at pp. 46–47.

11. *Manipulus*, 30.

12. Ray, *A Collection*, 232.

13. Taylor, *Surey Demoniack*, 53.

14. *The Beauties*, III, 94.

15. Of the importance of the dead in religious systems Steadman *et al.*, 'Universality'; and now Oesterdiekhoff, 'Why Premodern Humans?'.

16. *Rustic Speech*, 192.

17. Roberts, *Halifax*, 52.

referred to by Roberts).[18] If I had to translate 'boggart' into a single Standard English word, I would resort to the generic and philologically related 'bogie'. Going back to our earlier question, those hearing the sentence, 'I saw a boggart' would have had few limits placed on their imagination, for there is, in the words of one early nineteenth-century author, 'nothing systematic in the notions entertained by the country people' respecting boggarts.[19]

It might be useful here to sketch out all ambivalent or unpleasant entities, from Boggartdom (the territories where the boggart was known), and put them in relation to one another in a north-western folk taxonomy of the supernatural.[20] These 'scares' were collectively described as 'the feorin' (or an equivalent dialect term) meaning (supernatural) 'frightening things'.[21] The feorin broke down, in turn, into two categories. There were fairies (also confusingly called 'feorin' in some texts) and boggarts.[22] 'Boggart' was, as we have seen, an umbrella term for a whole series of different beings. By studying boggarts, we are actually studying all solitary feorin, as opposed to the social feorin (fairies). Some supernatural systems have terms like this: 'troll' and

---

18. There are tens of northern English texts that describe fairies from areas where 'boggart' was used in speech: not one describes a fairy as a 'boggart', save White, *Month*, 148, see further n. 294. The fairy was often quite sinister enough to be a 'boggart' in the Northwest: perhaps the difficulty was that fairies were plural or a collective and a boggart seems always to have been a solitary bogie. See further Young, 'Feorin', 57–58.

19. Burt, *Letters*, I, 227.

20. For other examples of folk taxonomies for the supernatural: Hengsuwan and Prasithrathsint, 'A Folk Taxonomy'; Brown *et al.*, 'Some General Principles', 78–80.

21. All of the following words ('freetnins', 'flaying', 'flaaens' etc.), derive from the local dialectal version of 'fear': there can be no question that 'feorins' were formed in the same way, and that they were, indeed, 'frightening things'. We have the following sentence from Furness (in what has been, since 1974, south Cumbria), 1867, [J.P. Morris], *T' Lebby Beck Dobby*, 3, 'we ol'as co'd 'em [ghosts] dobbies èr freetnins'. Whereas there are several references to 'flayings' from Cumberland, Westmorland and parts of Yorkshire: so in the late eighteenth century, A.W., *The Westmorland Dialect*, 45, 'I telt her haw I'd been flayd, an she sed ther wor flaying oa thor Fels, she her fel hed yance been sadly freetend, she saw a Horse wieawt a Heaad'; Pryme, *Autobiographic Recollections*, 32 '[t]he Dales-people called the re-appearances of the dead flayings, from flay, a north country word, to be frighted' (see also Wright, *Dialect Dictionary*, II, 392); Gibson, *Legends*, 3, '[g]hosts and hobgoblins come in, however, for a share of discussion [in north Westmorland], and places are still marked out where some murder has been committed, and where flayings are often seen'. Kirkby, *Lakeland Words*, 53: 'FLAAENS: Boggles, ghosts' are also attested from the Lake Counties. There is also, Burne, *Shropshire*, 114, 'frittenings' for Shropshire; and Barlow, *The Cheshire*, 122 (5 for the date) 'fearings' from Cheshire. An energetic search would turn up more variants across England and the Scottish Lowlands. I have looked at the feorin in detail in Young, 'Feorin'.

22. In folk taxonomies terms are often used in multiple *taxa*, e.g. pine for a type and pine for a species of tree. This kind of repetition is to be expected then.

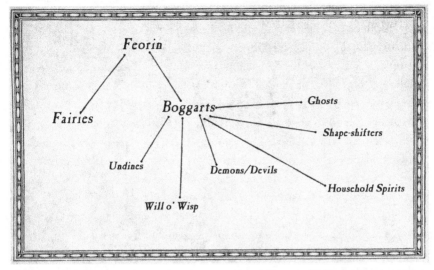

Figure 2: Supernatural folk taxonomy for Boggartdom.

'elf' in medieval and in early modern Scandinavian sources *could* be generic.[23] Others do not. In nineteenth-century Ireland, say, it is difficult to think of a word in English or in Irish, that could have served as an umbrella term for all solitary supernatural entities: 'banshees', 'fenodyree', 'glaistigs', 'lepre-chauns', 'pookas' etc.[24]

Say It Isn't So

The generic sense of boggart is straightforward in pre-twentieth-century sources, but it runs counter to what much modern folklore writing teaches us. Already in the early nineteenth century, there was a trend among some writers to cast the boggart more narrowly as a domestic spirit, what in the Scottish Lowlands used to be termed a 'brownie', and what in most of England was known as a 'hob'. This trend continued through the later 1800s and gradually took over in folklore writing in the 1900s. In 1959, for instance, the great postwar folklorist, Katharine Briggs, stated that the boggart 'is like a mischievous type of brownie. He is exactly the same as the poltergeist in

---

23. At least this might explain the range of meanings in: Jakobsson, *Troll*, 27; Simpson, 'Ambiguity'.
24. See, e.g., Croker, *Fairy Legends*; Yeats, *Irish Fairy and Folk Tales*; this is not just a problem of folklorists imposing a classificatory system. As the School Survey of the 1930s showed classification was clearly part of popular lore: https://www.duchas.ie/en/cbes [accessed 6 Jan 2019].

his activities and habits.'[25] This brownie-boggart is in full evidence in modern boggart folklore and fiction and will be the subject of Chapter 8.[26] The boggart of Victorian and Edwardian tradition could indeed be a household spirit, but the word was also used for other types of solitary supernatural entities.

Interestingly, not a single word in the list of twenty-seven definitions given earlier easily corresponds to a household spirit, the type of creature that aided and hindered families in English folk tradition. When household spirits appear in English texts in the nineteenth century they are sometimes described as 'hobs'.[27] They are sometimes referred to as 'brownies'. As noted earlier, 'brownie' was a Scots dialect word, but it became, in the course of the 1800s, a general term used by writers to describe household spirits anywhere in Britain.[28] Other writers referred instead to 'the lubber fiend', alluding to Milton's poem 'L'Allegro', which includes a household spirit—by far the most important occurrence in literary English.[29] Still others effortlessly combined two or three of these terms.[30] Again, it is not that it would have been considered wrong to call a household spirit a 'boggart'. We know, for instance, that T'Hob Thurs ('The Hob of the Wood')[31] at Barcroft Hall near Cliviger, was also called 'the Boggart of Barcroft Hall'.[32] It is just that the word 'boggart' covered so many more possibilities, from Sam's nightmare runner, to shape-changers, from murderous undines to poltergeists, from will o' the wisps to 'classic' ghosts.

---

25. Briggs, *Anatomy of Puck*, 186.
26. See, e.g., Edwards, *Hobgoblin and Sweet Puck*, 116; Larrington, *Green Man*, 148–49. It could be argued that Briggs pioneered this narrow definition, but see Hole, *English Folklore*, 151, who stated that the boggart was 'a form of house-spirit', compared unfavourably to the brownie (perhaps drawing on, as Briggs had, the Girl Guide tradition, see pp. 205–207) and the influential Burne, *Shropshire*, I, 45 for 1883. Note, too, that there has been a minority opinion that has preferred a generic definition, e.g. Simpson and Roud, *Dictionary*, 29.
27. 'The legends, legendary stories, and traditions of Derbyshire'.
28. Rhys, *Celtic Folklore*, II, 593; most folklorists qualify, e.g. Henderson, *Notes*, 266: 'this bespeaks him a sprite *of the Brownie type*' (my italics); an interesting example of the generic use in a title is found in Binnall, 'A Brownie Legend'.
29. Milton, *Poems*, 25–27 at 26. The poem is, to name just four folklore works, quoted in Keightley, *Fairy Mythology*, 318; Bottrell, *Traditions*, 173; Sikes, *British goblins*, 18; and Howells, *Cambrian Superstitions*, 111–12.
30. Take this example from the Lake District, Linton, *Lake*, 240, n. 9: 'Hob Thross, "a body all ower rough," like the Brownie of old time and Milton's lubber fiend'.
31. The name appears in a poem. Wilkinson, 'Barcroft Boggart' (1887): 'New clogs, new wood/ Thob [sic] Thurs will never do any more good'; then, Wilkinson and Tattersall, *Memories* (1889), 63. Compare Briggs, *The Remains*, 223 (for Millom): 'Thob [sic] thrush has got a new coat and a new hood/And he'll never do more good.' Hodgson, 'Surviving', 'A new coat, a new hood! Now little Hobberst will do no more good!', 117 (north-eastern Cumberland). These verses and others like them cry out for a study.
32. Wilkinson, 'Barcroft Boggart'.

It is difficult for those interested in British folklore to accept the original boggart in all its generic glory.[33] While writing this book I have often been told by colleagues, 'but ghosts are not boggarts!', or asked 'how can a demonic spirit be called a boggart?'. The household boggart of the reference works and fantasy fiction that we have read and that, in some cases, we have grown up with, has a powerful hold over us. I struggled for years to reach beyond the household boggart; the idea of an undead boggart, for example, just seemed *wrong*.[34] I console myself that even writers steeped in northern traditions who know boggart tales at first hand, find it difficult to accept the traditional uses of the word. Lancashire writer Aidan Turner-Bishop in one of the best modern works on north-western folklore, stated in 2010 that the boggart was 'an often mischievous, even malevolent, house brownie'.[35] Jessica Lofthouse, meanwhile, a South Pennine writer with considerable folklore knowledge, claimed that the boggart 'could be sly, full of mischievous pranks, his nuisance value high. But he rarely did serious harm and was so often helpful in the "good brownie" family tradition that he was usually tolerated.'[36]

Boggart Writing

Definitions complete, it will now be useful to set out some of the most thoughtful writing we have on boggarts from folklorists, historians, and linguists, from

---

33. Intriguing is Sayers, 'Puck', 52, who talks of the 'distinction between active agent [Puck] and menacing, potential agent [bog family]'. This distinction may have been present earlier in history; it is not there, though, in the nineteenth-century folklore of Boggartdom.

34. I write the following in penance to show how long it took me to grasp the generic nature of the boggart. Articles are given in the order in which they were written, rather than the order of publication. Young, 'Dialect', 1 'Boggarts are supernatural creatures associated, above all, with the north-west of England: they are frequently described as "fairies", sometimes as "ghosts"'; Young, 'Boggart Plays', 95–96: 'boggarts, in fact, conform only very loosely to contemporary ideas about fairies. They are large. They do not have wings, though some can fly. They shape-shift: often into animals. They are typically malicious. They are, at times the restless dead: nineteenth-century sources frequently define them simply as "ghosts"'; Young, 'Boggart Hole Clough', 119: 'boggarts, at least in the north west, typically fell into two categories. There were, first, house boggarts: these boggarts resembled domestic solitary fairies, helping and hindering families. There were, then, second, what we might call "country boggarts". These boggarts tended to haunt lanes, pools and woods and country boggarts, to continue with this (non-traditional) terminology, often appeared as animals, or even had the ability to shape-shift. If the house boggart frequently resembled a potentially friendly if more typically malicious brownie tied to a house and to a family, then the country boggart was closer to a troll: a dangerous guardian of a given locale out in the wilds'; Young, 'What is a Boggart Hole?', 73 'The boggart … was once a much feared bogey in the midlands and the north of England'; Young, 'Wright', 1 'The boggart is, of course [!], a ghost or a bogey'.

35. Turner-Bishop, 'Sites', 95.

36. Lofthouse, *Folklore*, 24–25.

1800 to the present. The first boggart authors were from Lancashire. Some of these have entered the canon of British folklore and are still read: chief among them are John Roby (1793–1850, despised father of Lancashire folklore and the author of *Traditions of Lancashire*), John Harland (1806–1868, a Yorkshire man by birth who made Lancashire his home), and Thomas Turner Wilkinson (1815–1875, a Burnley schoolteacher). Harland and Wilkinson wrote, together, the two most-quoted books on Lancashire traditions.[37] But there were others; for instance, two Preston writers, James Bowker (*fl*. mid to late nineteenth century) and Charles Hardwick (1817–1889). In his *Goblin Tales of Lancashire*, Bowker penned stylized boggart tales: 'boggarts and phantoms would begin to creep about to the music of the unearthly voices heard in every sough and sigh of the wandering wind as it wailed around the isolated dwellings'.[38] Hardwick authored *Traditions, Superstitions, and Folklore, (chiefly Lancashire and the north of England)*. His ambitious comparativism makes his work difficult to read today. The laying of the Grizlehurst Boggart with a cockerel is, for example, effortlessly elided, over seven long pages, with 'Aryan', Cornish, French, Greek, Jewish, Indian, and Roman traditions.[39]

Then there are a series of largely forgotten writers, men like John Higson (1825–1871) from Gorton. Higson, in sparse, hard-to-recover publications, gave detailed studies of the folklore of south-eastern Lancashire.[40] Tattersall Wilkinson (1825–1921, not to be confused with Thomas Turner Wilkinson) was an eccentric, instantly recognizable from the red fez he wore.[41] From the 1880s he wrote articles for the Burnley press on local history and in 1889 he published, with a rich relative, *Memories of Hurstwood, Burnley, Lancashire*. This book gives us an extremely detailed description of the supernatural landscape to the north-east of Burnley, around the village of Worsthorne.[42] Also in Burnley, John McKay gave a series of talks on 'The Evolution of East Lancashire Boggarts' at the Burnley Mechanics a year earlier (1888).[43]

---

37. *Lancashire Folk-lore*; *Lancashire Legends*.

38. *Goblin Tales*, 16.

39. Hardwick, *Traditions, Superstitions, and Folklore*, 132–38.

40. For Higson see pp. 79–84.

41. Spencer, *Tattersall*, for a marvellous evocation. He continued to be talked about for long after his death. Beilby, 'Boggarts' (1940): 'Miss Holroyd (a teacher): "Surely, you don't believe in such nonsense, Mister Tattersall." Old Tatty: "There are more things, Miss Holroyd in heaven and earth than are dreamt of in our philosophy."'

42. See also Wilkinson, 'Local Folklore', 1904.

43. I have placed these lectures online with extra passages from contemporary newspapers: https://www.academia.edu/28026366/McKay_The_Evolution_of_East_Lancashire_Boggarts [accessed 15 Jan 2019].

Figure 3: John Roby
(Roby, *Remains*, frontispiece).

These boggart pioneers had few twentieth-century successors. Consider this fact: from 1901 to 2000, *Folklore*, Britain's chief journal for popular traditions, had just thirty-one references to 'boggart'. There were 1,135 references to 'fairy' over the same period.[44] But a number of 'the few' (not from *Folklore*) are worth mentioning. In 1907, Charles Roeder (1848–1911) wrote a journal article on the folklore of Moston in the *Transactions of the Lancashire and Cheshire Antiquarian Society*, including references to several boggarts. In the years before the Second World War, the Lincolnshire folklorist Ethel Rudkin (1893–1985) described, on occasion, the boggarts of her home district.[45] In the late 1930s, and for the other side of the country, Christina Hole (1896–1985) dedicated a chapter of *Traditions and Customs of Cheshire* to ghosts and boggarts.[46] This Edwardian and interwar generation of writers was perhaps the most accomplished. They were still in contact with communities with boggart beliefs.

44. I searched on JSTOR using boggart/boggarts/boggard/boggards and fairy/fairies. The boggart references give some idea of the rise and fall of interest: 1903, 1903, 1914, 1918, 1923, 1928, 1932, 1933, 1936, 1938, 1952, 1955, 1956, 1957, 1958, 1959, 1962, 1971, 1972, 1975, 1980, 1981, 1981, 1984, 1984, 1987, 1988, 2000.
45. Rudkin, *Lincolnshire Folklore*, 34–38; 'Black Dog', 116–17. Note that Lincolnshire boggarts had been mentioned before, though, usually in passing: e.g. Balfour, 'Legends', see also pp. 65–66 for the farmer and the boggart, a possible Lincolnshire tale.
46. Hole, *Traditions and Customs*, 144–65.

After the war the great English fairyist, Katharine Briggs (1898–1980) often touched on boggarts, but in a rather idiosyncratic way. We shall have cause to look at her contribution to boggart folklore later in this book (p. 210). In 1962, Vera Winterbottom (1906–1969) wrote a chapter on boggarts in her *The Devil in Lancashire*.[47] In 1971, John Widdowson published an article on 'The Bogeyman', which proved to be one of the most important twentieth-century contributions in English to the subject of child fear and nursery monsters. It is cited frequently in Chapter 2. Another contribution was R.C. Turner's stimulating but misguided effort to link bog bodies, boggarts, Sir Gawain, and Beowulf (1986).[48] Then in 1989, Philip Leese published a study of the Kidsgrove Boggart (Staffordshire).[49]

After a quiet period in terms of scholarly boggart writing, interest in boggarts has picked up since around the turn of the millennium, particularly among those who write on north-western traditions. In 2007 and then again in 2011, John Billingsley published folklore volumes on Calderdale with reference to boggarts. Billingsley's 2007 book marks the beginning of contemporary boggart writing.[50] In 2010, Aidan Turner-Bishop brought out an article on Lancashire boggarts and fairies.[51] In 2011, Ceri Houlbrook wrote a precocious undergraduate thesis on Boggart Hole Clough in north Manchester (available online), which she has begun to publish as independent articles.[52] Boggarts and the supernatural Northwest also appear in Karl Bell's *The Magical Imagination* (2012).[53]

Kai Roberts included much boggart material in his excellent *The Folklore of Yorkshire* (2013), though frustratingly without notes. Roberts also authored a brief but useful article in 2014, on confusion over boggart traditions in Calderdale,[54] and in the same year, a book on supernatural Halifax.[55] In 2017, Andy Wood looked at the Towneley Boggart and made the case for a supernatural oral tradition which had endured some three hundred years.[56] Then, between 2013 and 2018, I published six articles on boggart beliefs.[57] My

---

47. Winterbottom, *The Devil*, 33–44.

48. Turner, 'Boggarts'.

49. Leese, *Kidsgrove*.

50. See especially, *Folk Tales* (2007), 19–22, 69–74 and *West Yorkshire*, 37–41.

51. Turner-Bishop, 'Sites'.

52. 'The Suburban Boggart' (thesis); and the first article 'The Suburban Boggart'.

53. See, e.g., 61–62.

54. 'Don't Boggart That Joint'.

55. *Halifax*; see also by Roberts, *Haunted Huddersfield*. These two books are among the very best of the 'Haunted' series.

56. Wood, 'Spectral Lordship'.

57. 'Dialect', 'What is a Boggart Hole?', 'Boggart Hole Clough', 'Joseph Wright', 'Lancashire Boggart Plays', *'Shantooe Jest'*.

articles have informed this work, but I offer in these pages a different approach and, in several cases, different conclusions.

The bibliography given here is, in terms of quantity, a slight foundation on which to construct a monograph-long study. Some of the writing is also lacking in terms of quality. The early authors never troubled to define a boggart with any care. The term was so familiar to them that it did not need much elucidation: 'Every [nineteenth-century] Lancashire man knows what a boggart is.'[58] Some of the later writers, particularly those from the 1960s to the 1980s, were detached from boggart-believing communities and on the basis of their limited sources, assumed that the boggart was a 'brownie', i.e. a household spirit. Our greatest postwar folklorist of the supernatural, Katharine Briggs, not only pushed the boggart-brownie in much of her writing but suggested that the Lanky 'Feorin', a related dialect term meaning, as we saw earlier, a 'frightening thing' had 'a Celtic sound'.[59]

It is crucial then, in attempting to elucidate Victorian and Edwardian boggart beliefs, to reach beyond our few secondary sources, be these the nineteenth-century folklore writers or postwar folklorists who only knew about boggarts second hand. I have for this book attempted to build up three alternative corpora to aid in discussions and analysis: (i) Boggart Ephemera; (ii) Boggart Names (BN); and (iii) a contemporary boggart folklore survey, the Boggart Census (BC).[60] The next sections deal with these three collections.

Corpus One: Boggart Ephemera

The first corpus has several forms of ephemera: broadsides, letters, magazines, and newspapers. Newspapers are by far the most important of these in terms of content and in terms of what has survived. Nineteenth-century journalists had far fewer filters than book authors. Journalists recorded stories that *incidentally* described supernatural beliefs. To give two examples that were included as legal items: a child died after being told a boggart story; and a night-time 'boggart' turned out to be a man wandering nude around the parish.[61] But writers for newspapers, particularly as the nineteenth century progressed, also felt increasingly able to recount, even if only with a 'voyeur's preoccupation

---

58. Price, 'Notes', 190.
59. *Fairy Dictionary*, 169. Note that Briggs knew and understood this term in other more familiar forms, e.g. 'English Fairies', 272 for 'frittenings'.
60. See Preface for details on viewing and downloading these open-access corpora, which together comprise *The Boggart Sourcebook*.
61. 'Death of a girl'; 'Commitment'.

with the mores of poor, illiterate and rustic people',[62] local beliefs as a subject in their own right.[63] They did so with more attention to content than contemporary folklorists, who were often distracted by folklore theory.

No one questioned that these lost folklore comments in nineteenth-century newspapers would be extraordinarily useful. The problem was how to recover the relevant sentences and paragraphs from the vast, difficult to access, physical collections held by British libraries. In the 2010s, however, digitization overcame that substantial barrier to research. For those researchers who are now lucky enough to have material in newspaper databases, potluck and days of drudge in stacks have been replaced by canny word searches and considerations about OCR quality. There has been what might be called a 'digital dividend'.

The magnitude of this technological change is best established by an example. If I wanted to take fifty years of a six-page Lancashire weekly newspaper and look manually for boggarts there, the task would be Herculean. I would have to look through 2,600 numbers. If I wanted to browse newspaper titles for promising material, then each newspaper would take about six minutes to read through; and thus the whole series would take about 260 hours.[64] If I wanted to browse, instead, the contents of each article, then each edition would take me thirty to forty minutes, and it would take about 1,500 hours to go through the entire series.[65] To offer a digital perspective, as of September 2018, the British Newspaper Archive has for Lancashire, for the period 1800–1900, scans from thirty-nine titles, covering various years and running to various lengths. There are in total some 96,473 different newspaper issues. By typing 'boggart' and variant spellings, I can do, with a simple search operation, what would have manually taken about 56,000 hours—or six and

---

62. Waters, 'Magic', 634.

63. Hobbs, *A Fleet Street*, 301–26 details the increasing use of dialect in Lancashire newspapers as the century progressed (spiking in the 1870s): the publication of local supernatural beliefs followed a similar pattern. For a more detailed look at how magic and the supernatural fell in and out of intellectual fashion from 1750 to 1900, Waters, 'Magic'.

64. Of course, looking at just titles means it is easy to miss interesting boggart-lore. Titles with boggart content in the present bibliography include such gems as: 'A Tuberculous Cow', 'A Determined Housebreaker' and 'Extraordinary Breach of Promise'.

65. None of this acknowledges simple physiological limitations. A human mind could *perhaps* stay alert while running through several dozen pages of titles without a break. But when skim-reading entire columns of small newspaper print, 'snow blindness' soon sets in (something this author has experienced): it is possible to 'read' several paragraphs before realizing that the mind has not taken in any information. It is worth paying tribute here to a very few supernaturalists who, in pre-digital times, recognized the importance of newspapers and who actually ploughed through physical collections: in the UK, principally, Owen Davies, as detailed in Waters, 'Belief in Witchcraft', 101–02; see also for the Netherlands, de Blécourt, *Termen*, 271–74.

half years without breaks for sleep or refreshment. To search through 'boggart' in all British and Irish newspapers, 1800–1900, we are carrying out the equivalent of several lifetimes of manual scanning in seconds.[66]

Of course, there are problems. Some issues are missing, some are faded, some have ruined pages or columns. The character recognition technology is not perfect, not least because of imperfect originals.[67] But here is a significant change in research gears. We can claw back tens of thousands of words written around boggarts, or, say, witchcraft or Spring-heel Jack—subjects which were ignored or misconstrued by earlier folklorists.[68] Certainly, my experience while writing this book has been that the boggart corpus from newspapers is many times more useful than the boggart writings, such as they are, of nineteenth-century folklorists. The evidence is more ample, more wide-ranging, and, usually, more straightforward.

Corpus Two: Boggart Onomastics

Boggart onomastics refer to two types of boggart-naming traditions. Firstly, there was the boggart personal name: nineteenth-century communities named local bogies with the word 'boggart', as in 'Aw'm heere agen, like the Clegg Hall Boggart'.[69] Secondly, in the same period, communities named places after boggarts—such as Boggart Bridge, Boggart Field, and so forth. Here, too, we benefit from the 'digital dividend', and we can access archives that have been digitized since the early 2000s to find these names. It is certainly much easier to dig out place and personal names in obscure records in the 2020s than it would have been even in the 1990s. Consider the following numbers for boggart

---

66. Of course, once the search has been made there is the time necessary to scan through the relevant texts.

67. I have seen, for example, 'Hoggarth', 'beggar', and 'suggests' mistaken for 'boggart'.

68. For witchcraft, Waters, *Cursed Britain*, 93; for Spring-heel Jack, Young, 'Folklore Survey', 185: 'Take, then, as a practical example, the fortunes of one British researcher who has spent much of his adult life in archives, physical and digital: Mike Dash. Dash has dedicated thirty years to the study of Spring-heeled Jack ... and has kept, while writing a larger analytical work, a file of sources'. This file should soon be published as the *Calendar of Spring-Heel Jack Sources*. 'From 1982 to 1996 he managed to gather about forty-five thousand words from contemporary writers, using microfilms and originals. By 2012, the number had shot up to 240,000 words, gathered more surely, and with far less effort, thanks to digitization ... As of September 2016 Dash had some 380,000 words in his database, a total that excludes all of the numerous duplicates that crop up in searches through the nineteenth-century press. In 2012 Dash thought that he might be able to reach half a million words "eventually" ... He now expects to pass that total by the end of the decade.' My experience of collecting boggart material, although of shorter duration, mirrors that of Dash.

69. Wright, *Rustic Speech*, 193.

place-names. The English Place-Name Society volumes collected—their authors using pre-digital research methods—twenty-six boggart place-names. In 2014, I was able, after many hours of searching, mainly in digital archives, to mark down some 108 boggart place-names. Since 2015, I have been able to reach 183, not least because digital archives have been growing.[70]

The 'Gamershaw Boggart' or 'Ogden Boggart' are boggart personal names: the first once employed in Flixton parish; the second in Newhey. Well-known local bogies were often given names in this way, and sometimes had more than one.[71] Supernatural personal names of any type represent a consensus view. The name only exists because a number of the community agree to use it. A journalist (in Bury) writes, for instance, '[t]here are persons now living who remember what was called the "Freetown Boggart"'.[72] There can be no question that 'Freetown Boggart' had been widely talked of in the area. An individual folklore writer cannot be so easily trusted. In nineteenth-century accounts from Lancashire, I know of authors who use the term 'goblin', 'elf', and 'sprite' in descriptions of a local bogie—although not typically as a proper name.[73] It is unlikely that these 'highfalutin' terms were employed in popular folklore. The authors were writing for an educated audience and consequently changed register or wished to vary their vocabulary.

Boggart place-names similarly represent a community consensus. They refer to 'uncanny' places—sometimes known only to a family, sometimes to an entire city—which are named after boggarts. It is certainly not the case that all supernaturally charged sites in Boggartdom were named 'Boggart'. There was, for instance, Blomoley Cloof at Middleton or Nell Parlour at Gorton, both the haunts of terrifying boggarts: respectively, Owd Blomoley and Nell Parlour Boggart.[74] But it is true that all, or the vast majority of, boggart

---

70. The EPNS numbers are based on BN—note that there will be many more when the Lancashire volumes are published; for 2014 Young, 'What is a Boggart Hole?', 97–106; for 2022 BN.

71. See, e.g., Fieldhouse, *Old Bradford*, 86–87: 'The Horton "boggard" ... was applied to the ghost of "Fair Becca" ... [or] "Rebecca," as the higher grade of Hortonians always spoke of the young woman'.

72. 'The "Freetown Pie"' (1862).

73. For examples of 'goblin' for boggarts P., 'Fairy Tales'; Thornber, *History*, 333; Waugh, *Sketches*, 234; for the only example I know of 'elf' being used in this way Wilkinson and Tattersall, *Memories*, 63; for 'sprite' Hampson, *Medii aevi*, I, 128–29; 'A Determined Boggart' (1842); Waugh, *Sketches*, 213 and (for a possible example where 'sprite' was used locally) Dawson, 'Spire-Holly's Sprite'. We arguably go in the opposite direction by using 'folksy' terms to replace generic words: e.g. James, *Lincolnshire*, 78–80 where a short story from Ruth Tongue about a giant and a dwarf, *Forgotten Folk-Tales*, 64–65 becomes a short story about a giant and a boggart.

74. Bamford, *Passages*, 45; Higson, *Gorton*, 16, for more on Nell and Nell Parlour Boggart: H., 'To and Through Didsbury'.

toponyms were viewed as being places of supernatural danger.[75] Typically, these places are simply 'Boggart' plus a landscape element, e.g. Boggart Lane. In a very few cases, there are instead names with the genitive, e.g. Boggart's Clough. These are not generally recorded for the nineteenth century and are probably more modern formulations.[76]

Boggart place-names are difficult to find. They (and this is true of most supernatural place-names) are typically micro-toponyms: bridges, meadows, houses, lanes, and the like. These were names known locally but not region-ally, save in exceptional cases when a boggart place-name happened to become famous. Boggart Hole Clough at Blackley, for example, earned a reputation as a gathering point for rallies;[77] the Old Boggard House in Leeds was an important Methodist chapel.[78] Micro-toponyms do not easily appear in docu-mentation and our knowledge of the vast majority of boggart toponyms depends on obscure sources. We only know that there was a Boggart Lane at Leigh because two boys were prosecuted for playing pitch and toss on that road in 1903.[79] Similarly, we only know of Boggart Lane in Mytholmroyd in the West Riding because a young man attempted to commit suicide there in 1907 (and because this appeared in a newspaper). In fact, of the 183 boggart place-names, 118 only appear in one source.

If obscurity is one problem, another related issue is status. There is, well into the nineteenth century, a demonstrable reluctance to use place-names with 'what are vulgarly called boggarts' in official contexts.[80] There is, indeed, the sense that 'Boggart' is an inappropriate name. In 1854, for example, Boggard Lane in Gringley in Nottinghamshire was rechristened Queen Lane.[81]

---

75. For a possible exception see p. 88.
76. Boggart's Barn (Wigglesworth, WRY): BC, Wigglesworth 1 (WRY); Boggart's Grave (Ogden, WRY): 'To be found along the woodland trail at Ogden Water Nature Reserve. A now fenced off, round stoned spring that unusually bubbles air as it emerges.' http://www.megalithic.co.uk/article.php?sid=12207 [accessed 20 October 2018]; Boggart's Green (Winteringham, Li): BC, Winteringham 4 (Li); Boggart's Lane (Pilling, La): BC, Pilling 2 (La); Boggart's Wood (Poulton, La): BC, Poulton 2 (La). There are two nineteenth-century examples. The first was perhaps a surname or a nickname originally (for more on boggart nicknames see pp. 223–25) Boggart's Inn Farm (Wirksworth, Db): 'The Like agreement to let to William Webster the house called Boggard's Inn', 1750, D/D An/Bundle 47/48417, Wigan Archives; Boggarts Hill (Prestbury, Ch): 1841 Census for Bosley 14, p. 8, adjacent, in the census, to 'Boggins Hill'.
77. Even appearing in a national history for a suffragette rally: Marr, *Modern Britain*, 55–56.
78. 'Wesleyan Missionary Society' (1863); Hardcastle, 'The story that the...' (1891).
79. 'Playing Pitch'; 'Desperate Attempt at Suicide'.
80. 'The Spaw "Boggart"' (1839).
81. 'Gringley' (1854). A study of 'submerged' boggart place-names has the opposite problem to a study of fairy place-names from the same period—e.g. Fairy Glen (Betws-y-Coed), Fairy Glen (Capelulo) and Morag's Fairy Glen (Dunoon). Modern fairy place-names often nudged out

There was, likewise, an attempt to rechristen Boggart Hole Clough, near Manchester, Bowker Hall Clough, a legal attempt that failed.[82] Note also the associated custom of placing the word 'boggart' in place-names in quotation marks in the 1800s: for example, 'as far as Leech House and [or?] "boggart house" as it was commonly called'.[83] One consequence of this kind of distaste was that there was often the official name of a place and there was the popular name, or by-name.[84] This was particularly true of roads and houses. In Baildon near Bradford, for example, Holden Lane was also known as Boggard Lane in 1875. In 1957, over eighty years later, the same two names continued to be used side by side.[85] The low status of boggart place-names made it even less likely that these names would be written about.

Boggart toponyms are of particular value because they offer something of a level playing field across the country. With boggart folklore sources we are ultimately the prisoners of local writers. If there is a lack of interest in local folklore then boggart-lore will not be collected. Boggart place-names, on the other hand, appeared in news stories and administrative documents irrespective of folklore or antiquarian interest. In fifteen cases we know about boggart toponyms *only* because they appear in census records; they were house, district, or lane names.[86] Unlike interest in folklore, the survival of nineteenth-century newspapers and administrative documents is equal across most of England. The data then does not depend on source biases. Of the 183 boggart place-names, two are from the East Riding; three from Nottinghamshire; three from

---

traditional names in the nineteenth century, as the English middle classes beautified, as they saw it, their mansions and holiday resorts: for modern fairy names Young, 'Fairy Trees', 19–20.

82. Waugh, *Sketches*, 225–26; Hardwick, *Traditions*, 151–52; Wentworth, *History*, 130.

83. 'Scotforth township' (1889).

84. For by-names see Redmonds, *Names and History*, 155–70.

85. Baildon and Baildon, *Baildon*, I, 16; 'Members Talk' (1957): note that by 2016 'Holden' had definitely won out, *Threshfield*, 16.

86. Boggard Bridge (Ovenden, WRY) 1841 Census Ovenden 2, p. 21; Boggard Cottage (Holme upon Spalding Moor, ERY): Census 1841 Holme upon Spalding Moor 21, p. 5; Boggard Houses (Greasley, Db): 1881 Census, Barford, Greasley, Enumeration District 11, p. 24; Boggard Houses (Horsley, Db): 1881 Census, Belper, Horsley, Enumeration District 6, p. 24; Boggard Town (Heanor, Db): 1871 Census, Heanor 3481, p. 43; Boggart Hole (Mellor Moor, Db): 1881 Census, Mellor, Enumeration District 9, p. 11; Boggart House (Bollin Fee, Ch): 1841 Census, Bollin Fee 5, p. 6; Boggart House (Dalton, La): 'Gildsley or Boggart House Dalton nr Southport', 1911 Census, Dalton, Enumeration District 1, p. 91; Boggart House (Kirkham, La): 1841 Census, Treals 10, p. 14; Boggart House (Matlock, Db): Boggart House 1891 Census, Wirksworth, Matlock, Enumeration District 16, p. 18; Boggart House (Strelley, Nt): 1911 Census, Strelley, Nt, Enumeration District 8, p. 65; Boggart Lane (Eccleston, La): 1881 Census, Prescott, Eccleston, Enumeration District 11, p. 30; Boggart Lathe (Keighley, WRY): 'Green Well Hobcote or Boggart Lathe', Census 1871: Keighley 4315, p. 2; Boggarts Hill (Prestbury, Ch): 1841 Census for Bosley 14, p. 8, adjacent, in the census, to 'Boggins Hill'.

Lincolnshire; thirteen from Cheshire; seventeen from Derbyshire; sixty-seven from the West Riding; and seventy-nine from Lancashire.

In terms of folklore-writing about boggarts, Lancashire dominates absolutely. Indeed, on the basis of how much is written about Lancashire boggarts one might expect three quarters or more of the boggart place-names to be in that county. This is not, however, the case: only about two fifths of boggart place-names come from Lancashire. The low numbers from Cheshire, Derbyshire, the East Riding, Lincolnshire, and Nottinghamshire can be explained because boggarts appeared in only parts of these counties. However, there are almost as many boggart place-names in the West Riding as there are in Lancashire. The West Riding is, admittedly, bigger than Lancashire, but the closeness of the numbers (sixty-seven versus seventy-nine) is striking, particularly given that not all of the West Riding seems to have had boggarts. Boggart place-names offer us a way around the severe lack of boggart documentation outside of Lancashire.

But what use can be made of 'mere' place-names or, for that matter, boggart personal names? I will argue in later chapters that these names are important resources for understanding boggart-lore and the supernatural. Not only do these two types help us to chart the limits of boggarts in geographical terms; put crudely, where we find boggart personal names or boggart place-names, we also find boggarts and, hence, often, boggart belief (Chapters 3 and 7). They also help us to situate boggarts in the landscape and allow us to start to see boggarts through our ancestors' eyes. We understand not only where to find boggarts, but we start to get some sense of *why* they were in this or that place (Chapter 4). These were questions that nineteenth- and twentieth-century folklore writers did not, for the most part, trouble themselves with.

Corpus Three: 2019 Boggart Census

As I was gathering in boggart reports and boggart names of various kinds, I was introduced to another possible source of information for nineteenth-century boggart beliefs. In March 2019, Dr Lynda Taylor interviewed her father-in-law, Arthur Taylor (born 1926), about his childhood memories of boggarts. Arthur talked in this interview of the fact that only grass will grow in a boggart field, the kind of detail that I would have expected to have found in a Victorian or Edwardian text.[87] Was it possible that Victorian and Edwardian traditions of boggarts had survived into the twenty-first century in the memories of men and women who had grown up before the Second

---

87. BC, Heywood 3 (La). For more on boggart fields see p. 230.

World War? Inspired by Arthur's words, I determined to gather in other boggart memories from those born between around 1920 and 1970 in the old boggart heartlands. My initial aim was to collect 100–200 replies from members of the general public.

I started collecting for the Boggart Census, as I termed it, in July 2019 and continued through to late October 2019. At first, I contacted various media outlets: *Radio Cumbria*, *Folklore Thursday*, and *Fortean Times*, among others, and editors and producers proved extremely open to the appeal. Articles were written, interviews were given, but the number of replies was disappointing and I began to despair at reaching even a hundred. In fact, I came often, in that summer, to remember Mrs Hodgson's advice for fairy folklorists, given at the end of Victoria's reign: 'The injudicious collector who hunts, so to say, with horn and hounds, will draw every cover blank; and even the aids to scouting formulated in folk-lore tracts may not always ensure success … Fairies, it is well known, thrive only in moonshine.'[88] Turning on a megaphone and shouting at the right demographics did not seem to be working.

In late August 2019, with serious misgivings, I switched to using social media to reach people more directly. This proved a happy choice for if fairies like moonlight, then boggarts thrive on Facebook. By general appeals and, crucially, targeted appeals within community groups on that platform, I was able to gather some 1,100 boggart memories. Collecting was facilitated by the semi-public nature of the replies: members of private forums wrote not just to me but to each other. In fact, often respondents were inspired by each other's memories. About 400 of these reports, one should note, were from the middle-aged and the elderly saying that they had never heard of boggarts while growing up. As I will argue later (Chapter 7), these negatives, from areas where the boggart had once ruled, were quite as important as the affirmatives in tracing the boggart's funeral cortège.

How relevant were these boggart memories to the boggart traditions of 1850–1914? The memories were fundamentally a snapshot of the boggart folklore that a given man or woman had grown up with, from 1920 to 1970. These memories could in no way be said to be pre-First World War folk-lore—the folklore around which this book is written. Indeed, I began being rather sceptical that there would be much continuity of ideas about the boggart. Was Arthur perhaps unusual, an exception even? After all, this was a period of immense change in British society. Not only was the boggart becoming less popular, as its disappearance from folklore publications suggested, as did the

---

88. 'On some Surviving Fairies', 116.

negatives in the Boggart Census survey. This was also a time when some of the traditional forms of transmitting knowledge—the fireside story, the ballad, and so on—were falling into abeyance (see pp. 109–37). There was massive population movement within Britain and new arrivals from overseas. British society also became, by most estimates, more atomized and less 'connected' as the century progressed.[89]

In any case, these folklore memories had been filtered through the decades and had been enriched by what might be called the 'popular culture boggart', who had started to appear in books and on the radio and television and, bizarrely, in the Girl Guides movement (see pp. 205–207). Here the boggart was no longer rooted in Boggartdom; it had become rather a national possession.[90] These popular culture boggarts, naturally enough, appeared in the survey. A BBC children's song, for instance, from 1970, the 'Railway Boggart' was recalled by five respondents who had sung this piece at school and were often almost word perfect a half century on:

> but rarer than these
> And very much nicer is such a rogue
> As the Railway Boggart, he doesn't clank chains
> But has lots of fun in railway trains.[91]

Many others, meanwhile, recalled boggart games in the Brownies when they were little girls.[92] I will look at these developments in the last chapter of the book where I refer to the 'goblinification' of the boggart. The Boggart Census is key to elucidating this process.

There were, however, also definite cases where older boggart traditions had been passed down. Thanks to memories given in 2019, for instance, I was able to solve two boggart questions from my earlier research. In 1867, the unexplained phrase 'making boggarts' appeared in open court in a sex abuse case, but what did it mean? A woman who grew up in the 1930s in Blackburn

---

89. Hall, 'Social Capital', read together with Grenier and Wright 'Social Capital': note that the authors of both studies admit that data from earlier in the century is poor or missing.

90. One set of boggart memories came from what was then Rhodesia, where a young British boy was terrified with boggarts by his elder sister; the family had no connection with the old boggart lands, BC, Zimbabwe 1 (Oth).

91. BC, Southport 7 (La); Upholland 1 (La); Brighouse 2 (WRY); Grindleford 1 (De); and Colchester 1 (Essex).

92. See, e.g., BC, Euxton 5 (La); Irlam 11 (La); Poulton 2 (La).

was able to explain that the sense was 'making a fuss' or 'trouble'.[93] 'In and out like a boggart' was given in a nineteenth-century Calderdale newspaper article. It was likewise opaque. A man who grew up in Haworth in the 1950s solved the problem. He recalled that 'as children, if we were running in and out of the house a lot, my grandmother would say "ee!, you're in and out like Butterfield Boggart!"'[94] There were also many, sometimes apologetic, claims that boggarts were 'ghosts', something that recalls the dialect definitions given earlier in this chapter rather than dominant ideas in modern folklore where the boggart is a brownie-style house spirit.[95] These memories were in no sense Victorian or Edwardian, but they came from those who had had Victorian and Edwardian parents and grandparents. As such, these memories can contextualize the Victorian and Edwardian boggart. Arthur's recollections were precious, but they were not that unusual.

Conclusion

The digital retrieval of data, be it from archives or social media platforms, has been crucial for this study. Indeed, it has been possible to gather hundreds of thousands of words, many of which will not have been read since the early 1900s and the vast majority of which have never been used by historians or folklorists. In some sense, it is easier to research Victorian boggarts in the 2020s than it would have been in Victorian times. We are, of course, cut off from the ideal for study: a living boggart-believing population. Modern boggart believers are, as the Boggart Census shows, few and far between.[96] An ethnographic survey of the men, women, and children (like Sam) who believed in boggarts (or, as interestingly, who did not believe) in around 1850 is now and forever beyond our reach. But we can, thanks to digitization, create an impressive series of boggart-lore files; one that would have taken far more time and effort to amass in 1890, and one that would have been unimaginable in 1990.

The key lesson of these corpora is that 'boggart' was, in all the parts of Boggartdom where enough documentation survives to allow us to judge, a

---

93. Young 'Wright', 7 (outside Lancaster) and BC, Blackburn 2 (La) see also p. 244.
94. Young 'Wright', 8 (Calderdale) and BC, Haworth 1 (WRY) see also p. 240.
95. BC, Blackpool 6 (La); Blackpool 10 (La); Britannia 1 (La); Great Harwood 3 (La). Littleborough 7 (La); Littleborough 18 (La); Littleborough 19 (La); Milnrow 7 (La); Out Rawcliffe 2 (La); Over Wyre 2 (La); Skelmersdale 1 (La); Skelmersdale 2 (La); Wardle 3 (La); Waterfoot 1 (La); Whitworth 1 (La); Aughton 1 (WRY); Esholt 1 (WRY); Hipperholme 3 (WRY); Stainforth 1 (WRY); Marple Bridge 1 (Ch); Hayfield 4 (De); Kinder 1 (De); New Mills 6 (De); and Conesby 1 (Li).
96. See, e.g., Moorside 1 (WRY); Strines 1 (De); or the remarkable Haslam, 'Rock-solid'.

generic word for solitary supernatural creatures. The brownie-style household helper is just a tiny part of the boggart story. It may have come to dominate modern boggart accounts, but those who go back to Victorian and Edwardian records will be confused if they are expecting a household helper. The generic nature of 'boggart' makes it a powerful lens through which to examine the supernatural in nineteenth-century Boggartdom. Writing about a boggart is not like writing about, say, *la llorona* or banshees—entities with a compact set of functions, which have been carefully studied by scholars and which both have monographs dedicated to them.[97] By studying boggarts—an umbrella term—we are actually studying the greater part of the supernatural in one of the most interesting regions of Britain in the 1800s. To use, with apologies, the kind of natural history metaphor that many folklorists object to, we are studying not a species, but an ecosystem.

---

97. Perez, *There was a Woman*; Lysaght, *Banshee*.

CHAPTER TWO

Boggart Origins

Introduction

Some of Britain and Ireland's supernatural beings are of considerable antiquity. The banshee that screams in contemporary Donegal or Clare can be traced back to Old Irish texts of the eighth century.[98] The leprechaun too has a long lineage: it is first attested in the same general period.[99] The English fairy is the descendant of the Anglo-Saxon elves, and Chaucer was already calling them by their modern name in the fourteenth century.[100] Puck is celebrated in *A Midsummer Night's Dream* in the sixteenth century and he was old then: almost certainly the early medieval *puca*, found in a score of English place-names from Kent to the Midlands.[101] *The Anglo-Saxon Chronicle* describes airborne dragons as the Viking depredations are beginning at the end of the eighth century, and there are still records of dragons being seen in England as late as the reign of William and Mary.[102] Of course, there is no guarantee that words like 'leprechaun', 'fairy', or 'dragon' meant the same thing to their earliest and later chroniclers.[103] But even if only the name and the belief in 'something' preternatural are transmitted across, say, a millennium that is still a fact worth recording.

Compared to the banshee or Puck, it must immediately be conceded that the boggart is a *parvenu*. The word 'boggart' is first written in English only in the sixteenth century. The first certain mention of a boggart in the landscape appears

---

98. Lysaght, *Banshee*, 193–34.
99. Winberry, 'Elusive Elf', 66–67; Bisagni, 'Leprechaun'. The reason that banshees (and perhaps leprechauns) cannot be traced back further into the past is the lack of a substantial corpus of writing in Irish prior to *c.*700 and in Hiberno-Latin prior to *c.*500.
100. Williams, 'Semantics', 466–68; Harte, 'Dorset', 68: for early medieval elves, Hall, *Elves*.
101. Sebo, 'Puca?', 169–70 (including one northern example); Harte, 'Dorset', 68.
102. 793 in the Chronicles (aurora borealis?); Simpson, *Dragons*, 41 (for the Henham dragon).
103. For a striking example of folklore continuity see Winberry, 'Elusive Elf', 66 (in the *Death of Fergus*); for examples of discontinuity, Jakobsson, 'The Taxonomy'.

in 1633: a Boggart Hole at Pendle.[104] From 1500 to about 1800, references to boggarts are intermittent and (for the most part) incidental, and (almost entirely) restricted to northern England. Although we can be sure that local populations believed in boggarts (in as much as their great-great-grandchildren demonstrably did), these beliefs were barely recorded. Then, from about 1800, the references climb steadily for a century, with a spike in the 1860s and the 1870s as the great works of Lancashire folklore are published.[105] References then drop away rapidly, almost to nothing, before the Second World War, to re-emerge only in the 2000s. Any student of boggarts is, therefore, obliged to concentrate on the ample nineteenth-century records, mostly centred on Lancashire. But that is very different from saying that boggart history begins in 1800. As noted above, there is earlier evidence that needs to be taken into account.

Etymology

What meanings did the word 'boggart' accumulate? where was it used? and where does it come from? These questions are best answered by looking firstly at the word's roots; secondly, at its associations; and thirdly, at its earliest occurrences. The supernatural 'boggart' has usually been assumed to belong to a family of English words based around Middle English *bugge*: 'bogy, hobgoblin, blackman, scarecrow'.[106] These include 'bog', 'bogie', 'bogieman', 'boggin', 'boggle' (from which English gets the verb 'to boggle'), 'bug' (from which American English probably gets its word for insects), 'bugbear', possibly 'bull-beggar',[107]

---

104. Crossley, *Discovery*, lxviii.

105. This spike comes out clearly in an N-gram (an online database, run off Google Books, to measure word frequency) of 'boggart': https://books.google.com/ngrams/graph?content=boggart&year_start=1500&year_end=2000&corpus=15&smoothing=3&share=&direct_url=t1%3B%2C boggart%3B%2Cc0 [accessed 21 August 2018]. For the limitations of N-gram, see Pechenick *et al.*, 'Google Books'.

106. *Middle English Dictionary*, B.5, 1212.

107. For Bull-beggar see Dragstra, 'Bull-Begger', 187–91 who effectively surrenders on the question of etymology. The first syllable is almost certainly 'boll', a supernatural terror, Nodal and Milner, *A Glossary*, 45. 'Beggar' is more curious: is it perhaps related to the 'bear' in bugbear, bearbug or bullbear (are these contractions?)? Some have wanted to derive 'beggar' from 'boggart' or some related form, not least the *OED v. Bull-beggar*; Jones and Dillon, *Dialect*, 62 note 'gally-bagger' in Hampshire; Wright, *Dialect Dictionary*, II, 546: 'gally-beggar'. Dundes, *Meaning of Folklore*, 220 points out the easy substitution of 'bugger' for 'beggar' in modern British English (see p. 30). Note that an element missing from all discussions is the original dialect distribution of bull-beggar before it was taken up into standard English. The name is often associated with the north (e.g. Wright, *Dialect Dictionary*, I, 436): but the few bull-beggar place-names—toponyms are missing from Dragstra, 'Bull-Begger'—cluster suggestively around London, see n. 236. Interestingly, most of the *OED*'s early attestations are from the south-east.

and very likely the American 'booger'.[108] Here is 'a remarkable cluster of forms which share … surprisingly closely linked' connotations.[109]

This 'cluster' has attracted, through the years, a certain amount of philological scholarship. As early as 1851, Hensleigh Wedgwood dedicated several pages to these forms in the *Transactions of the Philological Society*. In 1902, American philologist, George Flom, looked at 'big-bug' in relation to *bugge*. In 1911, Charles P.G. Scott touched on 'bogus' (and barghest). In 1935, Emily Allen discussed the *bugge* words and folklore beliefs. In the 1950s, Valentina Pavlovna Wasson and R. Gordon Wasson examined the bugge-family in their study of Russian mushroom culture. In 1958, P.L. Henry tried to trace 'boggart' and similar terms to the Celtic languages. Gillian Edwards gave a chapter to 'bugs, boggles and bogeys' in her popular look at folklore etymologies, *Hobgoblin and Sweet Puck*, in 1974. In 1994, John Timson reconstructed the evolution of the boggart in language and folklore terms in the popular review *Verbatim*. In 2000, Louise Sylvester discussed 'bug words' with special reference to Middle English. In 2005, Brian Cooper discussed 'boggart', 'bog', and other terms in relation particularly to Celtic, Slavic, and Germanic philology. In 2016, Maggie Scott looked at the Scots word 'bogle' in the online review *The Bottle Imp*. Finally, a paper has now appeared (2019) by the American scholar, William Sayers, entitled 'Puck and the Bogeyman'. What is most striking here is the disconnected nature of the debate. Almost none of the authors of these texts were aware of each other's work. Cooper, for example, the most important study listed, does not include any of the other names in his bibliography.[110]

The longer *OED* connects 'boggart' with 'bog', and makes the credible suggestion that *-art* or *-ard* (in the case of 'boggard') were an 'augmentative suffix'; i.e. a way of making a *bugge* into, we might say, 'a great big bugge'.[111] It is, also, worth noting that *bugge* (and, therefore, boggart) are possibly distant cousins of other supernatural nouns from Britain and Ireland including the

---

108. See e.g., Harris and Neely, 'Phantoms and Bogies'; and for a North Carolina booger place-name Hayes, *Queer Roots*, 249–53; see Wright, *Dialect Dictionary*, I, 433 for 'bugger': 'A hobgoblin, puck, ghost' for Gloucestershire.

109. Widdowson, 'Bogeyman', 107.

110. Wedgwood, 'On English Etymologies', 35–37; Flom, 'The Etymology of Big-bug'; Scott, 'Bogus and His Crew', an article that has gone almost unnoticed unlike Scott's celebrated 'The Devil and his Imps'; Allen, 'Two Related Examples', 1039; Wasson and Wasson, *Mushrooms*, 202–03; Henry, 'The Goblin Group'; Edwards, *Hobgoblin*, 83–101; Timson, 'The Evolution'; Sylvester, 'Naming', 280–88; Cooper, 'Lexical reflections'; Scott, 'Bogle'

111. Compare: 'braggart', 'dastard', 'drunkard', 'dullard', 'laggard' and 'sluggard'. Sayers, 'Puck', 54: 'boggard (aggrandizing suffix with comic potential)'. Note that most of the -ard words listed here date no earlier than the sixteenth century. 'Sluggard' is, according to the *OED*, the earliest with a first attestation in 1398.

bucca, pixie, Puck, pug (devil), and the Irish pooka, although the manner in which these words are related to one another (if indeed they are) remains controversial.[112] The linguistic history of Britain, and particularly England's supernatural fauna, has been neglected or left in the hands of dilettantes to general disadvantage. There is an urgent need for a proper study grounded in Celtic and Germanic, and, if necessary, wider Indo-European philology.[113]

The relationship of *bugge* and 'boggart' (and other similar words) is also informed by the distribution of the *bugge* family of words. There are four words that can be traced with some accuracy onto a map of central Britain: 'bogie' (and bogieman), 'boggart', 'buggin' and 'boggle'. 'Bogie' is the word of much of the English Midlands. 'Boggart' is to be found in Lancashire, the West Riding of Yorkshire, parts of Cheshire, Derbyshire, Staffordshire, and some of central England, including Nottinghamshire and Lincolnshire. 'Buggin' is a word associated with south Cheshire, perhaps influenced by or deriving from Welsh *bwgan*?[114] 'Boggle', meanwhile, dominates the eastern half of Yorkshire, Cumberland, County Durham, Northumbria, and the Scottish Lowlands; it is also to be found in Lincolnshire.[115]

As noted, most scholars who have troubled themselves with this question have assumed that the word 'boggart' is related to Middle English *bugge*. However, particularly in the nineteenth century, there were alternative theses that were sometimes offered by writers and that need to be disposed of here. The most incredible was the notion that 'boggart' was an adaptation of the predominantly North Yorkshire word 'barghest'. Now the barghest had, in supernatural terms, something in common with the boggart: Wright defines it as a 'ghost, wraith, or hobgoblin'.[116] The etymology of 'barghest' is mysterious and has been much debated. The second syllable is generally taken to be 'ghost'; the problem is the stubborn first element.[117] The word cannot be

---

112. Cooper, 'Lexical reflections', 90–93; Sebo, 'Puca?' I would presume that they are not related, although see Sayers, 'Puck'.

113. What is really needed is a philologist with knowledge of supernatural studies (Alaric Hall, William Sayers...?). Much will remain beyond proof, of course, but an act of rubble clearing, where scores of derelict theories are removed from the board, would be welcome.

114. Owen, *The place-names*, 9. Note that Turner, 'Boggarts', 170 relates 'buggin' to Manx 'buggane'. For Cheshire buggins see J.A. 'The Ghosts' and BC, Wirral 1 (Ch) and pp. 126–27. See also a 'Boggan' in Laxton (Notts), Haslam, *Ghosts*, 35.

115. The only general map: Orton *et al.*, *Atlas*, 'Bogey', L64. For 'buggin', Egerton and Wilbraham, *A Glossary*, 44.

116. Wright, *Dialect Dictionary*, I, 164. My impression (based on admittedly incomplete reading) is that the barghest is often or even typically a dog save in the extreme Northeast.

117. The *OED* has 'perh. ad. Ger. berg-geist mountain-demon, gnome; but by Scott referred to Ger. bahre bier, hearse, and by others to Ger. bär bear, with reference to its alleged form.' Roby,

assimilated to 'boggart', although the fact that such luminaries as John Roby, Thomas Crofton Croker, and William Henderson tried to do so means that the idea is often encountered, even in modern writing.[118]

A second, far less common notion was that boggart derived from 'Bulgard' (Bulgarian), a medieval word associated with heresy and homosexuality, more commonly 'Bougre' from which English-speakers get 'bugger'.[119] Were the connection with *bugge* not so convincing (with cognate forms), this etymology might be worth investigating. It is certainly possible that 'Bulgard', or a related form, influenced the development of 'boggart'. Perhaps this was a case of multiple etymologies.[120] Even if the word 'bugger' is not linked to 'boggart' genetically, 'bugger' and 'boggart' were confused in regional English: 'my Dad (born in Walton-le-Dale in the early 1920s) would sometimes use "boggart" in place of "bugger", as in "it's a bit of a boggart"'; 'My mum used the word "boggart" as you might say, "you little bugger", a non-swear word in Yorkshire'.[121]

Another idea was that the word 'boggart' and related forms were connected to mumming.[122] There *are* some interesting terms in British folk ceremonies, including in Lincolnshire 'boggans' (or 'boggins') at the Haxey Hood. In this curious event, eleven 'boggans', a fool, and their lord, take part in a series of rituals at Haxey and then play a bewildering team game.[123] But, if there is a

---

Traditions, II, 289 (with earlier etymologies). There are no folk etymologies known to me. Note that the *OED* dates the earliest reference to barghest to 1732. In fact, there is a mid seventeenth-century reference: Whitaker, *Richmondshire*, 168.

118. Roby, *Traditions*, II, 289, 295 [first series]; Henderson, *Notes*, 352: 'Barguest, Bahrgeist, Boguest, or Boggart'. I once encountered it in an (otherwise learned) peer review. Williams, 'Semantics', 461 connects 'barghest' indirectly with 'boggart' through a shared common etymology in 'bo': 'boghost (barghest)': Wright, *Dialect Dictionary*, I, 164 reports 'bohghost' for parts of North Yorkshire.

119. To the best of my knowledge the Bulgar-boggart suggestion was first made in 1838: Faber, *An Inquiry*, 339. Faber is, then, quoted approvingly by Gaster, *Greeko-Slavonic*, 78–79 in 1887; and as recently as 2019 Simon Bronner (as editor) references the Bulgar-boggart in Dundes, *Meaning of Folklore*, 213; see now Bronner, *Practice*, 85–116. For a modern discussion of the word and its origins Vasilev, *Heresy*, 32–36. Note that one of the medieval forms was 'bowgard', Ibid., 32; note also, an interesting fifteenth-century definition, Way, *Promptorium parvulorum*, 55 'Bugge or buglarde. Maurus, Ducius'. The connection between sodomy and heresy is, of course, longstanding: this would presumably be the hypothetical diabolical link between a Bulgarian and an English monster. Note that there are other instances of ethnonyms becoming supernatural entities in Britain and Ireland (and, indeed, further afield): the Danes and the Picts, Ó Giolláin, 'Exotic Foreigners': for foreigners and the supernatural more generally Beccaria, *I nomi*, 107–14.

120. Borghi, 'Grande Indoeuropa', 94 for 'etimologie plurime'.

121. BC, Walton-Le-Dale 2 (La) and Idle 1 (WRY).

122. Hampson, *Medii aevi*, I, 128–29; Harland and Wilkinson, *Lancashire Legends*, 141–42; 'New Year's Day' (1864).

123. Rudkin, *Lincolnshire Folklore*, 90–91; Turner, 'Boggarts', 171; Henricks, *Disputed Pleasures*, 62; and Pearson, '*In Comes I*', 151–62.

connection between mumming and boggarts, it likely goes from the supernatural to folk ceremony: ceremonials relying on *bugge* words, not *bugge* words
coming from ceremonials. Devils are frequently to be found in mumming and
other folk ceremonies.[124] Note, too, that there is an association in German
dialects between words in *bog-* and masks.[125]

There is finally the notion that 'boggart' and similar words relate in some
way to the word 'bog', wet spongy ground, or, in much contemporary English,
a marsh. 'Bog' entered English from Gaelic in the 1500s.[126] 'To bog', a related
form, was in early modern English 'to defecate',[127] a sense that survives into
the twenty-first century.[128] Indeed, in the 1500s a 'boggard' was also a privy.[129]
Even in the 2020s, the slang word for 'toilet' in much of England is 'the
bog'.[130] The late arrival of 'bog' and these related forms suggests that it is in
no way relevant to *bugge* or 'boggart'. Nor is there any sense that 'bog' influenced the popular view of the boggart in the nineteenth century. Surprisingly,
though, what is essentially a modern folk etymology for 'boggart' ('sounds
like bog')[131] has appeared in academic writing, particularly in relation to bog
bodies.[132] There is some evidence also that twentieth-century views and illustrations of the boggart, in as much as they exist, depend on slime and boggy
expanses. We come to the reptilian-amphibian goblin-boggart of modern

---

124. Cockrell, *Demons*, 42.
125. Cooper, 'Lexical reflections', 82: for the more general association between the supernatural
    and masks, see interspersed references in Allen, 'Influence' and Braccini and Braccini, 'Maschera'.
126. Bog, *OED*: 'In Scotland apparently from Gaelic, in England from Irish'. The earliest references
    are sixteenth century. A nice question is whether some of the many 'bog' toponyms in England
    were not originally *bugge* place-names. 'Bogs Lane' in Caistor, for example, in Moorlands, in
    Hambleton, and in Harrogate. There is Old English Bucga (personal name) and le Bugge (a Middle
    English surname). I accept that any individual toponym may be explained in this way. However,
    there are far too many place-names of this type to all be explained by what are rare personal
    names. Note that the surnames Bog and Bug are also rare.
127. Fischer, 'Non olet', 102–03.
128. Partridge, *Slang*, 109, strangely not in Wright, *Dialect Dictionary*, I, 325. For modern examples,
    BC, Lancaster 4 (La).
129. The earliest reference appears in 1572 in Huloet, *Huloets Dictionarie*, 'Siege [vox], iacques,
    bogard, or draft', unnumbered; other references include Ward, *The simple cobler*, 72 (1647); Heath,
    Clarastella, 157 (1650).
130. See, e.g., Billingsley, *Folk Tales from Calderdale*, 71.
131. Or a back formation. Consider, BC, Huyton 2 (La): 'Never heard the word used but I do
    know there was a lot of marsh and bog land around the area way back. Perhaps the word related
    to legendary stories about these areas i.e. Bog arts or stories'; and the ingenious, Barrow-in-
    Furness 1 (La), 'I'm just wondering if the name Boggart could have anything to do with the moss.
    I think [it] is called Bog Wart, I also think they maybe a medicinal value, and would naturally
    grow in Boggy ground'.
132. Stead, Bourke, and Brothwell, *Lindow Man*, 170; Turner, 'Boggart'; and Higham, *Frontier*, 97.

fantasy fiction.[133] Or consider the words of Lincolnshire dialectologist Joan Sims-Kimbrey in 1995, according to whom a boggart was a 'local mythological creature reputed to inhabit the dykes in the wetlands and the fens; a small and ugly, slimy green man with exceptionally long hairy arms'.[134]

This idea can also be found in twentieth-century boggart memories. 'Definitely heard the word "Boggart" associated with boggy areas'; there were 'boggy, marshy areas where the Boggarts might grab your leg and pull you into the bog so crossing boggy marshy ground was made quite exciting'; 'I associate boggarts with more of a rural area, of a person or being who lives in or around marshland'; a boggart is '[s]omething along the lines of a troll, or something that appeared out [of] a bog/marsh to cause mischief or terror!'; '[h]eard of the term [boggart] when I lived in Cheshire. Always thought it related to creatures of marshy places'; or 'grew up familiar with the word in the 1970s and understanding it was some kind of mythical marsh creature'.[135] Again, I have failed to find material like this from the 1800s.[136]

If the membership of boggart in the *bugge* family is straightforward, the deeper genealogy of the word is far thornier. Does Middle English *bugge* trace back to a medieval Welsh word *bwg*, both of which had a similar sense? One of these two words has borrowed from the other, or they both descend from an earlier word in another language. Whichever word has priority there is then also the question of where *bugge*/*bwg* (or a hypothetical common ancestor) ultimately came from. Suggestions have included Continental Celtic, a Germanic ancestor language, Persian, Slavonic, and proto-Indo-European.[137] 'Boggart' and *bugge* family words 'have been traditionally connected with a Celtic origin'.[138] In the nineteenth and for most of the twentieth centuries, scholars were overwhelmingly of the opinion that *bugge* came from a Brittonic language, perhaps Welsh.[139]

A Celtic ancestry was doubly pleasing in an age when folklore studies scrambled to trace modern words and customs to 'archaic' forms because it

---

133. See, e.g., Griffiths, *Lancashire Folklore*, 6 and ch. 8, passim.
134. *Wodds*, 33.
135. BC, Barrow 1 (La); BC, Preston 9 (La); BC, Great Harwood 4 (La); BC, Leyland 15 (La); BC, Liverpool 12 (La); BC, Southport 15 (La).
136. The earliest reference I know dates to 1955, Moorhouse, *Holiday*, 89.
137. Cooper, 'Lexical reflections'. Note that 'bôg' (god) in the Slavic languages is 'usually considered a borrowing from Iranian', Derksen, *Dictionary*, 50. For more on Slavic 'bôg', Trovesi, 'Famiglia'.
138. Ruano-García, *Lexis*, 242, who is referring to 'buggart' and 'boggle'.
139. See, e.g., Carr, *Horæ*, 59–60; Garnett, *The Philological Essays*, 164; Atkinson, *A Glossary*, 56; Nodal and Milner, *A Glossary*, 45; Skeat, *English Dialects*, 84 etc. This continued well into the twentieth century: e.g. Coatman, 'Lancashire Dialect', 122.

gave a potentially more ancient British pedigree for a supernatural word. Already by the late nineteenth century, there was also the strong association between 'the Celts' and visionary or supernatural experiences: was it not natural that the English or their Anglo-Saxon ancestors would have borrowed their bogies from the mystically inclined Celts?[140] I suspect that this conviction (which continues to the 2020s) is behind the striking number of respondents in the Boggart Census who claimed that 'boggart' had Irish origins.[141] Philology, though, points east. In 2005, Brian Cooper made a compelling case that Welsh borrowed English *bugge*.[142]

Given such a 'confusing periphery' and the danger of getting 'lost for ever within this labyrinth' of folk belief and language,[143] it will, I hope, be enough here to make three modest observations. Firstly, *bugge* emerged from a medieval context where Celtic and Germanic languages competed with and borrowed from each other. Secondly, the suffix *-art* in 'boggart', is certainly English,[144] and it should come as no surprise to find our earliest boggart references in a part of the country where English had been spoken for almost a thousand years by the time the word was first written. Thirdly, even if recoverable, any hypothetical origins of *bugge* or *bwg* in Euro-Asian prehistory would tell us little of use about the early modern or the nineteenth-century boggart, the subject of this book.

However, if we can put some questions to the side as distractions there are other considerations about the word 'boggart' that cannot be so easily dismissed. Firstly, an important secondary meaning of boggart is 'scarecrow';[145]

---

140. Sims-Williams, 'The visionary Celt'.

141. BC, Lancaster 1 (La): 'Boggarts were associated with Ireland'; Littleborough 12 (La) 'Yes – maybe something Irish, or to do with a demon'; Penwortham 4 (La) 'my dad ... said a common term in Preston while he was growing up and has Irish origins'.

142. Cooper, 'Lexical reflections', 92–93. Note that English 'fairy' may have made its way into Welsh in the same general period, Gruffydd, *Folklore*, 6–7; see also *coblyn* (recorded from 1547 in Welsh in the *Geiriadur Prifysgol Cymru*) from Eng. gobelin (OED records earliest attestation in the 1300s: likely borrowed from French). See now, for another point of view, Sayers, 'Puck'. I fail to understand why Scots Gaelic *bugh*, Sayers, 'Puck', 53, couldn't come from Scots (i.e. the English of the Scottish Lowlands) or a Scots ancestor rather than a hypothetical Brittonic form from Strathclyde.

143. Williams, 'Semantics', 460; Widdowson, 'Bogeyman', 106.

144. Although it came originally from a Romance language, presumably French or Anglo-Norman.

145. Sylvester, 'Naming', 286, leaves the question of priority open: 'It is difficult to discover which sense, that of terrifying supernatural phenomena or that denoting something deliberately set up to frighten birds came first.' There are many European examples of supernatural names being extended to scarecrows, e.g. Contini, 'Les désignations', 86–87. I take for granted (perhaps wrongly) that with bug-scarecrows there was a similar development of meaning, i.e. from spook to scarecrow.

the point here being perhaps that the 'boggart' scares birds, as boggarts scare people.[146] One instance of this in English popular culture is the famous illustration by Cheshire artist, Randolph Caldecott (1846–1886), of three fox-hunters meeting a boggart or scarecrow (see Figure 4).[147] There is, as it happens, a long history in English of scarecrows being named for supernatural beings, particularly beings with an initial bilabial plosive 'bo-'. Wright has some twenty examples in his *Dialect Dictionary*, including 'buccaboo' and 'bubbock' (see n. 994). This meaning also occurs in related forms in other languages,[148] which begs a number of questions about origins. While not of immediate concern here, these should at least be noted. The Welsh *bwbach* and *bwg* can mean scarecrow, as can Manx *boagandoo*, Swiss German *Bögg*, and German *Boggelmann*: all these words also refer to supernatural creatures.[149]

'Boggart' and related terms (including notably 'bogie') also mean 'dried mucous under the nose' in several English dialects.[150] This last point would hardly be worth mentioning were it not that there are cases in German dialects where a supernatural entity also has the same double meaning: monster/snot. As with the scarecrow we may have an association that dates back to a common Germanic form.[151] John Widdowson, in 1971, noted the tendency of 'bo-' words to be used for taboo and semi-taboo terms.[152]

Early Boggart References: 1500–1700

So much for etymology and the word's evolution. Can anything be deduced from the earliest uses of 'boggart'? We will examine the eighteen sources where 'boggart' is used from 1500 to 1700—what must be 'only the occasional

---

146. Williams, 'Semantics', 461. Note that given this fairly straightforward leap in meaning one could perhaps imagine the connection between scarecrows and supernatural creatures being made independently time and time again. It is much more difficult to imagine this kind of spontaneous association with masks—although see evolutionary theories for masks like Meuli, *Masken*—and supernatural creatures.

147. Famous enough that it was adapted by *Punch* (1943) in the Second World War: Churchill, Stalin and Roosevelt are the huntsmen and meet a scarecrow Hitler. 'One said it was a boggart, an' another he said "Nay, it's just a German Fuehrer and he's almost had his day"'. https://punch.photoshelter.com/image/I0000SzrBE75aPpc [accessed 17 Jan 2020].

148. *Épouvantail* for French, *spauracchio* for Italian, see further Profili, 'Les désignations'; Contini, 'Les désignations', 286–90.

149. Cooper, 'Lexical reflections', 79 and 82.

150. Wright, *Dialect Dictionary*, I, 316 for 'Boakie', I, 326 for 'Boggart', for 'Boggle' I, 327 I, 432 for 'Bug'.

151. Cooper, 'Lexical reflections', 82.

152. Widdowson, 'Bogeyman', 110.

Figure 4: 'One said it was a boggart, an another he said "Nay; It's just a ge'man-farmer. that has gone an' lost his way"' (Caldecott, *Three Jovial Huntsmen*, 5–6).

surfacing in literature' of slang and dialect words.[153] One should note that there is no question that 'boggart' could sometimes be employed as a personal name, albeit generally as a nickname. Indeed, we will come across a seventeenth-century example later in this chapter. However, I am not convinced that the rare English surname 'Boggett' comes from 'boggart', as suggested by the editors of the *Oxford Dictionary of Family Names*. The earliest reference dates to a will of one John Boget from 1502 in reference to properties on the Isle of Wight.

153. Ibid., 114.

Later 'Boggett' references are particularly associated instead with the North Riding of Yorkshire where 'boggart' was not generally used for the supernatural (see Chapter 3), at least in the 1800s.[154] I have not included, therefore, early references to boggart-sounding surnames in what follows. I have included, though, the far more straightforward evidence of boggart toponyms from the sixteenth and seventeenth centuries.

Foꝛ liƙe as a frayboggarde in a garden off Cucumbers ƙepeth nothinge, euen ſo are the ir goddes of wod, of ſyluer ꙅ golde: and liƙe

Figure 5: First occurrence of 'boggart' in English, *Coverdale Bible*, folio 54.

'Boggart', apparently, first appears in written English in 1535 in the Miles Coverdale (d.1569) translation of the Bible. 'Boggarde' here, however, refers to a scarecrow rather than to a supernatural creature: 'For like as a frayboggarde in a garden off cucumbers kepeth nothinge, even so are their goddes of wod, of sylver and golde.'[155] In 1555, Lawrence Saunders (1519–1555), a Protestant preacher, wrote to his wife, about a week before being burnt for heresy: 'be not afraide of fraybuggardes vvhich lye in the vvay, feare the euerlasting fire, fear the serpēt vvhich hath that deadly sting'.[156] 'Boggart' with the sense of 'a groundless concern' is particularly common in the early sources. In the late 1550s, a title deed from Midgley in the West Riding includes a reference to 'a messuage or freehold tenement of the said Tho. Oldfield called William Royde, alias Boggard House'. It has proved impossible to examine the original deed and thus there must remain some doubts about the

---

154. Hanks *et al.*, *Dictionary*, I, 270; National Archive prob/11/13 (Image Reference: 2177).

155. Baruch, 6, 69. Note also that Coverdale elsewhere uses 'bug' for supernatural creatures, Nordstrom, *Blood*, 101. Psalm 91, 5: 'So yt thou shalt not nede to be afrayed for eny bugges by night, ner for arowe that flyeth by daye.'

156. The letter was recorded in the first edition of Foxe (1563), *Actes and Monuments*, V, 1116. Note that in later editions Foxe changed the language: XI, 1711, 'Be not afrayd of fraybugges which lye in the way. Feare rather the euerlasting fyre: feare the Serpent which hath that deadly sting' (1570). 'Buggard' was presumably an unwelcome dialect term. Note that Foxe may have already begun this process of standardisation in his first edition. In the 1563 edition, Saunders was quoted as writing: V, 1112, 'Oh Lorde, howe lothe is this loyteryng sluggard to passe foorth in Goddes pathe? It fantasyeth forsooth muche feare of fray bugges.' 'Sluggard' suggests, at least to me, that in Saunders' original, there was 'fraybuggardes' here, too, and that Saunders had put the words together to create a jingle.

authenticity of the document.[157] It might be argued that 'boggard' in 'Boggard House' could have a non-supernatural meaning. To this I can only respond that I know of tens of examples of haunted boggart houses (admittedly most references are from the 1800s), but no examples where boggart had any other sense when applied to buildings.[158] Note also the 'alias' in the charter text: this is a by-name, something characteristic of haunted boggart house names (see p. 20).

In 1570, in his *Manipulus Vocabulorum*, an English rhyming dictionary, Peter Levins writes 'spectrum' (i.e. apparition) as a definition for 'a Boggarde'.[159] In 1575, William Whittingham (1524–1579) used 'boggart' metaphorically for troubles: 'Hereoff will all theis waightie discommodities growe that they two (ye muste vnderstande) maie not be in so great authoritie with all men nor be such buggarddes to the poore yff they maye not beare the bagge alone'.[160] The next attestation comes in a sermon by Robert Rollock (d.1599) on the Passion, given sometime between 1583 and 1599 in Scotland, but written up from notes after his death: 'It is not as men saye, to wit, Hell is but a boggarde to scarre children onelie: No, thy miserable soule shall finde in wofull experience the dolour and woe of that place'.[161] Richard Surphlet, meanwhile, in his 1599 translation of a French work, writes that the melancholic who tries to sleep is 'assayled with a thousand vaine visions, and hideous buggards, with fantasticall inventions, and dreadful dreames'.[162]

There are also references from the seventeenth century. In 1605, a Catholic apologist, John Radford, announced in his *A Directorie Teaching the Way to the Truth in a Briefe and Plaine Discourse Against the Heresies of this Time*: 'But these fellowes that deny Christ was in hell (the cloysters whereof hee once broke, binding that olde serpent) and so deny their Creede, no meruaile though they make so small reckening of Purgatorie, but account it as a buggard to feare children'.[163] Gervase

---

157. Sutcliffe, 'Midgley', 117–18 (refers to the reign of Mary and Philip). Note that if this deed has to be dismissed the next earliest record is in the parish records: 6 February 1657, burial of Thomas Oldfield of 'Boggard House', St Mary's, Luddenden.

158. See BN, passim; for a possible exception, Boggart's Inn Farm (Wirksworth, Db): 'The Like agreement to let to William Webster the house called Boggard's Inn', 1750, D/D An/Bundle 47/48417, Wigan Archives. The genitive is very unusual at this date (see further p. 19). Perhaps from a nickname or a surname?

159. *Manipulus*, 30. Sometimes said to be the first use of boggart: e.g. Serjeantson, 'Vocabulary', 70.

160. *A Brieff Discours*, 160.

161. *Lectures*, 132. The dates are based on Kirk, 'Rollock' and are the dates that Rollock had a chair in Edinburgh.

162. Du Laurens, *A Discourse*, 82. The translation is of du Laurens, *Discours*, 214: 'assailli d'un millié de phátosmes & spectres hideux, de fantasques chimeres de songes effoyables'.

163. McCoog, 'Radford', points out that the preface was dated 10 April 1594.

Markham (d.1637) uses the word 'boggard' four times in his 1617 work on horses to refer to anxious mounts. One chapter is entitled, 'How to correct a horse that is skittish, and fearefull, and findeth many Boggards'.[164] In 1633, there is a dramatic mention of a boggart place-name in a narrative describing some shape-changing witches near Pendle. A boy has escaped from a coven and is being chased: 'some of theire company came runninge after him neare to a place in a high way, called Boggard-hole, where this informer met two horsemen, at the sight whereof the sed persons left followinge him'.[165] This is almost certainly Boggard Hole at Fence. Another writer on horses, Thomas de Grey (aka Thomas de la Grey), claimed in 1639 that there was the danger that the horse would see 'boggards in his keepers face'.[166] In 1648, Charles Hoole produced an English-Latin dictionary. In a fascinating section on 'De Spiritibus' (which would repay study by folklorists) he translates 'Fray-buggards' as 'Maniae', presumably with the sense of 'bugbears'.[167]

John Webster (1610–1682) in 1677 referred to the different problem of impressionable men and women:

> These will take a bush to be a Boggard, and a black sheep to be a Demon; the noise of the wild Swans flying high upon the nights to be Spirits, or (as they call them here in the North) Gabriel Ratchets, the calling of a Daker-hen in the meadow to be the Whistlers; the howling of the female Fox in a Gill or a Clough for the male, when they are for copulation, to be the cry of young Children or such Creatures as the common people call Fayries, and many such like fancies and mistakes.[168]

---

164. *Cauelarice*, 112: the other references are in contents table, 17 and 24.

165. Crossley (ed.), *Discovery*, lxiii; Clayton, *Boy Witchfinder*, for the background to this case. Note that I can report an earlier uncertain reference to the Pendle Boggart Hole. In an article in 1952, Clitheroe historian, Arthur Langshaw, 'It Raineth', describes a flood where internal streams in Pendle erupted shocking local residents and reforming the terrain: 'in August [1580], when "Pendle brast its gurt sides" forming "Brast Clough" and "Boggart Hoil", spreading havoc in the hamlets along its western margin'. The quotations might mean a contemporary or near contemporary source: although I am sceptical. Another newspaper article 'Eruptions of Pendle' (1905): 'Those of "Brast", or "Burst Clough", and "Boggarts Hole", are known with certainty to have been' formed by water eruptions. This is in a description of the eruption of 1580 but the two cloughs are not said to have been caused at this time. I hope other researchers will be able to find the relevant source or clear up the confusion here. For another possible seventeenth-century boggart-style toponym see 'Bogger Furlong' (1649, Cavill, *Field-Names*, 37).

166. *The Compleat Horseman*, 28.

167. Hoole, *An Easy Entrance*, 145–47 at 146.

168. Webster, *The Displaying*, 60.

Echoing Webster, in 1678 the Essex writer, John Ray (1627–1705), includes a boggart saying in his *A Collection of English Proverbs*: 'He thinks every bush a boggard (i.e. a bugbear or a phantasm).'[169] In 1679, John Whitehall, in a critique of Hobbes' *Leviathan*, wrote that Hobbes 'approves very well of the word Infinitive (though he buggards at the word Entity) as useful'.[170] In 1681, the playwright, Thomas Shadwell (d.1692), has in *The Lancashire Witches* a yokel greet two sophisticated visitors with a description, in dialect, of a supernatural attack, which ends with the admonition: 'yeow mun [must] tack a care of your sells, the Plece's haunted with Buggarts and Witches'.[171] In 1697/1698, a pamphlet controversy took place among Dissenters and Anglicans over an exorcism in Lancashire, dating back to 1689/1690: 'the Surey Demoniack'.[172] In this controversy, Zachariah Taylor (1653–1705), who was critical of the exorcism, described a certain 'Boggard Fletcher', who lived near Whalley in Lancashire, and who had assisted the possessed man, Richard Dugdale.[173] Another author, N.N., blames Taylor for using the supernatural as an 'ill Boggard' in his polemic.[174]

There are two points worth making here about the early attestations of 'boggart': the fact that the word seems to be well established orally as it emerges into print; and the geographical range of the eighteen references. Let's start with the strong roots of boggart in early modern spoken English. Already in this period we have two boggart place-names (a Boggard Hole and a Boggard House), both in the South Pennines. Shadwell uses the word 'buggards' in a dialect passage. Of the other examples four refer to a saying. Rollock and Radford manipulate a locution: '*It is not as men saye* ... Hell is but a boggarde to scarre children onelie.' 'He thinks every bush a boggard' was also apparently a well-established saying in parts of England. (Both phrases can be paralleled with sentences employing other bog or bug words: e.g. 'A bug meet only to fray children'.[175]) Then even in our earliest example

---

169. Ray, *A Collection*, 232.

170. Whitehall, *Leviathan*, 18. The verb 'buggard' here likely comes from equestrian English.

171. Shadwell, *The Lancashire Witches*, 30: 1681 is the first recorded performance.

172. Westaway and Harrison, 'The Surey Demoniack'.

173. Taylor, *Surey Demoniack*, 53: 'As to what the said Fletcher pretends *to feel like a Dog or a Cat creeping upwards from his Knee towards his Heart, when he was in bed with* Richard, I take it to be a Dream, if not a Romance ... And so notorious a Fellow is this same *Fletcher* for such pretended Tricks as these, that he is known by the Name of *Boggard Fletcher*. A Boggard is a Bug-bear, or Spirit that Frights one; and at this *Fletcher*'s House, in former days, was such a Boggard as this pretended, from which he carried the Name of *Boggard Fletcher*. He was *Richard*'s Keeper for some time.' For 'Boggard' as a nickname see pp. 223–25.

174. N.N., *Lancashire Levite Rebuked*, 11.

175. Jewel, *The Works*, V, 199 in 1565 and Playfere, *Luke*, 'death was much like a Bugbegger which they fray children with', no page numbers in 1595.

of 'boggart', we have a compound word, a 'fray-boggarde' (a scarecrow), not the boggart itself. Either the boggart has displaced bugge in fray-bugge, an early modern word for a scarecrow,[176] or this form had evolved independently.

Eighteen instances from two hundred years are few, but taken together they suggest that 'boggart' was more common in conversation than in writing. Indeed, on this evidence it is very possible that 'boggart' was already used, albeit not yet written down, in the later Middle Ages. Should we see 'boggart' and related forms emerging around 1500 as part of a new supernatural vocabulary for Britain, taking up their place next to older forms like 'hob' and 'fairy'? It is true that with the exception of bugge, none is attested before the sixteenth century. The earliest reference to bugge in the OED is in 1388 by John Wycliffe (and his colleagues) with the meaning of 'scarecrow': 'as a bugge, either a man of raggis, in a place where gourdis wexen' (Bar. 6, 69). But is this a real or just an apparent absence? Perhaps dialect forms had not yet broken through into writing. After all, whether bugge has a Brittonic or Germanic origin, it must have been used over at least a part of the island in the preceding centuries; unless, of course, we imagine that bugge entered English from another (Germanic?) tongue in the later Middle Ages.

The second point to make is the geography of these authors. Of the eighteen instances recorded earlier, four are outside the areas traditionally associated with boggarts; eleven are within or close to that area; and two, Thomas de Gray[177] and John Whitehall,[178] we have been unable to place. Let me start with the four outliers. The first is Lawrence Saunders. Saunders was born in Northamptonshire in about 1520, although he left the county early for Eton and then Cambridge and London. It is possible that 'buggard' was used as far south as Northamptonshire in the 1500s; indeed, some doubtful nineteenth-century instances of Northants boggarts exist (see below pp. 64–66). However, another explanation might be Saunders' association with Staffordshire. From 1548 to 1552, Saunders worked out of Lichfield Cathedral and his wife Joanna seems to have come from that city.[179] Perhaps he acquired the word in Lichfield

---

176. Bale, *Yet a Course*, 41 for 1543.

177. It is possible that he was part of a landed Norfolk family based around Merton *Norfolk Lists*, 30–32. Thirty-six instances of individuals with the surname De Grey/De Gray feature in Archer's Software, *British 19th Century Surname Atlas* (a CD-ROM based on the 1881 census). The three counties with the most De Grays/De Greys are Kent, Staffordshire and Warwickshire. Of course, this is a very late source.

178. The surname Whitehall was particularly associated with Derbyshire and Staffordshire in Archer's Software, *British 19th Century Surname Atlas*.

179. Betteridge, 'Saunders'.

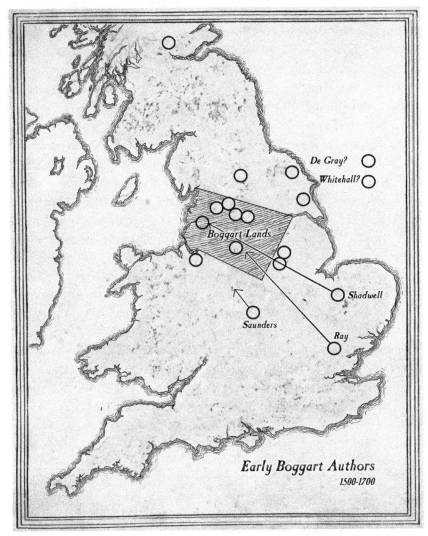

Figure 6: Early Boggart Authors, 1500–1700.

and used it in 1555 because he was writing a farewell to his wife, a Staffordshire woman. As we shall see, the word 'boggart' was certainly used in the 1800s in parts of Staffordshire.

The second outlier is Robert Rollock who was born near Stirling and lived in St Andrews, then later Edinburgh.[180] After his death, when many of Rollock's sermons and lectures were printed, there was an effort to publish some of

180. Kirk, 'Rollock'.

his works in English rather than Scots.[181] I suspect that 'boggarde' here ('Hell
is but a boggarde to scarre children onelie') represents one such 'translation'
from Scots: notice the English 'scarre' rather than Scots 'flay' and 'children'
rather than 'bairnes'. Elsewhere, Rollock has a similar sentence in this much
more Scots form: 'thinke not Hell a Bogill, for it is the sorest burning in the
world'; compare also Rollock's teacher, Melville: 'To these Hell is but a boggill
to fley barnes' (1584).[182]

　　The third outlier is John Ray who grew up in Black Notley in Essex and who
lived much of his life in East Anglia.[183] He was collecting, however, material
from throughout Britain. 'Boggard' does not appear in his 1670 edition. In
his 1678 edition, where it does appear, Ray mentions several individuals from
the north who had contributed proverbs.[184] The fourth outlier is Thomas
Shadwell, a Norfolk playwright who lived most of his life in London. His play
is entitled *The Lancashire Witches* and he went to some trouble to replicate
Lancashire English: 'the play exhibits a good example of the Lancashire
dialect'.[185] This is particularly true of his character 'Clod, A Country Fellow',
who uses the word 'buggards'. Shadwell had spent time at Chadderton Hall
near Oldham and had connections with East Lancashire.[186]

　　Let us turn now to those boggart authors in roughly the area later associated
with boggarts. Coverdale was, according to a contemporary, a Yorkshire man
(*ex Eboracensi patria*),[187] something that is also suggested by his use of Yorkshire
dialect words.[188] There is a tradition that dates back to at least 1822 that Coverdale
was from the Yorkshire village of Coverdale and that his surname was assumed
once he left that place.[189] This is late evidence, but I have reluctantly put him

---

181. Gunn, *Select Works*, I, xix-xx.

182. Rollock, *Fiue and Twentie*, 93; Melville, *The Autobiography*, 202. On the basis of Rollock 'boggarde'
is included in Jamieson and Johnstone, *Dictionary*, 76. It does not appear on the online (and
comprehensive) *Dictionary of the Scots Language* (http://www.dsl.ac.uk/), accessed 21 August
2018.

183. Belfour, 'The Life', ii.

184. There are nine names of contributors given in an unnumbered preface. The only candidate
from Boggartdom is 'Francis Jessop Esq of Broom-hall in Sheffield parish Yorkshire'. It is also
possible that Ray had read the saying in Webster, *The displaying*, 60.

185. Blake, *Language*, 105.

186. Slagle, 'Shadwell', 1114.

187. Bale, *Illustrium*, 241

188. Haylock and Appleby, *Manner of Speaking*, 73: 'Miles Coverdale's writings and Biblical
translations would reflect his Yorkshire upbringing'; Walsh, 'Something Old', 157; see also the
instances where East Riding dialect matches instances in Coverdale's own writing in Hoy, *Glossary*,
3, 183, 235.

189. For 1822, Langdale, *Dictionary*, 18; Guppy, 'Coverdale', 301: it would be unusual for an
Englishman to assign himself a surname in the sixteenth century in this way. Note that the surname

at Coverdale on the map. John Webster was from Thornton-in-Craven in the West Riding.[190] Levins was from Eske in East Yorkshire.[191] Charles Hoole was born in Wakefield and was 'sometimes Master of the Free-School at Rotherham in York-shire' before he moved to London.[192]

Zachary Taylor, the 'Lancashire Levite', was born in Bolton and lived much of his life in Wigan,[193] but his reference is to a local nickname and thus I have placed this on the map at Whalley. N.N. was a Lancashire man, or at least resident there.[194] Having no further clue to his location I have put him in the middle of the county. The Pendle place-name is, of course, from Lancashire: Boggard House is from just across the border in the West Riding. John Radford was certainly from the Midlands and probably from the Peak District, where I have placed him on the map.[195] Whittingham was brought up in Cheshire, perhaps in Chester, although his mother's family was from Lancashire.[196] Markham, meanwhile, was from Nottinghamshire. He 'was probably born at Cotham',[197] and Surphlet was also from that county and 'may have come from Holme'.[198]

Now, of the sixteen instances where we can place sources or authors, all save four (Rollock, Ray, Saunders, and Shadwell) fit within a narrow band of north-central England. The correspondence with the geography of later boggart belief, which appears to have covered about 10 per cent of Britain, is striking. On this evidence, several of the early authors betrayed their dialectal origins by writing 'boggart'. I have also included on the map a very approximate square of the area where boggart belief featured in England in the nineteenth century by using our best guide: place-names. This square reaches from the Humber estuary down into Nottinghamshire, from Nottinghamshire across to

---

Coverdale is quite rare. The *British 19th Century Surname Atlas* shows that the largest concentration of this surname was around Middlesbrough, with another important nucleus at Hull: see also Redmonds, *Yorkshire Surnames*, 187 (the early occurrences of the name are from the Yorkshire Dales). Note, too, that there are other places called Coverdale in the North Country. For example, Coverdale Clough, Brogden, Lancashire.

190. Whitaker, *Whalley*, 491–93. He spent the last twenty years of his life at Cliviger in Lancashire.

191. Wood, *Athenae Oxonienses*, I, 548.

192. Lupton, *Worthies*, 95–96: the quotation is from the frontispiece of Hoole, *An easy Entrance*.

193. Harrison, 'Taylor'.

194. *Lancashire Levite Rebuked*, 17: 'this county'.

195. McCoog, 'Radford', 'was born in the diocese of Lichfield, probably in Derbyshire because of his subsequent association with the Peak District ... Radford ministered to Catholics in the Peak District. On 3 February 1595, a spy reported that Radford dwelt at Mr Williamson's at Sawly until he kicked Mrs Williamson's dog down the stairs for making noise during mass.'

196. Marcombe, 'Whittingham'.

197. Steggle, 'Markham'.

198. Cooke, 'Surflet' 53, argues for a possible connection with Markham.

the Mersey estuary, and from the Mersey estuary up to Morecambe Bay (for more details, see Chapter 3). As can be seen on the map, six references fall within, and six fall close to that relatively small, circumscribed part of the island.

Boggart Writing, 1700–1800

We shuffle now slightly closer to the Victorian boggart, by looking at our few Enlightenment boggart sources. I produce here a map showing the nine boggart references known to me from eighteenth-century authors.[199] Here the distribution of boggart references conforms more closely to the boggart area outlined on the map. One reference from Hull and the most northerly reference from Westmorland fall narrowly outside the square. On some very slight evidence (particularly Peter Levins and John Webster on the earlier map),[200] we are possibly justified in seeing 'boggart' becoming more restricted over the period from 1500 to 1900, disappearing particularly from the North and East Ridings. Pockets of boggart belief in Cleveland (North Riding/Co. Durham) and around Skegness (Lincolnshire) in the mid and late nineteenth century—reviewed in the next chapter, pp. 66–69—might be taken as further pointers to a decline in the east. It must be reiterated, however, that we are dealing with very few sources.

Some of these eighteenth-century boggart mentions are inconsequential; for instance, a reference in a letter to the 'Cock Lane Boggart' from 1716—a reminder that 'boggart' often, perhaps invariably, referred to ghosts.[201] But we also see the first 'boggart tales' and I will quote these fully to give a sense of the boggart as it emerges into history. In 1730, a Dr Clegg (1679–1755) at Chinley in Cheshire tells in his diary the story of a local child who is touched by 'Ye Boggard' while sleeping in his parents' bed. It is our earliest boggart narrative:

---

199. I have not included eighteenth-century place-name references. Twemlow, *Twemlows*, 79 (1716) for Adlington (a letter about the 'Cock Lane Boggart' from Charles Legh of Adlington); Clegg, *Extracts*, 41 (1730) for Chinley (where Clegg lived); Bridges, *Homer Travestie*, 94 (1762) for Hull (Bridges was born there); *The Beauties*, III, 94 (1764) for Horton (a false boggart seen there); Bobbin, *Tim*, 327–28 (1764) for Milnrow (Tim Bobbins aka John Collier lived most of his life in Milnrow); Forster, 'Dear Sir', (1767) for Wakefield; West, *A Guide*, 256 (1778) for Chapel-le-Dale; Barlow, *The Cheshire*, 122 (c.1785), for Wilmslow; A.W., *The Westmorland Dialect*, 42 (1790) no location given, so placed at Kendal on the map.

200. Note, too, pp. 42–43, the possibility that Coverdale came from East rather than North Yorkshire.

201. Twemlow, *Twemlows*, 79. This is, of course, the famous Cock Lane Ghost: Chambers, *Ghost*.

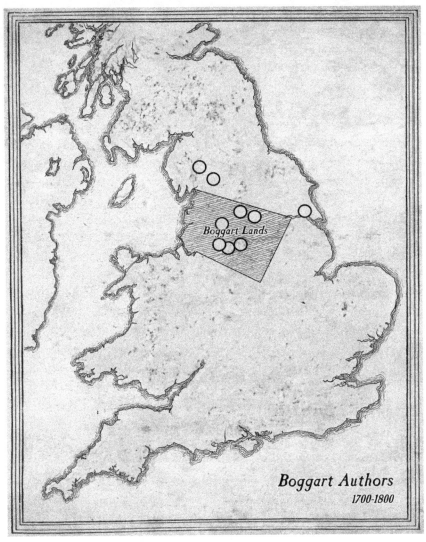

Figure 7: Boggart Authors, 1700–1800.

On the 18th [September] at night the wife of John Armstrong told
me the night her child was seized with the small-pox, her husband
being in bed with her and the child, both she and he heard a noise
as if some one had walked sharply over the chamber and gone
under the bed. The husband got up and searched the room but
found nothing. The child lay betwixt them but would needs be
removed to ye side next ye wall, but presently cryed out 'Ye
Boggard has touched me', and would lie betwixt them again. A

night or two before, ye wife being in ye house, herself heard a
dismal noise like ye cry of a child, ending in a mournful tone. Ye
like walking she heard again in ye chamber ye week but one after,
when her sisters child was seized. They were both seized with ye
most violent and deadly infection I had ever seen.[202]

In 1764, a Bradford newspaper described how a maid at Horton disappeared
from service, hid within the house where she had worked and was mistaken
for a 'boggart' by her employers. It is the first in a long line of comic boggart
stories:

The following very odd affair, we are informed, lately happened
at Horton near Bradford, in this country: a girl of about 17 years
of age, servant to one Mr. Swain, Woolstapler there, having been
charged with stealing a guinea, left her service privately, and was
missing upwards of two months: during this time several of her
master's family had seen her upon the stairs in the night-time,
which greatly alarmed and terrified them, all concluding it must
be her spirit or apparition. This confirmed the suspicion that she
had destroyed herself, and her master and father were at the
expence of 5l and upwards in searching the coal pits, ponds, &c
thereabouts for her body, but without success. At last, however,
she was found alive and above ground in the following manner;
all her master's family being gone to church, except one maid and
a child of six years of age, the child perceived her upon the stairs,
and cried out, [']That's no Boggard (Apparition) 'tis our Molly,[']
and made towards her, followed by the maid. The girl made what
haste she could into a working chamber, where [there] was a large
parcel of wool; but being closely pursued, and not having time to
hide herself in it, she jumped out of a window four yards high
into a barn, where she was, on her master's coming from church,
found concealed in the hay-mow. [203]

Then, in 1767, the Rev. Benjamin Forster shares, in a letter, tales about 'the
Boggard of Longar Hede' in Wakefield, a phantom dog that haunted the area
around Robin Hood's Well in that city:

---

202. Clegg, *Extracts*, 41.
203. *The Beauties*, III, 94.

Haistwell will tell you of a peculiar padfoot we have here of our own, hight 'Boggard of Langar hede': it is of old fame here; clanks its chain at a three lane end, and so parades it for a few hundred yards up the lane, under a long garden wall belonging to this house. It begins its stalk from a spot where is an old well (one of the three Robin Hood's wells in this Riding) under the present causeway. I have met with one person who saw it walk beside him for a quarter of a mile up the lane, and to be sure his aunt died that very night. It is white, with glaring eyes, four-legged (like all our goblins), and about the size of a cawf, and is the most dreaded of all the padfoots of this part. My lad, at supper-time, hardly dares to come to my apartment, which looks towards the garden-wall, and is a great way from the rest of the house; he hardly ever indeed does venture without bringing with him some one of the family, or enticing a glorious fellow of a mastiff to accompany him to the door. Mrs. Beale had a servant brought back her godspenny after she was hired, and would not live here, upon any account, no, not if you would give her the house and estate. Come and help me to exorcise this fierce fiend.[204]

These Wakefield experiences are the first boggart tales to be properly rooted in a landscape. The 'padfoot', note, is a Yorkshire name for a dog spirit.[205] 'Boggart' is here clearly being used in a general sense, much as Forster uses the Standard English 'goblin'. The 'godspenny' was the money given to serving staff upon being hired.

It is worth noting that not one of these three sets of early boggart stories appeared in a book: we have a diary, a letter, and a newspaper report. Even there note the colloquial nature of 'boggart'. The word appears twice in direct speech and once as a name. In not one case is it referred to by the author as part of his own vocabulary. Writing on the supernatural was rare in Enlightenment Europe, presumably because of the changing attitudes of published writers rather than changing attitudes among the general popula-tion.[206] The one area for which substantial supernatural writing survived in

---

204. Forster, 'Dear Sir'.
205. Wright, *Dialect Dictionary*, IV, 406. I hope to write on the padfoot, comparing this entity with barghest, gytrash and skriker.
206. Some recent writers have claimed that interest in the supernatural did not drop away in this period: e.g. Henderson, *Witchcraft*, 2. It is worth making a distinction between what the Enlightenment did to general beliefs (little and slowly) and what the Enlightenment did to the

the period 1680–1780 was, at least in Britain, ghost-lore. On this basis one might have thought that some boggart legends would have made it into eighteenth-century collections.[207] But the boggart ghost was perhaps too baroque for more classical eighteenth-century tastes. In the Enlightenment we see the creation of the modern ghost, with many previous forms of the undead (e.g. the shape-changer, the phantom army, the revenant, and so forth) being excluded.[208] It was only in the nineteenth century, and then only slowly, that the boggart would become commonplace in print.

Conclusion

As we come to the end of this chapter, we can leave aside questions of geography and distribution, of sources and survival, and ask instead questions about content. Taken together, what little can we learn about boggarts from 1500 to 1800? How were they imagined? Where did they live? What did they do? Folklorists are conscious of the fact that supernatural creatures are not static in human imagination; they will change from generation to generation. Yet on our admittedly limited evidence, the boggart remained in essence the same for over three hundred years. We have, for instance, early modern evidence that horses were scared by 'boggarts',[209] something well attested in later sources, too.[210] We see the country and the house boggart in the two surviving sixteenth- and seventeenth-century place-names: respectively, Boggart Hole (a 'clough' or steep valley) and Boggart House.[211] Modern boggarts were also associated, as we shall see, with both domestic settings and the outdoors.[212]

There are other points. We see a tradition of people mistaking things or persons, particularly at night, for boggarts: in bushes, for example, in the

---

beliefs of those who wrote about general beliefs (a great deal, very quickly). In a whole series of macro-areas (including superstitions, witchcraft and fairy-lore) Enlightenment writers were *far* less likely to write about the supernatural than their seventeenth-century predecessors and if they did so, they did so in a very different way. An interesting approach for measuring this is to put 'fairies', 'ghosts' and 'spirits' into an N-gram (for more on this database see n. 105). In all three cases there is a fall from about 1680, and a rise after 1750.

207. Handley, *Visions*, 1–6. Of course, boggarts could have appeared under different names. For some likely boggart accounts, without the word actually being used see *New Lights*, 6–7, 18, 42.

208. For some sense of the range of undead types in an earlier period of European history see Caciola, *Afterlives*, 3–5.

209. De Grey, *The Compleat Horseman*, 28; Markham, *Cauelarice*, 112; Whitehall, *Leviathan*, 18.

210. Wright, *Dialect Dictionary*, I, 326.

211. Crossley (ed.), *Discovery*, lxiii (country); Sutcliffe, 'Midgley', 117–18 (house); Taylor, *Surey Demoniack*, 53 (house).

212. See pp. 79–108.

seventeenth century; a supposedly dead servant in eighteenth-century England;[213] donkeys, drying laundry, and weather balloons, among many others in Victoria's England.[214] The boggart as a groundless fear was particularly important in our earliest sources. The boggart is also shown to be a monster that scares children—'Hell is but a boggarde to scarre children'—not least in the terrible illness-bringing boggart from Stodhart.[215] The boggart was, of course, still petrifying children in the north-west in the 1800s.[216] We see, perhaps in Levins and Ray and certainly in the 1764 case of the Horton servant, the boggart as a ghost: the nineteenth-century boggart was, as we have seen, generally undead.[217] We also have in the early sources a hint that 'boggart' was (as it remained afterwards) an umbrella term for a wide range of solitary beings: a dog spirit, a human ghost, a screeching noise.[218] On this admittedly limited evidence, the boggart that haunted Ellen Royd's farmhouse in the 1500s, the creature that stalked out of the Boggart Hole in Pendle around 1600, and the boggart that in the 1700s ran by Robin Hood Well, were all the same bogie that was talked about in those areas in the 1800s.

---

213. Ray, *A Collection*, 232; Webster, *The Displaying*, 60; *The Beauties*, III, 94.

214. Young 'Dialect', 2–3, for boggart jokes and 'A Balloon Mistaken' (1873).

215. *Lectures*, 132; Clegg, *Extracts*, 41.

216. See pp. 62–63.

217. Levins, *Manipulus*, 30; Ray, *A Collection*, 232; *The Beauties*, III, 94.

218. Forster, 'Dear Sir'; *The Beauties*, III, 94; Clegg, *Extracts*, 41.

CHAPTER THREE

Boggart Distribution

Introduction

Where were boggarts encountered in the nineteenth century? Those writing on British tradition and folklore have given a vast range of answers to that question. Some talk blithely of the north of England,[219] others of Lancashire,[220] others of Yorkshire,[221] others of both Lancashire *and* Yorkshire.[222] There are then more eccentric answers. Some write of boggarts in Devon and Cornwall,[223] in Ireland,[224] and Scotland—including a Gaelic-speaking boggart.[225] On very few occasions authors offer more exact, if suspect, homelands; for example, Kai Roberts states that 'boggart' is 'a common dialect term used throughout the West Riding of Yorkshire and East Lancashire';[226] while R.C. Turner is more ambitious—he states that 'boggart' 'occurs in Westmorland, Lancashire, Cheshire and Yorkshire'.[227] This confusion about the boggart's home regions is typical of British supernatural folklore writing which has a poor record for

---

219. Rockwood (ed.) 163, *Brewer's Dictionary of Phrase and Fable* claims 'boggard' is 'a north of England name'; see also Rose, *An Encyclopedia*, 45; Simpson and Roud, *Dictionary*, 29; Briggs, *Anatomy of Puck*, 186; Warren, *Lancashire Folk*, 11.
220. Spence, *Fairy Tradition*, 22; Morton, *Boggarts*, 9; Henderson, *Notes*, 274–75.
221. 'A Suspended Rule'; Drury, *Dictionary*, 35; Elton, *Origins*, 214; X [Goodrich-Freer], *Essays*, 80 (for her probable Yorkshire childhood, Campbell and Hall, *Strange Things*, 113–22, confirmed http://ehbritten.blogspot.com/2011/01/strange-story-of-ada-goodrich-freer.html [accessed 21 January 2020]); Walker, *The Woman's Encyclopedia*, 114.
222. Leach, *Funk and Wagnalls Standard Dictionary*, 153; Edwards, *Hobgoblin and Sweet Puck*, 95; Davitt, *Witches and Ghosts*, 13.
223. For Devon where 'boggarts abound', Cornish, 'Bridges', 812; for Cornwall, Grigson, *Freedom*, 88, and Barrett, 'Black Spider' (fiction); and Hill, 'Comlyn' (fiction) for a 'marsh boggart'.
224. Cockrell, 'Password', 24: 'a shape-shifting creature of Irish legend': see also n. 141.
225. *Century Dictionary*, III, 610; Frater, *Listverse.com's Ultimate Book*, 579; and, for a Gaelic-speaking boggart, Cooper's *The Boggart* (she at least had the excuse of fiction).
226. Roberts, *Halifax*, 52 (note this definition has the merit of identifying the area of maximum concentration of boggart evidence).
227. Turner, 'Boggarts', 170, we will see that there is very little evidence for Westmorland.

geographical exactitude, one of the consequences of poor data collecting in the 1800s.[228]

My aim in this chapter is to map out the supernatural use of 'boggart' in nineteenth- and early twentieth-century England; something that has not been done for boggarts (or, indeed, on this scale, for any other British bogie). The mapping is primarily an exercise in dialect studies. I am, after all, looking at the distribution of a word. But it is hoped that even a rough map of Boggartdom will provide the foundations for folklore-related and historical reflections in later chapters. I have tried four different but interlocking approaches to delineate where the dialect word 'boggart' was used: boggart place-names; boggart personal names (see p. 18); 'boggart' in Wright's *Dialect Dictionary*; and 'boggart' in the Survey of English Dialects (SED). This, it goes without saying, will necessarily be an approximate exercise. For the word 'boggart' we have only a few score data points. Compare this to the tens of thousands of data points available for similar exercises in other countries.[229] I will also put the word 'boggart' in relation to two other supernatural words found in the north of England: 'boggle' and 'dobbie'. All three, it will be shown, were generic terms for ambivalent solitary supernatural bogies.

Boggart Place-names

There are thousands of supernatural place-names in England. In some cases, these names recall a well-known supernatural being such as the fairy (e.g. Fairy Steps at Beetham in Westmorland);[230] in others they evoke more obscure beings such as the fearsome bullbeggar (e.g. Bullbeggar Lane near Woking, Surrey).[231] Supernatural place-names allow scholars to ask questions of popular beliefs when other sources fail us. Are, for example, fairies associated with

---

228. The historical-geographical approach (favoured in different forms in Scandinavia, Finland, Ireland and parts of northern Europe), see further Frog, 'Revisiting', naturally employed maps, particularly for story types, Tangherlini, 'Performances', 104–05. This map-making approach never caught on in Britain. A folklore atlas for Britain was proposed but never materialized, Sanderson, 'Towards'. The British folklore maps we have are all too often restricted to the folklore gazetteers that give a brief overview of folk traditions in different British counties, the best of which are Westwood and Simpson, *Lore of the Land*, and its predecessor Westwood, *Albion*. Rare folklore distribution maps of quality are to be found in Rudkin, 'Black Dog', 112, 115, 127, 129; and Brown, 'Black Dog', 177; and, an inspiration for me, Loveday, *Hikey Sprites*, 32, 34.

229. *Der Atlas der deutschen Volkskunde*, edited by Zender *et al.*, for Germany (in the 1930s), for instance, was based on questionnaires from some 20,000 points in German-speaking Europe; see further Wiegelmann and Cotter, 'The *Atlas*'; and, more generally, Wildhaber, 'Folk Atlas'.

230. OSWe 46 (1862).

231. See n. 236 for Bullbeggar place-names.

trees?[232] Did elves inhabit high or low places?[233] However, the most straight-forward way to use toponyms for supernatural research is as a geographical trace. If you find a 'boggart' place-name, boggarts will, at some point, have been a part of local lore. 'A supernatural place-name does not', of course, 'necessarily pinpoint a belief in particular beings', but it does demonstrate, 'a readiness to talk about them'.[234]

Place-names are useful in tracing popular beliefs because they represent a shared decision on the part of a community. If a given population has decided to, say, name a rise of land 'Boggart Hill', then it follows that at one time enough locals were prepared to repeat and establish the place-name. Admittedly, in some instances the community giving the names was likely very small: in the case of a Boggart Field in Blackley we might be dealing with a single farming family. The name appears on a tithe return.[235] But the principle remains that these are shared terms. Let us return to the example of the bullbeggar given earlier. In the places where these Bullbeggar place-names were coined, the bullbeggar featured as a part of local supernatural belief systems. There are nine English place-names with 'Bullbeggar' and these appear in the Home Counties, immediately around London, giving us an approximation to what might be called 'bullbeggardom'.[236] Can we trace boggarts in the same way?

The single greatest difficulty with supernatural place-names is that many are open to other non-supernatural interpretations. The element 'Hob', for example, in a place-name, is often reckoned to refer to a hob, a British soli-tary spirit that haunted houses and the countryside.[237] However, 'Hob' is also a diminutive of Robert; and it can also refer to grass tussocks.[238] Is Hob Wood, therefore, a haunted wood? Or a wood that once belonged to Robert? Or a

---

232. Young, 'Fairy Trees'.
233. Hall, 'Elves', 80; Hall, *Elves*, 66.
234. Harte, 'Ogre', 37, as long as, of course, the supernatural element is still understood.
235. DRM 1/15 (at http://archivecat.lancashire.gov.uk/), 1844 [accessed 12 October 2018].
236. Bullbeggars, Berkhamstead (Herts), '1936' (1952); Bullbeggars Farm, Caddington, Beds, *Book of Reference*, 54 [1880]; Bullbeggar's Farm, Elstree (Mid) OSMi S6 (1868), east of Elstree, 'Alleged Game Trespass' (1883); Bullbeggars Hole, Fortyhill (Mid), 'Copyhold Premises' (1831); OSMi 2 (1868), north-west of Fortyhill; Ford and Hodson, *Enfield*, 55 [1873]; Bullbeggars Lane, Godstone (Sur), Google Maps, south-east of Godstone; Bullbeggars Lane, Horsell (Sur), OSSur 16 (1873), just to the west of Horsell; Bullbeggars Lane, Hyde Heath (Bucks), Bennell, 'Great Missenden' (now Bullbaiter's Lane); Bullbeggar Mead, Cheshunt (Herts), DE/Wb/T16, Herts Archives and Local Studies, 'Of an unnamed farm at Cheshunt' (1813, 1819); Bullbeggar Wood, Wittersham (Kent), OSK 80SW (1899), north of village. There is also a Bullbeggar place-name in the United States (USA), Woodyard and Young, 'Three Notes', 65.
237. Dickins, 'Hobs'; Briggs, *Dictionary of Fairies*, 222–23; Henderson, *Notes*, 264; 'The legends' (Derbyshire, 1883); Westwood and Simspon, *Lore of the Land*, 828–29.
238. Wright, *Dialect Dictionary*, III, 183–84; Field, *Field Names*, 105.

wood full of rich growths of grass? This problem is ruinous for questions of distribution. Happily, with 'boggart', the potential for confusion is much less serious than with 'hob'. 'Boggart' meant 'scarecrow' in Cheshire and Lancashire.[239] However, it seems unlikely that this alternative would account for many boggart place-names, save *perhaps* in the case of the odd 'Boggart Field'.[240] There is also a rare surname 'Bogget', but this, as we saw in the last chapter, is not generally associated with Boggartdom.[241]

Despite these problems it has, as noted in Chapter 1, been possible to gather 183 boggart place-names. This is an important number of names and offers effective coverage. The collection of place-names for 'boggart' has been even across England. There are no obvious holes in the data collected: counties are equally served by place-name sources (see further pp. 20–21). Once placed on a map, the 183 boggart place-names give us an outline—however approximate—of Boggartdom. About two fifths of the names are from Lancashire. But boggart place-names also appear in northern Derbyshire, Cheshire, Nottinghamshire, Lincolnshire, the East Riding and, in large numbers, in the West Riding.

The only objection that might perhaps be brought against these results is the question of chronology. We suspect that boggart place-names were used from at least the sixteenth century, and we can document that they were used from the seventeenth century (see Chapter 2). Is it possible that the word 'boggart' dropped out of common usage, and that the place-name survived as a misunderstood fossil? An example of this process with supernatural place-names from the Northwest might be Alphin in Saddleworth, which *possibly* meant, when it was coined in the (early?) Middle Ages, the Elf Hill (or the Elf Stone).[242] No nineteenth-century resident would have

---

239. See pp. 33–34, and also the longer discussion of boggart scarecrows pp. 225–27.

240. The question of the meaning of Boggart Field and related names is a complex one, see further p. 230. Note that some of these names are for gates and stiles where a supernatural explanation seems the natural one, Spooner, 'Haunted': e.g. Boggart Yate, OSLa 43 (1848). For a late Derbyshire boggart encounter (possibly 1930s) at a fence crossing, MacGregor, *Ghost*, 163–64.

241. Hanks *et al.*, *Dictionary?*, I, 270.

242. Alphin is the dominant peak in the Greenfield district. Smith, *Place-Names*, II, 312 records, Alphenstone from 1468 and Alfin Hill from 1817 and suggests 'probably OE elfin (Merc ælfen) adj. from elf 'fairy', stān, hyll'; we would have then the Elfin Stone or the Elfin Hill. How likely is Smith to be right here? The fifteenth-century attestation is late and Anglo-Saxon elf toponyms have come under the scrutiny of Alaric Hall, who has showed that many have nothing to do with elves: 'Are There Any Elves in Anglo-Saxon Place-names?' However, Hall also notes that though the evidence, ibid. 80, 'of place-names for Anglo-Saxon beliefs is vanishingly slight… what there is is consistent with a wider range of evidence for medieval English elves' association with lonely hills and valleys'. Alfin satisfies these requirements, but it is much less satisfactory in linguistic terms.

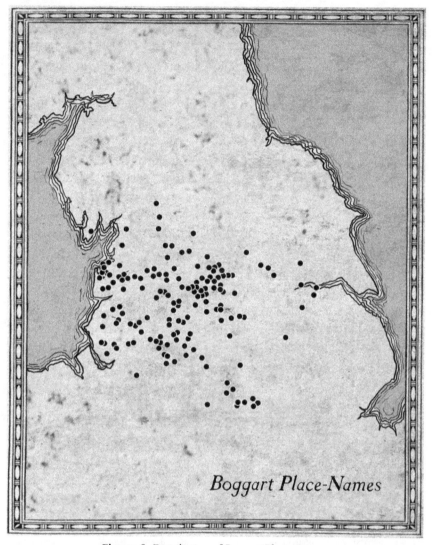

Boggart Place-Names

Figure 8: Distribution of Boggart Place-Names.

understood the word's original sense (if indeed it related to elves), although the area was associated with fairies well into the nineteenth century.[243] 'Boggart', as we shall see in this chapter, continued to be used in dialect in these regions throughout the 1800s. It is always possible that the name was understood, but that the belief system behind the name had collapsed. What,

---

243. I look at the fairies of Greenfield in Young, 'Public Bogies', 404–405.

for example, should we make of the three Nottinghamshire boggart place-names where there is in the 1800s no evidence of boggart beliefs in local folklore?[244]

Boggart Personal Names

Prior to the twentieth century there were many 'public bogies': spirits known and talked about by the entire communities.[245] Parts of Preston, for example, were haunted by a headless woman who sometimes turned into a headless dog. This boggart was known as 'Bannister Hall Doll'.[246] Around Windermere Lake there walked the spirit of a dead monk, a terrifying creature who was heard more often than seen. He was called the 'Crier of Claife'.[247] At Lowther in Westmorland, a bogie rode in a coach through the countryside. He skinned horses and was eventually laid by the local clergy. The folk near Lowther referred to this monster as 'the Auld Lord'.[248] All three names—'Bannister Hall Doll', 'the Crier of Claife', and 'the Auld Lord'—are examples of 'supernatural personal names'. In trying to establish Boggartdom, supernatural personal names are a valuable tool. If, in a given community, a supernatural entity was known as 'X Boggart' or 'the Boggart of X', then we can be sure that: (i) the word 'boggart' was used there; and (ii) the local population saw the bogie in question as a boggart.

I have catalogued several hundred northern spirits dating from the nineteenth and early twentieth centuries. A number of these are given supernatural personal names by the authors who describe them and in thirty-seven cases, the word 'boggart' features in this name; for instance, 'Gamershaw Boggart', the ghost of a murdered woman in Flixton (to the south of Manchester).[249] I have plotted these in Figure 9.[250] The distribution of boggart personal names

---

244. Boggard Lane, Gringley, 'Gringley' (1854); Boggart House, Strelley 1911 Census, Enumeration District 8, p. 65; Boggart Lane, Bulwell, 'An Alleged Dangerous Crossing' (1899). The only record of a boggart-like name in Notts folklore (known to me) is the 'Boggan' in Laxton, Haslam, *Ghosts*, 35.

245. Bennett, *Traditions*, 178–79.

246. An Enthusiast, 'Catching a Salmon' (1853); 'Literary Notices' (1867); Higson 'Five Days' Walks' (1872); Hardwick, *Traditions*, 130 (1872); Bowker, *Goblin Tales* (1883), 132; 'Preston' (1892); North-Westerner, 'Way' (1932); 'Ghost Legend' (1953); Coupe, 'A Spook' (1953); 'Readers' (1954): the only contemporary discussion known to me is Sartin, *Preston*, 27–28 and Karl and Yeomans, *Preston's Haunted Heritage*, 114–16.

247. Bowker, *Goblin Tales*, 212–20 for one of the many retellings of the story; Cowper, *Hawkshead*, 325–26 for an excellent critique of the Crier legend.

248. Sullivan, *Cumberland*, 158–60; ETA, 'Traditions and Superstitions'. The Auld Lord deserves his own study...

249. Lawson, *Flixton*, 109.

250. Note that in cases of multiple boggart personal names in one place I have included just the first.

looks like a rather limited version of the boggart place-name map: most of Lancashire and the edges of the West Riding are covered, as is northern Derbyshire. There is also a boggart personal name in Staffordshire. But on the basis of the distribution of place-names, we might have expected more boggarts to the east of the Pennines and also in the Midlands.

There are three obvious explanations as to why the distribution is more limited for boggart personal names than for boggart place-names. One possibility is that I have failed to pick up references to boggart personal names in Yorkshire and Midlands folklore. Another possibility, and the one that (perhaps for reasons of vanity) I would favour, is that folklore was not as well documented for Yorkshire and the Midlands counties as it was for Lancashire in the nineteenth century.[251] There were spirits with boggart personal names, but they (or at least their names) were not interesting to Victorian antiquarians and folklorists. It is, thinking in these terms, possibly instructive that four Lincolnshire supernatural boggart personal names are recorded only in the mid twentieth century.[252] A final possibility is that there was a slight shift in naming conventions from county to county, much as we find with human names. Possibly communities outside Lancashire, but still within Boggartdom, used 'boggart' in place-names but not for supernatural personal names.

Accrington (La): Aker-Whitt, 'The Dunkenhalgh Boggart'; Alton (De): Wigfull, 'Alton'; Ashton-on-Mersey (La): Sweeney, 'Dumber'; Austwick (WY), Hughes 'Acoustic Vases', 81–82; Bamford (De): Evans, *Bradwell*, 44–45; Blackley (La): Milner, *Country Pleasures*, 263–64; Blackpool (La): 'Superstition in the Fylde' (1857); Bradford (WRY): Fieldhouse, *Old Bradford*, 33; Burnley (La): McCandlish, 'Back O' Th' Hill Boggart'; Bury (La): 'The "Freetown Pie"' (1862); Chapel Le Dale (WRY), West, *A Guide*, 256; Clayton (La): Higson, *Droylsden* (1859), 69; Clitheroe (La): Clarke, *Clitheroe*, 59 [second run of page numbers]; Droylsden (La): Higson, *Droylsden*, 68; East Bierley (WRY): Parker, *Illustrated*, 278; Eyam (De) 'The Miner and the Ghost' (1887); Eccleston (La): 'The Copp Boggart' (1872); Fewston (WRY): Parkinson, *Yorkshire Legends*; 131–33; Flixton (La): Crofton, *Stretford*, III, 73–74; Glossop (De): Fizzwig 'From Glossop', (1866); Gorton (La): Higson, *Gorton*, 16; Hayfield (De): 'Hayfield' (1869); Helmshore (La): H, *Green Lane Boggert*; Heywood (La): Waugh, *Sketches* (1855), 225–28; Horton (WRY): Fieldhouse, *Old Bradford*, 86–89; Kidsgrove (Sta): Leese, *Kidsgrove*; Middleton (La), 'The Spaw "Boggart"'; Mowbrick (La): 'Boggart Renown'; Ramsbottom (La), Elliot, *The country*, 47; Preesall (La): Thornber, *History*, 332; Preston (La): 'Death' (1867); Ribchester (La): 'The Starling Bridge Boggart' (1894); Rochdale (La): Harland and Wilkinson, *Lancashire Legends*, 11–12; Salmesbury (La): McKay, *East*, 9; Wakefield (WRY): Forster, 'Dear Sir'; Wibsey (WY): Fieldhouse, *Old Bradford*, 89; Worsthorne (La), Young, 'Holden'; Wycoller (La): Carr, *Colne* (1878), 197.

251. The only English county that has a comparably rich late nineteenth-century written folklore tradition to Lancashire was Cornwall, James, *Folklore of Cornwall*, 8–21, and possibly Devon. Lancashire was characterized not by the quality of the work done there but by the quantity (particularly from the 1860s to the 1880s) and the *esprit de corps* among writers, many of whom knew and corresponded with each other.

252. See p. 68. As such they are too late for this survey where I have imposed the First World War as a cut-off date.

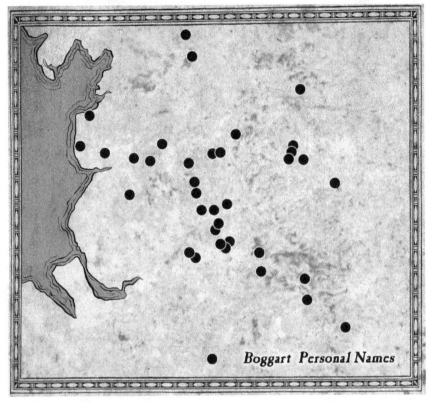

Figure 9: Occurrence of Boggart Personal Names.

Wright's *Dialect Dictionary*

Unlike British folklore collections, British dialect collections have a great deal of rich data. Indeed, there have been two massive national British dialect surveys. The first was Joseph Wright's six-volume *Dialect Dictionary*; and the second, the *Survey of English Dialects* (see the next section). In 1898, Wright's *Dictionary* listed the following places where 'boggart' was used with a supernatural sense (or an obviously derivative sense; e.g. scarecrow, scared horse, etc.): 'Cum[berland] W[est]m[orland] Y[or]ks[hire] Lan[cashire] Ch[e]s[hire] St[a]f[fordshire] Der[byshire] Not[tinghamshire] Lin[colnshire] Wor[cestershire]. Also Dev[on]?'[253]

253. *Dialect Dictionary*, I, 326. Compare with the *OED*: 'popular use in Westmoreland, Lancashire, Cheshire, Yorkshire and the north Midlands'; for the relationship between the *OED* and Wright's *Dialect Dictionary*, Durkin, '*The English Dialect Dictionary*'.

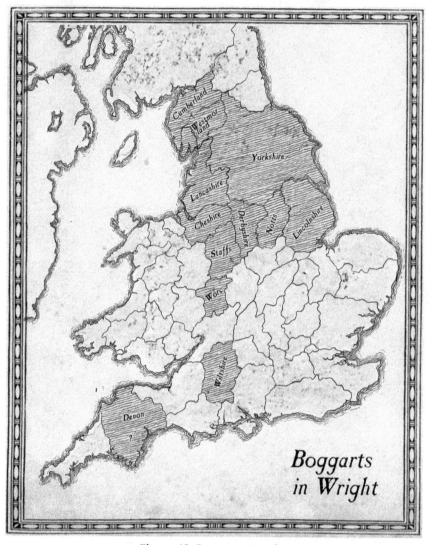

Figure 10: Boggarts in Wright.

To these, Wright subsequently added Wiltshire.[254] How did Wright achieve such
an exact series? Here it is important to look at his methods.

Wright had two ways of verifying and recording dialect words. The first
was to comb written works (published or otherwise), something that Wright
did with volunteer readers: 'There is need of others to read novels, agricultural
treatises, sporting books ... to make slips for the dialect words occurring

---

254. *Dialect Dictionary*, VI, 327.

therein.'[255] The second was that he relied on local knowledge. In fact, Wright
sent out, for the first of his six volumes, an incredible 12,000 queries to contacts
from what he called 'the Workshop', the study where the dictionary was put
together.[256] He listed almost 300 'Correspondents', most from Britain, in his first
volume, including the Peacock family in Lincolnshire (dialectologists and folklorists) and 'Wessex' novelist Thomas Hardy.[257] In terms of professions these were:
'country gentlemen, clergy, mill-workers, farmers, students, enthusiasts of all
sorts, both scholars and homely folk'. Many were not dialect speakers themselves
and were not consistently reliable authorities on particular local dialects. Following
what were often itinerant professions—such as vicar or teacher—they may have
confused information about the various parishes of districts in which they had
lived and worked; and we know that some of them were asked for information
about places that they had not visited for many years.[258]

However, Wright specifically noted contributions from individual correspondents under individual entries. Not only did he construct his entries
scientifically, he also took great care to allow future readers to check his
sources. In fact, even a passing acquaintance with Wright's six-volume work
leaves the reader bursting with admiration. Here, after all, was a man who
began his working life at six as a donkey driver in the West Riding, who only
learnt to read and write at fifteen,[259] and who, by his mid forties, had become
professor of comparative philology at Oxford. Characteristically, when Wright
failed to find a publisher ready to pay for the *Dictionary*, he tracked down
subscribers, taking ultimate financial responsibility for the venture.[260] Wright
himself grew up at Idle on the outskirts of Bradford, in an area where boggart
belief was present in the nineteenth century. In 1892, he had also published
a study of his hometown dialect, *A grammar of the dialect of Windhill, in the West
Riding of Yorkshire*, in which boggarts appear.[261] Wright was not, therefore,
while writing this entry, writing blind. He had an excellent sense of what
'boggart' meant in his home region.

Wright's firm knowledge of boggarts in one region does not in any way
guarantee, though, the quality of the distribution list. Here there are two

---

255. Wright, *The Life*, I, 358. I have not, note, used dialect word lists and dictionaries in establishing
     Boggartdom for the simple reason that Wright absorbed almost all into his dictionary, although
     see the comments on Cleveland pp. 66–67.
256. For 12,000, *Dialect Dictionary*, I, v; for life in the workshop, Wright, *The Life*, II, 378–91.
257. I, xiii-xiv.
258. Wright, *The Life*, II, 384; Sanderson, 'Folklore Material', 92.
259. Wright, *The Life*, I, 28 (for working) and I, 36 (for reading); see also Markus 'The Genesis'.
260. Wright, *The Life*, II, 369.
261. Page 218 (for definition).

important problems. Firstly, Wright's distribution lists were based solely on counties with little sense of where words were used within counties. After the nation, counties (along with parishes) were, in identity terms, the most important territorial unit in later nineteenth-century Britain. They were much more important than they are in modern British identity.[262] Wright understandably used these units, but we lose all geographical nuances. For example, Yorkshire is the largest English county. But although boggarts were to be found in the West Riding, there were, on the evidence of boggart place-names and boggart personal names, few to be found in the East and none to be found in the North Riding. A casual reader might think, however, that boggarts were to be found throughout Yorkshire: see Figure 10.

A second problem is that the frequency of geographical references in Wright's dictionary is uneven. Just looking at the first sense of 'boggart'—'An apparition, ghost, hobgoblin; and object of terror'—there are two sources for Cheshire, one for Cumberland, three for Derbyshire, one possible for Devon, seven for Lancashire, two for Lincolnshire, one for Nottinghamshire, one for Staffordshire, two for Westmorland, and five for Yorkshire.[263] It is, of course, entirely natural that the number of references is uneven: 'boggart' may have been used less in some areas than others and some areas produced a greater quantity of dialect literature (particularly, Lancashire and Yorkshire).[264] Some of the low-scoring areas should arguably not be in the list at all. Take the most doubtful case, Devon, where Wright speculatively links the word 'bawker' to 'boggart' on the basis of this sentence: 'Mothers frequently frighten their children away from dangerous wells by saying, "Doan', ee go there, my dear; there's a bawker in that will".'[265]

Little would be gained from the philological equivalent of house-to-house fighting, while working through Wright's 'boggart' entry. But there follows an examination of one reference from the list, just to give some sense of the limits of Wright's work. Wright's sole proof that the word 'boggart' was used in Cumberland comes from Elizabeth Linton's *The Lake Country*. The word 'boggart' does not appear in the main text of Linton's book, but it does appear

---

262. Colls, *Identity*, 226: as Morgan, *National Identities*, 219, notes 'the relationship between local and national identity is an area of study that has been largely ignored by British historians'.

263. *Dialect Dictionary*, I, 326.

264. Joyce, *Visions*, 265 who points out that of 131 pages on England in the English Dialect Society's list of 1877, 35 pages were given over to Lancashire, 23 to Yorkshire and 15 to Cumberland; over 50 per cent, then, to three north-western counties that cover, together, about 10 per cent of England.

265. This is taken from R.P.C., 'Bawker', his source, 'J.T.H., farmer, age 24, native of Hartland'. R.P.C. himself connected bawker and boggart.

in a list of 'provincialisms'. There we read 'Boggart, and Bogie, and Bogle, ghosts, and spectres, and evil spirits made visible'.[266] There is a great deal of evidence that 'boggle' was used in Cumberland in this period,[267] although I know of no reference to boggarts or bogies from the county. This phrase does begin to make more sense, however, when considered in the context of the author's life.

Elizabeth Linton grew up in Keswick and knew the Lakes well; she would certainly have encountered 'boggle' around her hometown.[268] The word 'boggart' was used instead in the south of the modern county of Cumbria, in parishes that were part of Lancashire prior to the county reorganization of 1974: 'Lancashire beyond the Sands'. Linton, in fact, spent ten years (1858–1868) in one of these parishes; it was here that she wrote *The Lake Country* and here she will have heard 'boggart'.[269] The evidence remains, then, but ceases to be for Cumberland, something Linton had never claimed; her provincialisms are for 'the Lake District' not for an individual county. Cumberland should be removed from Wright's list. Wiltshire and Worcestershire, which both have isolated references to scarecrows as boggarts, should perhaps also be removed.[270]

Survey of English Dialects

Another data set for boggart distribution appears in the Survey of English Dialects (1950–1968). This was a major postwar project carried out under the leadership of Professor Harold Orton—a project that in its ambition, recalls the heroic age of British scholarship to which Wright belonged. Some 313 locations were chosen in England, the Isle of Man, and parts of English-speaking Wales and questions were asked in these areas to elicit dialect words. The full questionnaire took about eighteen hours to complete. For this reason, often more than one informant (and sometimes as many as seven) was used

---

266. Linton, *Lake*, 297.
267. 'The St. Bees Boggle' (1844); 'Original Poetry. Scallow Beck Boggle' (1861); 'A Twin Brother of the Newtown Boggle' (1893) etc.
268. 'The Borrowdale Road Boggle' (1895), not supernatural but interesting for use of 'boggle'; 'A Tale of the Cuddy Beck Boggle' (1902).
269. Boggarts certainly were known in 'Lancashire beyond the Sands': e.g. 1851 OSLa 22; Newman 'Folklore Survivals', 101; BC, Barrow-in-Furness 2 (La); Grange-Over-Sands 1 (La). However, this was a transitional area where boggles and dobbies also appeared: e.g. Cowper, *Hawkshead*, 302–03. On the relationship between boggarts, boggles and dobbies see pp. 70–76.
270. Discussed at much greater length in the Appendix, pp. 225–27.

in a given location.[271] A typical question from the battery might be: 'What do you call that bird with large round eyes; it flies about at night?' Locals would give the word that they would use: throughout most of the 313 locations: 'owl'.[272]

SED is a useful source for boggarts because of this question: 'Sometimes, when children are behaving very badly, their mother will tell them that someone will come and take them away. What do you call this mysterious person? (L64)'.[273] North of the Trent there were five frequently repeated supernatural answers: the black-man,[274] bogie, bogie-man, boggart, and boggle. SED mapped these answers in the *Linguistic Atlas of England*.[275] But as the present study and the *Atlas* have different priorities, I have redone the part of the map where boggarts appear (see Figure 11).

How useful are SED's findings for boggart-lore and boggart belief? There are two problems: firstly, the question asked to elicit responses; and, secondly, the date at which these questions were asked. The question that elicited 'boggart' (or bogie or boggle...) was carefully phrased, but it must be remembered that the boggart is more than simply a child-scaring admonitory creature. The boggart is usually a supernatural creature (ghost or goblin), potentially believed in by the adult population. It is not *just* a bedtime bogie. 'Boggart' then has a series of derivative meanings, such as scarecrow or something that frightened a horse ('to take boggart'). SED's (necessarily) partial question and the answers it inspired might be the reason as authoritative a figure as John McNeal Dodgson wrote, 'The distribution of BOGGART in Map L64 seems incredible.'[276]

Had the questionnaire asked, say, 'what do you call a spirit who returns from the dead?', 'boggart' might have appeared in areas where it had lost, or perhaps never had, the sense of being a bogie for children.[277] Particularly interesting in this respect are the instances from Cartmel and Yealand (the

---

271. Orton *et al.*, *Atlas*, introduction 3.

272. Orton and Wright, *Word Geography*, 162.

273. Orton, *Survey*, 93.

274. I examine the question of black supernatural scarers in the Appendix, pp. 221–22.

275. Orton *et al.*, *Atlas*, L64. For the detailed results, see Orton and Halliday, *Survey of English Dialects*, 953–54.

276. Dodgson, 'Review', 152.

277. Note that I am not making any attempt to put boggart belief into chronological layers here. I do not think that boggart child-scarers necessarily came before their adult equivalents or necessarily survived the loss of belief in adult scarers. But I can imagine a situation—and SED might give us evidence for this—in which the word 'boggart' had slightly different semantic ranges in different regions. Here, for instance, meaning all scary things; there, meaning just child-scarers.

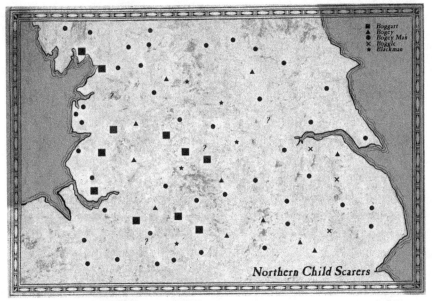

Figure 11: Northern Child Scarers after *The*
Linguistic Atlas of England (Orton *et al.*, *Atlas*, L64).

most northerly boggart squares on the map). Here (see the final section of
this chapter, pp. 70–76), 'dobbie' was used in preference to 'boggart' in
describing supernatural beings in the nineteenth century. Yet these findings
suggest that parents used 'boggart' to scare their children there. In dialect
questionnaires of this type, it is important to elicit responses indirectly. 'What
is a boggart?' is not a very satisfactory question. But for our purposes—it
goes without saying that SED had other priorities— that would have been the
most interesting approach.

The second problem is the date of the survey. As noted earlier in this
chapter boggart-lore was already a reality in parts of England by the sixteenth
century. Little is written about boggarts until the nineteenth century, when
much is put down. However, boggart-lore rapidly drains away after the First
World War. SED was carried out in the 1950s and 1960s. At this date, many
people had, as we will see in Chapter 7, no idea what a boggart was despite
living deep in what had been Boggartdom. It is true that SED staff deliberately
interviewed the oldest members of communities. Respondents had been born
between 1860 and 1900, when boggart belief certainly still featured: they had
to be 'over sixty years of age'.[278] Even so it must be acknowledged that the

---

278. *Atlas*, introduction 3.

survey was of the dialects as spoken after the Second World War. Its relevance for Victorian and Edwardian boggarts has, as with the Boggart Census, to be carefully qualified.

Red Herrings in Northamptonshire

A survey of boggart distribution is 'rescue' folklore: a desperate and necessarily approximate attempt to create data sets from place-names, dialect guides, and folklore writing, at a point where interviews with living populations can only give us limited information about the boggart beliefs of the 1800s. The four maps produced earlier represent four different approaches to the question of boggart distribution. None are perfect, but it is hoped that together they will give us a *sense* of the borders of Boggartdom. However, in gathering this data together, I have been struck by some boggart records unaccounted for in these four maps. These are records connected to Northamptonshire, Cleveland (between the North Riding and Co. Durham), and the Marsh in South Lindsey (Lincolnshire). In this and the following sections, I look, with some care, at these three regions and try and establish whether these are red herrings to be dismissed; or whether they are outliers, which would point to the limits of the method offered earlier.

Northamptonshire is the county to the south of Nottinghamshire and Lincolnshire and we have three pieces of evidence for boggart traditions there. In 1883, Alfred T. Story wrote in his *Legends and Stories of Northamptonshire* a tale of how the building of a county church was sabotaged by supernatural forces—a tale-type well known in Britain.[279] Who was the villain? 'Either Puck', wrote Story, 'or some unhallowed goblin—possibly Boggart (so well known to Northamptonshire children)—had been at work'.[280] A journalist from the county wrote something similar in 1912: 'Education and "common sense" have long ago disposed of these stories that used to be passed from father to son, and that drove in the children from the woods and fields when night fell for fear of the Boggart—an unholy goblin who played pranks on Northamptonshire folk'.[281] In 1886, Mabel Peacock reported a story about a boggart caught in a battle of wits with a farmer in Northamptonshire.[282]

---

279. Motif D2192.1, 'Supernatural agency moves new church foundations ... to another site at night'; ML7060. Baughman, *Type*, 133 (Baughman's list could be greatly extended).
280. *Historical Legends*, 49. Note that Story had previously published this tale in the press: 'Legends and Stories'.
281. 'Jaunts'.
282. *Tales*, 67–71.

At first glance these three pieces of evidence suggest boggart beliefs in a Midlands county in the nineteenth century, but on closer examination, the evidence becomes less impressive. The 1912 article is actually a rewritten version of Story's tale: they are both about the same church and the words in the 1912 article about boggarts and children are just an elaboration of Story's original sentence. How reliable was Story on matters of Northamptonshire lore? He was a Yorkshireman who spent many years abroad as a correspondent and worked on the Northamptonshire press before retiring to Sussex.[283] His stories were written, 'for the most part while the Author was resident in Northamptonshire, with a view merely to filling an occasional column of a newspaper'.[284] Story passed his childhood in North Cave (East Riding, near the Humber estuary) on the eastern fringes of Boggartdom. It is likely that he used 'boggart' growing up and gave it in 1883 instead of Standard English 'bogie'.[285]

Mabel Peacock's boggart can be dealt with more categorically. Peacock was a folklore collector from Lincolnshire and in 1886, she published a boggart story in her *Tales and Rhymes in Lindsey Folk-Speech* entitled 'Th' Man an' th' Boggard'.[286] The tale begins with the words: 'Ther' isn't noä boggards here-aboots 'at I knaw on, bud when I liv'd i' Northamptonsheer I heerd tell o' won 'at reckon'd 'at best farm i' lordship belonged to him.'[287] The reference is to a tale recorded in Lincolnshire about another county: it is nevertheless a Lincolnshire tale.[288] There is, as it happens, practically the same story told by Thomas Sternberg in 1851 about a Northamptonshire farmer and a bogie.[289] Note that 'bogie' was, according to other evidence, the preferred dialect term for a terrifying creature in Northamptonshire.[290] Is it possible that Peacock,

---

283. 'A Literary Celebrity'. Note that Victorian journalists were extremely mobile, Brown, *Victorian News*, 81–82.

284. Story, *Historical legends*, i: Story's own words.

285. One possible late piece of evidence for Northamptonshire boggart-lore, although I am sceptical (while not questioning the memory itself) is BC, Kettering 1 (Other): 'Me and my parents are originally from Northamptonshire and I recall dad calling me a "soggy boggart" when I had been out in the rain. My dad was born there but through his work we lived in different parts of the midlands. He would have called me this in the 1950s. I would think, then we lived in Stoke on Trent and Godmanchester near Huntingdon.'

286. 67–71.

287. 67. Note that it was reprinted in *Northamptonshire Notes and Queries* in 1888, Peacock, 'Th' Man'.

288. For the place of collection see note 309.

289. Sternberg, *The Dialect*, 138–41; see also Harris, *Folklore*, 65.

290. Sternberg, *The Dialect*, 138: 'The Bogie was the household spirit; the same with the Robin Goodfellow and Bogle of other parts of England'; Davies, 'Celtic', 7 gives 'bogie'.

in referring to Northamptonshire, was acknowledging that she had transposed a Northamptonshire tale into Lincolnshire dialect (perhaps she had read Sternberg)?[291] Or were these just similar tales in neighbouring counties, as Peacock would later claim?[292] In either case the evidence for boggarts in Northamptonshire boils down to a throwaway clause, written for copy, by a Yorkshireman temporarily resident there.

Boggart Outliers: Cleveland

Cleveland, on the border between North Yorkshire and Co. Durham, is more promising in boggart terms. In 1861, Walter White published *A Month in Yorkshire*. In his fourteenth chapter, White introduces us to the 'boggle-boggarts', 'a Yorkshire fairy tribe' based in Dunsley Bay. He continues: 'At Kettleness, whither we shall come by and by, they used to wash their linen in a certain spring, named Claymore Well, and the noise of their "bittle" was heard more than two miles off.'[293] This is a very curious reference: firstly, in hyphenating 'boggle' and 'boggart' together (for which I know of no equivalent);[294] secondly, in making a boggart (or boggle-boggart) into a fairy. It is tempting to disregard this reference altogether and put it down to a Londoner's failure to understand something told to him by a local. White certainly heard 'boggart' elsewhere in his travels in the three Ridings. Indeed, he describes the Hurtle Pot Boggart.[295]

However, there is other evidence from precisely the same area. In 1868, J.C. Atkinson, in *A Glossary of the Cleveland Dialect*, gave the following reference: 'Boggart, sb. A hobgoblin, a sprite. See Boggle.' Under 'Boggle' (a much more substantial entry) he included the following sentence:

> That the belief in Bogles or Boggarts was once very prevalent in the district might be inferred if there were no other means of knowing, from the many names involving the word Boggle; e.g. Boggle-house, Boggle-wood &c.[296]

---

291. See n. 289.
292. Gutch and Peacock, *Examples*, 326.
293. White, *A Month in Yorkshire*, 148.
294. Davide Ermacora suggests to me, pers. comm. November 2018, that White 'understood that they were essentially the same thing (as they are), and for practical reasons he put them together, hyphenating them'. I am suspicious of this explanation, while acknowledging that it neatly solves the problem. I wonder whether a local talked to White about '*boggles* 'n *boggarts*' and White understood them to be one species.
295. White, *A Month in Yorkshire*, 256.
296. Atkinson, *A Glossary*, 56.

'Boggle' is clearly, in Atkinson's mind, the dominant term in the area, but the independent entry 'boggart' in his glossary, plus this sentence, suggests that 'boggart' was also used for supernatural creatures. It might be hypothesized that Atkinson had taken 'boggart' from White.[297] But there is a third source that makes any such speculation unnecessary. In 1919, a Northumbrian writer named Howard Pease published a story in which a kneeling man is spotted in the night, though 'whether 'twere a boggart, as they say here, or some solitary shepherd seeking his sheep' was not clear.[298] The story was set in the country-side around Skelton Castle, close to Guisborough, in Cleveland. Pease was a Berwickshire man, but one with a great interest in the history of the Northeast.[299]

Taken together, these three references suggest that 'boggart' was employed for supernatural beings in the territory between Middlesbrough and Whitby. It is otherwise difficult to account for how the only three references to boggarts from the Northeast fall in the same tiny area. 'Boggart' seems to be a secondary word, used less than the typical north-eastern term, 'boggle', although if we had better records, perhaps we would see that some parishes preferred one form and some the other (see further pp. 71–75). In an earlier publication I expressed scepticism about 'boggart' as a 'coward' in a Whitby dialect guide from 1876.[300] I would, on the basis of these three sources, now take this term more seriously and would also note 'boggarty' in the nineteenth-century dialect of Whitby.[301] It looks very much as if Wright and other scholars have missed a small boggart island in north-eastern England. Likewise, the four interlocking methods in this chapter failed to pick up this boggart enclave.

Boggart Outliers: The Marsh

Lincolnshire certainly had boggarts: the difficulty is in establishing where boggarts were an object of belief in the county. The three Lincolnshire boggart toponyms that we have found are all present in the very north-west of the county.[302] In that same part of Lincolnshire, there are also four supernatural

---

297. It is unlikely. Atkinson knew the folklore of the area extremely well and had little patience with outsiders mangling local traditions, e.g. Atkinson, *Forty Years*, 66–67.
298. Pease, *Ghost Stories*, 157.
299. 'The Late Mr Howard Pease'.
300. Young, 'Wright', 4; Robinson, *A Glossary*, 21.
301. Ibid: 'BOGGARTY, or BOGGLY, adj. "A boggly bit", a spectre-haunted spot'.
302. Boggard Hall at Brumby, Cameron *et al.*, *Lincolnshire*, VI, 38; Boggart Lane near Roxby, Peacock, 'Water-Lore', 75; and Boggart's Green (Winteringham), BC, Winteringham 4 (Li).

personal names in 'boggart'. These were not included earlier in this chapter because they were written down only after the First World War. We have the Woofer Boggard (Wildsworth); Jinny On Boggard (Owston Ferry); Beggar Hill Boggard (Scotterthorpe); and Church Mere Boggard (Garthorpe).[303] There are also unnamed entities described as 'boggarts'. There is a boggard at Belle Hole (Kirton); a possible Civil War boggard at Lidgett's Gap (Scawby); and a boggard at Winteringham.[304] It is striking that these clump together again in the same part of the county. M.C. Balfour uses the word 'boggart' in her stories from the Carrs, in north-western Lincolnshire,[305] and Edward Peacock includes 'boggart' in his dialect survey of the region (along with 'bogey' and 'boggle').[306]

There can be no doubt then that boggarts were part of the lore of north-western Lincolnshire. The question is whether boggart-lore can be turned up elsewhere in the county. There is some fragmentary evidence that boggart belief featured in the Marsh (in the vicinity of Skegness). The Marsh was, in the nineteenth century, a boggy agricultural area with few urban centres.[307] We have already encountered Mabel Peacock's 'Th' Man an' th' Boggard' in relation to Northamptonshire.[308] This story was published in 1886, but in a 1908 publication it was stated that the story had been recorded at Mumby ten miles to the north of Skegness.[309] A second reference from the same general area came in 1902. In that year, the Reverend Heanley reported a conversation with an old man at Wainfleet, five miles to the south-west of Skegness. The Reverend had explained to his aged neighbour that he would very much like to excavate a round barrow there and the old man responded: 'The king of the boggarts is shutten up inside that thear, an' if thou lets un out it 'ud tek aal the passuns [parsons] i' the Maash [Marsh] a munth o' Sundays to lay 'un agin'.[310] A later Wainfleet reference from 1938 suggests that this

---

303. Rudkin, *Lincolnshire Folklore*, 37–38 for Woofer Boggard; Ibid for Jinny 34–36; Laughton 'Letters', for Beggar Hill; Ella, 'The Old River Don' for Church Mere (an 'old poem' apparently).

304. Rudkin 'Black Dog', 116–17; Belle Hole; Lidgett's Gap, Rudkin, *Lincolnshire Folklore*, 36–37; Gutch and Peacock, *Examples*, 51 for Winteringham. Note also that Caroline Oates kindly passed on to me an unpublished work of Mabel Peacock, *Folklore and Legends of Lincolnshire*, digitized by Gillian Bennett in 2010. In the third chapter of this unnumbered book, there are several references to boggarts from north-western Lincolnshire.

305. 264, 273.

306. *A Glossary*, 31.

307. Obelkevich, *Religion*, 4–6.

308. *Lindsey*, 67–71.

309. Gutch and Peacock, *Examples*, 326. Note that as Peacock was a coeditor of the volume, we might presume that this is accurate information.

310. Heanley, 'Vikings', 38–39; Obelkevich, *Religion*, 281–82. Note that the idea of a boggart

'round barrow' was Green Hill and mention is again made of the 'King of the Boggarts'.[311] A local talk in Wainfleet in 1933 included another nod to boggarts, as if they were part of the area's supernatural fauna.[312]

How is it that our evidence from north-western Lincolnshire is so strong, yet so weak from the Marsh in South Lindsey? It might be simply that there was less to collect. But I would suggest that, instead, East Lindsey is, in folk-lore and dialect terms, something of a black hole. Lincolnshire has a strong folklore writing tradition by the relatively poor standards of the English counties. But as so often happens in nineteenth- and early twentieth-century folklore collections, certain areas were favoured over others within a given county: for Lancashire the east, for Cornwall the extreme west, and for Lincolnshire the north-west.[313] Even in north-western Lincolnshire it is striking how much folklore material emerges for the first time in the twentieth century, thanks particularly to Ethel Rudkin.[314]

Nineteenth-century dialect surveys were similarly uneven. Surveys were made in the south-west and the north-west of Lincolnshire, but did not include all the coastal regions. We have no reference guide concerning the Marsh and we have no confirmation that 'boggart' was used there.[315] Of course, place-names are a 'level playing field' with similar quality sources in different parts of the same county. They allow us to step out of the straitjacket of folklore and dialect collecting. But boggart toponyms were, relative to Lancashire and the West Riding, not common in Lincolnshire and even in the north-west of the county we have only three. It is thus difficult to make much of their absence in East Lindsey generally and the Marsh more particularly.

Northamptonshire, Cleveland, and the Marsh offer interesting test cases that allow us to check the efficacy of the methods presented in this chapter. In all three cases there is nineteenth-century evidence, of varying quality, showing boggarts. In all three cases none of the four models employed picked

---

hierarchy might be picked up in Higson, *Gorton*, 16: Nell Parlour Boggart 'was always esteemed the "yead or arch boggart"'.

311. The Diarist, 'Men': Just possibly the Diarist gives independent confirmation: I suspect that this is from another published source but I have not been able to identify it.

312. 'Lincolnshire Legends'.

313. Rudkin's *Lincolnshire Folklore* has a misleadingly 'wide' title, when it is largely concerned with the north-west of the county.

314. See, e.g., *Lincolnshire Folklore*.

315. The word 'boggart' did not feature in the guide for the south-west, Cole, *A Glossary*, 18 ('boggle' did, but only in the sense of a horse shying); nor does 'boggart' appear in Brogden, *Provincial Words*, 27 (boggle for horses and bogie); ix for his Lincolnshire sources. 'Boggart' does appear in Sims-Kimbrey, *Wodds*, 33 but without any indication as to where it occurs in the county.

up any boggarts. In the case of Northamptonshire, the idea that boggarts were to be found in that county is based on a probably inaccurate clause. In Cleveland and around Skegness, the evidence for boggarts is persuasive. Indeed, these seem to have been two boggart islands detached from the rest of Boggartdom (see frontispiece). Cleveland and the Marsh stand as a warning. There may be—it is surely likely—other English regions where boggarts featured in the nineteenth century, but where the word 'boggart' did not register in undeveloped folklore and partially developed dialect collecting traditions.

Boggart Cousins

In the final section of this chapter, I wish to look not just at Boggartdom, but at all of the Northwest and to put the boggart in a wider context, with reference to two other supernatural terms: 'boggle' and 'dobbie'. 'Boggle' clearly shares, like 'boggart', a genealogy in *bugge* words: the *OED* compares 'boggle' to Welsh *bugail nos* (a night horror) and German *Boggel-mann*.[316] The 'boggle' spirit (with various spellings) is found from Cumberland through the Scottish Lowlands and much of north-eastern England and 'boggle' also appears in Lincolnshire folklore.[317] The dobbie, meanwhile, has a much smaller territory. He can be found in north Lancashire and in most of Westmorland and parts of south Cumberland and a corner of the West Riding.[318] The origins of the word are mysterious. Horses have been suggested, as has the personal name 'Robert', of which 'dobbie' might be a diminutive.[319]

A more exact analysis of the distribution of these two types would require extensive work with supernatural place-names and supernatural personal names. However, I produce a map here to give an approximate sense of how dobbies and boggles and boggarts interlocked geographically (Figure 12). I have taken all supernatural personal names for the Northwest in 'boggart',

---

316. Edwards, *Hobgoblin and Sweet Puck*, 92–93; Cooper, 'Lexical reflections', 81 for *bugail nos* and Brittonic relatives.
317. Orton *et al.*, *Atlas*, 'Bogey', L64: see also the re-elaborated map, Figure 11.
318. Briggs, *The Remains*, 219–21; Search 'Natland'; Smith, 'Dobbies'. Note that there seems to have been a small dobbie island in north-eastern England, e.g. Westwood and Simpson, *Lore of the Land*, 244–45 etc.
319. Allies, *British*, 414–15 for horse; Bardsley, *Chronicles*, 25 for a diminutive of Robert (which could be more credible). Ferguson, *The dialect*, 34, offers a desperate solution: 'Dobby ... Perhaps, by transposition of consonants for *boddy*. Hence same Sco. *boody*, from Gael. *bodach*, spectre, boggle. The converse transposition appears in Yorks. *body*, a simpleton (Ray), probably the same word as our *dobby*.'

'boggle', and 'dobbie' (known to me).[320] Boggarts, as has been seen earlier, dominate in most of Lancashire. Dobbies, on the other hand, are the spirits of north-western Lancashire, 'Lancashire beyond the Sands', and Westmorland. Boggles are the spirits of Cumberland and also parts of Westmorland.

North-western England can, on this evidence, be usefully broken down into three interlocking realms: Boggartdom, Boggledom, and Dobbiedom. There are three different words here—'boggart', 'boggle', and 'dobbie'—for three different regions, all with the same meaning of ambivalent solitary spirits. Yet here modern folklore has failed us. The boggart, the boggle, and the dobbie are typically given as three different types of supernatural creature, rather than what they really are: regional reflexes of a similar generic bogie.[321] The exact borders of their territories are uncertain, of course. These are cultural and above all linguistic divisions. They are certainly not the sharp lines of political frontiers. In the borderline areas the results bleed into each other.

An interesting example of this is the area in northern Lancashire where Boggartdom gives out to Dobbiedom. In Figure 13, I have used a battery of different evidence (supernatural personal names, toponyms, phrases, and so forth) to try to establish where 'boggart' and 'dobbie' were used.[322]

---

320. For boggarts see p. 57. For boggles: Armboth (Cu): Richardson, *Cummerland*, 99; Bowness-on-Windermere (We): 'To Correspondents' (1866); Carlisle (Cum): 'Carlisle' (1864); Cleator Moor (Cum): Litt, 'Henry and Mary', (1859); Eskdale (Cu): Rea, *Beckside Boggle* (1886), 1–30; Hawkshead (La): Cowper, *Hawkshead*, 328–30; Longtown (Cu): 'Local Superstitions' (1886); Reagill (We): Bland, *Lyvennet* (1910), 28; Whitehaven (Cu): Dickinson, *Cumbriana* (1876), 139; Workington (Cu): Jackson, 'The Curwens', 229–30. For dobbies: Bolton-le-Sands (La): 'Bolton Le Sands' (1870); Colton (La): 'A Ghost in Rusland', (1854); Furness (La): Bowker, *Goblin Tales* (1883), 152–58; Oxen Fell (La): Cowper, *Hawkshead*, 332; Natland (We): Search, 'Natland', (1867); Orton (We): 'A Westmoreland Ghost Story', (1849); Silverdale (La): 'In Sunny Silverdale' (1928); Ulverston (La): Davis, *The fancies*, 27. In the case of multiple boggle or dobbie names in one location I simply took the first. Note that there is not yet enough data to carry out this exercise, with place-names, over the north of England. A problem here also is the multiple meanings of 'Dobbie', note particularly for Yorkshire Dobbin/Dobby: 'A small, three-wheeled cart, used in quarries', Wright, *Dialect Dictionary*, II, 101.

321. Briggs, *Dictionary of Fairies*, 29–30 ('Boggart'), 32–33 ('Bogle'); and 103 ('Dobby' and, confusingly, 'Dobie'). The only folklorist I know who acknowledges the actual situation is Preston, *Cumbria*, 21: 'The term "dobbie" seems to belong to Lancashire, including the section "north of the sands". It changes to "boggle" in the Orton area, with various alternatives such as "boggart", "bogie" and "bogey man" elsewhere, and hob over in the direction of Millom.'

322. Boggarts: Barrow in Furness: BC, Barrow-in-Furness, 2 (La); Bolton-le-Sands: 'Bolton le Sands' (1870): Carnforth, 'Ghost Story', (1851); Cartmel: Orton *et al.*, *Atlas*, L64; Dendron, OSLa 22, 1851; Dolphinholme, 'County Petit Sessions'; Galgate: 'Scotforth' (1890); Silverdale, BC, Silverdale (La) 1; Yealand: Orton *et al.*, *Atlas*, L64. Dobbies: Bolton-le-Sands: 'Bolton Le Sands' (1870); Cark: Stockdale, *Annales* (1872), 389; Colton: 'A Ghost in Rusland' (1854); Cove: 'In Sunny Silverdale'; Furness (La): Bowker, *Goblin Tales*, 152–58; Skerton: 'Local Police Courts' (1880); Slyne: 'Bolton Le Sands' (1870); Ulverston (La): Davis, *The Fancies*, 27.

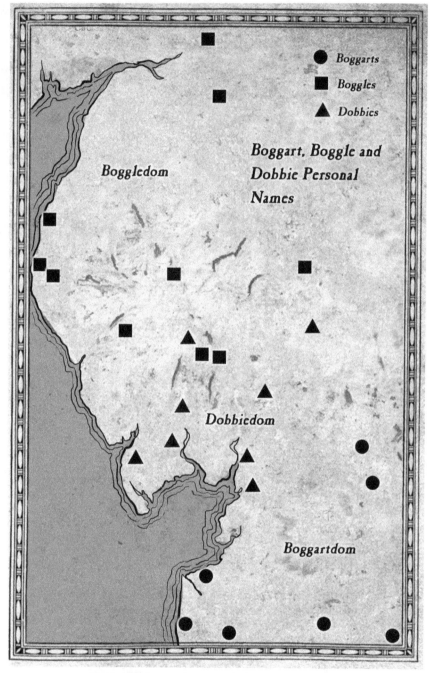

Figure 12: Boggartdom, Boggledom and Dobbiedom.

Boggarts dominate in the north of Lancashire, but there are references to dobbies around Lancaster. 'Lancashire beyond the Sands' has a boggart tradition in the south of the Furness Peninsula. Do we have overlap? At Bolton-le-Sands there was a dobbie, but the word 'boggart' seems also to have been used there with the sense of a child scarer. Or do we have, to use Jeremy Harte's phrase, a 'patchworked' territory?[323] This would mean dobbie enclaves within Boggartdom (e.g. around Lancashire) and boggart enclaves in Dobbiedom. There was likely an extremely complicated dialectal and supernatural mix in this area in the nineteenth century which would have been difficult to delineate even then. In the 2020s, with inadequate evidence, we can only flag up its complexity. Another interesting area for this kind of close study would be the North Riding.[324]

It is striking that in several instances, those who live on the borderlands effectively translate one of these words into another, for instance 'in Westmorland the word "dobbie" is applied to a bogle'.[325] Or Boggart Holes (cave) at Clapham are written up as 'Boggle Holes' by a writer further to the north;[326] or we have a Burnley journalist effortlessly editing Burns' famous lines:

> Glowering round with prudent cares
> Lest boggarts [instead of Burns' 'bogles'] catch me unawares.[327]

There is a Scottish politician who evoked a 'boggle' in a speech at Leigh in Lancashire: a man in the audience shouted, 'We call it a "boggart"!'[328] But perhaps most telling of all, a famous nineteenth-century solitary spirit was the Orton Dobbie, who was blamed for poltergeist activity in 1849 and entered local folklore.[329] We have one reference to 'Orton Boggart' from a writer who

---

323. Harte, 'Dorset', 72 for pixies and fairies. Do we have overlapping or tessellation?
324. Note that Harland, *A Glossary*, 7 establishes that 'boggle' and not 'boggart' was used in Swaledale. He also suggests there that barghaists had a special role in the district: for that, see also Routh, *Rambles*, 69 *via* Gutch and Peacock, *Examples*. Is it even possible that 'barguest' became generic terms in parts of the North Riding?
325. See, e.g., Lonsdale, *A Biographical Sketch*, 9.
326. 'Ancient Coin' (1848).
327. 'Towneley Hall' (1902).
328. 'The Liberal Candidates'.
329. 'Orton Dobbie' first appeared in 1849 as a poltergeist flap (see p. 140 for the term 'flap'), 'A Westmoreland Ghost Story' and Leighton, 'Editor': although it was usually referred to, in that year, in the newspapers as the 'Orton Ghost'. The first appearance of 'Orton Dobbie' was in the newspaper 5 May of that year ('The Orton "Dobbie"', note inverted commas: this was likely the vernacular term from the beginning). The name then entered regional lore. Apart from the endless regurgitations of the happenings of spring of 1849, in 1880 (A Liberal, 'Canvassers'), 1892 (Back

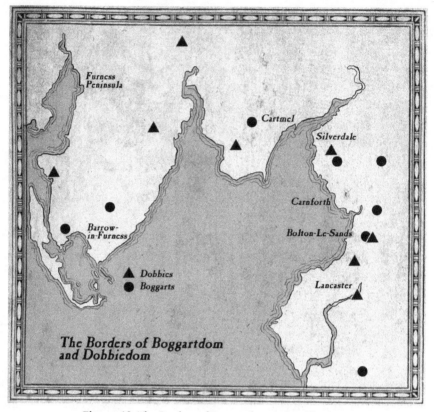

Figure 13: The Borders of Boggartdom and Dobbiedom.

travelled on the railway and heard Lancashire enginemen talk of the bogie.[330] A Cumberland newspaper, meanwhile, referred to the Orton Dobbie as a 'boggle'.[331]

Sometimes the terms mix in interesting ways in the same piece of writing. The *Lancaster Gazette*, for example, was sold in an area that straddled Boggartdom and Dobbiedom (see Figure 13 earlier and the relevant discussion for this complicated, in dialectal and supernatural terms, region). In the *Gazette*'s pages in January 1851 a supernatural encounter was described. A carter heading up from Bolton-le-Sands (in Boggartdom) towards Kendal market (in Dobbiedom) had a supernatural experience near the Carnforth

---

O' Birket, 'Sir') and 1901 (Vae Victis, 'Rejected') 'Orton Dobbie' appeared in rhetorical tropes in letters to Westmorland newspapers; then, both a championship dog, 'Some of Sir Humphrey' (1898) and a carriage, 'A Ride' (1849), were named after the spirit.

330. Leighton, 'Editor', 336 'was well acquainted with the enginemen and others employed upon it'.
331. 'The Westmoreland Boggle' (1849): calling it 'Orton Ghost' in the body of the article.

Boggart House. The newspaper reported the clearly relevant toponym, taking for granted that its readers would understand it. But the journalist introduced the spirit with the following sentence: 'last week the "dobby strain" made its appearance much to the terror of an inoffensive carter'.[332]

In reading reports of boggarts, boggles (at least those in north-western England), and dobbies, it is clear that there are no substantial differences between them: they are all solitary spirits. As with boggarts there are ghosts. The boggle at Salterbeck, for example, seems to have repeated an action which had been tragic in life. He appeared 'in the startling shape of a coffin borne by four drunken sailors, staggering along and vanishing suddenly with a loud cry as they reached the middle of the water-course'. Legend says that four men shouldering a coffin were swept away by a flooded stream here.[333] Another ghost is the dobbie seen at Elinghearth Brow:

> a female form, clothed in white, [who] often has appeared, and, according to the testimony of a Rusland man ... its approach was generally heralded by a strange 'waffling' sound in the coppice near the road. Sometimes it only accompanied foot passengers up the hill, but often it seated itself in the cart ... and it 'waffled' away as mysteriously as it appeared.[334]

As with boggarts, there are dobbie and boggle shape-changers: '[the Waterside Boggle of Hawskhead] takes on a variety of shapes. It has been seen as a man in light blue, as an animal neither calf nor donkey ... or as a white fox or foxes.' The Dalehead Park Boggle, meanwhile, was seen by one shepherd as a pile of lime and on another occasion as a ball of a fire. The Newtown Boggle was primarily a warner: 'Whitehaven has been noted in old times for a Newtown boggle, which occasionally rendered night hideous by its howlings, and especially before fatal accidents occurred in the collieries.'[335] Then there are instances that remind us that these categories have fluid boundaries. The versatile Crosby Hall Dobbie seemed, for example, to work as a shape-changer, a ghost, a threatening spirit, *and*, on occasion, a household spirit. To some, he was seen

---

332. 'Ghost Story' (1851).
333. Gibson, 'Ancient Customs', 109.
334. Cowper, *Hawkshead*, 331.
335. Ibid., 328; Richardson, *Cummerland*, 98–105; Dickinson, *Cumbriana*, 139.

as a white bull looking through the windows at midnight; to others
as a sheeted figure waving a knife; and to one in particular [the
dobbie] appeared and disclosed the whereabouts of some hidden
treasure, [and] at the same time told them the period of its [their?]
death.[336]

The previous pages have been largely a study in dialect, but with these
north-western bogies and their extraordinary acts we move back into folklore.
The approximate boundaries of Boggartdom have been established. The next
chapters can, then, concentrate on the folklore boggart.

---

336. Whitehead, *Legends*, 72.

II: Lived Boggart Folklore

The good people of Worsthorne have been recently disturbed from their usual placid condition by the strange appearance in their midst of one of those unearthly visitants from the regions of darkness or elsewhere commonly called 'boggarts'.

A Villager, 'A Boggart at Worsthorne'.

Figure 14: Nineteenth-century Worsthorne (postcard).

CHAPTER FOUR

Boggart Landscapes

Introduction: John Higson and the Boggarts

John Higson (1825–1871), a Lancashire historian and folklorist, was born in the heart of Boggartdom. His home village was Gorton, to the south of Manchester. His family were impoverished farming folk—their fields have long since disappeared under the concrete and tarmac of the conurbation. Although Higson 'received little if any education',[337] he struggled hard to become an author.[338] When he died in his mid forties he had been working as a cashier, but he had also long written for the press; he had even been involved, as a prospective editor, in an attempt to set up a south-eastern Lancashire newspaper.[339] His writing was unashamedly antiquarian: 'At a comparatively early age he conceived a passion for local antiquities and folk-lore, and became an industrious collector of items of regional history and records of ancient manners and superstitions.'[340] While his work is to be found in newspaper articles,[341] local and national journal pieces,[342] and several local history books,[343] much remained unpublished at his death, with some of these texts being exploited by later Lancashire writers.[344] From his various publications, I have been able to gather about 10,000 words on north-western boggart-lore.[345] Higson also wrote in dialect and a boggart poem of his has come down to us.[346]

---

337. 'Death of Mr. John Higson' (1871).
338. Ibid; and, movingly, 'Late John Higson'; Crofton, *Newton*, I, 4–5.
339. 'Death of Mr. John Higson' (1871).
340. Ibid.
341. Crofton, *Newton*, 4. The task of tracking these down in databases is made considerably more difficult by the fact that Higson used, as his assumed name, in the *Ashton Weekly Reporter*, 'H'; see 'Death of Mr. John Higson', 1871.
342. Higson, 'Boggarts and Feorin', 'Boggarts, Feorin, etc', 'Walton-le-Dale Folk Lore'.
343. Higson, *Gorton* and *Droylsden*.
344. Crofton, *Newton*, passim. A project that cries out for a young Manchester researcher would be the digitization of Higson's unfinished 'Glossary of the Lancashire Dialect', Manuscripts/1/244, Chetham Library (thanks to Lucy Evans for this reference).
345. Now collected together in Higson, *South Manchester Supernatural*.
346. 'The Boggart of Gorton Chapelyord'.

Higson, like several other Victorian authors, was intrigued by boggarts. But more than almost any of his peers he was fascinated by the way that boggarts inhabited the landscape.[347] During his short life he lived in three south-eastern Lancashire communities not more than ten miles apart. The first, as noted earlier, was Gorton. In his twenties he moved east, to Droylsden; then, in his very early forties, he arrived in what would be his home at the time of his death, Lees, on the Lancashire–Yorkshire border. When he came to remember the folklore of Gorton, Droyslden, and Lees (the first two in books and the third in *Notes and Queries*), he ignored the conventions of British folklore writing. He did not, as was typical at that date and indeed still is, concentrate on 'the stock local haunt',[348] the most famous of a number of bogies haunting an area. Rather, he gave a census of the horrors to be found there.[349] The coverage is impressive, so much so that one assumes that when he composed these three accounts, Higson sat at his desk and mentally walked around the village, lane by lane and then field by field. We see, thanks to him, the way in which the supernatural had saturated the landscape of south-eastern Lancashire.

Here is a slightly curtailed version of Higson's description of the boggarts of Lees, the last of the three communities in which he lived. This text was published in 1869, just two years before his death:

> Dividing our parish from Oldham, flows Lees brook, one of the three main heads of the river Medlock, and this was specially the gamboling ground of several varieties of 'feorin'.[350] One form of boggart displayed itself in the shape of headless trunks or 'men 'bout yeads' [without heads], as the villagers termed them; and another in the semblance of 'horses 'bout yeads' [without heads]. In addition, to these uncouth travelers along the bed of the brook, or rather on the surface of its waters, was the 'brook rider', in the form of a wild white horse, which used to come galloping down the stream. Strangely enough, considering its name, this terrible horse was destitute of rider. One

---

347. The only three other nineteenth-century north-western authors of whom this could be reasonably said (known to me) are Bamford, *Passages*, I, 44–48, for Middleton and Cowper, *Hawkshead*, 325–33 for Hawkshead, and Wilkinson and Tattersall, *Memories*, 48–92 for Worsthorne.
348. Cowper, *Hawkshead*, 325.
349. *Gorton*, 16; *Droylsden*, 68–69; 'Boggarts and Feorin', 508; note that Higson also created a similar but less complete account of upper Saddleworth (near Lees), 'Boggarts, Feorin, etc', 157.
350. For 'feorin' (frightening things) see p. 8.

Figure 15: John Higson, 'from Photograph by C.A. Jackson[,] Oldham: John Higson historian of Gorton, Droylsden etc.' (frontispiece in Crofton, *Newton*, I).

of our thoroughfares, formerly called Sorcey Lane, but latterly designated Church Street by our local board, was once noted for the many unearthly forms which, after dark, flitted along its short length. One of the old dwellings acquired the name of 'Boggart House', in consequence of its being haunted by a hobgoblin having the appearance of a calf, some said with a cap on its head, and others a frill round its neck. A cellar in the same lane was occupied by an old woman, who, it was believed, had 'made away', with two children, whose restless spirits, in consequence of non-interment in consecrated ground, were often seen wandering about the spot where they dwelt when in the body. Occasionally in the plashy meadows 'Jack' or 'Peggy-with-Lanthorn' was visible after dark, dancing and gamboling away in impossible jumps, and folks there were who ...: 'Had been kept at bay,/ By Jack-with-lanthorn till 'twas day'. Within a short distance of us, just within the borders of Yorkshire—for boggarts never trespass on each other's domains—the 'padfoot' was seen, but the spectator was safe from his assaults when gaining the Lancashire side of the border. A boggart of some description, though what was not clearly defined, once infested a footpath beside a fence in Leesfield, below the site of our present church. One night a roistering braggart declared he

would go and see the boggart. Something he saw which acted
as a purgative, but what it was he never did nor could tell—but
he became an altered man. A short distance away lies the hillside hamlet of Hartshead, and there a suicide, having been
interred at a 'three lane ends', a boggart, in the language of our
informant, was ever after to be seen or dreaded.[351]

The reader will find this account (Lees) and those of Gorton and Droylsden
drawn up here. These graphics are based on the nearest contemporary six-
inch OS maps: Gorton and Droylsden, particularly, have changed out of all
recognition.

In some cases, Higson gives a marker that I was not able to find. In other
cases, he is just too vague for the reader to get any kind of bearing: take his
description for Lees of Peggy/Jack-with-Lanthorn alight in the 'plashy
meadows', with no clues to which of the many meadows surrounding the
town was inhabited by a will o' the wisp. The screaming faces represent one
of the unpleasant boggarts that Higson described—a point of danger for the
nocturnal walker. We will see again and again that the boggart is an ordeal to
be faced in the dark: 'It's getten to th' edge o' dark; and there'll be boggarts
abroad in a bit.'[352]

This was a period when street lighting was modest, even in the centres
of towns and cities.[353] It was also a period when the need to get to places
on foot or on horseback meant that workers—think of a farmer taking his
goods to market—often had to leave their homes long before dawn and
could expect to get back long after midnight. There are many evocations of
this experience in our sources. Sometimes travellers mistook objects for
boggarts (a calf dragging a chain was a favourite);[354] sometimes those out
at night ran into others pretending to be boggarts (see further pp. 149–55);
then sometimes nocturnal strollers met horrors (at Preston, a female boggart

---

351. Higson, 'Boggarts and Feorin', 508.

352. Waugh, The Chimney, 359; consider also Clarke, Clitheroe, 59 [second run of page numbers]:
'Had [boggarts] been more prone to wander forth at mid-day, the mysteriousness which had so
enshrouded them would have vanished as quickly as a snow-flake on the river …: true to their
instincts they would only venture forth at the solemn and bewitching hour of midnight'.

353. Wilson, Lighting, 3: sixteen urban centres in Lancashire already had gas lighting by 1826, but
it took many more years and often 'municipalisation' of the gas supply for street lighting to
become comprehensive.

354. See, e.g., Chip, 'Cuttock'; Wrigley, Saddleworth Superstitions, 21–23, see p. 153.

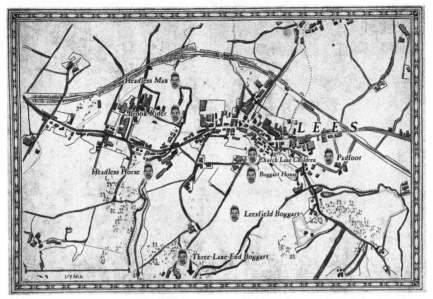

Figure 16: Supernatural Lees.

hurled her own head after her prey—Figure 19).[355] Boggarts even attacked those on carts and horseback: take, for instance, the fearful Pillion Lady who jumped behind riders on the roads near Garstang.[356] It goes without saying that walking or riding on a horse is very different from the protected experience of driving in a car.

Here, thanks to Higson, we are able to conflate 'the mundane and the fantastical',[357] reproducing something of the supernatural geography of three small communities in Boggartdom in the nineteenth century. In fact, we glimpse the landscape in both emotional and practical terms.[358] There are two elements which these maps have in common, and which would also apply to other parts of Boggartdom and perhaps to the supernatural in most parts of nineteenth-century Britain. Firstly, the boggarts on these maps congregate not within, but on the edges of communities, often in a radial pattern; they dwell in relation to humans, but not in their midst.[359]

---

355. Bowker, *Goblin Tales*, 131–39.
356. Ibid., 77–82; compare with the Boggart of Cave Ha, Hughes, 'Acoustic Vases', 81–82.
357. Bell, *Magical Imagination*, 239.
358. Paraphrasing Devlin, *The Superstitious Mind*, 81.
359. I suspect that were we to talk to an inhabitant of the northern part of Lees *c.*1870, we would

Secondly, they are sometimes found at strategic points—junctions, boundaries, bridges, and rivers. Think of the three brook bogies in Lees (the
brook marked the boundary with nearby Oldham) or the padfoot on just
the other side of the Lancashire–Yorkshire border (marked on the Lees
map). If you were setting out from Droylsden, Lees, or Gorton in 1850
on a journey after dark, you would have been painfully aware of the
monsters around about: '[W]hen you step into this space, you step into
legend.'[360]

Boggarts, Boggarts Everywhere

Boggarts 'were supposed to be lurking in almost every retired corner, or
sombre-looking place; whence they come forth at their permitted hours, to
enjoy their nocturnal freedom'. 'Every lane and dingle and brookside had its
own particular ghost or boggart.' 'In one parish the spectre was a black dog
which galloped through a certain lane. In another it was a headless woman
who paced a certain garden. In a third it was a figure in white which haunted
a certain field.' 'Every lonely lane and field path was haunted. East Bank House
… had its "boggart." Even a spot in the sandhills near South Hawes, where
an old white horse was buried, was a place to be avoided at night, for the
worn-out old animal was reputed to "walk"'. 'Each shady sequestered lane
had its apparition; sometimes an ill-favoured dog appeared suddenly to the
passer-by and as suddenly disappeared; sometimes an ill-defined but frightful
form would terrify the benighted rustic. Headless women in white haunted
the brooks, waited for wayfarers on the bridge or expected their approach
sitting on the stiles.'[361] 'This place', to use, finally, a dialect version of Higson's
description of Lees, 'had a boggart, an' that place had a padfeet; at th' three
lone eends a suicide is buried wi' a stake i' his insoide, an' i' spoite uv that
he ust to ger up eawt uv his hoyle, an' walk deawn th' cowd lones for
amusement'.[362]

---

hear of a monster that had passed Higson by and that guarded the northern road. Higson lived
at Birch Cottage, to the south of Lees. Note, for classical instances of suburban ghosts, see
Doroszewska, 'The Liminal Space'.

360. Gunnell, 'Power', 27.

361. Bamford, *Passages*, I, 47; Milner, *Country Pleasures*, 277; Sydney, *Early Days*, II, 71; E.R.B. 'The
Southport', 142; Weld, *Leagram*, 151.

362. Axon, *Black Knight*, 54. The connection between Higson's work and Axon's still requires
elucidation: Lucy Evans is working on this and other questions relating to Axon's life.

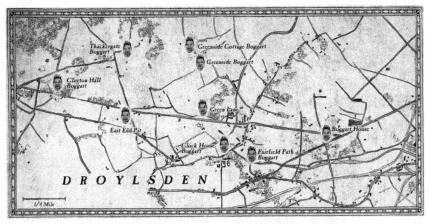

Figure 17: Supernatural Droylsden.

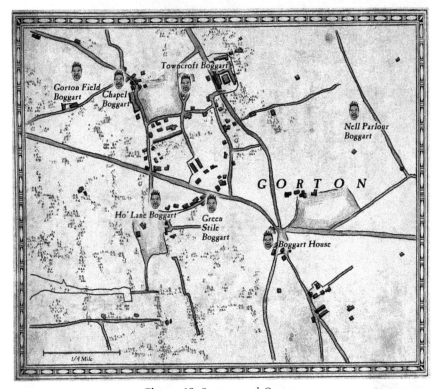

Figure 18: Supernatural Gorton.

Figure 19: A boggart throws its head after an escaping pedestrian
(Bowker, *Goblin Tales*, 136).

But what was it actually like to be in one of these infernal points, alone, after dark? The finest description of a night-time boggart walk comes from the pen of Edwin Waugh. It is the passage that perhaps takes us closest to the experience of being 'boggart-feart'. Ben is alone, after sunset, in the haunted clough, desperately trying to find Dimple, his escaped jackass. Note the combination of prior landscape associations ('many a wild "boggart" story') and Ben's intense physical reaction to the night:

> He had sat by the fire on winter nights, when a lad, in his father's cottage on Lobden moor, listening in eager excitement to many a wild 'boggart' story, the scene of which was laid in the solemn clough where he was then wandering to and fro so lonely in the dark. He could have kept his heart up better if he had even had his poor jackass by his side; but, bereft of Dimple, he felt strangely cut off from human society, and left entirely at the mercy of those fearful beings who are said to wander back to us from the confines of the invisible world. He tried to get the better of his fears, but he could not; for, in spite of himself, the awful stillness and the deepening gloom sank every moment more heavily upon his spirits. He began to be afraid of his own footsteps; for his senses were so unnaturally quickened by a morbid imagination, that those thin undersounds which creep about lonely corners of the world all through the night-time came now with strange distinctness upon his ears and loaded with undefinable horrors. He pulled his hat down upon his brow, and he turned up the collar of his coat, to shut out things he dreaded seeing; and he trod the ground with softer footfall than before, lest he should awake the anger of some lurking wanderer from the land of shade. The unhealthy activity of his senses left him no rest. Now, a leather-winged bat, flitting athwart the gloom, made his heart leap with sudden terror, and he glared aloft, and muttered tremulously, 'What's that?' Sometimes he fancied he heard strange whisperings a few yards off; but, too terrified to look, he hutched closer into his clothing, the last poor citadel left to protect him from the powers of darkness. And now and then, even when the wind was still, a stealthy rustle crept through the trees behind the mill, as if the dusky wood swarmed with goblin wings. He began to keep nearer to the building, for there was more of human association in that than in the gloomy clough. But even

there he was haunted by the terrors of the night; for as he paced by the door it gave a drowsy jolt that made him start aside. There was something in the sound that told him it had not been stirred by the wind, nor yet by earthly hands, and the poor fellow's flesh crept upon his bones. And then, when the wind came moaning up from the dark, like a thing in pain, it seemed to pause where he stood, and coil itself about him maliciously; and he felt as if it had left its hollow cell solely to wail an inarticulate warning against his intrusion upon the mysteries of the night. Everything around him seemed to be waiting to go on with some weird business as soon as he should go away. And, heaven knows, poor Ben had no desire to make or meddle with such things. He would have been glad to go, if he could only have got hold of his jackass; for he was terrified, and even the faint sounds of life which came, by fits, from little folds upon the heights in the distance, only served to deepen his sense of the solitude around him.[363]

Of course, we should not make the mistake of thinking that all places with a supernatural place-name or reputations were primarily frightening. Some supernatural place-names might have originated from a joke: Boggart Plat at Goosnargh, for example, was the place that a well-known local had wrongly thought he had seen a boggart.[364] There are also British place-names recalling heroes with a background in the supernatural (primarily Arthur and Robin Hood), which would have been unlikely to cause fear.[365] There are likewise place-names relating to giants and dragons in a period when we might suspect no one believed in these bogies; or that, if they did, they thought of them as something from the past, rather than a present danger. Typically, this is 'a point in the environment which is subjectively perceived as being so exceptional and significant that a mythical

---

363. *Besom Ben*, 28.
364. Of Boggart Plat Ghost, Cookson, *Goosnargh*, 311 'there is a well authenticated story: that it arose through the vagary of one William Cowell… He having imbibed pretty freely of what he had a liking for at the village, and having occasion to take the bier and pall home to keep overnight in readiness to pass on north-wards the following morning… he put down the bier on a small piece of waste land near to the said plat, covering himself with the pall to have a nap and refresh himself; and being found by a passerby in that unusual position, it gave rise to the legend of Boggart Plat.' Of course, if you had an anxious temperament, such a name would still have, in the right circumstances, the potential to trigger a strong personal reaction…
365. There are some examples, though, where boggarts are associated with such places. Forster, 'Dear Sir' (Robin Hood Well at Wakefield), see further p. 88; Proctor, 'The Manor', 95 ('King Arthur's pit', 'there were boggarts and ghosts to be seen in the vicinity of this pit').

story is circulated to account for its existence'.[366] The story *explains* an unusual landscape feature. So, to think of a common English example, a pile of rocks, was, according to local storytellers, dropped by a giant.[367]

The places inhabited by boggarts do sometimes include tales about landscape minutiae: marks in the road, permanent 'blood-drops' on the ground, the failure of grass to grow where a man was killed, even the smell of thyme.[368] But they are principally spots that are believed to be inhabited by dangerous spirits, for intrinsic reasons (the 'feel' of the place) or for external reasons (typically a death or burial): 'a murder or a suicide takes place, and the people promptly crowd the site, so to speak, with bogeys'.[369] As haunted sites they are also—and this is a neglected question—places of power. We know that a witch-bottle was buried at Boggart Hole (Fence, Pendle);[370] and that in Boggart Hole Clough at Blackley, young men met together to carry out magic rituals: 'Gasping, and with cold sweat oozing on his brow, Plant recollected that they were to shake the fern with a forked rod of witch hazel, and by no means must touch it with their hands.'[371]

British folklorists and historians have been, as many of their Continental counterparts, sensitive to the intensely local nature of fearful supernatural spaces.[372] Historical apparitions, as one author notes, have 'a rootedness in place, and a concern with features of the landscape and topography'.[373] But there have been few attempts to actually put bogies on maps, either nationally, as we saw in Chapter 3, or, as I've attempted to do here, locally. Ethel Rudkin used maps to track local hauntings.[374] Karl Bell has looked at hauntings in three British cities in the nineteenth century,[375] while John Reppion edited a collection of essays on *Spirits of Place*, with several striking local studies (2016).[376]

---

366. Simpson, 'God's visible judgements', 57. See also now, Harte, 'Names and Tales', 376–82.
367. Barrowclough and Hallam, 'Devil's Footprints', 93–96.
368. For an overpowering thyme smell at Poulton Thornber, *History*, 38 and Clarke, *Windmill Land*, 118–19 for haunted thyme at Freckleton; see also Addy, 'Death'.
369. Cowper, *Hawkshead*, 327.
370. Daisy, 'Green Head House'.
371. Bamford, *Passages*, II, 119–25 at 123.
372. For works on supernatural landscapes from the late twentieth and early twenty-first century see: Basso, *Wisdom*; Doroszewska, 'The Liminal Space'; Dragan, *La représentation*; Franceschetto, *I capitelli*; Hand, *Boundaries*; Harte 'Names and Tales'; Hrobat, 'Conceptualization of Space' and 'Emplaced' Tradition; Gunnell, 'Power'; Puhvel, *The Crossroads*; Simpson, 'God's visible judgements'; Thomassen, *Liminality* (not only in landscapes); Walsham, *Reformation of the Landscape*, 497–515.
373. Marshall, *Leakey*, 229, with comments for the seventeenth century.
374. Rudkin, 'Black Dog', particularly 127, 129.
375. *Magical Imagination*, 227–59.
376. Only a few of which, though, were about Britain.

Typically, though, British scholars have dealt with supernatural landscapes in general terms.[377] Some of the most grounded landscape writing comes, instead, in popular or alternative publications on the supernatural. A new trend in ghost publications has been to corral ghost references for a given place, the History Press's *Haunted* series is perhaps the bestselling example in the UK.[378] There is also the school of 'ley line' studies in Britain and Ireland. I am (to say the least) suspicious of the idea of ley lines. However, ley-liners often offer valuable insights into the relationship between a territory and those that inhabited it, not least because the students of that discipline visit, measure and scour the places that they write about.[379] 'We should study the land, not the map.'[380]

Boggart Houses and Boggart Lanes

With this exhortation let us turn to the position of Boggart Houses and Boggart Lanes in the landscape. Boggart Houses were the most common boggart toponym: 'Surely there is something mysterious about this name: something to make one, if superstitiously inclined, look askance as one passes it by night'.[381] In Standard English we would perhaps call them simply 'haunted houses'. Needless to say, these were houses that one would not choose to live in. We have story after story—many lived accounts rather than local legends—of families fleeing from Boggart Houses, when the boggart became active.[382] Further, as we will see in Chapter 6, haunted residences could become tourist attractions with crowds gathering outside anxious to spot spectral occupants. The periods in which a house like this was empty only added, with its 'creepy name',[383] to its reputation: a vicious circle of haunting and neglect kicked in.

You would not willingly buy a property called 'Boggart House',[384] and frequently occupiers fought a losing battle with the local population in an attempt to change the unhappy name.[385] In the twenty-first century, we perhaps think most easily of the fate of those who lived *in* the Boggart House. However,

---

377. A rare exception, Harte, 'Haunted Lanes'.
378. See, e.g., Roberts, *Halifax*; Roberts, *Haunted Huddersfield*.
379. See, e.g., Devereux, *Spirit Roads*; Broadhurst and Miller, *The Sun*.
380. Harte, 'Haunted Lanes', 5.
381. One Highly Interested, 'Boggart House Farm' (1879).
382. See, e.g., Price, 'Notes', 192, for other examples see pp. 141–42.
383. Clarke, *Windmill Land*, 118.
384. BC, Widnes 6 (La).
385. We often, in the sources, see competing names: the official and the boggart name e.g. 'Scotforth township' (1889), see further, p. 20; and BC, Midgley 1 (WRY), Boggart Farm to Allswell.

our Victorian ancestors were, on the evidence of surviving sources, also concerned about walking by a Boggart House after dusk. This is the fearful experience of walking or riding at night again. The following is a description of 'Boggart House' on the road to the south of Lancaster:

> Many a one, in passing this dreaded spot upon hearing the slightest sound, the faintest rustling of the leaves, has felt a curious sensation run down his back and ooze out at his toes, and not a few who had great pretensions to fearlessness when coming into immediate proximity with the 'boggart house,' have felt themselves compelled to 'whistle to bear their courage up.'[386]

Or here is a memory of a Chesterfield Boggart House:

> Despite its pleasant situation the old house had an evil reputation. It was said to be haunted and after nightfall children and the timid would not pass it if they could help it.[387]

Indeed, one local publican there used to see his guests off with the encouraging words, 'Good-night, take care of the ghost in the lane'![388] Passers-by in boggart spots, understandably, developed stratagems. One young man closed his eyes as he walked past; others took care to only go there in company; others whistled or sang psalms; while others took off their shoes and crept past.[389]

There were yarns about how these houses gained their reputation, but typically 'the story is somewhat clouded in mystery'.[390] Often this meant that there were competing tales. The Warton Boggart House, for instance, naturally had a bad reputation:

> It has freetenin' in it—when there's a storm on there's chains rattlin' an' ghosts of men runnin' about'; and, most startling of all, soothers aver, a phantom ship that drives on the house, as on a rock, and envelops the building like a mist.[391]

---

386. 'Ghost Story' (1851).
387. 'The Spital Estate' (1932).
388. Ibid.
389. Brushfield, 'Reminiscences', 15; Fizzwig, 'From Glossop to Disley' and 'A "Ghost"' at Bolton' (1887); Bamford, *Passages*, I, 44; Hardwick, 'Ancient', 277.
390. Robertson, *Rochdale*, 171.
391. Clarke, *Windmill Land*, 116. For frightenings and feorins, see p. 8.

Some claimed that the chains were actually a noise created by a smugglers' gang who used the premises. Might this account for the ghostly vessel, too? Others, however, insisted on the supernatural: either a daughter had been baked alive by her mother in an oven; or a great black dog haunted the house and gardens.[392]

These Boggart Houses, with their amorphous tales, were no more spaced randomly through the landscape than other supernatural place-names. To illustrate this, I took all twenty-six Boggart Houses to be found in the county of Lancashire and broke them down into four categories.[393] Urban Boggart Houses (i.e. ones in the midst of a given community); outskirt Boggart Houses (those on the edges of a community or within five-minutes' walk of that community); rural Boggart Houses (those in open countryside); and houses whose position I was not able to identify with any confidence. In positioning the houses, I endeavoured to use OS maps published as close as possible to the period to which their haunted name was first attested.

In six cases I was not able to identify the position of a Boggart House, or at least not precisely enough to satisfy the criteria given earlier.[394] In thirteen cases Lancashire boggart houses were to be found in open countryside.[395] In

---

392. Allen Clarke, *Windmill Land*, 117 wisely wrote, while setting out the different versions: the house 'may have more [stories] – I should not be surprised.'

393. I avoided, for the purposes of this exercise, the boggart barns and boggart halls and boggart farms, which would have skewed the sample towards the countryside: I only used places with the word 'house'. But the Lancashire Boggart Houses did not, as the numbers above show, need any help in being dragged away from the city lights.

394. Boggart Heawse (Middleton, La) 'A Ghost Story' (1839); Boggart House (Dalton, La): 'Gildsley or Boggart House Dalton nr Southport', 1911 Census, Dalton, Enumeration District 1, p. 91; Boggart House (Kirkham, La): 1841 Census, Treals 10, p. 14; Boggart House (Rufford, La): BC, Rufford 1 (La); Boggart House Farm (Newsham, La): 'Boggart House Farm' (1879); Boggart House Farm (Out Rawcliffe, La): 'Melancholy Suicide' (1848).

395. Boggard House (Warton in Fylde, L): 'Boggard House Field', Warton in Amounderness tithe apportionment entry, DRB/1/194 [at http://archivecat.lancashire.gov.uk/]; Boggart House (Burtonwood, La): Tithe Maps 1836–1851, Burtonwood, Plot 955; 'Boggart House', OSLa 108 (1849); Boggart House (Carnforth, La): 'Ghost Story', (1851); Boggart House (Galgate, La): 'Scotforth' (1889); Boggart House (Hindley, La): OSLa 94 (1849); Boggart House (Whalley, La): BC, Blackburn 13 (La); Boggart House (South Tunley, L): OSLa 85, (1845); Boggart House (Wardle, La): 'On Sale' (1915); BC, Wardle 2 (La); Boggart House (West Derby, La): Dickinson, 'Flora', 104; Boggart House (Westhoughton/Hindley, La): OSLa 94 (1849); Boggart House (Winwick, La): OSLa 108 (1849); Buggard House, The (Stretford, La): Crofton, *Stretford*, I, 160; Buggart House (Walton on the Hill, La): 'Certificate regarding the road within Kirkdale ...', QSB/1/1781/APR/PT2/36 [at http://archivecat.lancashire. gov.uk/], Certificate 24 Apr 1781.

seven cases they were found on the outskirts of communities.[396] And I did not find a single instance of a Boggart House within a settlement in Lancashire. Boggart Houses are to be found in the darkness on the edge of town or in the fields beyond: they are not in a principal square or on the high street. We see here a pattern that we have already encountered with John Higson's supernatural word maps of Droylsden, Gorton, and Lees (see earlier pp. 79–84).

This is not to say that Boggart Houses were independent of towns and villages. In fact, they were often located on roads on the edge of a given settlement, or at a nearby junction, where they would be passed. In other words, while they might not be a physical part of a community they belonged to its imagination. Indeed, many Boggart Houses stood as sentinels over spaces so that it was difficult to avoid them without taking a long detour. Carnforth Boggart House, for example, sat between Carnforth and Bolton-Le-Sands, close to the single most-frequented road in the area. In 1851, a carter had an unpleasant experience just next to this Boggart House. His first hint that there was trouble came when his horse became scared:

> On looking to ascertain the cause, he perceived as he imagined a large sheep lying in the middle of the road, to which he proceeded with the intention of applying his whip to force its removal. He struck, the blow fell upon vacancy, the supposed sheep aroused itself and as if with indignity at the insult, swelled out as the man affirms, into the size of a house, and then giving him a look of ineffable contempt flew away in a flame of fire.[397]

No wonder that the story made the local press. This was not just a bizarre experience and a chance to laugh at a neighbour. It was an event on the most important highway out of Carnforth. A further boggart incident was reported a generation later, on a road about ten miles to the south, when a horse shied close to Galgate Boggart House. Many of the readers, one suspects, will have

---

396. Boggart House (Audenshaw, La): OSLa 105 (1848); Boggart House (Broughton, La): 1881 Census, Preston, Broughton, Enumeration District 18, p. 9; Ditchfield, 'Lancashire', 93; Boggart House (Gorton, La): Higson, *Gorton*, 16; Boggart House (Helmshore, La): BC, Helmshore 1 (La); Boggart House (Lees, La): Higson, 'Boggarts and Feorin', 508; Boggart House (Skelmersdale, La): BC, Skelmersdale 1 (La), Skelmersdale 7 (La); Boggart House (Wigan, La): Holme House OSLa 93 (1849).
397. 'Ghost Story' (1851), perhaps *corr.* to 'size of a horse'.

come to their own conclusions about what caused the horse to take fright and left the rider 'seriously hurt'.[398]

Boggart Lanes follow much the same pattern as Boggart Houses: indeed, they are sometimes coupled, with a Boggart House standing on a Boggart Lane.[399] They are found, again, not in the middle of settlements, but on the outskirts and sometimes they cross a stretch of countryside. Thus, in Hipperholme, Boggard Lane was a bridleway between Bramley Lane and Northedge Lane, higher up the valley, away from the houses. In Oughtibridge, Boggart Lane was a narrow track running around the back of Hagg Stones quarry. In Cawood, Boggard Lane was an L-shaped road just behind the Lodge and about half a mile out of the village. In Skelmanthorpe, Boggart Lane ran to Emley Moor Collieries.[400] This list could go on: there are thirty-eight Boggart Lanes known to me.[401] What is important to note is that none of these examples is 'urban' in the sense of being part of the mesh of streets in the centre of a settlement. They are all on the outskirts or in open country. My impression is that while Boggart Houses are more likely to be found in the open countryside than on the outskirts of towns, the reverse is true of Boggart Lanes.

What was it like walking on one of these lanes at night? Are we once again like poor Ben in the clough? In most of the Boggart Lanes mentioned above it would (I think) have been possible to see the lights of houses while strolling, although these lights would, of course, have been much weaker before electricity. But there would also have been a strong sense of detachment from the community as the pedestrian traversed the haunted stretch of road. Perhaps the lights indeed 'only served to deepen [the] sense of ... solitude'.[402] In other cases, the darkness may have been even deeper than in the nearby countryside. Several Boggart Lanes are sunken (see Figure 20) and at night light will not have penetrated much. Other boggart sites—and this may have been true of some Boggart Lanes—had thick vegetation around them, producing similar effects.[403]

---

398. 'Serious Accident' (1891); compare with 'Wheatley Lane' (1897) for an accident at Boggart Hole Farm and 'S Bend Collision' at Boggart Bridge (Burnley) in 1935.

399. See, e.g., Droylsden OSLa 105 (1848) where Boggart House (presumably the primary name) sits on Boggart Lane: I omitted the name from the map in Figure 17 because it seems to be secondary.

400. Turner, 'Fragments' (1869) and see BC, Hipperholme (WRY) multiple entries; OSY 288 (1855); OSY 206 (1851); OSY 261 (1854).

401. BN.

402. *Besom Ben*, 28.

403. See, e.g., D.S. 'Depledge', 'My depledge "used to be a boggart place", a dark mass of trees';

Gloomy or otherwise, there would usually have been silence in these lanes. It is interesting, though, how many Boggart Lanes cross railway tracks. Boggart Lane in Skelmanthorpe went under the railway on the way to the colliery. Boggart Lane in Sowerby Bridge passed over the top of a railway tunnel. Boggart Lane at Bramley crossed over the Leeds-Bradford-Halifax line, on a small bridge. Boggart Lane in Droylsden ran under the railway there. A Boggart Lane crossed the railway between Rochdale and Milnrow.[404] None of this is to say that you need a railway to have a boggart: indeed, in tradition there was the idea that the supernatural was scared off by trains (see further pp. 114–15). But the infernal noise of a train passing and the sense of isolation might together have helped to jar the night-walker's senses out of their customary grooves, with terrifying consequences. As one mid twentieth-century writer put it, do not go up Boggart Lane: 'The gobbelins might git yer if yer don't watch out.'[405]

I have stressed throughout this section that Boggart Houses and Boggart Lanes are not urban. It will be useful to look now at two telling exceptions to this rule. The first of these is the Old Boggard House in Leeds, 'the cathedral of Methodism' in the north.[406] This building no longer exists—it was demolished in 1834—but it stood close to what is, today the Playhouse in the centre of the modern city. The name 'Boggard' here apparently dates back to a period before Leeds expanded, when the fields there were known as Boggard Closes. The name was then given to a house that was built up, under Wesley's direction, into the great Methodist chapel. The name survived because of the prestige of that chapel. One suspects that late eighteenth-century Methodists enjoyed the triumph over supernatural evil suggested by keeping 'Boggard' for a place of worship.[407] There are other cases that we know of

---

compare with Parkinson, *Yorkshire legends*, 131, 'Near Fewston ... is a spot named Busky or Bosky Dike – no doubt from the bushes, locally called "busks" or "bosks", with which the sides of the narrow gill ... were at one time covered. The place has now been denuded of its bosky appendages, and has at present no trace of the former dark and gloomy character which made it the haunt of the bargest or boggart'; and Elliot, *The country*, 47: 'They took away th' high hedge and hollins, and after that t' boggart wur ne'er heard of. That simple job laid th' Crowlum boggart.'

404. OSY 261 (1854); OSY 230 (1908); OSY 217NE (1894); OSLa 105 (1848); OSLa 89NW (1894).

405. North, 'More' (1939).

406. 'Ten Hours Factory Bill' (1835).

407. 'Wesleyan Missionary Society' (1863); and particularly Hardcastle, 'The story that the ...' (1891). The Old Boggard House deserves a longer study. Davies 'Methodism' for Methodists' proactive stance against supernatural evil.

Figure 20: Nineteenth-century postcard of Hipperholme's Boggart Lane.

where Boggart Houses were absorbed into growing cities.[408] But in these instances the Boggart Houses did not survive: one imagines that the very fact that they had earned the name 'boggart' made them buildings that were less likely to be preserved.

The other interesting exception is Boggard Lane in eighteenth-century Bradford. The earliest reference to this thoroughfare comes in 1756.[409] In the Victorian city it stood between the Bradford Interchange and St James Market. There was an effort in the 1830s to change the name to Eastbrook Lane—a typical act of nineteenth-century gentrification.[410] But the two names were used side by side for the next twenty years. Indeed, both names were still

---

408. Some just disappeared, take Gorton's Boggart House, which had vanished by OSLa 105 (1910). Others were renamed: take the Boggart House of Droyslden OSLa 105 (1848) which became Oak House, OSLa 105 (1910).

409. The property of Joseph Buck and Mrs Hannah Marshall, adjoining Boggart Lane, Dead Lane, and the road from Bradford to Wakefield, Bradford (now bottom of Wakefield Road and Leeds Road), Sep 1756, DB38/C1/page 149, WY Archives (*non vidi*).

410. 'To the Editor …' (1837); for another example, 'Gringley' (1854).

being used interchangeably in 1850.[411] There is a journalist's comment from 1843: 'One street was called Boggard Lane and indeed it was the most appropriate name which could have been chosen.'[412] Does this mean that the street was judged to be uncanny at this date? Or perhaps we have a secondary meaning of the word 'boggart', namely that the street was particularly dirty or disreputable? (see further pp. 227–28). How did a Boggard Lane find its way into central Bradford? The explanation here again is that a rural name was absorbed by the growing city. In fact, on our earliest six-inch OS map in 1852, the lane in question—labelled already at that date 'Eastbrook Lane'— is a two-minute walk from the countryside, with an iron foundry and mill flanking the route out of the city.[413] In 1756, when Bradford, a modest town of under 5,000 inhabitants, stood to the west, the entire lane would have been lined with fields and farms.

What we have then with these two 'urban' boggart names in the West Riding are actually cases of absorption and (temporary) survival. We do not have the inhabitants of a city choosing to give a boggart name to a familiar building or street. There is, in fact, very little evidence of supernatural place-names in city or town or for that matter village centres. This is not to suggest, for a second, that there was not supernatural folklore in Bradford, Leeds, Manchester, Liverpool, and Sheffield, the great cities of Boggartdom. Karl Bell has taught us just how supernatural Victorian urban spaces could be.[414] And we will see examples in the next chapter of how social relations were electrified by supernatural conversations in both town and countryside. In many instances, the word 'boggart' was used by urban populations trying to make sense of the impossible and houses were certainly identified as having spirits.[415] But there was not the habit of giving supernatural place-names to sites in the heart of cities, towns, and, for that matter, villages. When there are urban supernatural place-names, they are usually names that predate urban growth and even these do not, as a rule, long survive the 'tide of bricks and mortar', which engulfed so many acres of Boggartdom in the 1800s.[416]

---

411. 'Board of Surveyors' (1850).
412. 'Public Meetings' (1853).
413. OSY 216 (1852).
414. Bell, *Magical Imagination*.
415. 'A Ghost' (1835) for Manchester. The word 'boggart' was not used in this report, but it was likely, given Manchester's place in the heart of Boggartdom, used by the crowds who gathered there.
416. *The Village Atlas*, 1.

Boggart Holes

Let us move now to another sort of boggart name, the Boggart Hole. Supernatural entities are often associated with 'holes' in the landscape. There are, in England and the Scottish Lowlands, Hob Holes, Mermaid Holes, Boggle Holes, and Fairy Holes. As part of this series, 'Boggart Hole' was used to refer to caves; to tight steep dells; to small rooms in houses; to a pond in which dead bodies had been found; to holes in woodwork; and to holes in the ground, big or small (see pp. 231–32). What, if anything, can be said to bring these different types of hole together? In 1898, in the first volume of his *Dialect Dictionary*, Joseph Wright defined a boggart hole as 'a haunted hollow; a mythical place of terror invented with the idea of frightening children into good behavior'.[417] Wright is correct on both these points, but his words are focused on outcomes rather than meaning. I would suggest that a better definition is that a Boggart Hole was the boggart's lair or the doorway into that lair. This is summed up very neatly in a late Derbyshire boggart phrase: 'now then, surree, ast put boggart into boggart 'ole?' ('Have you, friend, put the car in the garage?').[418]

We know of seventeen Boggart Hole place-names: some of which survive to this day.[419] The Boggart Hole toponyms cover much of north-western

---

417. Wright, *Dialect Dictionary*, I, 326.

418. BC, Buxworth 1 (De).

419. The names in Figure 21 are as follows: Bogard Hole Close (North Bierley, WRY): WY Archives, 68D82/14/35, 'concerning a capital messuage in North Bierley, with closes of land called the Bogard [sic], Hole Close', 1705; Cavill, *Field-Names*, 37 has Bogard Hall Close; Boggard Hole (Fence, La): 'Boggard Hole' 1633, Crossley, *Discovery*, lxiii; Boggard Hole (Oldham, La): 'Hannah daughter of James Andrew of Boggart Hole', 'Giles Shaw Manuscripts – Handwritten Transcript of Oldham St. Mary Parish Registers', 1784, available on findmypast.co.uk [accessed November 2018]; Boggard Hole (Peak Forest, Db): Heathcote, 'History', 17; Boggard Hole (Skipton, WRY): Smith, *Place-Names*, VI, 71; Boggart Cave, The (Great Eccleston, La): 'The Copp Boggart'(1872); Boggart Clough (Lumb, La): BC, Lumb (La) 1; Boggart Hole (Bolton, La): OSLa 87 (1850); Boggart Hole (Clitheroe, La): 'Pollution' (1880); Boggart Hole (Goosnargh, La): Cookson, *Goosnargh*, 51 and 311; Boggart Hole (Greetland, WRY): Longbotham 'Lambert', 70c; Boggart Hole (Littleborough, La): BC, Littleborough 4 (La); Boggart Hole (Mellor Moor, Db): 1881 Census, Mellor, Enumeration District 9, p. 11; Boggart Hole (Newsham, La): noted in Field, *Field Names*, 24, no reference. Has there been confusion with Boggart Hall? See further Boggart House Farm (Newsham, La) in *BPN*; Boggart Hole (Stacksteads, La): Referred to in the historical section of the *Bacup Times* www.bacuptimes.co.uk/stacksteads.htm [accessed 31 January 2020]; Boggart Hole Clough (Blackley, La): see Young, 'Boggart Hole Clough'; Boggart Holes (Chapel-le-Dale, WRY): Speight, *Craven*, 254; Boggart Holes (Clapham, WRY): 'Ingleton' (1885); Boggart Holes (Higher Blackley, La): OSLa 96 (1848); Boggart Holes (Metham, ERY): Cavill, *Field-Names*, 37; Boggart Holes (Ribchester, La): 'Fatal Result' (1889); Boggart Old Clough (Cronton, La): BC, Cronton 1 (La); Boggart Old Clough (Rochdale, La): BC, Rochdale 1 (La); Boggart Pits (Treales, La). BC, Treales 1 (La); Boggart's Clough (Sabden, La): Kenrick, 'Tramps'.

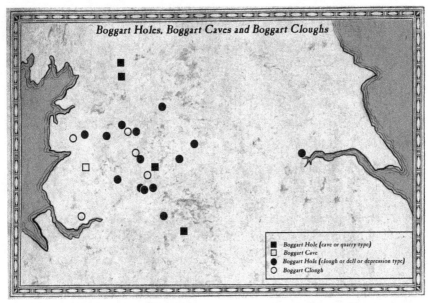

Figure 21: Boggart Holes, Boggart Caves and Boggart Cloughs.

England—I have found no examples in the Midlands or Lincolnshire.[420] They range from the Yorkshire Dales down to the Peak District and from the Ribble Valley in the west to Calderdale in the east—with a fascinating outlier in the East Riding. A Boggart Hole changed its shape from place to place, likely as a result of the radically different landscapes found across this area. In three cases a Boggart Hole referred to a cave or mine shaft; in the others (where we can with confidence identify the hole in question), a Boggart Hole referred to a clough or, in one case, a small quarry set back from the road. The most famous Boggart Hole cave type is the Boggart Holes near Clapham—a series of vertical potholes, enlivened by the cries of the boggart below (the waters or echoing rock falls).[421] The most famous dell-style Boggart Hole is Boggart Hole Clough in Blackley—a steep valley with a supernatural reputation; a site which we will examine further in Chapter 6 (see pp. 183–88).

All these Boggart Holes (and indeed other types of supernatural holes, including Fairy Holes) have in common the idea of a trip into the depths. In the case of the caves, there is a journey into a subterranean world; one that in the nineteenth century might well have been deadly. The Victorian

---

420. I know a fictional example for Staffordshire, Traice, 'Velvet Shoe'.
421. 'Ingleton' (1885); compare with Hurtlepot Boggart, West, *A Guide*, 258.

author Sabine Baring-Gould was fascinated by these drops into the dark at
boggart cave sites and included them in two of his works of fiction; in one
case in a fine horror story.[422] But even in the hollows and cloughs of Lancashire
and the South Pennines there is a sense of a descent from a high point into
a steep and often wooded valley. The boggart's lair was not necessarily
underground, but it was certainly 'below'. Here is an extract from a Victorian
Lancashire romantic novel. The hero fears that his friend Ada has strayed
into Boggart Clough:

> He had to be cautious; for the way was boggy and uncertain, and
> the light from his lantern scarcely penetrated a yard before him.
> At length, after what seemed to him an interminable period, he
> reached the brink of the clough, a deep gully that had been fretted
> away by the action of water. The sides were steep and uncertain,
> the edge ragged and treacherous, while the gully was being contin-
> ually widened by landslips, which broke away at any moment, and
> in the most unexpected places.[423]

If a fictional evocation is not enough, I offer here two maps of dell-style
Boggart Holes, one at Fence, Pendle (the oldest attested Boggart Hole), and
the other, Boggart Hole at Ribchester, the westernmost in the series, to give
some sense of the kind of landscape we are dealing with.[424] In both cases we
see the hillside falling off steeply into the 'hole'. Even looked at from below,
there is the sense that the land is dropping away.

In this talk of descent into holes, it is useful to compare Boggart and Fairy
Holes. As shown in Chapter 1, boggarts and fairies are very different types
of supernatural creatures. Fairies are social spirits, working together in a
society. 'Boggart' is instead the preferred term in Boggartdom for solitary
spirits, be they demons, ghosts, shape-changers, or deadly undines. Fairies
and boggarts are distinct tribes who are kept apart in the folklore of
Boggartdom; surprisingly so given how porous folklore boundaries usually
are. As to their holes, both fairies and boggarts had underground residences.
But, in landscape terms, entrances into fairyland tended to be on high: they
were often large and even majestic sites with caves that were sometimes

422. *Margery of Quether*, 129–30; and (the horror story) *Yorkshire Oddities*, 326–39 (first published 1867).
423. Hocking, *Real Grit*, 45–46.
424. Boggard Hole (Fence, La): 'Boggard Hole' 1633, Crossley, *Discovery*, lxiii; Boggart Holes (Ribchester, La): 'Fatal Result' (1889).

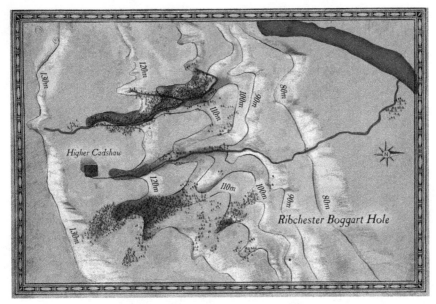

Figure 22: Ribchester Boggart Hole.

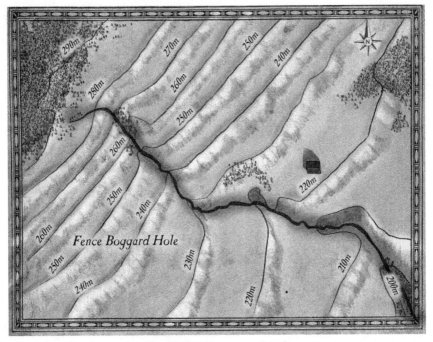

Figure 23: Fence Boggard Hole.

referred to as 'churches'.[425] The entrance into the boggart's home, however, was scary (vertical drops in the case of potholes) or was limited to 'umbrageous cloughs'.[426]

Then there were also different interiors. The fairy world was magical and full of marvels and light and, of course, fairy glamour. The boggart's lair was, on the other hand, a place of terror and darkness. We 'were always wary of dark spaces as we [were] made to believe these were boggart holes'.[427] These are the words of a mid-twentieth-century child. Boggart Holes were, in the 1800s and, indeed, the 1900s, frightening for the young threatened with a trip to the ''ole'; evoked by the likes of Wright, who may have been remembering his own Bradford childhood. The following extract is a Lancashire lad who played in Boggart Hole Clough in the 1960s. His mother had provided him with her own boggart theology:

> the 'Boggart' was a naughty imp who, if it found children being naughty, would encourage them to be even naughtier so as to get them in more trouble and on occasions would tempt them into the depths of the Clough to take them to their lair never to be seen again.[428]

These dell-style Boggart Holes should perhaps be related to other items of boggart vocabulary: 'boggart meat' (ferns), 'boggart flowers' (poisonous dog's mercury), and 'boggart muck' (owl pellets), all items that could be found in a steep Lancashire dell, particularly near running water (see Appendix). There were similar fairy objects to be found in or near those dells: 'fairy pipes' (old clay pipes), 'fairy shot' (flint arrowheads), 'fairy's horse' (ragwort, which would change into a fairy flying steed), 'fairy gloves' (foxgloves), and 'fairy butter' (various types of fungi).[429] Note

---

425. Young, 'The Fairy Placenames', 44–45; and on high elf names, Hall, 'Are There Any Elves in Anglo-Saxon Place-Names?', 80; Hall, *Elves*, 66; Semple, *Perceptions*, 186.
426. 'The Peel Family'.
427. BC, Clitheroe 4 (La).
428. BC, Crumpsall 3 (La). Lest the reader should think that such threats are a thing of the past, consider BC, Manchester 15 (La): 'I'm twenty-five and I used the boggart to scare my children (five and three) into being good whilst we're in the Clough. We spend a lot of afternoons/weekends there. They both think the boggart comes out when it starts to get dark, but hides out in the Clough watching for naughty people during the day, so that he can eat them when it's dark. Been told his favourite meal is naughty children. It works. They play nicely and behave when we're there.'
429. For fairy pipes, *Varii*, 'Fairy Pipes; for arrows, Hall, 'Getting Shot'; for fairy gloves and ragwort, Vickery, *Vickery's Folk*, respectively, 273 and 557; for fairy butter, Westwood and Simpson, *Lore of the Land*, 242–43 and 773–74.

how the fairies here are credited with civilization: they dressed, they fought with weapons, they prepared food rather than just scavenging.

The boggart was, on this evidence, an ignoble savage: he scoffed uncooked leaves and shat barely digested small mammals and beetles. There is a temptation, with the dell-dwelling boggart, to create a Lanky troll or, according to tastes, an English sasquatch: it has often been done in modern boggart fiction (see Chapter 8). But this urge should be resisted. There is nothing in nineteenth-century folklore, at least, that suggests that the boggart of the Boggart Hole was a goblinoid hiding in the high bracken—goblin-type boggarts are, as we have seen, rare in the 1800s.

I have been struck by how almost none of these Boggart Holes have stories attached to them; Boggart Houses do better in this regard. The Holes were places of potential terror: think of Ben looking for his lost jackass in a haunted clough. The inhabitant of the Hole was left largely to the imagination. Its indeterminacy, of course, was the source of much of its power:[430] here were the 'vaguest, unnameable, and therefore perhaps most frightening terrors'.[431] Perhaps the primitive nature of the boggart—when compared to louche, sophisticated fairies—left it usefully inchoate in the minds of victims.

There were Boggart Holes in houses too. Attestations for these are rare in the nineteenth century, although we have descriptions of visits to the boggart's room at Towneley Hall and to Pegg's Place (the room in which water demon Peg O'Nell was reputed to have lived) from the 1800s.[432] There are many more from the Boggart Census that give some sense of how widespread the domestic boggart hole must once have been. They were probably too proletarian and too private to have been recorded in the Victorian period: 'We called the opening into the roof space at the top of the stairs, the Boggart Hole.' 'We were told of the bogart as kids and that the loft hatch was the bogart ole (hole) and he would come down it and get us and take us away if we didn't behave.' 'When I was growing up in Rastrick in the late 1950s/early 1960s, we had a walk-in cupboard under the stairs, that we always called the boggard-'ole.' 'There was a cupboard under the stairs and we always called it the Boggart Hole.' And, *sic transit gloria mundi*, 'We had a boggart room in our house. It is a shower room now.'[433]

---

430. For more on supernatural indeterminacy, Beville, *Unnameable Monster*.

431. Sylvester, 'Naming', 281. Compare, Brown, *The Fate*, 17 on bugges 'it is a horror of the darkness of chaos known to all children and to most adults as well'.

432. Kerr, 'Marriage and Morals', 'the reputed quarters of the boggart in a small and rather inconvenient hole, close to the great clock, in one of the higher rooms'; Redding, *History*, 209.

433. BC, Clitheroe 4 (La); BC, Clitheroe 7 (La); BC, Rastrick 3 (WRY); BC, New Mills 4 (De);

The reaction of some residents suggests that these holes were, or could become, more than just a family joke. This comes from children who grew up with a Boggart Hole loft:

> When upstairs if we heard a noise creak [or] the wind up in the attic there would be a stampede down the stairs to take refuge behind the settee where our mum and dad sat.[434]

The lack of stories about Boggart Holes in dells and houses brings us to a larger question about the boggart and, indeed, other British folk creatures: perhaps one we should have attempted to answer earlier. What is actually meant by a Boggart Hole? Do we have a single monster, linked to a series of traditions and stories— stories which have perhaps not come down to us? Or do we have something, in its way more terrifying: a stretch of land which is open to all kinds of supernatural influence? Some spots certainly have a specific association. The boggart of Boggart House in Lees, therefore, was, according to John Higson, a spectral calf, 'some said with a cap on its head, and others a frill round its neck'.[435] This ridiculous get-up begs a narrative. Some sites, meanwhile, have a *generally* terrifying air. Take Higson, for instance, describing Green Lane in Droylsden: 'th' owd Green Lone ... swaarmt wi fairees, witches, un boggarts'.[436] That word 'swarmed' is used again and again in the Northwest and the Midlands in the nineteenth century, to describe the exuberance of supernatural evil.[437] My suspicion, for what it is worth, is that most boggart sites were, or under the yoke of imagination at least had the potential to become, *generally* haunted spots. A story was replaced by simple menace, made so much worse by unknowing.

Boggart Versus Fairies

Where do boggarts dwell in the landscape? In the preceding pages I have argued, using Higson's writing, that boggarts prefer spaces in relation to but not inside human communities. But there are other questions. Do boggarts choose high or low places? Wooded or open spaces? Or do boggart-haunted

---

BC, Burscough 3 (La).
434. BC, Clitheroe 7 (La).
435. Higson, 'Boggarts and Feorin', 508.
436. Higson, *Droylsden*, 68.
437. Burt, *Letters*, I, 227 (combined with a related word 'infest'); Lawson, *Letters*, 51; and Waugh, *Sketches*, 214, etc.

spots emerge with little thought for what a landscape looks like? I have gathered, over a number of years, 183 boggart place-names, most recorded in the nineteenth century. It is true that not all areas haunted by a boggart have a supernatural place-name; or even if they do, that the word 'boggart' is necessarily used. However, by breaking these place-names down into landscape features we get a sense of where those living in Boggartdom in the 1800s expected boggarts to be found. The percentages in the figures that follow are rounded.

Sixty-five of the boggart toponyms were for buildings: halls, houses, barns, cottages, and even a church (36%); thirty-eight were lanes and roads (21%); twenty-six were fields and meadows (14%). Boggart fields (including gates and stiles) are the most problematic of the boggart toponyms because there is the danger that a field or meadow has been named after a scarecrow rather than a supernatural force; 'boggart', it will be remembered, also meant 'scarecrow' in parts of the Northwest (see pp. 33–34 and 225–27). Twenty more were dells or valleys (11%). Most of these dells were 'Boggart Holes', the term examined in the last section. Then there are the minor boggart names: woods scored just nine (5%); caves, cliffs, and rocks, seven (4%); bridges, six (3%); collieries and mines, five (3%); rivers, streams, and wells, four (2%); and heights (hills, etc.) three (2%).[438] Do these numbers help us better understand boggarts? Or do they simply represent a typical northern landscape?

In drawing out special characteristics it is useful, again, to contrast the boggart with fairies, or, more specifically, two small samples of fairy toponyms from the same general region. In 2019, I published a handlist of thirty-six fairy place-names from the modern county of Cumbria. Cumbria has more highland territory than Lancashire and the West Riding, but the two regions have similar styles of folklore.[439] The breakdown of the thirty-six names was, in landscape terms, as follows. Of the Cumbrian fairy names, twenty-one were caves, cliffs, and rocks (58%); eleven were rivers, streams, and wells (31%); two were fields (6%); and two were high places (6%).[440] It is important to stress that, despite landscape differences, these types of fairy names

---

438. BN.

439. Instead of fairies and boggarts, central and north Cumbria have either fairies and boggles or fairies and dobbies: there is the same division (social versus solitary spirits) with different terms, see further pp. 70–76.

440. Young, 'The Fairy Placenames'. For the purposes of these calculations, I ignored three fairy toponyms from the region which had been concocted by individuals: two house owners determined to beautify their properties (Fairy Glen and Fairy House), and a name given by a potholer (Fairies Workshop).

conform to the fairy names found elsewhere in the north. Thinking of the nineteen fairy toponyms that I know of for the historical county of Lancashire,[441] for instance, we have: nine for caves, cliffs, and rocks (47%); two for high places (11%); two for lanes and roads (including a possibly modern invention, a Fairy Street in Everton, 11%); two fairy wells (11%); two fairy trees (although one of these was originally the Fair Oak not Fairy Oak, 11%); one fairy building (5%), which might have arisen from confusion with Fair House; and one fairy bridge (5%).[442]

On this evidence, boggarts and fairies inhabit very different parts of the landscape. Fairies are to be found, above all, near impressive rocky crags and running water or wells. Combining rocks, water, and high places, we have a score of 95 per cent for Cumbria and 69 per cent for Lancashire. In fact, this preference is even stronger because several of the names from the Northwest combine rocks and water: for instance the Fairy Kettle at Caldbeck, a boiling rock pool; or the Fairy Castle at Brackenhill, a rock by a river. It is also perhaps unfair to state that *only* two fairy toponyms for Cumbria were 'high places'. So, just two had place-name elements that identified them as such: Fairy Knowe (a hillock particularly associated with fairies in Scots) and Fairy Knott. But several of the others are in hilly or mountainous areas, for example the Fairy Graves in the Upper Duddon Valley. Several of the rocks, meanwhile, tower above their locality: e.g. the Fairy Crag at Rosgill. Northern English fairies are, on this evidence, likely to be found near eye-catching boulders and/or around water. Most of these sites (Fairy Street in Everton is a conspicuous exception!) are also well away from human habitation.[443]

---

441. I've not included Lancashire beyond the Sands (southern Cumbria) because these are included in the Cumbrian figures.

442. Fairy Bridge (Little Bowland): Young, 'Fairy Trees', 16; Fairy Buttery (Entwistle): OSLa 79 (1850), NW of Turton reservoir; Fairy Chapel (Healey Dell): 'The New Railway' (1870); Fairy Chapel (Morecambe): 'The Fairy Chapel was a distinctive rock formation and tourist attraction at the base of Heysham Head, just to the north of Half Moon Bay', http://morecambe.myzen. co.uk/detail.html?id=10 [accessed 14 January 2020]; Fairy Hill (Cheetham): OSLa 104 (1848); Fairy Hill Cottage (Quernmore): OSLa 35 (1847), top NW corner; Fairy Hole (Warton Cragg): OSLa 18 (1848); Fairy Hole Wood (Little Bowland): Young, 'Fairy Trees', 16; Fairy Holes Cave (Whitewell): OSLa 46 (1847); Fairy House (Lowton): OSLa 102, S of Lowton Common; Fairy Lane (Cheetham): OSLa 104 (1848); Fairy Oak (Little Bowland): Young, 'Fairy Trees', 19–21; Fairy Steps (Beetham): 'Silverdale' (1933); Fairy Stones (Bidstone Hill): 'Fairy Superstition' (1859); Fairy Street (Everton): OSLa 106 (1851), and 3 July 1842, St Peter, Liverpool baptism of one George Upton resident on Fairy Street; Fairy Tree (Stalmine): Lancashire Archives, DRB/1/180, accessed 12 July 2016 at http://archivecat.lancashire.gov. uk/calmview/; Fairy Well (Golbourne): OSLa 102 (1849), SW corner; Fairy Well (Preesall with Hackinsall): OSLa 38 (1848) just to the north of the village; Queen of the Fairies Chair (Tatham): OSLa 26 (1847).

443. All examples in this paragraph are in Young 'The Fairy Placenames' save Fairy Street for which

	Boggarts Toponyms	Cumbrian Fairies	Lancashire Fairies	North-Western Fairies
Buildings	65 (36%)	N/A	1 (5%)	1 (2%)
Roads	38 (21%)	N/A	2 (11%)	2 (4%)
Fields	26 (14%)	2 (6%)	N/A	2 (4%)
Dells	20 (11%)	N/A	N/A	N/A
Woods and Trees	9 (5%)	N/A	2 (11%)	2 (4%)
Rocks and Caves	7 (4%)	21 (58%)	9 (47%)	30 (55%)
Bridges	6 (3%)	N/A	1 (5%)	1 (2%)
Mines	5 (3%)	N/A	N/A	N/A
Water	4 (2%)	11 (31%)	2 (11%)	13 (24%)
Hills	3 (2%)	2 (6%)	2 (11%)	4 (7%)

Figure 24: Supernatural Toponyms. Note that 'North-Western Fairies'
puts Cumbrian and Lancashire Fairies together.

Boggarts have, it will be seen immediately, a different pattern of habitation. Most boggart place-names are associated with either buildings or with roads: they tend to be much more closely tied to humanity than fairies are. Indeed, if we include bridges and mines, then 54 per cent of boggart toponyms are linked to human objects in the landscape. This could not be said of a single one of the Cumbrian fairy names and only a handful of the Lancashire ones. The number should be even higher. After all, fields are, for the most part, human in that they are spaces that have been fenced and farmed. But we cannot safely include these because of the possibility, noted earlier, that 'boggart' in certain cases refers to scarecrows. There is also a handful of boggart rocks and woods and caves, which would be, on the evidence given above, acceptable to fairies. Unlike the fairies, just 6 per cent of boggart names are linked primarily to rocks and water. Boggart Holes (mostly dells) belong here, but as we have seen, even in these cases there is some contrast with Fairy Holes.

How could we sum up these differences between fairy and boggart toponyms? We can perhaps usefully talk of supernatural physical and supernatural human geography. Fairies dominate the supernatural physical geography of the north. They are much more likely to be found in places away from humans with dramatic rocks and wild streams. Boggarts are, on the other hand, part of supernatural human geography. They are found above all in connection with places and objects that humans have created: 'Fairies are not human, but they resemble humans and live lives parallel to theirs.'[444] They carry out the same activities (hunting, smoking, love-making, feasts, food preparation, war, and

---

see n. 442: another example of a fairy site close to a human community is Preesall, Fairy Well: OSLa 38 (1848).

444. Bourke, *Burning*, 28.

so on). They offer a mirror to human society, just set apart in the wilderness (or what passes for wilderness in England). Fairies and humans rely on each other, but they only occasionally come into contact, usually with painful consequences. Boggarts, on the other hand, are not the mirror, but rather the shadow of their victims. The solitary spirits of Boggartdom—the ghosts, the shape-changers, and various other ghouls and goblins—may appear, thinking of examples from this chapter, as calves with frills, as women who can throw their heads, or as ballooning sheep. But they are, in an important sense, much more human than the aloof fay.[445]

---

445. The Irish legend where the fairies are damned because they have not a drop of human blood is worth recalling here, e.g. Andrews, *Ulster*, 99.

CHAPTER FIVE

Boggart Beliefs and Transmission

Introduction

In the early and mid 1800s, the Staffordshire village of Kidsgrove, the nearby canal tunnel, the mines, and the countryside around about were haunted by Kidgrew Boggart, 'for years the terror and dread' of the area. Kidgrew Boggart sometimes appeared as a dog, sometimes as 'a dancing and flickering light', and sometimes as a headless maid in its iterations around this rapidly industrializing area: 'perhaps no village or hamlet in England was ever more completely possessed, or more fully believed in a goblin than did the one in question'. The boggart screeched, despite its missing head, something taken to presage a disaster in the collieries. It also occasionally sang like a nightingale 'and hundreds of colliers with affrighted faces gathered to the spot to listen'. Like many bogies, Kidgrew Boggart had an impressive range of forms and roles. It was even credited with stealing rabbits.[446]

According to some, the boggart had been a boatman's wife, killed and decapitated in a quarrel with her vicious husband. According to others, she was a travelling Liverpudlian who was raped and beheaded on the canal: 'Many [were] the tales told as to the origin of this village phantom, all of them differing in detail.' In the 1850s, when Kidgrew Boggart was a power in the land, there must have been hundreds of stories about her escapades and encounters with terrified locals. When a lonely collier returning home or a gamekeeper out at night met Kidgrew Boggart, 'the news went round to every cottage household, with the usual results, that the boggart had been seen'. Unfortunately, almost none of these accounts survive for few writers took up the challenge of recording Kidgrew Boggart's lore: Staffordshire folklore went largely uncollected. There are just some nineteenth-century

---

446. All the quotations in this paragraph and the next come from 'Up and Down the Country' (1879).

newspaper articles and a useful but necessarily short pamphlet published by Philip Leese in 1989.[447]

Here, in essence, is our difficulty with recreating boggart stories and experiences. We know that boggarts had an important role in Victorian communities, particularly in the Northwest. Sometimes, as with Kidgrew Boggart, we see the ripples that these experiences and stories caused. However, we can only partially reconstruct the boggart beliefs and tales of one place, such as Kidsgrove. There are not enough sources about the super-natural, even for the best covered areas, such as Burnley or Saddleworth, never mind for a poor community in the Potteries, like Kidsgrove. In looking at boggart belief and the transmission of boggart tales, I have resorted here to the next best thing: an overview of boggart belief and boggart transmis-sion in the Northwest, taken from a medley of different sources: there is simply not enough boggart-lore from the nineteenth-century Midlands or Lincolnshire to justify their inclusion.

In this medley I have attempted to draw on boggart memories from different kinds of communities. There are rural scenes, such as a bridge dripping blood in the Colne countryside. There are villages like Helmshore, where the Dumber Boggert terrified passers-by. There are mill towns like Littleborough and Preston, with their own boggart legends: Littleborough trembled at Clegg Hall Boggart, the inhabitants of Preston at Bannister Hall Doll. Then there are cities, including Bradford, which in 1832 had a boggart who defended the workers against the factory owners in the struggle for a ten-hour day.[448] Ronald Hutton is certainly correct that there was a 'tremendous idealisation of rural England' starting in the 1700s and reaching its 'apogee between 1880 and 1930'. This idealization defined folklore collection, which favoured the rural over the urban.[449] But, happily, enough non-folklore sources are available to allow us to trace boggart-lore, not just in Pennine farms and in Fylde hamlets, but also in the mills and factories, the tenements and the industrializing civil parishes of the Northwest.

---

447. Leese, *Kidsgrove Boggart*. Leese's account could now be improved upon with 'Up and Down the Country' (1879), and 'Conviction' (1843).
448. These examples are given in this chapter, with the exception of Bannister Hall Doll, for which see p. 55.
449. Hutton, *Triumph*, 117.

Beliefs

A necessary preliminary to the question of how stories were transmitted is the question of belief. What percentage of the population believed in boggarts? What does belief in boggarts even mean? Belief in supernatural forces is, it must first be acknowledged, *extraordinarily* hard to measure. Even in days of scientific polling the question of what percentage of the population believes, say, that we survive death continues to be difficult to measure.[450] So much depends on definition: there are, for example, those who do not believe in 'ghosts', but who believe that their dead loved ones communicate with them.[451] There is also the suspicion that supernatural belief is more malleable than some parallel belief systems: a man out for a walk on a stormy night in the countryside will be more likely to believe than that same man strolling down the high street in broad daylight. People 'can go from being sardonic cynics one moment to ardent believers the next'.[452] Then there is the difficulty that many keep their supernatural opinions to themselves for fear of ridicule; the paranormal equivalent of the 'shy Tory'.

How then can we possibly start to measure belief in nineteenth-century Britain when there are not even skewed survey results to refer to? We are told of the beliefs of individuals and this at least gives us some sense of the range of possibilities within a community. There are what we might call 'the mystics' who see 'things' on a regular basis; those born, for instance, between 'twelve and one at night', who can perceive 'both boggarts and spirits'.[453] Take Jem Hill, 'th' King o' Dreighlsdin', who used to master boggarts on the edges of Droylsden; or Weasel: 'There was not a boggart in all the countryside ... with which he was not on nodding terms.'[454] There are those who have one-off boggart experiences: the servant boy who was chased by a fireball at Cartmel in 1809; or the 'jolly butcher of Blackpool' who came face to face with his dead wife on a road outside the town.[455] There are those who give nuanced answers: 'Nay ... aw connot say 'at aw've fairly sin [a boggart], but aw've thowt aw hed, an' aw've just bin as weel freeten'd as iv aw'd sin id ever sooa.'[456]

---

450. For an overview of modern polling and the supernatural: Bennett, *Alas*, 10–12.

451. Bennett, *Alas*, 15; for terminological problems with the supernatural in research see also Day, 'Everyday', 151–54; and Cowdell, 'City', 83.

452. Waters, *Cursed Britain*, 8 for flexible witchcraft beliefs, another 'imaginative, uncanny and wishful way of thinking'.

453. 'Folklore' (1857).

454. Higson, *Droylsden*, 88; Snowden, *Tales*, 120 (fictional, but based on Yorkshire realities).

455. Stockdale, *Annales*, 389; 'Superstition in the Fylde' (1857).

456. Aker-Whitt, 'The Dunkenhalgh Boggart'.

Then there are the sceptics. Some of these belong to the local middle classes and have little patience for such beliefs: for instance Thornber, a Fylde clergyman who wrote an extensive but 'ridiculous list of still lingering feelings of superstition'.[457] But there were also more sympathetic disbelievers among Lancashire's intellectuals: 'For our part, we have far less patience with the vulgarity of the man who laughs at the aged East Lancashire believer in boggarts, than we have with the so-called vulgarity of the man who has not yet wholly lost all power of belief in the supernatural.'[458] There were also, it must not be forgotten, members of the working class who disbelieved. 'Folk talk a deal o' them boggarts', said one Lancashire gamekeeper, 'but I dunnot believe in them. I've been aboot o' neets mair nor [than] maist folk, an' if there wor any boggarts agait I mun [must] ha' leet o' [come across] one, for sure.'[459] Old John, a Clitheroe gravedigger, said to a man pretending to be a ghost: 'If thou'rt nowt tha can't harm me; but if thou'rt owt, I'll warm thee', at which the 'boggart' fled.[460] Any given community is a tapestry woven with these different strands.

What proportions are—to use familiar terms—atheists, agnostics, and believers? Were these proportions different in 1800 and 1900; and did they change from plain to hills or from farmstead to city? The temptation—and it must be resisted—is to extrapolate on the basis of isolated comments. In 1844, for instance, Cyrus Redding visited Boggart Hole Clough (Blackley) and asked a young man whether he had seen the boggart. The local replied, 'There's noa Boggart neaw'.[461] Does this mean that boggart belief had ended in the locality? Not a bit of it. We could be seeing a generational difference. We could be dealing with a single eccentric view. The 'young man' may have been irritated at being patronized by an outsider, as he apparently replied 'with an archness of meaning that language is quite unable to convey'.[462] Or Redding could have invented or embellished the episode.[463] Certainly we

---

457. *Blackpool*, 332. Bell, *Magical Imagination*, 141–49 is very good on folklore collectors as 'conflicted agents'.

458. McKay, *East Lancashire*, 20.

459. T.H.H., 'Letter'.

460. Clarke, *Clitheroe*, 59 (in the second run of page numbers in the volume). This may be a folklore episode but, if so, it is all the more interesting for scepticism in tradition itself, see Roper, 'Folk Disbelief' and Correll, 'Believers'.

461. Redding, *History*, 162.

462. Ibid., 162.

463. It is extremely easy to make these kinds of deductions: e.g. for this passage, Bell, *Magical Imagination*, 186: 'Such a response did not deny the possibility that a ghost had once haunted the locality, but if it had, it had been believed in by the previous generations, not the boy's'.

should not be surprised that some forty years later, George Milner (whose knowledge of the area was greater than Redding's) reported seeing a group of scared children at the entrance to the Clough in the gloaming: 'Probably they are still believers in the existence of the Boggart.'[464]

Much more valuable are general comments from astute observers. In 1890, for instance, Ab' O' Ned, an aged man, talking of south Lancashire, told a woman who visited him: 'I' my young days ... everybody i' eawr country side believt i' boggarts an' witches, an' uncanny things o' that sooart.' Edward Kirk, describing life in the north of Lancashire in the 1830s, wrote, 'The belief in boggarts, when I was a boy, was implicit: to doubt them was heretical'; and again: '[t]o doubt the existence and presence of boggarts was to doubt your own being'. John Higson wrote of Gorton in the early part of the century and for an allied belief system (fairies): 'Few of the villagers disbelieved the existence of these imaginative [sic] beings.'[465]

Supernatural beliefs are often projected back into the past and thus we need to be careful with such sentiments.[466] Nevertheless, the principle of a decline in traditional supernatural beliefs during the reign of Victoria is evident in the comments of Higson, Sydney, Kirk, and Ab' O' Ned and it is insisted upon again and again in our sources. Henry Cowper, perhaps the most perspicuous north-western writer of the period, claimed that belief had fallen away in the later nineteenth century in Hawkshead; the result, he suspected, of cheap publications penetrating the farming valleys.[467] Joseph Lawson writing on Pudsey, between Bradford and Leeds, ascribed various causes to a similar decline there, including the arrival of gas in houses, education, and even Pepper's Ghost.[468] Henry Houlding, in a fascinating 1892 talk at Burnley, suggested that it was new political ideas after the French Revolution that had spelled the end of traditional beliefs: 'That star [of liberty] was then only glimmering in the horizon, but somehow there was less talk of the Pendle

---

464. Milner, *Country Pleasures*, 266. Consider, too, BC, Accrington 1 (La): 'Forty-odd years ago [1970s] when I was in my early twenties, I used to live very close to Boggart Hole Clough ... and worked at the children's hospital opposite the clough. Local children seemed very aware of the malicious nature of the boggarts who, according to the folklore, lived there so they tended to stay away from the clough when it was dark, if they had any sense.'

465. Hamer, 'Ab' O' Ned's "'Witchins'"'; Kirk, 'A Nook of North Lancashire'; Kirk, 'The Folk of a North Lancashire Nook', 105; Higson, *Gorton*, 17.

466. The finest discussion remains Rieti, *Newfoundland*, 35–87 (a doctorate chapter on Newfoundland fairy traditions—though the principles Rieti establishes are applicable to the supernatural more generally). This chapter was missed out of Rieti's later monograph on Newfoundland fairies. See also, Waters, 'They', for witchcraft.

467. Cowper, *Hawkshead*, 302–04.

468. Lawson, *Letters*, 48–54.

Forest witches after its uprising.'[469] Other writers made the fundamental point that if the traditional supernatural was declining, it was being replaced by different supernatural forms, among them table-rapping and Spiritualism: 'superstition is not extinct, but merely modified'.[470] Spiritualists, indeed, had striking success in the northern working classes in the later 1800s: 'The only clear thing one can say about the geographical pattern of plebeian spiritualism is that it remained predominantly northern and Pennine until the 1900s.'[471]

Scholars concerned with the 'disenchantment of the world' would find much of interest in these reflections by intelligent writers on changes that they had lived through in their own communities.[472] I am interested in the direction and speed of that change, as opposed to the reasons behind any shift. As such, I am most struck not by the quality of comments, but by their sheer quantity. Cowper, Lawson, and Houlding had thought the matter through carefully. Others employed instead the falling away of belief as a rhetorical trope—a trope that was trotted out to fill newspaper columns or round off chapters: 'During the last few years the railway engine, the telegraph, and the schoolmaster have frightened into oblivion all the shadowy marauders of our forefathers' peace.' 'Science lectures, school boards, and long chimneys are fast sweeping all these old tales away, and in a few more years they will be all forgotten.' Or again: 'Owd Ned [the steam-engine], un' lung chimblies; fact'ry folk havin' summat else t'mind nur [than] wanderin' ghosts un' rollickin' sperrits.'[473] Such comments from nineteenth-century writers could be multiplied many times over.

A particularly interesting instance of these formulaic assertions about the decline of traditional belief is the topos that boggarts (and other supernatural creatures) fled from the train. The idea that supernatural beings hated din has a long pedigree in British folklore.[474] 'Since the railway ... invaded the sylvan and rocky recesses of Cliviger the Towneley boggart frightened, possibly, by the advent of the steam courser, has evidently "made tracks"'; 'the railway whistle echoes in the cloughs and denes where the boggarts and warlocks

---

469. Houlding, 'Local Glimpses', 70. Compare, Potter, *Lancashire*, 99: 'With all their progress and their politics, the weavers were steeped in superstition; believed devoutly in "boggarts" and "signs of death"'.

470. Higson, 'Boggarts and Feorin' (1869).

471. Barrow, *Spirits*, 104.

472. Walsham, 'The Reformation'; Josephson-Storm, *The Myth*.

473. 'Chip', 'Cuttock'; Wilkinson, 'Barcroft Boggart'; Higson, *Droylsden*, 71.

474. 'Young, 'Fairies and Railways'. For boggarts see also the disappearance of Fair Becca (Horton Boggart): Cudworth, *Rambles*, 171, 'her non-appearance is accounted for by the fact that she had been "flayed away" by the whirr of machinery at Cliffe Mills'.

once dwelt'; 'railway trains began to snort and rumble hourly through solitudes where the "little grey folk" of past days had held undisturbed sway, laden with multitudes of busy, curious people, who recked little of witchcraft'; '[t]he shriek of the railway engine has driven away many a boggart from old haunted manor houses'; 'at that toime there'n no new fangled thinks code [called] foire engins, an railway styemers scroikin [screeching] away through th' country, enew to flay [frighten] a buggart eawt o'th' greawnd.'[475]

Why did so many authors indulge in such tropes? Nineteenth-century north-western writers—and similar phrases can be gathered from other parts of Britain[476]—did not just observe the decline but approved it. By putting down phrases like this, authors were affirming their membership of an educated club whose creed was, they believed, superior to that represented by the traditional supernatural world. There is little doubt that traditional supernatural beliefs *were* falling away in the nineteenth and the early twentieth centuries: the Boggart Census demonstrates this for boggart-lore (see Chapter 7). But we should be suspicious of the enthusiasm of those applauding at the boggart's wake. In the end the descriptions of supernatural events that appear in Chapter 6 are a far more reliable index of belief than any of those offered above. In the tens of episodes described, we will see men, women, and children acting on their convictions, sometimes in ways that confounded the expectations of educated contemporaries.

Tellers of Tales

The basic unit of the social supernatural was the tale. These could be stories of personal experiences, which folklorists call 'memorates'—for instance: 'The girls who sat up to roast [the annual joint] were frightened by a boggard and left the beef, which was burnt to a cinder long before morning.'[477] Very often they were, instead, traditional tales about local bogies which belonged to a wider pool of European stories: 'Of the adventures of the said boggart, and the pranks it plays, the inhabitants of the dale tell many a tale; some of these stories bear a strong family likeness to the tales of other boggarts in other parts of the world.'[478] The Boggart Census suggests that a number of these formulaic stories are still told in the early twenty-first century, although

---

475. Kerr, 'Summer Rambles' (1892); Dobson, *Rambles*, 104; Waugh, *Sketches*, 215; Old Yew Tree, 'A Day in Cheshire' (1869); Lahee, *Betty*, 6.

476. See, e.g., Middleton, *Spirits*, 201–03.

477. A Parish Apprentice, 'Passages', 76.

478. Axon, 'Gallowsfield Ghost'.

print not voice now seems to be the typical medium of transmission.[479] Personal experiences and traditions, needless to say, easily come, with retelling, to resemble each other.

We cannot speak of a class of professional storytellers in the north of England in the nineteenth-century. These still operated in Ireland in the 1800s and, at least to some extent, in Cornwall.[480] However, there was clearly a culture of storytelling and some north-westerners had the reputation of being good tellers of tales. Of one Lancashire woman, it was written that she had 'a store of "boggart-tales", which are the delight and wonder of the country-side'. About one young man preparing for the ministry, a friend remembered, after his premature death: 'Of "boggart" stories and anecdote he had a never-failing source.' Thomas Turner Wilkinson, Burnley schoolteacher and historian, became famous for his 'ballads and sayings and stories'. Old Robin o' Giles was 'a rare living repository of local legendary lore'.[481]

Sometimes the fame of these storytellers came to extend outside a narrow network of friends and family. Benjamin Brierley, in one of his most thoughtful essays, talks of social circles where, in the early nineteenth century, gifted raconteurs told stories to each other:

> This habit of rubbing shoulders together at these domestic clubs produced many a semi-professional tale-teller, who went about the country after the manner of itinerant theatricals ... I knew one of this fraternity who was in great request at gentlemen's houses for miles round.[482]

We glimpse another of these 'semi-professionals', 'Old Robert Dillrume' of Saddleworth, in Thomas Shaw's poem 'Shantooe Jest':

> [Robert's] mind had treasur'd up
> Much antient [sic] strange record
> And on a winters' [sic] night
> When by a neighbours fire
> He free declar'd

479. For a rare orally transmitted tale BC, Bolton 1 (La).
480. Delargy, 'Story-Teller'; James, *Folklore of Cornwall*, 22–35.
481. Francis, 'Tales', 123; Shaw, *Local Notes*, 224; 'The Burnley Antiquary'; Aker-Whitt, 'The Dunkenhalgh Boggart'.
482. *Lancashire Wit and Humour*, 7.

What he had seen and heard
Sleep could not overpow'r
Till evening grew late,
If Mr. Dill had come
To be our company,
Times usual rate
Seem'd quicken'd while he sat.[483]

Dillrume was a typical late eighteenth- or early nineteenth-century English 'bard',
caught between the literate and the oral. He combined lofty commentaries on
Milton's betrayal of Charles I with Saddleworth legends of giants, fairies, and, of
course, boggarts. This class of informal Georgian and Victorian tale-tellers badly
deserves its own study; I know of no attempt to write their history.[484]

Storytelling in the Family

If the basic unit of the social supernatural was the tale, then the typical setting
for storytelling was the family hearth, particularly in the winter months. This
was before electricity and even gas had become commonplace; so these stories
were often recounted around the flames as night drew in:

The pitch darkness outside, and the comparative darkness within,
and the howling moaning winds, and perhaps heavy raindrops
pattering against the window panes, cause everyone's imagination
to be in full vigour, ready to drink in the weird stories.[485]

Frequently in our sources, reference is made to stories being told before
the burning coals:

And now with open mouth and dilated eyes, with strained ears
and excited brain, they draw nearer to the fire, whilst the aged
parent retails many an ancient and oft told tradition of ghosts and
haunted places, or narrates reminiscences of personal encounters
with boggarts and feeorin.[486]

---

483. *Recent Poems*, 124.
484. The closest is perhaps Kreilkamp, *Voice*.
485. Lawson, *Letters*, 48.
486. Higson, *Droylsden*, 70. Fire continued to work its magic into the twentieth century BC,

It was only as the nineteenth century progressed that private reading (see further pp. 129–31) started to replace family storytelling in working-class families. Instead of communal gatherings and tales, 'we sat reading *Pickwick* and *The Old Curiosity Shop*'. [487]

It was, above all, the responsibility of the oldest in a household—'the elder branches of the family', [488] or 'the hoary farmer or elderly female, in her trim tally-ironed cap' [489]—to tell supernatural tales, so that

> children sitting round the fire,
> Could hear the wearied talk
> Of what their grannies oft had seen,
> When nights were cold and dark. [490]

Preference was given either to the personal experiences of the storytellers or to those of other family members, past or present: storytellers 'will recount the spiritual visitors they, their father, mother, or some of their family have seen'. [491] Sam Bamford, for instance, remembered years later how his aunt had told him, as a child, about seeing her sister's ghost—Sam's mother: 'I and she being alone in the house, she gave me an account which made my heart to thrill and the tears to gush from my eyes.' [492] It is striking the number of encounters there were with deceased relatives. One West Riding man was shocked into sobriety after a boggart experience—a meeting with his dead mother in the dark. [493] I insisted in the last chapter that the supernatural was rooted in localities. It was also personal. [494]

If the stories came from senior members of the family, they were particularly loved by the young, with children clamouring to hear these terrifying tales:

Rochdale 6 (La): 'I was born in 1955 and my mum used to say that we were watching the Boggarts if we stared into the coal fire when it was lit. She said Boggarts lived in amongst the orange and yellow flames of the coals.'

487. Houlding, 'Local Glimpses', 70. Elbourne, *Music*, 96, offers this paradox about increasing literacy: 'While potentially instruments for the homogenization of culture, writing and print may also provide the capacity for individual isolation within the "global village"'.

488. Briggs, *The Remains*, 219.

489. Chip, 'Cuttock'.

490. Anderson, 'There are no Boggarts Now' (1902).

491. Chip, 'Cuttock'.

492. *Passages*, 144.

493. Lawson, *Letters*, 50.

494. I am reminded of Gillian Bennett's comment from her 1980s survey into supernatural belief, *Alas*, 28: 'It seems to be sociability itself – interest in others, and especially love of family – that most often predisposes women towards belief [in the supernatural].'

"'Grandfather," said the eldest boy, "you promised us, when we had learned our tasks, to tell us some fairy-tale or ghost-story'". 'Many is the time when as a youngster have I heard my revered granny relate this weird story on a dark winter's night in a room lighted up with a half-penny candle, which made the darkness look blacker in the corners.'[495] Enlightenment and post-Enlightenment thinkers disapproved of the effects of these tales on young minds, even if told by familiar faces in a familiar setting, ignoring the therapeutics and pleasure of fear.[496] There are two nineteenth-century news stories that claimed that Lancashire children had died from hearing spooky tales.[497] One book for young people published in 1849 in Halifax raged: 'It is a very foolish, as well as a very wrong thing, to fill the minds of children, with old women's stories about ghosts, hobgoblins, and raw-head and bloody-bones, &c.'[498] Joseph Baron, meanwhile, wrote in the 1890s: 'Boggart lore is the earliest pabulum upon which the child's hereditary supersti-tions feed.'[499] Children were certainly, at times, left 'boggart-feart'. Tattersall Wilkinson as a boy listened 'to those stories to such an extent that he could scarcely venture home after dark across the village green at Worsthorne'.[500]

It is a good question how often elder members of the family believed in the stories with which they terrified their young charges. In some instances, there was clearly great sincerity: 'I have heard old Aunt Ailse … relate the pathetic story of the wronged Lucette', who became Dunkenhalgh Boggart after her suicide, 'while tears have trickled down her cheeks'.[501] In other cases we have references to parents deliberately producing anxiety in their sons and daughters and the use of boggarts as 'domestic policemen', as shown here:[502]

> It was a common practice of parents when their little ones were naughty to tell them there was a black boggard up the chimney, or coming down to fetch them; also for them to make noises in

495. Riley, *Juvenile Tales*, 86; 'Towneley Hall' (1902).
496. The earliest British reference I know dates to 1711: Addison, *Works*, III, 37: 'I took notice in particular [during the ghost story] of a little boy, who was so attentive to every story, that I am mistaken if he ventures to go to bed by himself this twelve-month'. Handley, *Visions*, 115–18 for a fuller view of Addison's writing on ghosts. For the therapeutics of fear, Warner, *No Go*, 5–6.
497. 'A Child Frightened to Death by "Boggarts"'; 'The Cruel and Wanton Folly …', from Spring-heeled Jack rumours.
498. Riley, *Juvenile Tales*, 92. Note this followed on from the tale of Horton boggart!
499. Baron, 'Lancashire Boggarts'. Baron went on to claim, with some bitterness, that as the child grew older: 'Then that purgative – Education – is administered, and exit Superstition to make room for something more sensible, – theosophy, and table-turning, for instance.'
500. Wilkinson, 'Folk Lore'.
501. Aker-Whitt, 'The Dunkenhalgh Boggart'.
502. Brushfield, 'Reminiscences', 14; repeated in North-Westerner, 'Way' (1932).

secret, or knocks, said to be 'Tom knocker,' to intimate the presence of boggards.[503]

Supernatural monsters were also created as wards for children in the dangerous
outdoors. The intention was both to stop children damaging the countryside
and to stop the countryside damaging children. There was, for example, the
nut nan: 'Her office was to seize children who purloined nuts before they
were ripe.'[504] Then, of course, there was Jenny Greenteeth and other blood-
thirsty undines, invented by parents to keep children away from dangerous
pools—although her remit would eventually be extended to dental hygiene,
slippery rocks, and railways, too.[505] Families went to some lengths to convince
children of the reality of such beings. We know, for instance, that one child
in Cheshire was taken out to listen to 'Jenny' (the wind) howling in the trees;
and that children in south Lancashire were shown false teeth with green enamel
as a proof of Jenny's existence. A young Charles Hardwick was told that the
boggarts would be more likely to get him if he didn't believe in them.[506]

It will come as no surprise that these adult creations took on a life of their
own. Jenny Greenteeth is a particularly interesting example of this. Our folklore
primers claim that Jenny was, as noted earlier, associated with dangerous bodies
of water and that she would pull children below the surface to devour them.[507]
Yet we find her in other roles, too, and bothering adults as well as the young. In
one account she lived in a subterranean tunnel and came after any intruders with
a blade. In Newton Chapelry she was said to guard treasure in a haunted lane:
'when John Ravenscroft in 1842 found some old coins buried near Rose Hill,
about three feet below the surface, he was so afraid of Jennie's wrath that he
would not pass that part of the Common after dark without some one with him'.
At Preston, meanwhile, 'superstitious old women used to tell strange tales of one
"Jenny Greenteeth", who was said to be occasionally seen riding on a broomstick,
cutting wonderful capers'.[508] This all suggests that the bogies of inventive parents
could become real to children and adults alike. These bogies easily broke out of
the supernatural reservations into which they had been ineffectually corralled.[509]

---

503. Lawson, *Letters*, 51.
504. Higson, *Gorton Historical Recorder*, 12.
505. Young, 'Jenny Greenteeth'.
506. Higson, 'Boggarts Feorin, etc', 57; Hardwick, *Traditions*, 131.
507. Briggs, *Dictionary of Fairies*, 242.
508. Vollam, 'In Evil Days' (fiction based in the Burnley area); Crofton, *Newton*, 164; A Prestonian,
    'Preston'.
509. On possible adult beliefs in the existence of bogey figures Widdowson, *Aspects*, 142–45: for an
    Icelandic bogey that was first seen by children but began to be seen by adults, Jakobsson, *Troll*, 99.

Storytelling in the Community

Storytelling also took place outside families, of course, within the wider community. For one, stories were told in pubs and clubs:

> There were two or three other songs given in excellent style by various members, after which, in order to vary the amusement, it was proposed that 'Lung Nathan' should be solicited to give them his ghost story; and immediately thereafter three or four were besieging that individual's chair, persuading him to gratify the wishes of the company. Nathan observed that 'somb'dy wur like t' do summut t' pass time on,' and after rapping the ashes out of his pipe on the toe of his thick boot, and taking what he termed a 'startin droight' at his ale, immediately commenced his tale, which he designated 'A Ghost Story'.[510]

Such accounts are particularly common in dialect writing where storytelling in the pub or in a domestic club (i.e. one based in a private dwelling) becomes the frame for a tale; perhaps a family setting with children would have precluded more adult themes, such as drunkenness?[511] Indeed, drunkenness and getting home late were identified as among the reasons for seeing boggarts: 'Get whoam wi' thee, an' doent stop rakeing aet ov a neet, an' th' boggards will noen bother thee!'[512] Pub tales, of course, more easily went outside a narrow family circle:

> Another told a story, which he said,
> Was told to him some years since, by his cousin,
> Who heard it from a friend, (alas! now dead!)
> Who heard it from old men, at least a dozen.[513]

Boggarts were, in the wonderful words of one nineteenth-century writer 'a quotable institution'.[514]

---

510. Dawson, 'Th' Club Neet'.
511. Axon, 'Gallowsfield Ghost'; 'Eyam, Stoney Middleton, Calver and District'; compare Axon, *Black Knight*, where friends meet in a private house to tell tales. Drunkenness often plays a part in boggart tales: particularly when it transpires the boggart experience is based on a misunderstanding.
512. A.L., *Forty Years*, 12.
513. Davis, *The Fancies*, 35.
514. Kerr, 'Typical "Chips": No. 1' (1894).

Workplaces, too, were fertile territory for boggarts and boggart tales; something suggested by the Boggart Collieries and Boggart Mills recorded in the nineteenth century.[515] In one account from Bradford, an old man remembers how, in the early 1830s, during late-night shifts in a textile mill as a child, he and his fellow workers would stare out of the great mill windows towards Horton 'and many a night [we] have looked ... to try and see "Fair Becca," the Horton boggart, but she never appeared'.[516] One boggart flap in 1903 began in a Burnley fabric factory: news that two Spiritualists had visited a house led to workplace gossip that the house was haunted.[517] And ghosts could be seen *at* work. Weavers became so frightened by a boggart at a mill at Lostock in Lancashire, 'that they enter the premises collectively'.[518] Agricultural workers also exchanged supernatural tales. Edwin Waugh's most important boggart informant was Robin, a 'cow lad' at Blackstone Edge.[519] There are also many stories of rural labourers and servants tricking fellow workers with bogus boggart experiences.[520]

As we have seen in Chapter 4, the landscape itself had important supernatural associations. At times there were confirmations of these places' reputations in landscape features. A pair of carved scissors (probably a 'Greek cross') marked the place a tailor had been killed in the Civil War: he had returned as a boggart.[521] An inscribed stone had entrapped a boggart at Longridge and woe betide the one who moved it.[522] More rarely, new points emerged to confirm older superstitions. Thus blood issued forth from the bridge at Colne, demonstrating that a murder had taken place there long before.[523] Dunkenhalgh Boggart was the ghost of, Lucette, a French governess who had committed suicide on a bridge; the finding of a shawl pin during renovation of that bridge was taken as proof of the traditional legend.[524] There were also frequent discoveries of bones in the walls of houses that explained hauntings: their uncovering sometimes ended troublesome presences.[525] At other

---

515. BN under 'Buildings' and 'Collieries and Mines'.
516. 'Churchyard Stories', (1877): should we understand from this that Becca was sometimes seen as a light?
517. 'Ghost Rumours at Burnley' (1903).
518. 'A "Ghost" at Bolton' (1887).
519. Waugh, *Sketches*, 214.
520. See, e.g., 'Kendal Natural History' (1841); 'Droylsden Customs', (1855), 4; Potter, *Lancashire*, 99.
521. Carr, *Colne*, 195–96.
522. H.S. 'The Stone Shackled Ghost'.
523. Carr, *Colne*, 199–200; compare with the bleeding tree-initials in Aker-Whitt, 'The Dunkenhalgh Boggart'.
524. Aker-Whitt, 'The Dunkenhalgh Boggart'.
525. See, e.g., Weld, *Leagram*, 156.

Figure 25: 'An Old Chimney Corner in Chadderton Fold'
(Waugh, *The Chimney Corner*, frontispiece).

times bone hunts proved fruitless, something that could just as easily be turned into a tale.[526]

On top of this there was a nascent nineteenth-century tourist industry. A group trip to Pendle Hill ended with stories told by a group of daytrippers (recorded by the poet William Billington):

> Strange tales were told of witches, long ago ...
> Of Demdike's wrinkled rival, Mother Chattox–
> The abbot Paslew—the Dule-upo'-Dun—
> The Pig bewitched—enchanted spades and mattocks—
> The Dog Familiar and the Magic Gun;
> Such webs were woven and such yarns were spun,
> Of many a monk transformed into a tike,
> And nymphs allured to fates they could not shun,—
> Of faries [*sic*], banshees, boggarts and the like
> All wound up with a song, 'The Devil and little Mike'.[527]

---

526. H., 'Lines'.
527. Billington, *Pendle Hill*, 19.

William Axon set his *Black Knight* tales (a Lancashire *Decameron*) with boggarts and demons on an outing to the Black Lad festival in Ashton.[528] Local guides would refer to supernatural traditions as they took guests around estates. One late nineteenth-century visitor to Towneley Hall 'was shown, by the *cicerone*' the boggart's room.[529] Other tourists visited the statue of headless Peg o' the Well at Clitheroe, or the boggart's lair at Boggart Hole Clough. We have here the ancestor of the modern ghost walk.[530]

Stories also spread through casual conversation. We can no longer trace the networks of supernatural gossip, but we can sometimes get a sense of their range. In 1869, one James Heaton wrote a newspaper article including several supernatural stories from the countryside to the east of Burnley.[531] He mentioned, quite routinely, his contacts for these tales—the kind of material unfortunately lacking for Kidsgrove. A woman called Stanfield had seen a brownie at Brownside while out walking one night.[532] Heaton had been told (by unknown individuals) of fragments of fairy dresses and fairy pipes being found in a meadow at Rowley. A joiner, one William Chaffer, had seen an Elizabethan boggart at Rowley House, while a milkman, known to Heaton had been magically interfered with by the same bogie. Heaton's own uncle had seen various 'supernatural visitors' and knew when members of his own family were to die. In this short article we have an informal listing of the contacts that a local, even a sceptical one like Heaton, might have in writing or talking about an area's supernatural facts. Presumably tales were established in family circles and, if remarkable or attractive enough, they were picked up by the wider community.

Boggart Poems, Talks, and Plays

Supernatural stories have survived down to our times: most families and many circles of friends have them. But poetry has all but vanished as a public form. In

---

528. Axon, *Black Knight*.
529. Kerr, 'Marriage and Morals' (1892).
530. Redding, *History*, 208–09; Hardwick, *Traditions*, 151–52; McEvoy, *Tourism*, 107–26.
531. Heaton, 'Stray Notes'.
532. The brownie was associated with the Scottish borders. In the nineteenth century, though, the word became commonplace in Standard English, and began to be used as a term, often the preferred term, for 'household spirit', see p. 10. Burnley is nowhere near the area that 'brownie' was traditionally used, and we should assume that this brownie was a backformation from Brownside. Compare a similar phenomenon for nearby Saddleworth: Bradbury, *Sketches*, 203, for claims that Brownhill was named from brownies that were said to live there; other supernatural traditions for Brownhill Bradbury, *Sketches*, 114–15 and 206–07 and Howcroft, *Tales*, 8–9.

the nineteenth century, poetry was still learnt by rote and recited,[533] and boggarts often graced poems either incidentally or as a plot device. Boggarts, for example, make an appearance in the most famous English dialect poem of the 1800s, Edwin Waugh's 'Come Whoam To Thy Childer an' Me': 'Has th' boggarts taen houd o' my dad?', asks a young boy missing his absent father.[534] The same is true of Bealey's 'Courtin' Neet', where boggarts impede the poet's work, making time drag until he can be with his sweetheart.[535] Then there are the many dialect poems about boggarts; typically involving a night-time encounter with something that is reckoned to be uncanny, but that turns out to be nothing of the sort. In Higson's 'The Boggart of Gorton Chapelyord', for instance, the boggart is a drunk; in 'The Dumber Boggert', the wife goes to investigate an alleged boggart:

> A little farther they saw the flaming eyes, the club feet and the hair,
> For Jimmy's Boggart was nothing but the Rector's old Brown
> Mare.[536]

These boggart poems were typically local affairs—tied to a particular community—and what becomes clear from the sources is the manner in which poems were freely exchanged in ways that are rare in the twenty-first century. They were much more than just words on pages. We know that working-class poet William Bennett used to give impromptu performances in Glossop of his poem 'The Spire-Holly Boggart': 'the author often recited the foregoing piece in public', presumably in a tavern.[537] Saddleworth supernatural poems were also learnt by heart and recited.[538] We even have evidence of newspaper poetry duels at Hayfield in which local boggarts appeared:

> And there he saw the boggart house,
> Where th' Highgate witch is seen
> By moonlight at some midnight hours,
> Dancing on Highgate green.[539]

---

533. Robson, *Heart Beats*.

534. Waugh, *Poems*, 3–6 at 5.

535. Bealey, *Field flowers*, 37.

536. Sweeney, 'Dumber'.

537. This extract was found on: http://freepages.genealogy.rootsweb.ancestry.com/~glossopfamily/news.htm [accessed 14 April 2016]. The date is unknown.

538. Bradbury, *Sketches*, 177; Young, '*Shantooe Jest*', 12.

539. Sandy Banks, 'Criticism'. 'Witch' here should be understood in the sense of hag, i.e. non-human bogey.

In the Victorian West Riding 'town-songs' ('satirical verses made and sung in a village') included boggarts.[540] As late as the 1940s, a mother sang her child to sleep at Siddal in the Upper Calder Valley with a Yorkshire boggart poem, 'At' a' the'ere' Boggart?'; the 'child', in his seventies, remembers the title, but the words have long since been forgotten.[541]

Some of the most interesting rhymes were those exchanged primarily by children in play or in jest. These infant poems were unfortunately not collected systematically in the nineteenth century, at least in the Northwest.[542] But occasionally a fragment has come down to us. Most famous perhaps is the 'Old Woman at Baildon' limerick, repeated in several sources from 1871: she met a horned boggart.[543] Other rhymes come to us, by chance. Take one about Jenny Greenteeth:

> Hey lads! Hey, lads, run for yo're life,
> Owd Jinny Greenteeth's comin' with a knife.

I first came across these two lines in an obscure piece of Lancashire fiction from 1891. I wondered whether they had been confected, but then found them in a Cumbrian folklore collection from 1979.[544] Other children's rhymes arrived through the Boggart Census: 'I remember singing moonlight starlight. I hope there are no bogarts tonight', wrote one ninety-two-year-old from Littleborough.[545] This was recalled by another grown child who had heard it in the late 1950s or 1960s as a skipping rhyme in Southport: 'The stars are shining, the moon's so bright, the boggart can't come out tonight.'[546]

Another jingle comes from Tattenhall in Cheshire and concerns a buggin rather than a boggart.

---

540. Addy, *A Glossary*, 265.
541. BC, Siddal 1 (WRY): John Widdowson writes, pers. comm., 14 February 2020: 'This is a fairly accurate phonetic rendering of how West Riding dialect would sound, though perhaps not with quite so many apostrophes. The speaker is actually saying "Art thou there, Boggart?" and phonetically the dialect would sound like "At a theer" (with voiced "th").'
542. Northall, *English folk-rhymes*, 85 has only one supernatural verse from Boggartdom, but then generally he collects few ghost and monster verses. Does this reflect his personal preferences or a real lack of material?
543. Andrews, 'Yorkshire', 204; Rayner, *Pudsey*, 187: 'There was an old woman at Baildon,/ Whose door had a horse-shoe nail'd on,/ Because on one night/ She had such a fright/ With a boggart that was horned and a tail'd un'.
544. Vollam, 'In Evil Days'; Preston, *Cumbria*, 22.
545. Littleborough 18 (La).
546. BC, Southport 13 (La). See Wright, *Dialect Dictionary*, I, 326.

Come thou yarly, come thou leet,
Beweer of the Buggin at th' Poo' Yed Gate.[547]

There must have been dozens of these local rhymes which had no attraction and made no sense beyond the boundaries of the parish and have, as a result, been lost for ever. One rhyme that did become relatively famous with the Lancashire folklore writers was the lament of the Towneley Boggart, where the boggart, the spirit of Sir John Towneley (fl. 1490s–c.1520), regrets his greed in enclosing common land. The first reference appears in 1818:

Lay out, Lay out
Horelaw and Hollinhey Clough[548]

And a longer version was published in 1844:

Be warned! Lay out! Lay out! Be warned!
Around Horelaw and Hollinhey Clough;
To her children give back the widow's cot
For you and yours there's still enough[549]

And another version in 1873:

Lay out! Lay out!
Give back to the poor!
Hore-law and Hollin Hey Clough
For me and mine, there's land enough![550]

---

547. Haworth *et al.*, *Cheshire Village Memories*, II, 93: for another buggin jingle, see Brown, 'The Ancient Parish', 59.

548. Whitaker, *Whalley*, 342. Note that Wood, 'Spectral Lordship', 110, claims that Whitaker, 'couldn't establish the identity of the encloser'. Whitaker, in fact, wrote 'the spirit of some former and hitherto forgotten possessor of this estate' and then went on to reveal the spirit to be Sir John Towneley (although he does not identify which Sir John or date him). In popular tradition the boggart may simply have been identified as 'Owd Towneley' or some such.

549. Redding, *History*, 189.

550. Wilkinson, 'Ancient Mansions' (1873); Wood, 'Spectral Lordship', 110, quotes a manuscript version of this poem from the Cheetham Library and ascribes it to 'Thomas Turner'. I suspect that this is Thomas Turner Wilkinson. Note that in 1860, Wilkinson, 'On the Popular Superstitions', 92 had preferred Redding's version.

A Sir John Towneley did enclose Horelaw and Hollin Hey. As Andy Wood (and before him, in vaguer terms, Thomas Whitaker) suggested, there is a *prima facie* case to be made here for an oral tradition lasting some three hundred years, from about 1500 to the early nineteenth century. How else, it is argued, could the knowledge have been retained in the Burnley area?[551] The quote was so well known, note, around the town that in 1903 one bored Burnley writer (or his editor) clipped the verse: 'that noisy spirit who was accustomed to call "Lay out, lay out," etc.'.[552]

Poetry also appeared in formal readings in public places where stories and essays were read, too. In fact, 'Penny Readings', on occasion with celebrities appearing to declaim their own or another's writings, proved extremely popular in mid-Victorian Britain and continued to be enjoyed until the end of the century.[553] The boggarts naturally made their appearance here. Some scattered examples follow to give a sense of the sheer range of performances. In 1867, Mr T. Lockhead encored an evening performance with 'A queer sort of a boggart' ('a Lancashire sketch') in Bury. In 1869, 'Th' Boggart Hunt' was offered up for public enjoyment by a Mr P. Whiteside, at the Iron Works Reading Room, Carnforth. In 1877, a Mr Hutchinson read the 'Hazel Clough Boggart' in Catforth. In 1884, Mr Meyee sang 'Th' owd boggart' a humorous piece at St Andrew's School in Wigan. And, straying for a moment outside the Northwest, in 1909, in Hull, 'The Boggart o' Scar Wood' was recited in West Riding dialect (in the East Riding) for the Esperanto Society.[554]

Other venues for the supernatural were the various working men's associations. We know—to give one instance from many—that the Burnley Literary and Scientific Club had occasional talks on the supernatural. Thus, in the 1888 'syllabus' there were twenty-one papers: one was on folklore and one on boggart-lore; other subjects included 'Water Gas' and 'Norway and the Land of the Midnight Sun'.[555] These evening meetings made time for questions and answers afterwards and sometimes earnest conversations were recorded in the club periodical. In 1905, in the same Burnley club, after a local vicar gave

---

551. Wood, 'Spectral Lordship'; Whitaker, *Whalley*, 342. This argument is attractive. I do wonder, though, whether the phrase was originally Towneley's. The first and, particularly, the second version could be someone berating Towneley (or a descendant?). Note, too, that Redding, *History*, 189 claims that Sir John 'died calling out, "lay out, lay out"'.

552. 'Notes and Comments'.

553. Beaven, *Leisure*, 19–27.

554. 'Entertainment at the Baptist School'; 'Carnforth Readings'; 'Concert at Catforth'; 'Entertainment at St. Andrew's School'; 'Hull Esperanto Society'.

555. 'Syllabus'. For more on the subject of supernatural talks, Water, 'Magic', 640–41.

his view of hallucinations, members discussed the reasons for ghost sightings.[556] We even have one instance of a young men's club in Preston in 1857 formally debating the existence of boggarts; a vote at the end affirmed belief in the supernatural.[557] Talks and discussions were sometimes subsequently written up for local newspapers, which, of course, brought the ideas therein to a wider public.[558]

Finally, we must also acknowledge the presence of boggarts at the theatre. Local dialect writers quarried boggarts for their plays, much as they did for poems and stories. The earliest example known to me is *Th' Boggart Blacksmith! Or the return of the Boggart Bridge Ghost* (1863) by Edward Slater, who was to become the most important Burnley writer and composer of his generation.[559] Other boggart plays followed in the Pennines and the Northwest, including *The Boggart of Newsight Park* and *The Bunderley Boggart*.[560] These all seem to have been—in as much as we can read contemporary descriptions and, in some very few cases, examine scripts—comedies based around a misunderstanding or a joke. Then there were theatrical shows where bogies came running out of the wings, including in the 1870s and the 1880s, a Lancashire gymnastic troupe called the Bounding Boggarts.[561]

Boggart Prose and the Reading Revolution

Many of the poems listed above were oral compositions that happened to be preserved in print; others were print compositions that were presented orally—e.g. in penny readings. However, for boggart folklore and folklore transmission, it is crucial to recognize the growing importance of *private* reading, as Britain experienced, in the nineteenth century, a veritable reading revolution. There were two interconnected aspects to that revolution: rapidly growing literacy levels; and the greater availability of printed material. When Victoria came to the throne, in 1837, a little more than half of all adults were literate.[562] By the time Victoria died in 1901, literacy levels were not far from where they stand in the twenty-first century. This was an extraordinary

---

556. Ormerod, 'Psychology', 21–22

557. 'Debating Societies' (1857).

558. See, e.g., McKay, *Evolution*: the local paper here did a better job at printing all of McKay's talk than the learned proceedings in which the text was formally published.

559. Young, 'Boggart Plays', 100–02 and for Slater, Young, 'To Sound Cheerily'.

560. Young, 'Boggart Plays', 99–100; Metcalfe, *Bunderley*, 11–79. See also Moorman, *Plays of the Ridings*, 27–42 for 'An All Souls' Night Dream'.

561. 'Alarming Accident'.

562. Vincent, *Literacy*, 22–23; Lloyd, 'Education' estimates about 60 per cent for 1840.

achievement, managed over a long generation. It was the result, in part, of
legislation. School became compulsory and Parliament accepted the principle
that it would fund elementary education.[563] It was primarily, though, the result
of a change in working-class culture. Even very poor families came to expect
their children to be able to read.[564] 'Reading', we learn in an 1854 letter from
Preston, 'is becoming necessary to the working man'.[565]

The second shift was the increase in the availability of the printed word.
In the 1820s, a triple-decker set of novels, say one of Scott's (then) new titles,
retailed for thirty-one shillings and sixpence, about 10 per cent of a labourer's
annual wage. Newspapers sold for as much as eight pence; magazines cost
anything from one shilling sixpence to six shillings.[566] If you were poor in the
early 1800s and had a shilling to spare for reading, then you would have been
obliged to buy penny broadsides or chapbooks with stories, poems or ballads
(for more on broadsides see pp. 131–33). From the 1830s to the 1850s, a
series of technological and legislative changes meant that it became cheaper
to print sheets and books. By the 1890s you would, with your shilling, have
been able to buy one decently stitched novel. Alternatively, you would have
been able to buy a newspaper a day for a week. Prices for newspapers had
gone down and the numbers sold gone up after the end of stamp duty in
1855: 90 million newspapers were purchased in 1854 in the UK; by the mid-
1860s about 550 million were sold annually.[567]

The reading revolution had, naturally, consequences for folklore and folklore transmission. Henry Cowper, for instance, judged the Crier of Claife tale
to be 'in great part a modern invention' while accepting that there was older
local folklore about supernatural screams on Windermere.[568] If he is correct
then the story must have seeped down into Hawkshead lore through the
numerous published versions of the tale that were produced in the second
half of the nineteenth century: 'The fact that the country people now know
the story, is worthless as evidence, since it has been repeated by guide book
after guide book for at least thirty years.'[569] We have similar problems with
the Clegg Hall Boggart, the subject of many narratives from the 'primitive

---

563. For an overview of the reform process Larsen, *The making*, 29–50.
564. Vincent, *Literacy*, 53–66.
565. Clay, *Prison*, 545–47 at 547 in relation to the number of books pawned, via Hobbs, *A Fleet Street*, 58.
566. Altick, *English Common*, 263, 322, and 319.
567. Hobbs, *A Fleet Street*, 5.
568. Cowper, *Hawkshead*, 325–26.
569. Ibid., 326.

people of the hills' in the mid nineteenth century.[570] Had these narratives been evolving slowly for generations with little reference to the outside world, or had they been influenced by John Roby's fictionalized version of that very boggart in his *Traditions of Lancashire* in 1831?[571] The cross-pollination of oral and literary traditions is well known from English, and indeed, world folklore.

An elusive category of boggart literature is what might be called the boggart broadside. The broadside was a single-sided sheet of paper usually printed with a news account or a ballad of some description. These very cheap works—typically costing a penny or half-penny in the nineteenth century—are classed as ephemera.[572] Broadside publishers did not have high production or editorial values and any printed poetry rarely rose above the level of doggerel. The result was that relatively few broadsides have survived from the nineteenth century, at least in relation to the numbers that we know were printed.[573] However, thanks to those that have come through to the modern age we can see that the supernatural—along with public executions and marvels—was one of the areas most favoured by broadside publishers. Indeed, we have from nineteenth-century Britain such titles as 'Wonderful Just & Terrible Judgement on a Blasphemer' and 'Apparition of a Ghost to a Miller to Discover a Hidden Murder'.[574]

The only example of a boggart broadside known prior to 2019 was a poster-sized political broadside from 1832 entitled 'The Boggart', which includes the following threat to Bradford factory owners put into the mouth of that monster:

> I am coming every week (by the special conjuring of the worsted spinner who has lately been very guilty himself, but now repents) to haunt those factory masters in this town, who are working, and have been working their mills from 6 to 8 or 9 o'clock, and in some cases longer than that, without any breakfast time, and only 30 minutes at noon for dinner.[575]

---

570. Waugh, *Sketches*, 214; the best description of the boggart remains Harland and Wilkinson, *Lancashire Legends*, 10–12.

571. Roby, *Traditions*, second series, 3–53.

572. Corfe, 'Sensation and Song'.

573. Elbourne, *Music*, 57.

574. Hindley, *Curiosities*, 24 and 26; see also, for an earlier period, Harvey, *Scottish*, 107–15. It is a very crude metric, but http://ballads.bodleian.ox.ac.uk/ [accessed 7 February 2020] has 144 executions in its database and 167 ghosts (using the site's thematic index).

575. 'The Boggart!!!' in 'The following placard ...', where it is reported, 89, that it 'created a sensation'. See also Hepburn, *A Book*, I, 255.

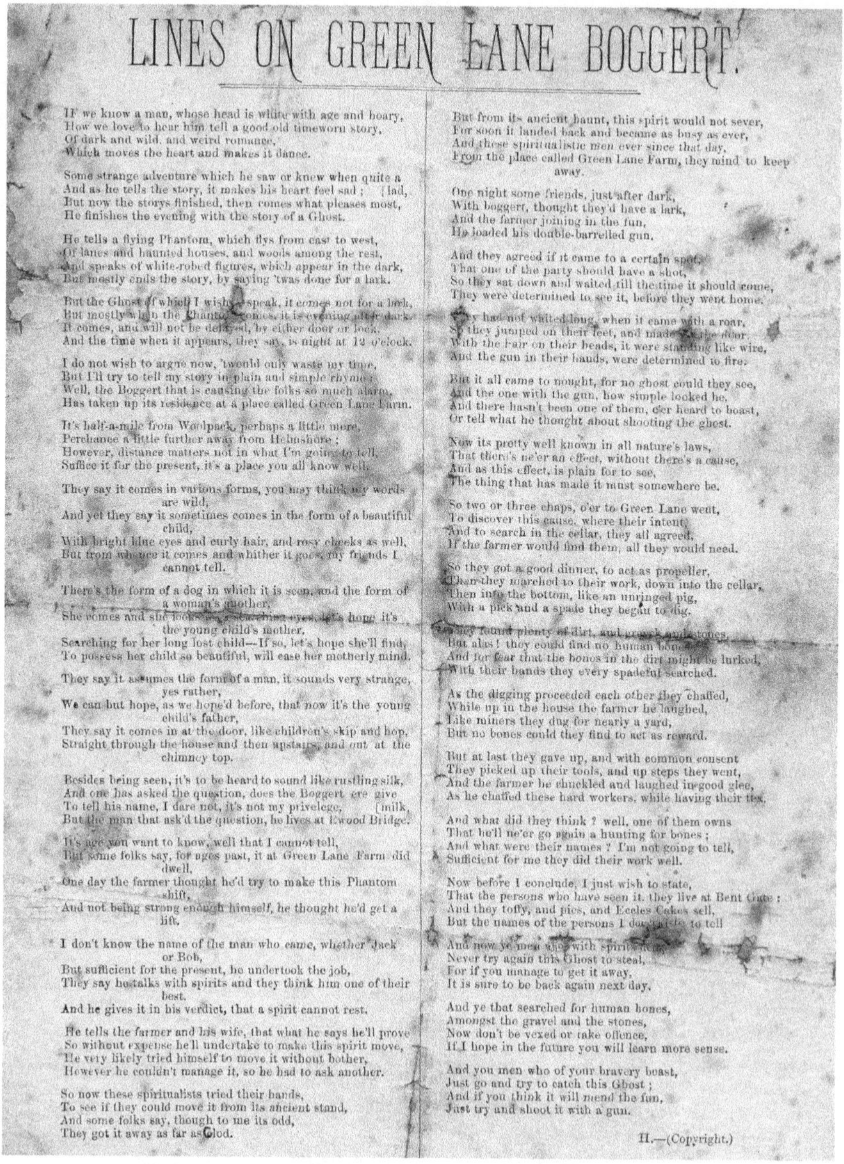

LINES ON GREEN LANE BOGGERT.

If we know a man, whose head is white with age and hoary,
How we love to hear him tell a good old timeworn story,
Of dark and wild, and weird romance,
Which moves the heart and makes it dance.

Some strange adventure which he saw or knew when quite a lad,
And as he tells the story, it makes his heart feel sad;
But now the storys finished, then comes what pleases most,
He finishes the evening with the story of a Ghost.

He tells a flying Phantom, which flys from east to west,
Of lanes and haunted houses, and woods among the rest,
And speaks of white-robed figures, which appear in the dark,
But mostly ends the story, by saying 'twas done for a lark.

But the Ghost of which I wish to speak, it comes not for a lark,
But mostly when the Phantom comes it is evening after dark,
It comes, and will not be delayed, by either door or lock,
And the time when it appears, they say, is night at 12 o'clock.

I do not wish to argue now, 'twould only waste my time,
But I'll try to tell my story in plain and simple rhyme;
Well, the Boggert that is causing the folks so much alarm,
Has taken up its residence at a place called Green Lane Farm.

It's half-a-mile from Woolpack, perhaps a little more,
Perchance a little further away from Helmshore;
However, distance matters not in what I'm going to tell,
Suffice it for the present, it's a place you all know well.

They say it comes in various forms, you may think my words are wild,
And yet they say it sometimes comes in the form of a beautiful child,
With bright blue eyes and curly hair, and rosy cheeks as well,
But from whence it comes and whither it goes, my friends I cannot tell.

There's the form of a dog in which it is seen, and the form of a woman's mother,
She comes and she looks ... eyes, let's hope it's the young child's mother,
Searching for her long lost child—If so, let's hope she'll find,
To possess her child so beautiful, will ease her motherly mind.

They say it assumes the form of a man, it sounds very strange, yes rather,
We can but hope, as we hope'd before, that now it's the young child's father,
They say it comes in at the door, like children's skip and hop,
Straight through the house and then upstairs, and out at the chimney top.

Besides being seen, it's to be heard to sound like rustling silk,
And one has asked the question, does the Boggert ere give milk
To tell his name, I dare not, it's not my privelege,
But the man that ask'd the question, he lives at Ewood Bridge.

It's age you want to know, well that I cannot tell,
But some folks say, for ages past, it at Green Lane Farm did dwell,
One day the farmer thought he'd try to make this Phantom shift,
And not being strong enough himself, he thought he'd get a lift.

I don't know the name of the man who came, whether Jack or Bob,
But sufficient for the present, he undertook the job,
They say he talks with spirits and they think him one of their best,
And he gives it in his verdict, that a spirit cannot rest.

He tells the farmer and his wife, that what he says he'll prove
So without expense he'll undertake to make this spirit move,
He very likely tried himself to move it without bother,
However he couldn't manage it, so he had to ask another.

So now these spiritualists tried their hands,
To see if they could move it from its ancient stand,
And some folks say, though to me its odd,
They got it away as far as God.

But from its ancient haunt, this spirit would not sever,
For soon it landed back and became as busy as ever,
And these spiritualistic men ever since that day,
From the place called Green Lane Farm, they mind to keep away.

One night some friends, just after dark,
With boggert, thought they'd have a lark,
And the farmer joining in the fun,
He loaded his double-barrelled gun.

And they agreed if it came to a certain spot,
That one of the party should have a shot,
So they sat down and waited till the time it should come,
They were determined to see it, before they went home.

They had not whit-a-long, when it came with a roar,
They jumped on their feet, and made ... door,
With the hair on their heads, it were standing like wire,
And the gun in their hands, were determined to fire.

But it all came to nought, for no ghost could they see,
And the one with the gun, how simple locked he,
And there hasn't been one of them, e'er heard to boast,
Or tell what he thought about shooting the ghost.

Now its pretty well known in all nature's laws,
That there's ne'er an effect, without there's a cause,
And as this effect, is plain for to see,
The thing that has made it must somewhere be.

So two or three chaps, o'er to Green Lane went,
To discover this cause, where their intent,
And to search in the cellar, they all agreed,
If the farmer would find them, all they would need.

So they got a good dinner, to act as propeller,
Then they marched to their work, down into the cellar,
Then into the bottom, like an unringed pig,
With a pick and a spade they began to dig.

They found plenty of dirt, and gravel and stones,
But alas! they could find no human bones,
And for fear that the bones in the dirt might be lurked,
With their hands they every spadeful searched.

As the digging proceeded each other they chaffed,
While up in the house the farmer he laughed,
Like miners they dug for nearly a yard,
But no bones could they find to act as reward.

But at last they gave up, and with common consent
They picked up their tools, and up steps they went,
And the farmer he chuckled and laughed in good glee,
As he chaffed these hard workers, while having their tea.

And what did they think? well, one of them owns
That he'll ne'er go again a hunting for bones;
And what were their names? I'm not going to tell,
Sufficient for me they did their work well.

Now before I conclude, I just wish to state,
That the persons who have seen it, they live at Bent Gate;
And they toffy, and pies, and Eccles Cakes sell,
But the names of the persons I dare not to tell

And now ye men also with spirit ...,
Never try again this Ghost to steal,
For if you manage to get it away,
It is sure to be back again next day.

And ye that searched for human bones,
Amongst the gravel and the stones,
Now don't be vexed or take offence,
If I hope in the future you will learn more sense.

And you men who of your bravery boast,
Just go and try to catch this Ghost;
And if you think it will mend the fun,
Just try and shoot it with a gun.

H.—(Copyright.)

Figure 26: 'Lines on Green Lane Boggert' (a broadside).

In the next chapter (p. 154), we will see how boggarts were sometimes given a political edge.

While gathering boggart memories, I discovered two other examples. Interestingly, both were preserved in the communities where they had been set in the nineteenth century. The first, *Lines on the Green Lane Boggert* by a certain H. was passed on to me by Helmshore History Society; the second,

The Dumber Boggert by one P. Sweeney, was held by a family at Ashton-on-Mersey, and was likewise sent upon request. Both are medium sized with no illustrations and tell the story, in verse, of boggart encounters. *Lines* covers various incidents concerning a famous local boggart; *Dumber Boggert* describes an encounter between a drunk gardener and a horse. As is typical with broadsides there is no date, although looking at the printing, I would estimate that they belong to the second half, and possibly the last quarter, of the nineteenth century.[576] The chance survival of these two broadsides suggests that there will have been many more boggart broadsides in the 1800s. With some luck, others may yet be uncovered.

The most interesting point about *Dumber Boggert* and *Lines on the Green Lane Boggert* is that they are extremely local productions. *Dumber* was set in the town of Ashton-on-Mersey, more specifically Dumber Lane, with references to local places and local individuals. *Lines* was written about Helmshore, with several sly nods to members of the community:

> And what were their names? I'm not going to tell,
> Sufficient for me they did their work well.

Both use convincing local dialect in dialogues. Both authors evidently knew the area intimately: the author of *Dumber* gives his address as 'Church Lane' in Ashton. This is a very different model from that found in nineteenth-century London where a template story was fixed onto a locality to improve sales. The Liverpool Tragedy (parents accidentally murder their son when he comes home from sea), for instance, was taken and applied to, say, Bermondsey and then sold as a local event.[577] The two boggart broadsides detailed here are local works, written by locals, and are dense with local references.

Much easier to find today than these extremely rare boggart broadsides are the many boggart dialect pamphlets in prose, which typically revolve around the 'mistaken' boggart. I have already had cause to mention Axon's *Black Knight* tales. But there were dozens of other boggart stories sold cheaply in small paperback volumes. The most prolific boggart writer by a long way was Benjamin Brierley. His first boggart story was *The Hazel Clough Boggart*, published in 1860 (the 'boggart' is a helium balloon). Later works by the same author included *The Boggart of Fairy Bridge* and *Th' Boggart o' th' Stump* (in this

---

576. These would need to be associated with 'ghost' broadsides from the Northwest including, for example, 'Dean Church Ghost!', described in Bell, *Magical Imagination*, 241.

577. Mayhew, *London*, I, 222; for the 'Liverpool Tragedy' Bennett, *Bodies*, 142–85.

last the 'boggart' is a stuffed monkey).[578] The always interesting M.R. Lahee
published, in 1882, *Trot Coffie's Boggart*, about a man who is thought to be his
dead wife (Trot), while dressing in her clothes. Ammon Wrigley included
several boggart tales in his Saddleworth volumes: for instance Moll's boggart,
which is, it transpires, a pudding bouncing down a hill.[579] Then in 1926 Frank
Ormerod gave the title of a boggart yarn to a short-story collection, *The Cock
Hall Boggart*: a man trapped in a cellar plays his flute and convinces the
community that he is a boggart.[580]

Boggarty Newspapers

Much more important for boggart-lore were newspapers.[581] Newspapers, it
must be remembered, were passed from hand to hand and from house to
house. This was particularly so in the early nineteenth century when they were
still expensive: 'they were sixpence an' eightpence a piece!'[582] In the 1800s,
there was a well-developed tradition of clipping and keeping stories of interest;
newspapers were not as disposable as we consider them.[583] Supernatural
newspaper stories or features could resurface a generation later, often without
reference to an earlier newspaper source. In 1888, Self Weeks wrote an article
about the haunted houses of Clitheroe. This article reappeared in Burnley
newspapers in 1900 and then again in 1918.[584] Weeks was at least acknowledged. When James Heaton published his article on Burnley ghosts in 1869,
the editor would not, I suspect, have imagined that in 1880, 1888, and 1889
this material would be recycled without any reference to Heaton.[585]

Supernatural stories could appear, particularly in the second half of the
1800s, in the most surprising places in newspapers, even adverts.[586] Indeed,
newspapers during this time became forums for discussing the supernatural.
The letters pages served to contest or add opinions. In one striking instance,

---

578. *Nights with Ben Brierley*, 11–19; *Bunk Ho*, 56–64; *Popular Edition*, 5–43.
579. *The Wind*, 294–97.
580. Ormerod, *The Cock Hall Boggart*, 11–25.
581. For nineteenth-century British newspapers, Lee, *The Origins*; Brown, *Victorian News*; Hewitt, *Dawn*; Jones, *Powers*; Hobbs, *A Fleet Street*.
582. Hamer, 'Ab' O' Ned's "Witchins"'.
583. Brown, *Victorian News*, 27–28; Heesen, *The newspaper*, 47–76 for clippings (Germany but applicable to Britain). Note also the existence of thematic books or files of clippings for the UK, e.g. Boyle, *Black Swines*, 1–9; Bell, *Magical Imagination*, 269.
584. Weeks, 'Haunted Houses' (1900 and 1918).
585. Heaton, 'Stray Notes'; 'Legends of Worsthorn'; McKay, 'The Evolution', 9; H.H., 'Some Lancashire Boggart Tales'.
586. 'Was it a Ghost They Saw?' for Mother Seigel's Syrup.

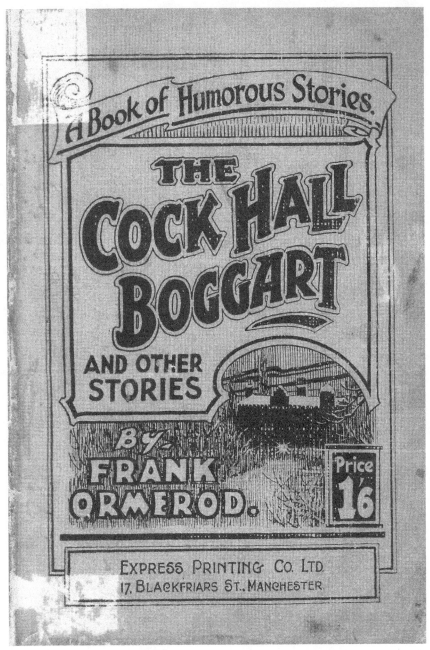

Figure 27: Frank Ormerod, *The Cock Hall Boggart* (1926).

a church owl at Deeside was taken to be a boggart and the week following, 'the Deeside Owl' wrote a disgusted letter to the newspaper.[587] In another newspaper 'ANTIQUARIAN' argued for the superiority of Mowbrick Boggart over Weeton Boggart:

> Other places may have boggarts possessing various qualities enti-tling them to notoriety in one form or other, but for being dreaded, for working mischief, and for all evil, the Mowbrick boggart licks them all put together.[588]

A nice example, meanwhile, of how journalists transmitted stories from local oral tradition is illustrated in an 1887 article entitled 'Rossendale Boggart Tales'. In August of that year, a story did the rounds in Crawshawbooth that some footballers had been joined in a game by a 'gentlemanly personage dressed in black':

> The ball at length rolled to his feet, and unable to resist the temp-tation, he took it in his hand, and gave it a kick that sent it spinning into the air; but instead of the ball returning to *terra firma*, it continued to rise until it vanished from the sight of the gaping rustics. Turning to look at the stranger who had performed such a marvelous feat, they espied what they had not observed before—the cloven foot and barbed tail (just visible from underneath the coat of his Satanic Majesty).[589]

We have two accounts of this episode with differing details.[590] Here the news-papers have become just another linkin the chain of 'a good story'. These are oral creations captured in print before, presumably, being absorbed back into an oral pool of tales.

A key question is how reliable newspapers were in recounting local lore. Some nineteenth-century newspaper traditions did not particularly value truth. The American press of the period, for instance, often ran made-up stories, without too much fear of a backlash from readers.[591] The contemporary British

587. 'A Boggart in a Church' (1883); The Deeside Owl, 'A Hoot'.
588. 'Boggart Renown'.
589. 'Rossendale Boggart Tales' (1897). Devil detected by his hoofs: G303.4.5.3.1. For other contemporary examples from the English-speaking world Smith, 'Killing'.
590. 'Rossendale Boggart Tales' (1897), both versions are included in the article.
591. Goodman, *Sun*, passim and Fedler, *Media Hoaxes*.

press, it is fair to say, took the ideal of truth more seriously, even to the point of being rather priggish, perhaps not least because in a relatively small, well-connected country, lies were quickly found out.[592] Thinking now of supernatural reports, we might wonder whether jobbing north-western journalists, getting paid per word, did not sometimes just invent episodes. This likely happened in large urban centres when individual experiences were reported. The lack of names in such pieces from the UK is sometimes striking.[593] But rural or town papers relied on networks of informants whose reputation would suffer were untruths to appear in print. If invention did take place, then the newspaper (or a rival) would publish—as very occasionally happened[594]—letters disputing a report. All this to say that the reports in the next chapter should largely be taken on trust. These reports—even if dramatized—reflected real beliefs in communities.

---

592. One example must stand for many. In 1904, a story about an eagle carrying a baby away was passed down from the Scottish Highlands. Subsequently, a fake was admitted. Consider the language used by one newspaper on reporting this fake, 'The Eagle': 'the original informant confessed that he invented the story; and it is understood *that the matter is to be dealt with accordingly*', my italics. This was not a correspondent but a tall-tale-telling member of the public. See difference in urban/rural coverage Hughes, *News*, 150–51.

593. Dash, 'Spring-heeled Jack', passim.

594. 'Boggart' (1860); Elos, 'The "Boggart"'; A True Volunteer, 'The "Boggart"'.

—————

CHAPTER SIX

Social Boggarts

Introduction

In 2010, in Gabon, a bricklayer was tied to a post and beaten viciously: he had, it was claimed, stolen a stranger's penis with a handshake. In 2013, a mermaid was filmed on a rock in Israel; to date the video has been watched on YouTube over a quarter of a million times. In 2013/2014, there were protests in Iceland against road building on the Álftanes peninsula near Reykjavik; the new road, some of the protestors said, would disturb a clan of elves. In 2014, in Wisconsin, two twelve-year-olds tried to sacrifice a friend to a supernatural being: a media storm followed. In 2016, community leaders in a remote settlement in Peru decided to kill a witch; the images of her horrific death were caught on a cell phone—she was burnt alive. Later that year, a school was thrown into crisis in Malaysia after a mysterious black figure, glimpsed in the corridors, created unease, and students and teachers suffered from inexplicable physical and mental ailments. In December 2017, some one hundred people gathered together in the middle of Mexico City to watch an unexplained white light in the sky on a bright sunny day.[595]

The list could go on and, indeed, it will. For all that we are living in a 'rational age', the supernatural shows no sign of abating, let alone disappearing, although, as the references to YouTube and UFOs here remind us, the forms and channels that the supernatural take, change. However, for the purposes of this chapter, the most important point about this list is not the dates but their social dimension. Some of these events began as individual experiences: for example, the 'victim' in Gabon in 2010 knew that his penis had been stolen because he felt a tiny electronic shock in his genitals when the bricklayer shook his

---

595. Bonhomme, 'The dangers', 205–06; https://www.youtube.com/watch?v=T_JN9Sc_F20; 'Elf Lobby'; Maddox, 'Of Internet born', for media coverage; 'Woman burned'; Wong and Asher, 'Malaysia school'; 'Crowds stop'.

hand.[596] But all of them became communal events, shared and, in some cases, acted upon. The Gabonese bricklayer was almost beaten to death; two school-girls stabbed a classmate; Peruvian villagers dowsed an old woman with petrol. The supernatural may or may not have some existence external to the human brain, but it is most certainly a 'social reality'.[597] Supernatural beliefs have social consequences.[598]

In this chapter, I look at what might be called the social boggart and the different forms social boggatry took. There are 'flaps' when communities become convinced that a supernatural being is among them. There are 'crowds' when large groups gather to observe a boggart. There are 'hunts' when crowds (in some cases children) pursue a supernatural entity or someone pretending to be one. There are 'fakes' when individuals pretend to be a boggart; occasionally this is associated with crime, but more often with illicit nudity and jokes. And there are 'misunderstandings', when some natural phenomenon—typically an animal—is believed to be a boggart. These terms—'flaps', 'crowds', 'hunts', 'fakes', and 'misunderstandings'— are used here in relation to the Northwest, but similar events are recorded for all the UK.[599] There were, it is true, no boggarts to be seen in Cornwall or Aberdeenshire. But there were, depending on local belief systems, fairy hunts, mermaid crowds, and demon flaps. The name changed, but the social dynamics were the same.

Curiously, the social dimension of the Victorian supernatural has been—with some important exceptions—little explored. Take the area that has, at least in the English-speaking world, proved most attractive to twenty-first century scholars: ghost-lore. We have historical studies on the theology of ghosts, ghosts in high and low culture, and the imagined ghost.[600] There are also studies on ghost belief and ghost experiences; particularly stimulating are

---

596. Bonhomme, 'The dangers', 205–06.

597. Hall, *Elves*, 9.

598. McClenon, *Wondrous Events*, 3: 'wondrous events are *sociologically* real because they have real effects on those who experience them and their societies'; compare Bamford, *Passages*, I, 46–47, 'The noticing of these supposed supernatural appearances may seem puerile to some readers. The suppositions in themselves may be so; but taken in connection with, and affecting as they did, in a degree, the minds and manners of the rural population of the period, they are of more consequence than may at the first glance be apparent.'

599. Middleton, *Spirits*, xv-xvi suggests that 'prowling ghosts' pooled in some areas: I suspect that Middleton is measuring not the number of incidents but the readiness of journalists to report them.

600. Bann, 'Ghostly Hands'; del Pilar Blanco *Ghost-Watching*; Handley, *Visions*; Hudson, *Ghosts*; Smajic, *Ghost-Seers*; Smith, *Ghost Story*.

those written by folklorists and ethnographers.[601] But there have been relatively few studies on what might be called 'social ghosts'—the social dimension and consequences of ghostly experiences.[602] Perhaps we have here an aspect of the past that is too close temporally but too distant temperamentally: superficially familiar but ultimately jarring. After all, in our more autonomous—some would say socially fragmented—age, we no longer find hundreds of people turning out to watch a shadow at the window of a boggart house; miners hunting a boggart with weapons; or fearful workers travelling in groups to pass a boggarted spot in company.

Boggart Flaps

The flap, as applied to the supernatural, is a term borrowed from the writing of David Clarke.[603] By a 'flap'—an early twentieth-century word (*OED* 'a state of worry, agitation, fuss or excitement')—is meant here the conviction in a given community that there is an unusual spike in supernatural activity: typically, an entity has recently been encountered by several individuals. A 'community' can, for these purposes, vary in size. Sometimes the flap is limited to a single family. Sometimes a community can be all, or a large part of, a city.[604] There are still paranormal flaps in the early twenty-first century. But apart from very special circumstances, supernatural flaps in contemporary Britain are limited to families or institutions (hospitals, schools, etc.). There are no longer the beliefs and perhaps more importantly no longer the social networks to sustain a ghost flap in a modern British town or village, certainly not without media interest.[605] Many of the events described here would be unimaginable in the UK in the 2020s.

Nineteenth-century family flaps typically revolved around a house. A family and (if the family were of high enough social level) the family servants might, for example, experience poltergeist activity, as shown here:

---

601. Cowdell, 'City'; Bennett, *Traditions*; Day, 'Everyday'; and from continental tradition Raahauge, 'Ghosts'; Valk 'Liminality'.

602. Some honourable exceptions: Davies, *The Haunted*; Middleton, *Spirits*; Clarke 'Unmasking'; Bell, *Magical Imagination*; Bell, 'Cities'; Dash, 'Spring-heeled Jack'; and briefly Williams, *Religious*, 80; for Australia Waldron and Waldron, 'Playing the Ghost'.

603. Clarke, 'Unmasking', 47.

604. For a good example of an urban flap (Sheffield), Clarke, 'Unmasking'.

605. The closest we perhaps come in the 2020s are occasional flaps over alien animals in the British countryside: e.g. Rees, 'Monsters', 398–403.

At the dead of night, sounds would be heard as if persons were holding a conversation in whispers; doleful cries would break forth, or a crash would resound as if every piece of crockery in the dwelling was broken, when, in the morning, everything would be found in its place.[606]

There was also more classical ghostly behaviour, as in the old hall at Leagram: 'Strange and unaccountable noises, the opening and shutting of doors, footsteps and rustling of dresses were ... of frequent occurrence.'[607] Sometimes the confusion got so bad that families had to decamp. At a boggart house near Wrightington 'during the sickness of one of the inmates ... the visitations of the house ghost became so frequent and terrifying, that the inhabitants fled in terror'. In another 'flit'—a northern dialect word, 'to move from a house with the household goods'—this time near Middleton, an elderly couple 'fled at once from the house, and several days elapsed before they durst return for the purpose of taking away their furniture'. In Burnley it was the Clark family that was driven out of a house after a boggart continually pulled bed clothes off those sleeping there: 'th' boggart hes driven William Clark eawt of his heawse; he flitted th' last Friday'.[608]

Often these stories remained in small circles. We only know of the flit from Wrightington, for instance, because an antiquarian happened to have a conversation with a neighbour of the flitting family. The antiquarian then, perhaps surprisingly, reported the conversation.[609] The elderly couple in Middleton also seemed to have been little talked about. We know of their misfortunes because they were mentioned, as an aside, after a later haunting in the same house.[610] The Burnley boggart flit had an afterlife of sorts. Accounts relating to the Clarks' 'flit' in 1844 appeared in the local press, on and off, for fifty years after the actual haunting.[611] A poem was then published in 1895, loosely based on the Clarks' experiences.[612] The Orton Dobbie of 1849, however—just beyond the edge of Boggartdom—became a national sensation with reports being given, not just in the north-western

606. Bamford, *Passages*, I, 46.

607. Weld, *Leagram*, 153.

608. Price, 'Notes', 191–92; Nodal and Milner, *A Glossary*, 131; 'A Ghost Story' (1839); Redding, *History*, 182.

609. Price, 'Notes', 191–92.

610. 'A Ghost Story' (1839).

611. 1844 is the year it was first reported—Redding, *History*, 182; for later records Booth, 'A Ramble' (1883); 'Ghost Stories' (1895).

612. McCandlish, 'Back O' Th' Hill Boggart'.

but also in the London and Irish press.[613] Hundreds crossed the hills to visit
the house and an engine driver from the local railway reported that his hat
was slapped across his face by the spirit.[614]

More typically a village or town flap began not with events in a single
house, but with a number of sightings outdoors. A night-time walker, say, had
an experience and the next day: 'a flaming account of the adventure, a rich
treat for the gossips, both male and female was extensively circulated through
the thinly populated locality, detailing at length, and gathering minuteness and
improvement with transmission'.[615] An 1860 flap at Whaley in Derbyshire, for
example, started with a 'boggart' ('with long ears horns tail &c') being seen
in a mill pool. The local journalist suggested that an otter had been glimpsed
in the dark.[616] At Coddington in Cheshire in 1886, a young farmer came across
a tall woman in white who walked through a gate. An 'evening or two later'
another nocturnal walker encountered a giant man 'again in white (of course)'.
Subsequently a young gardener bumped into the boggart and his mind 'was
almost unhinged in consequence'. Then, a coachman met a carriage that disappeared as it passed him on the road.[617]

For a twenty-first century reader it is not at all clear why these different
events at Coddington were connected. Shape-shifting is one thing, but a
change of gender is difficult to parallel in English supernatural tradition.[618]
Indeed, the journalist who reported the flap was facetious on this point:
'[the locals] say they wouldn't object so much if the "boggart" would keep
itself respectable, but to appear first as a woman, then as a man, and then
in some other fantastic form, such conduct is extraordinary.'[619] Perhaps the
association depended on something as simple as the apparitions being seen
on the same stretch of road. Perhaps they somehow linked into earlier
legends of which we know nothing. As so often happened there is too little
information given in our one report on the case. These four sightings were,
in any case, only 'samples of the stories that are agitating the minds of the
good people in the locality'.[620]

613. The story appeared in, to give a representative sample, the *Cork Examiner*, the *Dumfries and Galloway Standard*, the *Exeter Flying Post*, the *Leicestershire Mercury* and the *Morning Post*. See further pp. 73–74.
614. 'A Westmoreland Ghost Story' (1849).
615. Higson, *Droylsden*, 70.
616. 'Boggart' (1860).
617. Rambler, 'Out and About' (March 1886).
618. Though see Middleton, *Spirits*, 228.
619. Rambler, 'Out and About' (March 1886).
620. Ibid.

Agitation is, of course, at the heart of the flap: shared communal fear and curiosity. '[T]he susceptible people of Whalley have been put into great fear.' The 'chief topic of conversation in Clayton-le-Woods for some days past' has been the boggart. The 'inhabitants of the neighbourhood [of Dial Street, Warrington] ... are just now somewhat exercised in their minds'. 'Considerable alarm has been caused at Lostock, Bolton.' At Blackley the population was thrown into 'considerable excitement'. The 'good people of Worsthorne have been recently disturbed from their usual placid condition'. '[T]he inhabitants [of Garstang] have been considerably concerned.' A 'story of a boggart' in Church and Oswaldtwistle 'has been food for gossips for more than a week'. '[T]he neighbourhood of Seed-hill ... has been in a state of extraordinary excitement' over noises in a house. The village of Egton was 'in a state of considerable excitement' in consequence of a ghost. On 'the more timid of the populace' of Dungley the boggart 'has made a great impression'. '[A]bout Broughton, the stories handed down are really thrilling.'[621] One curiosity is that flaps are associated in our sources with rural or semi-rural areas. Of the examples given in the last paragraph, only Dial Street has an urban setting; Seed Hill was still semi-rural at this date.

Why sometimes a single haunting and why sometimes a series of apparitions were needed to whip up excitement in a community is unclear and will have depended on local conditions which are now beyond analysis. We can, at least, signal that flaps—in the rare instances when we can trace their origins—might depend on something as trivial as a minor earthquake; the visions of a pregnant woman; or on the conviction of an aged couple that they were having their bedclothes pulled off by a departed neighbour.[622] In perhaps the most famous supernatural news item of the nineteenth century from Lancashire, a flap got its foot up into print because a postman from Garstang resigned his position to avoid meeting a boggart on country lanes. The story was widely reported in London and even appeared in the *Illustrated Police News* (Figure 28).[623] One 1839 flap from near Middleton started, meanwhile, with strange noises, but then became a regional news story once a local miner visited the haunted house and challenged a boggart there to a wrestling match:

---

621. 'Boggart' (1860); 'The Dungley Boggart', (1892); 'Mill Haunted' (1889); 'A "'Ghost'"' at Bolton' (1887); 'Extraordinary Superstition at Blackley' (1852); A Villager, 'A Boggart at Worsthorne'; 'A Troublesome Ghost' (1881); 'A Ghost Story' (1865); 'The Seed-Hill Ghost' (1855); 'A Ghost at Egton' (1864); 'The Dungley Boggart' (1892); 'A Ghost in 1852' (1852).

622. 'The Earthquake' (1843); 'A Ghost Story' (1865); Rambler, 'Out and About Chester' (June 1887).

623. 'A Troublesome Ghost'; 'The Garstang Ghost'. For another example of a boggart-feart postman 'Longnor' (1874).

Figure 28: The Garstang Boggart transformed into the Garstang Ghost
in the *Illustrated Police News* (17 September 1881), 1.

At a beer-shop in a place called Stocks, which is very near the
house in question, there lodges a man named Isaac Unsworth, a
collier, who, for one of his calling, is said to be a quiet orderly
man, when sober. On the first night of the present year, however,
as might reasonably be anticipated, he came home a little elevated
with liquor; and after sitting a short time by the fire, he started
up, about ten o'clock, and declared he would go to the 'boggart
heawse.' ... On coming up to the place he 'punsed' at the first
door, when it flew open, and he went in; and, having danced a
step on the floor, called out: 'Ho! if there's ony one here, let

him come!' Nothing, however, appeared; and he went to the second door, which, in like manner yielded to his foot, and he there in like manner, repeated his summons without effect. 'The third time', however, according to a vulgar adage, 'pays for all'; and so according to the story, Isaac Unsworth found it. On approaching the door, he found it open, and there he had no occasion at all to repeat his summons; for, as he entered the door, a little girl, having a bonnet on, with a bow of ribbon on one side, went in before him, and stood in the middle of the floor; on which, being apparently in a humour for dancing, he danced a step round her, when she suddenly disappeared. At that moment a man entered the room, as if pursuing the girl. The new comer was of very formidable appearance, but Isaac Unsworth had had too many new-year's gifts to be frightened at trifles ... and he therefore resolutely challenged the stranger to wrestle for half a gallon of ale! The challenge was as promptly accepted; they closed, and Isaac, though he put in all he could found himself immediately lifted from his feet, and thrown with great violence against the wall where he lay stunned and senseless for several minutes. On coming to himself he beat a speedy retreat, unmolested when a voice called after him, that he must return at two o'clock, and pay his debt. This demand greatly troubled him for being a man of honour in his way, he did not like to 'levant,' as the sporting phrase is; but he had very little stomach for facing his formidable antagonist a second time. Fearing, however, that worse might come of it if he failed, he determined to keep the appointment; and, accordingly, a little before two o'clock, he sallied forth on his way to the place of meeting. Whether he duly carried with him the half-gallon of ale he had lost, or whether he meant to tender 'dry money' (which, we should imagine, would be an affront to any ghost of respectability), the story is unfortunately silent; but it records, that, on arriving at the house, he saw his old antagonist, who now seemed of gigantic stature, and who offered him a handful of money if he would try two more falls. Isaac Unsworth, however, had had quite enough in the first encounter, and very prudently declined the offer; on which the spectre, according to all ghostly etiquette, 'vanished in a flame of fire,' letting the money fall upon the ground, which

Isaac did not stop to pick up, but made his way back home with all the speed he could master.[624]

A correspondent sent this in and the editor published the letter. But the editor chose to put some distance between himself and his correspondent's extraordinary account: we 'cannot avoid expressing a belief that some designing persons for some purpose or other, are imposing upon the "good folks" of the neighbourhood. The age of superstition is past, and can only be revived in a rural district.'[625]

The explanations given for flaps are of interest. When a boggart appeared at Worsthorne, for instance, the village consensus was that this was the result of a recent bad death: 'A short time ago a very worthy resident departed this life, and as it has been alleged that some of his actions during his career were not altogether what some people expected, they presumed he would not be able to rest in his new abode.'[626] In other cases, the local storytellers dug out obscure events from the recent or distant past: 'blood-curdling tales at the same time being told as to what occurred in the locality some time ago'.[627] In one Cheshire town, 'the people firmly believe that' the boggart 'was real, and are quite ready to quote numberless instances reaching far away down the vista of time of others who have been favoured by similar visits'.[628] Note the existence of authorities, men and women like Old Billy: 'should there be seen a "boggard" in Fairy Vale, he is the first to whom the tale is told, and it is for him to say what is the meaning of the apparition'.[629]

Occasionally, it is possible to link flaps to the established boggarts of the area. Sometimes this is done in a straightforward fashion. A tradition existed, for instance, that Dungley Boggart appeared 'on the 7th and 14th day septennially and haunted the rooms at Dunkenhalgh during the witching hour at

---

624. 'A Ghost Story' (1839). This motif of the braggart appears again and again in our sources: in both fiction and what purports to be fact, e.g. Higson, 'Boggarts and Feorin', 508; 'The Starling Bridge Boggart'; 'A Ghost Story' (1869); 'The Miner and the Ghost' (1887); and 'Eyam, Stoney Middleton, Calver and District' (1903). A man claims that he is brave enough to visit a supernatural location and doing so encounters and suffers the wrath of a local boggart. This is the nineteenth-century equivalent of twentieth- and twenty-first-century legend tripping, see further Bird, 'Playing with Fear', and as such deserves a longer study. There seems to be no folklore motif: the closest is perhaps N81(c) 'Wagers on approaching a dead man'.
625. 'A Ghost Story' (1839).
626. A Villager, 'A Boggart at Worsthorne'.
627. 'Mill Haunted by the Screaming Lady'.
628. Rambler, 'Out and About Chester' (June 1887).
629. A.L., Forty Years, 12.

midnight'.[630] Naturally, the servants in the hall saw the boggart at the appointed time, and this news then spread through the wider area where it caused consternation. Indeed, a committee of investigation was called into being.[631] The fact that boggarts could occasionally escape from where they had been 'laid' also had obvious potential in the context of a flap. The uptick in boggart sightings was due, it was believed, to a boggart who had eluded imprisonment (see pp. 243–44). In other cases, strange events were elided imaginatively with pre-existing figures. When a railway embankment continually gave way in northern Derbyshire, it was blamed on the most famous local boggart, Dickie, a screaming skull, who resided in a nearby farmhouse.[632] Even if the events could not be explained by older boggarts, flaps had the potential to re-energize traditional tales: 'All the rare old Ghost stories of many generations were told in improved and enlarged editions.'[633]

Boggart Crowds

Boggart flaps sometimes necessitated people coming together in one place. There are, for example, several instances of what might be called the 'village conference' where community elders discussed how to deal with a boggart.[634] These might be usefully seen as the precursors of the scientific investigation of paranormal events which also began to appear in Boggartdom towards the end of our period.[635] It sometimes happened that people found safety in numbers. When Bank Hagg Boggart was active 'Crowds of persons going to their work in the early morning were wont to wait [at a corner of the road] from fear and lack of courage to pass, until their numbers became such as to assure their courage, and enable them to pass with safety the haunted place.'[636] However, the best attested gatherings of people for supernatural purposes were what I will term 'boggart crowds'.

---

630. 'The Dungley Boggart' (1892).
631. Ibid.
632. H. 'A Tramp in Derbyshire'.
633. 'A Ghost in Rusland'.
634. See, e.g., 'Extraordinary Superstition at Blackley'. The most remarkable of these—and it is well documented—took place in 1845, a little outside Boggartdom, in Cumberland. After a man had received a message from a ghost, a local landowner—suspected of the murder that had led to the haunting—was obliged to dig up the victim's body and touch its corpse (to see if blood flowed) while twenty-three neighbours looked on: 'Nichol Forest Ghost Story'. The reference is, of course, to cruentation, the old European belief that a corpse bleeds when touched by its murderer: Gaskill, Crime, 227–30.
635. See, e.g., 'More Wyke Wonders' (1909).
636. Fizzwig, 'From Glossop'.

The 'boggart crowd' might be defined as tens, hundreds, or, in some cases, thousands of people coming together to see or hear boggarts. Such crowds have a long history in Britain. Indeed, the presence of crowds interested in seeing or hearing supernatural events dates back at least to the seventeenth century in England and continued as late as the 1930s.[637] In the nineteenth-century boggart crowd, typically a bogie of some description had been spotted in the window of a house or in a cemetery and a crowd turned out to enjoy the show. Entertainment seems to have been paramount. In 1835, footsteps were heard in an architect's studio in the centre of Manchester when no one was there in the evening. Large groups appeared to listen to the steps: 'the place is nightly visited by crowds of idle persons, all anxious to hear the ghost, and it is amusing to witness the effect produced upon them when any mischievous wag announces that the ghost is coming'.[638] The noises were eventually traced—at least to the satisfaction of the local constabulary—to a nearby pub. The crowds, though, continued to gather and the police had difficulty in clearing the streets.

The 1835 Manchester boggart crowd was by no means an isolated incident. Equivalent crowds are to be found throughout Victorian Britain, although very few scholars have acknowledged this fascinating phenomenon.[639] Restricting ourselves to a selection of north-western examples from the nineteenth and early twentieth centuries, we have the following. '[C]rowds of people' came from Colne and other places to see blood seeping from Laneshaw Bridge. In Huddersfield, a house was 'regularly besieged by crowds of people, all anxious to see and hear for themselves the marvellous doings of the ghost'. In Bury, 'gaping thousands' turned up to look into a haunted house there. '[H]undreds of persons' went to visit some haunted buildings near Middleton. A house at Burnley was besieged after a false rumour had got out that it was haunted by a little man dressed in khaki. In the hamlet of Upholland, near Wigan, 'crowds of peoples ... gathered in the neighbourhood' to hear knockings in a haunted house near the parish church. 'Crowds of scared inhabitants gathered at the foot of Goodman's End' (Bradford) to watch the wavering form of a ghost at

---

637. Bath and Newton, 'Belief', 11: 'there seems to have been a shift in the later [sic] half of the seventeenth century from visits to haunted places being the preserve of the elite to a more democratised attempt to experience the supernatural'. I am sceptical, but the evidence allows us to go no further. The earliest reference known to me for ghost crowds is: Hunter, 'New light', 27.

638. 'A Ghost!' (1835).

639. An honourable exception for ghost crowds in London, Bell, 'Cities', 102–03, 107; and Davies, The Haunted, 90–94.

a window—it turned out to be some loose wallpaper. Large numbers also turned up at Blackley at a boggart house there.[640]

It will be seen from these examples that most ghost crowds gathered around a building: there needed to be a clear focus for groups to congregate after dark, particularly in the winter months.[641] There is also a bias towards urban sites, although note the mysterious spectral blood at Laneshaw Bridge near Colne. People were clearly prepared to travel long distances to see something remarkable. We might wonder what the mood was like in these crowds. The occasional reference to public order problems and the intervention of the police (there was also pickpocketing)[642] suggests that the boggart-watchers could become raucous.[643] They were festive, too. In the case of the Blackley boggart crowd we are told that 'publicans and beersellers' reaped 'a rich harvest from the boggart hunters'.[644] In a crowd at St Helens, hundreds of people turned up to watch a spectre, 'giving the streets the appearance of a fair': 'Fried fish sellers and hot potato vendors drove a roaring trade.'[645] Jacob Middleton has described the 'somewhat celebratory atmosphere' of a crowd in Derby.[646] It has been suggested—and the matter is certainly worth consideration—that boggart crowds declined in the early twentieth century because of cinemas.[647] For those who lived in a house surrounded by crowds, things rarely ended well. We have reports of stolen food and nuisance knocking.[648]

Boggart Hunts and Fake Boggarts

A more energetic form of the social supernatural was the boggart hunt.[649] In these cases, adults gathered together to capture someone masquerading as a boggart, often with a white sheet over their head. This was a world in

---

640. Carr, *Colne*, 199–200; 'The Seed-Hill Ghost' (1855); 'The "Freetown Pie"; 'A Ghost Story' (1839); 'Ghost Rumours at Burnley' (1903); 'In these enlightened days'; Fieldhouse, *Old Bradford*, 82; 'Extraordinary Superstition at Blackley'.

641. For interesting reflection on ghost seasons, see Middleton, *Spirits*, 80.

642. 'A Ghost!' (1835).

643. Davies, *The Haunted*, 92–93; Bell, 'Cities', 107, 'a temporary but highly unpredictable communal reclamation of the streets'.

644. 'Extraordinary Superstition at Blackley'.

645. 'A St Helen's Ghost Story'.

646. Middleton, *Spirits*, 220.

647. Clarke, draft article, 'A ghost, a bear and a devil, the folklore of Spring-heeled Jack', refers to 'the competing attraction of new forms of working-class media, such as the music hall and the film show'. I thank David for allowing me to see this article before publication.

648. 'Not a Case for the Psychical Research Society'; 'Ghost Rumours at Burnley'.

649. For more on this term in dialect, see p. 232.

which an 1862 headline like 'The Sweetclough Boggart Caught at Last' made perfect sense.[650] Harsh measures were sometimes meted out or at least threatened. At Tyldesley, for instance, in 1881, 'Scores of colliers and others' paraded 'the district armed with sticks and bludgeons, and one of the colliers … fired several shots at the latest arrival from spiritland.' At Garstang in the same year, so strong was the sensation about the boggart 'that each night bands of young men patrol the lanes, armed with cudgels'. A boggart was actually captured in the late nineteenth century in Burnley by a group of locals who handed him over to the courts. One fake boggart in Cheshire had a dog set on him. Another was publicly abused in the newspaper: 'We heard that the perpetrator of this foolish trick is known, and that should he repeat his "boggart" freak, it is not improbable but a horsewhip may touch his "feel-ings," and teach him in future to conduct himself better.'[651] Presumably both the hunters and the hunted derived atavistic pleasures from these chases through the moonlit countryside. Duels between the 'boggart' and its hunters died away in the early twentieth century, but some tales entered tradition. Here is a remarkable example that was recorded in 2019 which had survived through the twentieth century in a Moston family:

> I can't confirm the veracity of this story, but here it is as told to me by my grandmother in the early 1950s … Someone has already mentioned Boggart Hole Clough. Apparently it got its name following a series of incidents when a ghost or Bogart, used to jump out of the bushes and frighten young women walking through this isolated area. It would have been sometime in the late 1800s when her father (or grandfather, I can't remember) was walking through the area when he saw the Boggart up to its usual tricks, frightening a young woman. He [the father/grandfather] was on his way home from work and was carrying a tin plate which he took with him to eat his meals from at the mill. When he saw the Boggart he threw the plate at him (bear in mind this was before the invention of the frisbee) and it struck him [the boggart] on the head knocking him to the ground. On getting closer he [the father/grandfather] saw that he actually knew the man well, who with his dying breath said 'Aye Tom, tha's killed me' … So there

---

650. The boggart, it transpires, was a cat: but the editor plays with expectations in the title.
651. '"Boggart" Hunting at Tyldesley'; 'A Troublesome Ghost' (1881); E.C., 'Sandygate Boggart'; Rambler, 'Out and About Chester' (February 1887); 'Another New Hall Boggart'.

we have it, my Great Grandfather killed the Ghost of Boggart Hole Clough. Either that or my grandmother was a good storyteller.[652]

The question of fake boggarts (or elsewhere in Britain, fake ghosts—see Figure 29) is the best-studied aspect of the British social supernatural: in 2014, Jacob Middleton dedicated an entire monograph to the question.[653] The motives for fake hauntings were various. The most common was what could very loosely be called a 'prank' played either by an individual against a community or against a friend or friends. As one northern poet put it: a storyteller 'mostly ends the [ghost] story, by saying 'twas done for a lark'.[654]

Here is a fictional example of pranking, but one that presupposes a background in Lancashire life. Note the use of the term 'boggartin'':[655]

> Quifter an' Billy were owd cronies; an' they wur al'ays up to some mak o' witless marlocks [jokes], particular when they had a gill [drink] or two. Well, as they coom maunderin' eawt o'th public-house at th' side o'th church one winter's neet, about nine o'clock, Nukkin looked up at th' churchyard, an' he said, 'Billy, it's too soon to go whoam. Let's have a go at boggartin'! Go thee an' borrow two sheets, an' two white neet-caps; an' we'n see if we connot stir some o' these sleepy bowster-yeds up a bit as they walken by'.[656]

The two pretend to be ghosts and ambush passers-by.

There are many factual examples of similar 'marlocks' from the Northwest. In one instance a young man created clanking sounds outside a cottage where a game of cards was taking place to terrify those within (this was an age where ghosts still had chains). We have a fragmentary account of Satan appearing on Wilsden Hill and 'spitting blue-fire': 'it was a huge joke'. In another jest, a goose was dropped down a chimney ruining a Methodist gathering. The congregation, convinced that the Devil was among them, fled. In yet another case, a man guarding a tomb (from body snatchers) was scared by some young men pretending to be a boggart. Then, of course, there were disgruntled or bored servants producing poltergeist phenomena: for instance, a twelve-year-

652. BC, Moston 7 (La).
653. *Spirits*; Davies, *The Haunted*, 165–86; also now for Australia, Waldron and Waldron, 'Playing the Ghost'.
654. H, *Lines*.
655. For another term, 'playing the boggart', see p. 238.
656. Waugh, *Tufts*, 46.

Figure 29: Fake Ghost Hunt in Devon, *Police News* (29 September 1894), 1.

old Irish maid in 1855 who convinced many in Huddersfield that a house there was haunted.[657] These boggart games survived, in one form or another, until the Second World War. This comment refers to shenanigans in Bentham in the 1940s. Note the continued use in dialect of 'boggartin'':

> On 4 Nov (mischief night) the teenagers went Boggarting which involved rolling up a newspaper and pushing it up the roof drainage down pipe and setting fire to it which made a loud moaning noise.[658]

While not in the same tradition, an April Fools' joke in the same spirit ran in *The Independent* in 1988 claiming that a hybrid badger-fox, named a 'bogart', had been discovered in the Cumbrian mountains.[659]

---

657. 'A Boggart' (1856); Speight, *Chronicles*, 268; Heaton, 'Stray Notes'; 'The Midnight Robbers'; 'The Capture'.

658. BC, Bentham 4 (La).

659. 'Naturalists foxed'. This, note, is the stuffed boggart which has long been on display at the Twa Dogs in Keswick: 'Not to be missed is our world famous Cumbrian Boggart, which is a cross between a fox and a badger, animal which roams the Cumbrian fells', http://www.twadogs. co.uk/pub.htm [accessed 24 January 2020]. Peter Harding, the landlord in 2020 and the proud possessor of the Cumbrian boggart, tells me that the hunter in Brian Duff's photograph was Gordon Hallett, in 1988, the landlord of the Twa Dogs. Peter remembered in a phone conversation, 18 December 2020, that Gordon won a contest as 'the world's biggest liar' for his boggart shenanigans. For a nineteenth-century pub boggart relic, see Ward, *Moston*, 155–56.

Figure 30: 'Bogart' captured in Cumbria, 1988.

Related to the joke boggart was what might be called 'the misunderstood boggart'. These were particularly common in dialect literature. Indeed, almost always in published dialect tales and poems about boggarts, the 'boggart' turns out, as we have seen earlier, to be something else seen at night: perhaps a white cow, perhaps a dog with a chain, perhaps an escaped bear.[660] It would be easy to explain these tales as yarns that were in line with the presiding rational spirit of the time, as indeed they were. But, in fact, narratives about fake and misunderstood supernatural beings were also there in traditional folklore.[661] Certainly many of these episodes entered (or came from) a local pool of tales, with similar yarns being repeated from place to place. Take, for example, a story about a black-and-white boggart from Lancashire which echoes that of the black-and-white bucca from Cornwall.[662] There are also autobiographical descriptions of people mistaking some object at night for a boggart. A man and a woman, for example, walk down a haunted lane and hear a clanking chain: the woman fears the worst but the man rightly identifies the noise as coming from a tethered donkey.[663] A sound-recording from the 1950s has a seventy-six-year-old from Skelmanthorpe recall how, as a young man in the late nineteenth century, he mistook a woman searching out her cat for a local ghost.[664]

---

660. Young, 'Dialect , 2–3; for a rare late example BC, Lytham 1 (La).
661. Roper, 'Folk Disbelief'
662. H, 'Reminiscences of Droylsden'; Bottrell, *Traditions* (1870), 143–44; for more on this motif, Smith, 'The Devil'.
663. 'Bolton-Le-Sands' (1870).
664. Lancashire sound archives, 'Skelmanthorpe, Wilsey Dyson, aged 76 yrs, miner and weaver' (Y031), 25 October 1952.

Another motive for fake hauntings was crime. In one case near Saddleworth, a ghost jumped out and, after terrifying passers-by, its partner (another man) would demand a 'tax'.[665] In Staffordshire thieves assumed the appearance of a boggart to rob farms.[666] More typically, a boggart was used to keep the police and the public away, a use of the supernatural that will be familiar to anyone who has ever watched a *Scooby-Doo* cartoon. We have already met smugglers at Warton.[667] What about the 'huge coffin, draped in black, and borne on the shoulders of four stalwart fellows' from south Lancashire which was believed to be a boggart? It turned out to be a ruse dreamt up by a group of sheep-stealers. They packed the sheep into the 'coffin' and the ghostly procession had free run of the countryside.[668] In a dialect story from the same region, a man had a trained pony walk on two legs and imitate the Devil to frighten off excise men: the pony's owner ran an illegal distillery.[669] There are many similar stories concerning smuggling and wrecking from other parts of the country.[670] There are also some intriguing hints of boggarts being used to shield the identity of radicals during strikes.[671] Indeed, there has long been an association between outlaws and the supernatural.[672]

A final type of fake ghost is what might be very loosely called the sexual haunter. On a number of occasions—and it has even been suggested that there is a concentration of such cases in Lancashire[673]—'ghosts' were seen wandering around naked at night. One respected Wesleyan, for instance, enjoyed a three-year reign of terror near Winsford in the early 1830s. He would stroll nude in the dark, apparently to frighten local women. He was finally captured by a publican and punished by the magistrates.[674] In an age when semi-nudity in public was much rarer than in the twenty-first century—though there were some examples of nude male swimming—and when nakedness was unacceptable in some private residences, the shock of a bare body must have been considerable. This would have been particularly so at night, when white skin

665. Sugden, *Slaithwaite Notes*, 251; compare with Middleton, *Spirits*, 68.
666. 'Up and Down the Country' (1879).
667. Clarke, *Windmill Land*, 116.
668. Higson, 'Boggarts and Feorin', 508–09; see also Axon, *Black Knight*, 53–60.
669. Chip, 'Smelt Mill Boggart'.
670. Menefee, 'Watch'. See also the British films around this theme including *Doctor Syn* (1937); and the sublime Will Hay in *Ask a Policeman* (1939).
671. Shuttleworth, *Scarsdale*, I, 60–61; Hepburn, *A Book*, I, 255.
672. Harte, 'Subversive or What?'.
673. Middleton, *Spirits*, 147–48.
674. 'Commitment'.

has a slightly luminous quality.[675] We have some hints that nudity could excite unexpected reactions. On one occasion a boy threw a stone at a urinating man, because he believed that the man was a boggart;[676] likewise a dead baby discovered in an attic was thought to be a boggart.[677] Next to nudity we might consider cases of transvestism—there are only hints from the Northwest— where men dressed up as women and walked around after dark.[678]

Children and the Supernatural

Children had their own social supernatural experiences which were woven into their games, their rituals, and their adventures. This is a rich field of study that would certainly repay careful work in the archives. One of the earliest cases to be recorded from the Northwest comes from the pen of a man in 1827 remembering his childhood trips—in the late 1700s—to the Fairy Holes at Lamplugh: 'so often the scenes of sportive gaiety to the *brethren* of the adjacent schools, in all generations prior to the present'.[679] This is not admittedly, a Boggart Hole, but the children's actions are instructive.

> Often have I entered this cavern with the trembling company of youngsters, with lighted candle to explore the extent, and armed with a pistol to protect ourselves in case of an attack from the airy beings on whose mansions of darkness we were intruding, and as often emerged to the light of day in unsuccessful safety: for with all our precautions of laying pebbles, and chalking the sides, as marks whereby to retrace our steps, we never yet found an end but the one we entered by.

The possibility of bumping into something supernatural clearly gave a not unwelcome edge to these expeditions—note the pistol. The boys on some occasions mistook the red eyes of a rabbit in the dark for a fairy, and the

---

675. Middleton, *Spirits*, 145–48.

676. 'Assault Upon a Child' (1858).

677. 'Extraordinary Case' (1832). For another interesting human 'boggart', a woman who had cut her throat and bled profusely was described as a 'red 'boggart', 'Attempt at Murder'.

678. See, e.g. Rambler, 'Out and About' (March 1886) and see also Lahee, *Trot*. For a particularly striking case from Somerset, 1927, 'A Minister's Masquerade': the local vicar 'had heard that many girls and young women got into trouble or got molested, and he had posed as a lady to see if that were true'.

679. W.D., 'Recollections'.

children also played tricks on new gang members by convincing them that they had encountered one of the fay. Trips to the Holes were undertaken, in fact, for gang initiations and the boys would make oaths in the 'chapel'—a large central cave—about, say, 'the plunder of an orchard or the "barring out" of the master before the Christmas holidays'.[680]

Another journey into a subterranean space is recorded for the mid nineteenth century: a gaggle of children on the southern boundaries of Bradford went into a tunnel to find the Low Well Boggard. The raid entered legend:

> A party of juveniles, ranging in age from ten to fourteen, planned a visit to the supposed hiding-place of the boggard. Saturday afternoon was selected for the excursion. Candles, oil lamps, and matches were provided in abundance, and the party set forth upon their perilous adventure, under the guidance of a certain valiant youth. The tunnel is short, but towards the middle there is a slight bend which renders that part of the passage perfectly dark. It crosses beneath Manchester Road, and comes out in the low ground on the other side, flowing towards the brick kiln. The expedition entered at the Dewhirst Mill end. The water was shallow, and by tilting from side to side they managed to keep their shoes tolerably dry. All went well until the dark portion of the tunnel was reached. Their progress became slower and more cautious at that point, and the regular thud of their footfalls was all that could be heard. In another moment the leader of the expedition would have passed the bend, but the supposed boggard, infuriated by such a rude intrusion upon his privacy, leaped to his feet and rattled his chains until the water splashed in all directions, and the underground passage vibrated with his terrible menaces. The 'expedition' were in one huge mass, each member in his turn, and sometimes before his turn, getting a sound drenching. It was some time before the confusion sufficiently subsided to enable the adventurers to retreat in the direction whence they started. Meantime, the person who had undertaken to play the part of [the] boggard, had escaped unobserved at the other end. Although the Low Well boggard did not give another such practical demonstration of his presence, his existence was never afterwards questioned, and many people charitably concluded that he had fallen into a trance.[681]

---

680. For the custom of 'barring out', see *The Black Non-Conformist*, unnumbered dedicatory epistle.
681. Fieldhouse, *Old Bradford*, 85–86. I wonder if Fieldhouse himself was not part of this expedition.

There were also deliberate rituals to conjure up supernatural forces: the boggart was expected to come to the children, rather than the children to the boggart. At its most banal this could be a dare, such as the Burnley children who kicked the door of the ghost of St Paul's Vicarage: 'if one of us dared to kick the door, we were thought to be brave indeed'.[682] Rather more serious were spells involving mirrors and the Devil.[683] Other rituals were more elaborate still. Take this extraordinary account from Calverley near Bradford in 1874: the author remembering his childhood some forty years previous and how he and his friends had obliged, on several occasions, 'Old Calverley', to appear. 'Old Calverley' was a boggart who had been laid under a stone in Wood Lane:

> The modus operandi was as follows. About a dozen of the scholars having leisure, and fired with the imaginative spirit, used to assemble after school hours close to the venerable old church of Calverley … and there we used to put down on the ground our hats and caps in a pyramid form. Then taking hold of each other's hands we formed a 'magic circle,' holding firmly together and making use of an old refrain—'Old Calverley, old Calverley, I have thee by the ears, I'll cut thee in collops unless thou appears.' While this incantation was going on, crumbs of bread (left from our dinners) were strewed on the ground, mixed with pins, while at the tune we tramped round in the circle with a heavy tread, and some of the more venturesome had to go round to all the church doors and whistle aloud through the keyhole, uttering the bewitching couplet that was being repeated by the other small boys. At this culminating point the figure used to come forth ghostly and pale … for, although old Calverley was conjured down, he was obliged to break open his prison-house. The figure that we saw was like that in the finishing canto of Don Juan, called Fitz-Fulke.[684] In our hurry to escape detention and to avoid the fearful grasp of a ghost, we used to fall down over each other, our hats and caps being lifted behind a buttress or scattered over the ground, while we scampered off afraid of the spirit we had thus called forth.[685]

682. Wiseman, 'A Local Boggart Tale'.

683. Bell, *Magical Imagination*, 188 (undated in the *Middleton Guardian*).

684. The author seems to have confused the ghost of the sable Friar with the Duchess of Fitz-Fulke whom Juan mistakes for a ghost: Canto 16 'And in the doorway, darkening darkness, stood/ The sable Friar in his solemn hood'. On this passage, Beatty, 'Unknown Modes', 44–45.

685. Phantom, 'Calverley'.

In 1928, another form of the social supernatural was recorded in north-western newspapers: the school scare.[686] Children in the Yorkshire town of Barnoldswick became convinced that a ghost with a three-cornered hat was planning to blow up their schools with dynamite! To judge by their reactions the children believed that they would be in class when these all-too-real bombs would be set off:

> The little folks have got the fever badly, and boys and girls have been observed running to and from the various schools in the town crying, 'Come and see the ghost.' One teacher was amazed to see a whole class in tears over the matter, and mothers have complained of their children shouting out in their sleep in terror.[687]

This is a late record for Victorian and Edwardian boggart-lore. But in Britain, the social supernatural seems to have survived more convincingly among children than among adults. Indeed, there are even later examples. In Liverpool in 1964, for instance, hundreds of children ran wild in the city centre trying to capture, of all things, leprechauns.[688] Then, to finish on a boggart note, we have in the same decade an incident where several schoolboys were chased by no less than Towneley Boggart in the grounds of Towneley House (Burnley) '[l]ate one winter night'.[689]

---

686. For similar cases both from Britain and internationally, Bartholomew with Rickard, *Hysteria*.
687. '"Ghost" in Three-Cornered Hat at Barnoldswick'.
688. Watson, 'Case'. The tradition of children's hunts can be paralleled elsewhere: Irish children sought a leprechaun in 1908, Wentz, *Fairy-Faith*, 71; and in Glasgow in 1954, scamps chased 'vampires', Cornwell and Hobbs, 'Hunting'.
689. BC, Burnley 9 (La).

III: The Death and Rebirth of the Boggart

[What was a boggart for you?] 'At first, probably a nameless horror, but as I read fairy stories and saw illustrations in them, I think my idea of a boggart developed into a goblin or troll type of creature.'
BC, Greenfield 1 (WRY).

Figure 31: A still from the film *The Spiderwick Chronicles* (2008).

CHAPTER SEVEN

Boggart Death

Introduction: 'Boggard House', Esholt

The scenic village of Esholt stands on the northern edge of the Leeds-Bradford conurbation. Little has been written about Esholt folklore, but at least something of its nineteenth-century supernatural beliefs is caught in the aspic of a toponym: an isolated cottage near the village hall is known to this day as 'Boggard House'.[690] The building in question was constructed in about 1800 at a three-way junction and 'Boggard House' was evidently well enough established as a name to convince an OS official to include the words on a map surveyed 1847/1848.[691] Luckily, a couple of sentences were written a generation later about how the cottage acquired its moniker. In the 1870s, a Bradford journalist, William Cudworth, described a walk there:

> we take the road in the rear of the hall, passing the Boggard House, so named because it was some time untenanted, and the simple rustics in the neighbourhood imagined that they saw lights in the house after the death of a person named Strothers.[692]

Strothers must have lived there sometime in the early 1800s: in the years between the house being built and the publication of the OS map. The spirit of Strothers was supposed, Cudworth tells us, to have played marbles with other ghosts in the empty building; a curious tradition but one that is worth

---

690. It is a grade two listed building and is described, in the official listings, as an '[e]arly C19 estate cottage': https://historicengland.org.uk/listing/the-list/list-entry/1314421 [accessed 7 January 2020].

691. OSY 202 (1851) To the best of my knowledge, this is the first appearance of the name in print. It is worth noting that the name appears in the census returns only in 1901 (Esholt, District 8, p. 3) when it was occupied by a gamekeeper and his wife. I have not been able, with certainty, to identify the house in previous censuses.

692. Cudworth, *Round*, 422; note that this had appeared in the newspapers a year earlier [Cudworth], 'Round About' (1875).

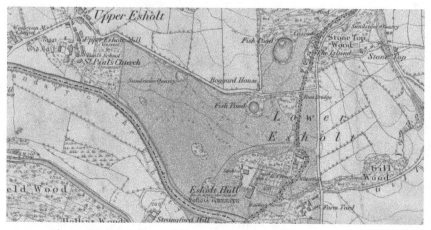

Figure 32: Esholt Boggard House in the late 1840s (OSY 202, 1851).

comparing with records from the 1800s of supernatural creatures gathering for occasional meetings in English folklore.[693]

It is difficult to trace historical beliefs in phantoms in a village with a weak written tradition like Esholt. But it is also difficult to trace the fortunes of the word 'boggart' there over subsequent decades, a period when very little is written on boggart-lore either by folklorists or local historians. Yet here, too, there are clues. In the *Shipley Times*, 9 May 1945, there appeared a question: 'how did Boggard House at Esholt get its name?'.[694] The very fact that this question was asked is perhaps telling. Then, 30 May 1945, in the same newspaper, the occupier of the house, a Mrs English, frustrated that no one

---

693. A legend from Worsthorne, Booth, 'A Morning Ramble' (1884), has a man passing close to the Tithe Barn who sees a congregation of different supernatural spirits from the parish within the building. He accidentally banishes them by invoking God (F382.3, Use of God's name nullifies fairies' power; G303.16.8, Devil leaves at mention of God's name). That this is not a chance motif is suggested by a near-contemporary north-western poem describing local spirits meeting in a Westmorland tithe barn: Master Quiz, 'Hugh', (1842) 'When before him he chanced the Tithe Barn to espy/ A place always famous for Dobbie and Tay/ Which the priests of all England could never allay.' The tithe barn is a communal space with unpleasant connotations (taxes) and would be a suitable enough place for boggarts to gather. Two examples do not a folk type make, but more research might—I am optimistic—turn up others. Indeed, the story of an encounter with groups of boggarts may link into learnt and popular traditions of witch sabbats, Sharpe, 'Sabbat'. In 'Tam O'Shanter' by Burns *Works*, 146–48, Tam encounters witches feasting with the Devil and the dead and only escapes by crossing running water: was this perhaps a Lowland cousin (twice removed) of the boggart get-together in Worsthorne? For a meeting between boggles, see Wilson, 'Thirlmere', 61.

694. 'Idle Quiz'.

had given an answer, stated that she, too, wished to learn why. She had heard vague traditions of supernatural marbles tournaments—which had evidently survived in village lore—but she was unclear as to what the word 'boggart' itself meant. 'So far as we know,' she wrote, 'a boggart is a kind of devil'.[695] On this evidence 'boggart' did not feature in the English family's vocabulary, except, of course, as part of their address. It is unlikely that anyone living in the Bradford area seventy years before, let alone the residents of a haunted house, would have failed to understand that word. See the way Cudworth, a Bradford man writing for a Bradford audience, takes its sense for granted in the passage quoted earlier: 'Boggard House, so named because …'.

From 1965, the Cook family took up residence in this Boggard House: the parents would live there for the next fifty years. Their children, who grew up in the 1960s, were likewise unclear as to what a boggart was, although, 'At some point myself and two older sisters were told that a Boggart was a mischievous Yorkshire ghost who, amongst other things, liked to place a cold clammy hand on the face [of] people while they were sleeping'. That 'mischievous' brings us very much to modern fantasy traditions of boggart house spirits (see pp. 211–15), something that constituted only a tiny part of nineteenth-century boggart-lore. Traditionalists will be glad to know that even if the word 'boggart' had drifted from its nineteenth-century moorings, a definite aura of the supernatural persisted in the house in the later twentieth century. 'I remember mum's electric sewing machine started working on its own despite being turned off at the switch and my friend's car once moved around in the driveway despite the handbrake being engaged and doors locked.' As the member of the Cook family who provided these memories noted, such happenings were, 'Not terrifying but definitely weird'.[696]

In this brief account of a single building—Esholt's Boggard House—we see the decline of the Victorian boggart. In the nineteenth century, 'boggart' was a commonplace word for any sinister or ambivalent solitary supernatural being. The very fact that the name was given to a house in Esholt shows that 'boggart' was indeed used in local dialect in the early to mid-1800s; as it was in much of the rest of the West Riding. However, it is clear that by the middle and later twentieth century, the word 'boggart' or, to give it the more Yorkshire form, 'boggard' was no longer easily understood in the area. Mrs English wrote 'So

---

695. English, 'Boggart House'. The English family eventually decided to change the house name to 'The Firs' which suggests that they were uneasy with it, BC, Esholt 1 (WRY).

696. BC, Esholt 1 (WRY).

far as we know'; the younger Cook girls '[a]t some point ... were told'.[697]
Indeed, one suspects that the word survives here because 'boggart' had become
attached to a house where it became something that needed to be explained,
particularly by those who lived there. In an important sense Strothers' ghost
has come through to the modern age in the poltergeist spasms of sewing machines
and parked cars. But the word 'boggart' was no longer part of a community's
shared supernatural. No modern Esholtite hurries by the three-way junction of
the Boggard House at night, 'boggart-feart'.

'Boggart' in Dialect

In Chapter 5, we have seen the danger of taking self-proclamations about the
boggart's decline at face value (pp. 113–14): just because someone says 'there
are fewer boggarts about today than when I was a lad', does not mean that
this is necessarily so. Men and women have always romanticized their glory
days and there is very definitely a supernatural version of this: 'back then
everyone believed in fairies' and the like. But through the twentieth century
we can see, in the old boggart heartlands, the disappearance of something
integral to belief in boggarts: the decline of the word itself. This chapter is,
in fact, a survey of how 'boggart' dropped out of day-to-day speech: a dialect
study with folklore ends. A nice question is whether the death of the word
meant the death of the concept behind it; something we will postpone to a
discussion in the final part of this chapter.

The generic term 'boggart' belonged to dialect and dialect caused embar-
rassment in a country and a period in which Standard English was a
prerequisite for any kind of upwards social mobility. As such, 'boggart' was,
in Hardy's words, one of those 'terrible marks of the beast to the truly
genteel':[698] witness the many Victorian texts where 'boggart' was used only
with apologies.[699] The decline in the use of dialect can be measured in authors
from Boggartdom in the years after the First World War: whether writing in
Standard English, or Lancashire, Yorkshire, or other northern dialects.[700] It
should come as no surprise that this is the period in which the use of the
word 'boggart' nose-dived throughout much of the Northwest. In the 2020s,
many ten-year-olds in the north of England know the word 'boggart'. They

---

697. English, 'Boggart House'; BC, Esholt 1 (WRY).
698. Hardy, *Mayor*, 163.
699. The most common indication of this is the use of inverted commas: see, e.g., 'Scotforth
    township'.
700. Russell, *Looking North*, 111–46; Beal, *Regional*, 2–7.

do so because, since the 1970s and particularly since the 2000s, 'boggart' has appeared in fantasy film and fantasy fiction: crucially, a boggart makes an appearance in the *Harry Potter* universe. 'Guess today's children probably think a boggart is just a shapeshifter from the Harry Potter novels', wrote one respondent from the Boggart Census.[701] 'Boggart' is no longer a dialect word. It belongs rather to Standard English and is used not just in the Northwest but also in Minneapolis and New South Wales. The knowledge of this modern boggart comes from the page *and* from the screen. It has not, except in very rare instances, been passed down by grandparents to those born in the twenty-first century.

In the SED survey in the 1950s, 'boggart' (admittedly with the narrow sense of child scarer) was only found in parts of the Northwest (see pp. 61–64). This fall off in the use of 'boggart' had been trailed for some years before, however, in the comments of local writers. In 1933, for instance, a Lancashire journalist explained that ghosts were 'still called "boggarts" by villagers', placing the use of such words outside urban centres like Blackpool and Preston.[702] In the nineteenth century 'boggart' had been used routinely in those two towns.[703] In the 1940s, Philip Ahier wrote some six hundred pages on Huddersfield legends, history, and folklore, in a period when such careful local studies were not common. Ahier frequently mentions supernatural forms, but he only uses the word 'bogard' twice, once in a quotation and once in a place-name—a word not long before current in Huddersfield dialect.[704] In 1946, a correspondent wrote to a Burnley newspaper specifically to explain the word 'boggart' to readers ('a bogey, ghost or apparition') and also examined the expression 'off at the boggart'.[705] In, say, the 1870s, a Burnley editor would no more have put a letter of this type in their paper than they would have included a missive explaining what a tree looked like. The loss of 'boggard' from day-to-day vocabulary in Esholt in the twentieth century was, it will be seen, part of a larger pattern.

---

701. BC, Failsworth 2 (La).

702. North-Westerner, 'The Way' (1933).

703. See, e.g., 'Superstition in the Fylde' (1857) for Blackpool; 'Another New Hall Boggart' (1866) for Preston.

704. *Legends*, I, 153; I, 157. The unusual spelling, 'bogard', suggests that Ahier might not have been familiar with boggart writing. Indeed, we cannot be *absolutely* sure that Ahier understood what the word meant, though I, 157 includes ghostly goings on. For previous uses of the word Haigh, *Huddersfield Dialect* (1928), 13.

705. F.B., 'Letters' (1946).

Boggart Attrition

The loss of words from a language is referred to by linguists as 'lexical attrition'.[706] This term is often applied to bilingual communities or individuals where two languages are spoken, but where one of them is dominant. Frequently a word is forgotten in a native language and the word is replaced by words from a second language. English words, for instance, creep into the Spanish conversations of a second-generation Mexican family in the USA, displacing, as they do so, Spanish words. 'Lexical attrition' also takes place, of course, between a standard language and a dialect, in periods where the standard version of a tongue takes the upper hand—although attrition between mutually comprehensible dialects/languages is clearly more difficult to measure.[707] Dialect words are gradually lost as Standard English words take their place; so in Geordie a 'pissiemoor' becomes an ant, a 'tanklet' becomes an icicle.[708] There can also, on rare occasions, be different processes: a dialect word survives the demise of a given dialect and continues to be used in the spoken English of a given area, perhaps even being absorbed into Standard English.[709] What was the trajectory of 'boggart' as it disappeared from much of northern England? This is no easy thing to chart as there is almost no relevant scholarly work,[710] and '[f]inding out which words a person knows, but rarely if ever uses, is, of course, very difficult to elicit "naturally"'.[711]

In early 2019, I had determined to chart the use of 'boggart' over Boggartdom and particularly from those born between around 1920 and 1970 in a Boggart Census. My hope (discussed in Chapter 1, pp. 21–24) was to gather in boggart memories that might contextualize nineteenth-century boggart beliefs which can often be frustratingly obscure. However, I was early on encouraged to add another dimension to these enquiries. In my questions I asked not only for memories about boggarts, but memories from those who could emphatically state that they had never heard 'boggart': 'negatives', I stated in my promotional literature, 'are interesting'.[712] Happily, members of the general public took me at my word. I received some 1,100 answers to my boggart enquiries, ranging from a brief sentence to many paragraphs. Of these, about 400 were negatives, people from Boggartdom, born roughly 1920

---

706. Schmid, *Language*, 38–47.
707. Millar *et al.*, *Lexical Variation*, 9–11 and 13–14.
708. Simmelbauer, *Dialect*, 178.
709. The word 'boggart' was ultimately to follow this path.
710. Apart from SED, Orton *et al.*, *Atlas*, L64 and Dewsbury, 'Vanishing', 67–68.
711. Millar, Barras and Bonnici, *Lexical Variation*, 3.
712. BC; I thank John Billingsley for this insight.

to 1970, saying that they were *not* familiar with boggarts. Apart from a handful of answers (from Lincolnshire, from southern England, and some very few locations abroad), all responses, positive and negative, came from the Northwest of England.[713] I know of no other study of an English dialect lexeme on this scale, concentrated in one region.

The crucial dynamic in the period 1920–1970 was the decline of regional dialects, into what has been called 'regional Englishes'.[714] With great respect to modern champions of dialect, what we have, in 2022, are, for the most part, geographically based versions of Standard English with different accents rather than with different lexemes and different grammar. In much of Britain, on the other hand, in the nineteenth century, there were county tongues, which were not always immediately comprehensible to English-speaking outsiders. In the Boggart Census, the data for which was collected in 2019, there was little by way of dialect, in terms of how people wrote: the replies were all written primarily in Standard English. But there were frequent references to memories of a world where 'strong' dialects could still be found. 'My dad was also born in Leyland and spoke very broad Lanky.' 'Boggarts were definitely mentioned by people who spoke the dialect, like my Uncle Jim.' Or there was a woman from Siddal in the West Riding who used to recite a boggart poem to her son 'in broad Yorkshire'.[715] A turn to Standard English meant that 'boggart' was less likely to be used: 'I doubt that I'd have heard of such a thing [boggart] at that time. This is because my mother and sister were both educated at the convent school and "talked posh".'[716] Women, it has sometimes been suggested, are more likely than men to conform to a standard form of a language.[717]

Dialect was no guarantee of the presence of boggarts—one grandmother used such Lanky markers as 'thee, thou and tha', 'clempt' and 'skrieking' but never 'boggart'.[718] However, the word 'boggart' was frequently associated with dialect or dialect phrases in responses to the Boggart Census. Indeed, dialect emerged in responses in direct quotation. When grown children remembered how they had heard about boggarts from parents and grandparents, they often

---

713. About 95 per cent in terms of word count.

714. Beal, *Regional*, title.

715. BC, Leyland 18 (La); BC, Oldham 10 (La); BC, Siddal 1 (WRY).

716. BC, Littleborough 11 (La).

717. SED, Orton *et al.*, *Atlas*, unnumbered introduction, preferred men to women 'since women seemed in general to encourage the social upgrading of the speech of their families'. For a subtler view from Italy, Dal Negro, *The Decay*, 63–64.

718. BC, Cadishead 1 (La).

remembered in dialect. '"T'boggart'll get you", was a threat to misbehaving children.' 'Owd Georgie Jammy', in a grandmother's story, 'came leathering down t' street, his face as white as a puddin' clout (cloth for rag puddings), shoutin' "do let me in, I've sin a boggart!"'. 'My Granddad used "Yon Boggart in't coal house" to scare me.'[719] There is a sense that sometimes the respondents drop, almost unconsciously, into dialect as they recall their childhood. 'I was born in Whalley in the 1950s, but brought up in Accrington. My Grandfather would often talk about t' boggart.'[720]

Boggart Talkers, Boggart Knowers, and the Boggartless

If dialect was one (perhaps the primary) marker for the use of the word 'boggart', then the population can be usefully broken down into, in boggart terms, three categories. There are those who use 'boggart' in conversation: 'the boggart talkers'. There are those who understand or at least are familiar with the word 'boggart' but who do not use it: 'the boggart knowers'. There are then those who did not understand 'boggart' and so did not use the word: 'the boggartless'. Working backwards through this list, the boggartless included those who are confidently ignorant. 'Born in Ashton in 1940 and left in 1966 and I have never heard the word "Boggart"'; 'Born and brought up in the 1940s, 1950s in High Bentham. I too have never heard the word "boggart" in any context.'[721] Other times, ignorance had to be carefully deduced, memory itself not being trusted. One thoughtful woman from near Huddersfield remembers that she visited Boggard Ing in the 1940s: 'We never felt anything spooky about the farm or its fields, and as children we never questioned the name; to us it just sounded boggy. This implies that the word "boggard" was meaningless to us youngsters.'[722]

Then occasionally there are those who are caught between 'the boggartless' and the 'boggart knowers'. They did once understand 'boggart' but the word has long since rusted up in their memory. 'My Mum', wrote a Fleetwood woman, who had grown up in the 1960s, 'used [boggart] if I was maybe a bit cheeky etc. I heard her use it quite a lot, but it was long forgotten until I read your post!'[723] 'I never heard the word "boggart", bogey man yes, boggart no', wrote one woman from Wigan who had also grown up in the

---

719. BC, Pendle 2 (La); BC, Milnrow 6 (La); BC, Great Harwood 7 (La).
720. BC, Whalley 1 (La).
721. BC, Ashton-Under-Lyne 8 (La); BC, Bentham 3 (La).
722. BC, Berry Brow 1 (WRY).
723. BC, Fleetwood 1 (La).

1960s. But then, later in the conversation, perhaps spurred by other answers
on social media, she changed her mind: 'Just remembered that my dad used
to say, "That horse has taken boggarts". Meaning the horse has run off.'[724]
Maybe the shock of a horse bolting and a strange expression from her father
had fixed the word somewhere deep in her unconscious. Consider also this
memory from the 1970s: 'New Mills … Long hair just got out of bed, when
I came in [Mum said] … "eh up the Boggart returns". It never crossed my
mind to wonder what a Boggart was. It wasn't til I saw this. It jogged my
memory.'[725]

The 'boggart knowers' typically restrict the word in their descriptions to
the language and habits of previous generations. This comes from a woman
born in Accrington in 1962:

> I'm familiar with the word 'boggart' and remembering hearing
> some older Accringtonians use it when I was growing up. But it
> was certainly a rare word … My mother, who grew up in Clitheroe
> in the 1930s and 1940s, used to recall a story of when she and
> her friends dressed as ghosts and a neighbour exclaimed: 'Eeeeh
> boggarts!'[726]

Here the word 'boggart' seems to have run its course in the individual's life.
It was heard occasionally in the respondent's childhood, not least because it
is fixed in direct speech in an anecdote of her mother. But it is unlikely, on
this evidence, that she herself ever uses the word. Here, on the other hand,
is a Nelson memory from a woman who grew up in the 1950s:

> The word 'boggart' was used in our house, all through my child-
> hood, in the same way as 'bogeyman'. In fact, I always thought
> that the bogey part was a shortening of 'boggart' … but by the
> time my three sons were born, in the late 1970s and early 1980s,
> I never heard the term 'boggart' used, only 'bogeyman'.[727]

---

724. BC, Wigan 3 (La).
725. BC, New Mills 14 (De).
726. BC, Accrington 11 (La).
727. BC, Nelson 3 (La).

There are also cases where family members presumed that parents or grand-parents had invented 'boggart', suggesting that they never heard the word outside their own houses:

> My dad has used the word 'boggart' for as long as I can remember when hearing or seeing something he couldn't identify. I just thought it was a word he'd made up.[728]

Another interesting development, thinking of this 'hearing or seeing some-thing he couldn't identify' comment, is when 'boggart' is used without any knowledge of its supernatural roots. Consider 'to take boggart', typically used of a panicked horse: the original notion was that a boggart had spooked the horse. This phrase has a fascinating history and was easily adapted to many circumstances (see p. 245). Indeed, as horses disappeared from everyday life, its survival as a phrase depended on its ability to adapt. One respondent from Nelson recollected, 'I'll have heard the word "Boggart" used in the context of "She were off at Boggart to the shop before it closed". So I took that to mean running fast. This was in the 1940s.'[729] The man in question clearly had no idea that 'boggart' had a supernatural background, something true of another Nelson respondent: 'I grew up in Nelson in the 1940s/1950s. If anyone was running as fast as they could, they were said to be off at Boggart.'[730] When asked what a boggart was, the same respondent answered: 'Just someone going fast. We had so many sayings in those days, you just seemed to copy off your mum and dad and grandma and granddad.' Take another Nelson memory—'taking boggart' to mean running is evidently well established in the town:

> Lived in Nelson from 1957 to 1986. Bogart meant speeding off with the wind behind you, possibly fear. Running it. Moving very fast ... as a child you understood that it was not normal as in normal human behaviour. There was a mystery attached to it as you only said 'I ran like Boggart' if you were scared.[731]

---

728. BC, Leyland 16 (La); see also Chorley 1 (La).
729. BC, Nelson 6 (La).
730. BC, Nelson 8 (La).
731. BC, Nelson 9 (La).

That 'if you were scared' is the closest these comments came to giving a supernatural explanation to the Nelson runners.

Turning now to 'boggart talkers', those who used boggart in conversation, there are some heartening examples where 'boggart' is clearly still employed across the generations and with a supernatural sense. This is from a Preesall woman living on a farm, born 1973. She has even brought a southern husband into her 'boggart' circle, although note that the frequent use of 'boggart' is placed in the past:

> Hasn't died out in my family ... and boggart is still a word I hear when family is about. I was born and bred Over Wyre in Preesall and lived on a farm till I was twelve. Youngest of three daughters, others are sixty-three and fifty-six. Boggarts were under your bed or at the back of the barn and messed with things in mischief ... And my parents (still alive at eighty-three and eighty) used it all the time. There's also the saying 'there's no bigger boggart than yourself' that I still say now to my kids. Even my southern husband knows what a boggart is after being married for sixteen years![732]

Here is an equivalent memory from Over Wyre. The reference again to a farm, i.e. a rural setting, might be important. The self-confident 'all over Lancashire' is as magnificent as it is wrong, but it gives a sense of how deeply 'boggart' is embedded in this particular family's vocabulary. Interesting also is the traditional definition of boggart as a ghost (see p. 6):

> I grew up in Out Rawcliffe in the 1960s/1970s and yes the word 'bogart' was often used in and around our very old farmhouse, usually to try and keep us kids out of mischief. 'Don't go in there, Boggarts will get thee!' etc etc. Anything that was a bit scary was always down to boggarts, chuckle. I'm from a very big Over Wyre family and I think everyone young and old will still know what a Boggart was. I would say boggarts are still going strong all over Lancashire. To us they were another word for ghosts.[733]

---

732. BC, Preesall 4 (La).
733. BC, Out Rawcliffe 2 (La).

Even more impressive, in their way, are some comments from Longridge near Preston (something of a boggart stronghold). These comments suggest the easy daily use of 'boggart' in conversation in an extended community. Consider this incredulous reply to an inquiry about the old Lancashire word 'boggart': 'We use the word "boggart" all the time! I think "Susan" might have also used it on the odd occasion.' 'Susan' at this point chipped in, 'I used it yesterday at work in fact!'[734]

Later, in the same stream of answers on a Longridge community group on Facebook, another woman writes that she '[u]sed [boggart] growing in the 1970s'. She then explains that she had also resorted to it in the previous days as an insult for a 'scruffy boggert', who had been fly-tipping 'up Chapel Hill'.[735] If 'boggart' is being used in a given community, employed in chit-chat at work, and spat out at a fly-tipper, then we should assume that the word is in excellent health there.

Factors in Survival

What are the factors that determine whether a given person is a 'boggart talker', a 'boggart knower', or 'boggartless'. A crucial point is age. Indeed, it will be clear from reading the previous paragraphs that the shift is often generational. It can be summed up in this glum exchange from Rochdale: 'Did your parents and grandparents use the word [boggart]?' 'Yes.' 'Do your children, nephews and nieces use it?' 'No.'[736] Sometimes respondents can fix the death of the word on a human death:

> I was born in 1944 and my granddad used to use the phrase 'don't do that the boggart will get you' or 'don't go in there the boggart [is] in there'. My dad didn't really use the phrase after granddad died. The saying fizzled out in our family, but [I] can still hear him saying that.[737]

It is certainly striking that respondents often heard of the word from their grandparents rather than their parents.

---

734. BC, Longridge 5 (La): 'Susan': invented name.
735. BC, Longridge 9 (La).
736. BC, Rochdale 1 (La).
737. BC, Blackburn 31 (La).

> My Wigan grandparents ... mentioned boggarts when we were
> young: it would have been anything from 1964 to 1975 when they
> chastised us for cheekiness: 'tha'r a boggart!' and even 'tha'r a
> marsh boggart!' Once we'd stopped laughing we begged to know
> what a boggart was, or the difference between ordinary boggarts
> or marsh boggarts but I don't remember getting a description![738]

If a word, particularly in a telling off, is greeted with hilarity in this way then
it is less likely to be reproduced. How did the grandparents, we might ask,
feel about this treasured threat being ridiculed? The grandchildren, from this
point on, used the word 'boggart' among themselves as a joke word.

Another important factor is the rural–urban divide. Folklore certainly exists
in cities—something perhaps not sufficiently appreciated by previous generations of western folklorists who only turned to urban folklore in the 1970s.[739]
But folklore continuity is more difficult in an urban setting. The landscape of
cities is more liable to change than the landscape of rural communities; not
just buildings but streets disappear, particularly in periods of expansion.[740]
Then, there is usually much greater population turnover in cities than in rural
areas and populations are more likely to arrive from further away.[741] These
forms of physical and demographic dislocation—things that make 'fermenting'
cities so exciting to live and work in—naturally have consequences for folklore,
chief among them is that the continuity of ideas starts to break down. A tradition linked to a building or a name becomes more difficult if the building and
name disappears and if the people who remember the name move elsewhere.[742]

A useful example here might be Bradford, the city just to the south of Esholt
and its Boggard House, and a place the boggart ruled in the nineteenth century.
In 1801, Bradford had a modest population of around 6,000 inhabitants and by

---

738. BC, Aspull 1 (La).

739. Smidchens, 'Urban Folklore'.

740. Bell, *Magical Imagination*, 227–59.

741. Dégh and Vázsonyi's 'conduit theory', usefully summarized in Dégh, 'Conduit', suggests that
folklore ideas are passed easily in culturally and socially stable environments. When there is social
and cultural change, folklore ideas die or they are adapted to new social and cultural realities.
For an example of a nineteenth-century conduit failing in the face of new ideas, take the Irish
servant (with non-Lancashire ideas) in Blackpool who denied that a boggart was a ghost:
'Superstition in the Fylde' (1857), 'because a ghost never did or could appear after twelve o'
clock at night'. Bell, *Magical Imagination*, 196–97 points out how population turnover changed
from area to area within a city.

742. For a contrary view, Bell, *Magical Imagination*, 234–35. I don't doubt, incidentally, the possibility
of creating urban memory maps, just the ability to keep the map through time as so much in the
physical geography of the city changes.

1851 some 100,000. In 1897 when the town was, by royal decree, made into a city there were some 200,000 souls living there. As of 2021 about 350,000 dwell in Bradford.[743] These jumps in population could not, of course, be supplied solely by the surrounding countryside. Bradford had an influx of German and Irish migrants in the nineteenth century.[744] Then, in the postwar period, tens of thousands of migrants came from the Indian subcontinent. Indicative of this is the fact that about a quarter of modern Bradfordians are Muslim.[745] These kinds of changes had fascinating consequences for Bradford's folklore. But this level of population turnover hardly favours the survival of such nineteenth-century Bradford boggarts as Fair Becca or the Paper Hall Boggart.[746] It is not that boggarts and cities cannot coexist—boggart-lore was demonstrably found in cities in the nineteenth century. The issue is rather that cities are not good places for boggart memory.[747]

For us, in the 2020s, it is perhaps uncomfortable to look at questions of population continuity but I would submit that for a folklorist, it is necessary. In determining the likelihood that a given person or family would use 'boggart' in conversation, their background clearly mattered. We have, for instance, in the Boggart Census a family from Cornwall, who in 2019, still recounted how their father/grandfather, as a child in the 1940s, met a boggart on the moor 'in our ancestral homeland', Lancashire.[748] The story is an entertaining one, but what are the chances that a boggart tale will survive in Cornwall, at least under the name 'boggart'? Clearly the odds will be lower than in Lancashire. Similarly, the make-up of families is important. Indeed, when respondents trouble to describe their genealogies, it is often striking how complicated they are. One Rossendale man, born in the 1960s describes a maternal grandmother from Burnley, paternal grandparents from London,

---

743. Hall, *Bradford*, 92.
744. Ibid., 65–78; for a vivid episode, Wright, *Life*, I, 57.
745. https://www.bradford.gov.uk/open-data/our-datasets/population/ [accessed 7 January 2020], numbers for 2017.
746. Fieldhouse, *Old Bradford*, 82–91.
747. There are presumably two forms of dislocation in folklore belief systems. In the first, less radical form, folklore details are lost (names of boggarts, boggart stories), but a folklore system (boggart-lore) survives. In the second, more radical form, the folklore system itself is adapted: boggart-lore is replaced with another supernatural system. One might imagine that a growing Lancashire mill town in the nineteenth century, relying on the populations of surrounding parishes and shires, experienced the first. On the other hand, a large city like Bradford, which drew on populations from far outside Bradford, experienced the second. Consider this comment from the BC, Liverpool 8 (La) on the failure of boggarts to survive in that city: 'You must know that Liverpool is really not part of "old Lancashire", but more Irish, Welsh and Scots etc mixture'.
748. BC, Bacup 2 (La).

and wife and parents-in-law from Colne.[749] These different voices from different regions will certainly, as he himself acknowledged, have altered the boggart equation.

Many respondents actively boast of having deep roots in a given area: they feel that this gives them more authority. 'I grew up in Scarisbrick, born 1970. My granddad and my nan were both born there in the early 1900s; the family goes back generations in Scarisbrick, Halsall, Rufford.' 'The whole family was Todmorden born for about three generations.' Grandparents 'were born in Keighley in the early 1900s and their ancestry remains within a ten mile radius of Keighley back to the beginning of the 1600s'.[750] Sometimes there is even an enjoyable element of one-upmanship. When one respondent found herself in a minority in her hometown in remembering boggarts, she was firm that this was because her family had been there longer. 'My Dad came from an old Winteringham Family going back several hundred years. Strange that I saw someone else around my age had never heard of them [boggarts] but I know her father was not a local.'[751] Population continuity— something, until the 1980s, usually more assured in the countryside—makes a difference in the transmission of folklore beliefs, not least because it suggests relative isolation.

That the rural–urban divide had an influence on boggart belief is the view of several respondents in the Boggart Census. There seems to be the idea that boggarts are more of a country thing. 'I always thought [boggart] was just a country name', writes a man who grew up in Leyland in the 1940s; his mother had been from Blackburn, giving him perhaps a wider perspective. 'In my mind I associate boggarts with more of a rural area, of a person or being who lives in or around marshland.' 'I think I was a teenager before I heard of boggarts and [I] thought of them as being in the rural areas.' 'For me a Boggart is a slightly malevolent rural dwarf.' 'I grew up in a town', writes a Prestonian who was terrified by his parents with the bogey man in the 1950s, 'but it was more country people used "boggart"'. A contemporary from Irlam writes of how she was terrified with boggart stories by her country cousin, who lived on a farm on Chat Moss.[752] Of course, just because these loosely held ideas exist does not mean that they are right. Compare with the absolutely fallacious notion, frequently found in the Boggart Census, that boggarts had something

---

749. BC, Rossendale 1 (La).
750. BC, Scarisbrick 2 (La); BC, Todmorden 3 (WRY); BC, Haworth 1 (WRY).
751. BC, Winteringham 5 (Li).
752. BC, Leyland 15 (La); BC, Great Harwood 4 (La); BC, Blackburn 7 (La); BC, Lancaster 1 (La); BC, Preston 3 (La); BC, Irlam 1 (La).

to do with Ireland and the Irish (see n. 141). But such ideas are, nonetheless, worth considering.

The Boggart Census depended on respondents themselves saying where they had grown up and, for very understandable reasons, respondents (the majority of whom were approached by a complete stranger on social media) did not give precise details. They talked, for the most part, of towns and cities, not streets and parishes. However, there is the suspicion that when boggarts survived in cities and large towns, they were more likely to do so on the rural outskirts than in the city centres where population change was often more rapid. Again, I will give a concrete example: Warrington, a community of some 200,000 on the Cheshire–Lancashire border. Warrington has little folklore writing and little writing about supernatural traditions; it is difficult therefore to cross-reference the Boggart Census for the town with anything else.[753] Fortunately eighteen people from Warrington responded to questions about boggarts.

Of these eighteen, four had come into contact with traditional boggart-lore: the other fourteen had not heard of boggarts, although they gave some fascinating insights into Warrington folklore; Warrington deserves a special study. Of those four who had come across boggarts, two were from Bewsey on the northern outskirts of the town, and referred to the gully (a wild valley) there and its boggarts. One had heard of boggarts from his grandmother (b. 1912): 'She was originally from the Moore area but lived most of her life in Fearnhead', again on the edge of the town. The final person used the phrase 'crow boggart', comparing friends to scarecrows; no detail is given as to where in Warrington the individual came from, but the suspicion is that there was some contact with the surrounding countryside.[754] There is also the record of a Shropshire family who had come from Warrington and who took the boggarts away with them. The mother and father (a gamekeeper) came from, respectively, Latchford and Orford in Warrington, both also on the outskirts of the town.[755] With only rather general locations being given, it is not possible to analyse a single community in geographical terms. But we can make educated guesses of the type given here.

Beyond age and the rural–urban divide there will have been other factors that would be worth measuring.[756] It would have been particularly interesting

---

753. Wally Barnes has written a series of enjoyable books about frightening tales of 'Old Warrington', e.g. *Ghosts*, which are well known in the town, BC, Warrington 7 (La) and Warrington 11 (La). These, though, are more, I am told, fiction than folklore.

754. BC, Warrington 13; 15; 14 and 16 (La).

755. BC, Shropshire 1 (Oth).

756. Millar *et al.*, *Lexical Variation*, 164–69 look at geography, age and gender. I did not examine gender, although I was intrigued by BC, Little Lever 1 (La): boggart 'was a term that was mostly

to learn about parents' jobs and so get some sense of social class. Here, too, there are chance references to parents being weavers, teachers, farmers, and labourers, but nothing that allows for any kind of systematic survey.[757] It would, likewise, be interesting to establish the education level of the respondent, which is, for the mid twentieth century, a proxy for class. For both these issues, the Boggart Census proved inadequate: those who wrote about their boggart memories did not feel like sharing these kinds of details in a semi-public forum. Perhaps it will be possible in the future to pick one particularly promising north-western community and carry out a series of face-to-face boggart interviews there, enquiring, in person and with sensitivity, into these more delicate points of background.[758] Here, though, we only acknowledge that there are many unanswered questions.

Mapping Boggart Death

How do we judge the moment of boggart death in a given community? I would suggest that it comes when there are no longer 'boggart talkers'. 'Boggart knowers' are vital for research, but these individuals hardly constitute a community in which the word exists in any useful sense. Again, with slight data of the kind offered by the Boggart Census even an estimate of this kind of 'death'—the end of conversations about boggarts—is impossible to establish. But looked at community by community, interesting results do emerge. While organizing the census results, I broke down the 1,100 entries geographically. I put them into the pre-1974 counties as chapters, then ordered the individual chapters alphabetically by town, village, or parish. Even a flick through the different chapters shows that there are areas where boggart traditions are all but non-existent.

Nineteen responses came from Bradford, and not one gives the definite use of the word 'boggart' with a traditional supernatural sense; yet it was the Bradford region that gave us our first comic boggart story and whose countryside was teeming with boggarts in the nineteenth century.[759] The closest was the bizarre memory of one respondent about his father who 'referred to the white dot that appeared in the middle of the telly when it was turned off

---

used by the women in the family'. This was the only gender-specific comment in BC. Of course, much else could be deduced.

757. See, e.g., BC, Rochdale 6 (La) (weaver), Burnley 4 (La) (teacher).

758. Ceri Houlbrook carried out such face-to-face interviews for her writing on Boggart Hole Clough, Houlbrook, 'The Suburban Boggart' (thesis).

759. *The Beauties*, III, 94; Fieldhouse, *Old Bradford*, 82–91.

as "a Boggart" in the 1950s'![760] I suspect that the word 'boggart' had all but disappeared by the time television sets were arriving in the city in significant numbers. No wonder that the boggard of Elsholt's Boggard House (just to the north of Bradford) was something of a mystery by the postwar period. There are similarly disappointing results for other large urban centres in the Northwest, including Leeds, Liverpool (indeed all of Merseyside), and, to some extent, Sheffield. The rural–urban division seems to matter, then, with the exception of Manchester, which we will examine later in the chapter.

There are other communities where 'boggart' clearly survived until the relatively late twentieth century, and in some parts of those communities into the 2020s. As one Chorley woman, born in the early 1940s, charmingly put it: '"Boggerts" was used a lot in my childhood ... I've been known to say [boggart] to this day!'[761] Seventeen responses came, for instance from New Mills on the Cheshire–Derbyshire border. Of these, sixteen had evidence of supernatural boggart beliefs, or associated phrases.[762] Eleven responses came from the small town of Longridge (noted before for references to boggarts at work and a 'scruffy boggert' fly-tipping). Nine of these included references to boggarts in local families and traditions; the other two respondents knew what boggarts were but had not grown up with them.[763] These communities could realistically claim that the word 'boggart' had never died there.

Most communities stood, of course, somewhere in between the boggartless cities and the more conservative boggart strongholds like New Mills and Longridge and offer contradictory accounts. I have been particularly struck by the area I grew up in, the upper Calder Valley. A number of my peers and I are convinced that we did not encounter the word when we were children in the late 1970s and the 1980s.[764] But John Billingsley, a prominent West Riding folklorist who lives there, claims that the word was used across the generations in the same period—he arrived, as a young adult, in 1975.[765] We

---

760. BC, Bradford 7 (WRY).

761. BC, Chorley 2 (La).

762. See BC, New Mills (De) 1–17.

763. See BC, Longridge (La) 1–11.

764. BC, Hebden Bridge 1 (WRY); BC, Hebden Bridge 2 (WRY), two classmates, both born in 1973.

765. Pers. Comm. July 2019. John had taken exception to something I had published on the decline of boggarts and gently took me to task: 'I guess you know from your own experience that "boggart" has been in use locally here in upper Calderdale in the time I've lived here (since 1975), by a mixture of generations.' In a subsequent email, John recalls: 'You've read my Folk Tales books [see Bibliography], so you'll know that through the late 70s, and to a declining extent in the 1990s, I heard most of the tales in the books orally, not through documentary sources. In other words, the stories were still being remembered and passed on—and I suspect boggart references went along with that sort of thing. But from the mid-90s on, I began hearing fewer and fewer

are all, doubtless, right: different circles of 'boggart talkers', 'knowers', and 'the boggartless' will have coexisted. The Boggart Census offers witnesses from the area for whom the word 'boggart' had died out as early as the 1950s, and others for whom 'boggart' survived into the 1990s.[766] Boggart death is, on this evidence, messy: not a bang but a long, drawn-out whimper. Somewhere, in the brambles and bracken, on the beautiful banks of the Calder, there is the grave of the last local boggart and it reads 'obit *c.*1970—give or take thirty years'.

How can we use this data to put survival on a map? The survey has unfortunately very uneven coverage. Thinking of the examples I gave before, there were: nineteen responses from Bradford with a population of about 350,000; and seventeen responses from New Mills with a population of some 12,000. I decided, therefore, to use a very rough initial measure, which is given in Figure 33. I limited myself, firstly, to those born between 1920 and 1970, although some born later had also answered the questionnaire. Secondly, I included as positive answers only those that concerned traditional boggarts or associated language (as opposed to, say, boggart games played in the Brownies or childhood glimpses of boggarts in fantasy fiction).[767] I then divided communities into four groups: (i) those where more than three individuals had known of traditional boggarts; (ii) those where more than three had not known of traditional boggarts; (iii) those where at least three individuals had known of traditional boggarts and where three had not (in the same community); and (iv) those where none of these three conditions was met—usually there were too few responses. Finally, I mapped the first three onto a map of Boggartdom.[768]

local tales as I wandered about, and that was when I decided the books needed to be written. Of course, in the 90s that was when the demographic and economic balance of the upper Calder valley shifted not necessarily to the advantage of local people—becoming less able to afford property or rents, or indeed to find local jobs ... the communities who shared the stories were displaced.'

766. BC, Heptonstall 1 (WRY); Midgley 1 (WRY); Mytholmroyd 2 (WRY); Sharneyford 1 (WRY); Todmorden 7 (WRY). The survival of boggart-lore in Todmorden is, in a very small sample, striking. Holly Elsdon suggests to me, pers. comm. 18 October 2019, that this might be the result of less population turnover there. There is, frustratingly, next to no boggart writing from the area prior to the 1990s to give context. For a rare exception: Hopkins, *Ghosts*, 108–20.

767. I review contemporary boggart-lore in the next chapter.

768. *Positive*: Accrington; Aspull; Atherton; Bacup; Banks; Billinge; Blackley; Blackpool; Burnley; Bury; Chorley; Clitheroe; Collyhurst; Colne; Crumpsall; Euxton; Great Harwood; Haslingden; Hayfield; Hazel Grove; Heywood; Leyland; Littleborough; Longridge; Lumb; Manchester; Middleton; Milnrow; Moston; Nelson; New Mills; Newhey; Oldham; Openshaw; Penwortham; Pilling; Preesall; Rawtenstall; Rochdale; Rossendale; Saddleworth; Salford; Skelmersdale; Slaithwaite; Smallbridge; Smithy Bridge; Thornton-Cleverley; Todmorden; Wardle; Whitefield. *Mixed*: Ashton; Blackburn; Burscough; Droylsden; Edgworth; Preston; Prestwich; Sheffield;

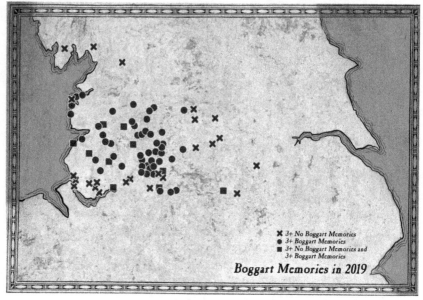

Figure 33: Boggart Memories in 2019.

The patterning on the map justifies this approach, I think. In the 1800s, all the symbols would have fallen within Boggartdom. In the 2020s, the southern edges of Lancashire and northern Cheshire have no significant living memory of boggarts. These correspond to a belt of highly urbanized and (previously at least) highly industrialized communities. The important exception to this rule is the Greater Manchester area—one of the most urbanized parts of Western Europe. Here, for reasons we will discuss further on, the boggart remained a crucial part of local folklore, especially among children. The boggart was successful, too, in the more rural parts of central and northern Lancashire on both sides of the Ribble. The lack of either negatives or positives in the Lancaster area and in 'Lancashire beyond the Sands' (the north of the map) perhaps reflects the fact that this was, in the nineteenth century, the area where the boggart competed with the dobbie (see pp. 71–75). It may also be a question of failure on my part to collect enough data from these areas. Another striking point was the boggart's death in most of the West Riding. This includes very urban areas (like Bradford and Leeds), but also far more rural areas, such as Calderdale and Kirklees.

Southport; Stockport; Warrington; Wigan. *Negative*: Almondbury; Audenshaw; Baildon; Bentham; Bootle; Bradford; Cadishead; Cheadle; Cronton; Doncaster; Fleetwood; Huyton; Hyde; Irlam; Kirkdale; Leeds; Liverpool; Netherton; Rainhill; Storth; Swallownest; Ulverston; Wakefield; Widnes.

A second figure offers a slightly different approach to mapping boggarts in the mid to late twentieth century. Here I have placed the twenty-five instances from the Boggart Census where respondents referred to a named local boggart; a concept which I introduced earlier (see p. 18).[769] Remarkably, it was still possible in 2019 to record a number of these named boggarts, including such luminaries as Ogden Boggart and Staining Boggart. As I argue in Chapters 1 and 3, the existence of a supernatural personal name suggests that there is a shared communal tradition. One girl in the 1980s, for instance, heard the 'rumour' (a suggestive word) that Aughton Boggart lived in a barn on her farm; the Aughton Boggart clearly enjoyed some kind of celebrity status in the village.[770] In other instances we have not a shared communal tradition, but the memory of one. Take the Pall Mall Boggart, which was described to a Blackburn child in the 1960s by his father who had heard it in turn from his mother when he was a child (probably in the 1930s).[771] This is very likely a nineteenth-century Blackburn monster: the Pell Mell Boggart, who has been unhappily assimilated to a London Monopoly address.[772]

The pattern in Figure 34 is very similar to that seen in Figure 33. The heavily urbanized parts of northern Cheshire and south Lancashire are largely lacking boggarts with personal names, save in Greater Manchester (again, we will look at Manchester in the next pages). Audenshaw and Openshaw are the other Greater Manchester sites with named boggarts, both connected, interestingly, to water.[773] The one Merseyside example here is 'the boggart of Cherry Lane in Walton', although this bogie may be confused with another Walton.[774] There is also the relative absence of named boggarts from the West Riding, something which once more corresponds to Figure 33. Indeed, the only named Yorkshire boggart is the Rag Hole or Raggle Boggart from Ogden. Unfortunately for the honour of the West Riding, this boggart, too, might be based on a misunderstanding.[775]

---

769. BC, Aspull 3 (La); Audenshaw 1 (La); Aughton 1 (La); Aughton 2 (La); Barnoldswick 4 (WRY); Blackburn 14 (La); Blackrod 2 (La); Chorley 5 (La); Chorley 7 (La); Clayton-Le-Moores 2 (La); Euxton 11 (La); Littleborough 1 (La); Littleborough 20 (La); Newhey 2 (La); Ogden 3 (WRY); Openshaw 1 (La); Preesall 5 (La); Rishton 2 (La); Stalmine 1 (La); Thornton-Cleveley 1 (La); Walton 2 (La); Walton-Le-Dale 1 (La); Weeton 1 (La); Whittingham 1 (La); Whitworth 1 (La).

770. BC, Aughton 1 (La).

771. BC, Blackburn 14 (La).

772. For the Pell Mell Boggart, Bill-o'-Jacks, 'Bits'; Young, 'Dialect', 9.

773. BC, Audenshaw 1 (La); Openshaw 1 (La).

774. BC, Walton 2 (La); for doubts, Liverpool 9 (La).

775. BC, Ogden 3 (WRY). Compare Newhey 1 (La): 'I used to say "Raggle Boggart". Think it may mean a ghostly shape?'. I worry that Ogden 3 (WRY) is actually giving a (to me) obscure boggart idiom here. Note 'raggil', a dialect word in Cheshire, Lancashire and Yorkshire, meant: Wright,

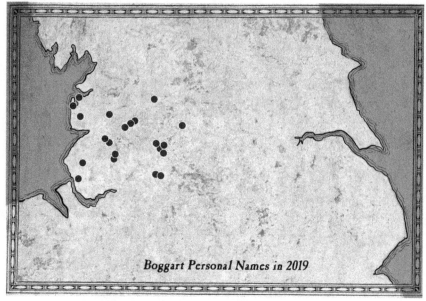

Figure 34: Boggart Personal Names in 2019.

These two maps, with their similar results, suggest that the boundaries of Boggartdom have narrowed dramatically since 1900. I say this because the results here do not reflect the reality in the 2020s. Rather, they are based on twenty-first century memories of an interwar or postwar reality. Think again of the Pall Mall boggart in Blackburn which was based on a conversation between a mother and son before the Second World War and which has been passed on in oral tradition. Most of the individual records—with the possible exception of the boggart or boggarts of Boggart Hole Clough, more of which in the next section—have boggart traditions set in the past. As such, these maps, which reveal so clearly the ending of boggart traditions on Merseyside and in south Lancashire and north Cheshire, relate to a mid twentieth-century reality rather than the situation as it is in the 2020s. Indeed, Boggartdom in 2019 would be Greater Manchester and an archipelago of tiny rural islands on the map of the Northwest: Longridge, New Mills, and a sprinkling of other boggarted communities.

Dialect Dictionary, V, 14 'A rascal, scoundrel, worthless vagabound; a careless or mischievous person'.

Main Entrance, Boggart Hole Clough. Williams, Post Office, Barnes Green.

Figure 35: Main Entrance, Boggart Hole Clough (Blackley, Manchester).
Edwardian postcard.

The Charisma of Boggart Hole Clough

In the previous section I made the uncontroversial suggestion that it is
more likely that boggart-lore will survive in the countryside than in cities;
and also explored the more difficult point that population continuity may
be an issue in folklore survival. However, in the Northwest, there is one
striking exception to these rules: Manchester. In Greater Manchester, as
Figures 33 and 34 suggest, boggart-lore hurtled past the Second World
War. Indeed, in some senses, boggart-lore has a brighter future in Gorton
and Moss Side than in any other part of Britain, although we will see that
this boggart-lore is not, in any sense, 'Victorian'. Why? The Boggart Census
suggests that the answer is a small park within the conurbation, Boggart
Hole Clough. Indeed, the Boggart Census shows that Boggart Hole Clough
is a boggart Mecca, the central focus of a faith that stretches far beyond
the city.

Boggart Hole Clough is a park bordering what were once the villages of
Blackley and Moston to the north of Manchester city centre. These villages
were sucked into Manchester in the early twentieth century. But happily, in
the 1890s, the Clough was bought in parcels by Manchester City council and
was preserved. It covers some 200 acres and is on the border between two
parishes; something that probably gave it a supernatural cachet in centuries
past. In the mid nineteenth century, the Clough was already celebrated by

writers trying to escape the smog and stress of the city centre.[776] It remained
a place of escape and adventure over subsequent decades and, indeed, remains
so in the 2020s: an island of green in a sea of red and grey roofs. However,
it also became famous in the Victorian and Edwardian periods for large public
meetings: Emmeline Pankhurst and Keir Hardie spoke there in 1896.[777] The
Clough was used, too, as a place for various sporting events and this likewise
meant that its name was repeated in the media. These speeches and races are
also part of the story, as they helped, usually via newspapers, to fix the name
in the public imagination.

'Boggart Hole Clough is', one respondent to the Boggart Census wrote, 'a
grand northern placename'.[778] The 'hole' is, as we saw in Chapter 4, a reference
to the lair of the boggart. In most of Lancashire, a Boggart Hole was a small,
wooded valley or a clough and, in fact, the name Boggart Hole Clough is, as
is the case with many place-names, pleonastic: the 'Clough' is redundant.[779]
As the twentieth century rolled on and as the word 'boggart' became less well
known in Lancashire, the name began to be misunderstood. Some gems
included 'Bucket Ho Clough' and 'Bucket o Clough'.[780] But the lesson of
Boggard House in Esholt is that place-names demand an explanation. A name
with the prestige of Boggart Hole Clough meant that 'boggarts' were a subject
of conversation within the conurbation and beyond. In fact, it is extraordinary
just how often Boggart Hole Clough was brought up in the Boggart Census.

In Figures 36 and 37, I show mentions of the three most popular north-
western boggart landmarks.[781] In Figure 36, I map mentions of Boggart Hole

---

776. Young, 'Boggart Hole Clough'.

777. Bartley, *Emmeline*, 58.

778. Colne 3 (La).

779. Pleonastic names usually occur when a word is no longer understood, which would be strange
for the nineteenth century. There are several Boggart Holes and Boggart Cloughs in the Northwest,
see pp. 98–103. It is just possible that the 'hole' referred to something within the clough: a hollow
perhaps or dell—there are no caves there.

780. BC, Collyhurst 3 (La); Collyhurst 6 (La).

781. All references to BC. *Clegg Hall Boggart*: Hollingworth 1 (La); Littleborough 1 (La); Milnrow
1 (La); Ogden 3 (WRY); Prestwich 6 (La); Smallbridge 2 (La); Smithy Bridge 1 (La); Wardle 3
(La). *Boggart Treacle Miners*: Accrington 14 (La); Blackpool 7 (La); Burnley 11 (La); Burscough 1
(La); Clitheroe 2 (La); Colne 2 (La); Euxton 7 (La); Helmshore 2 (La); Pendle 1 (La). *Boggart
Hole Clough*: Accrington 1 (La); Almondbury 7 (WRY); Ashton-Under-Lyne 2 (La); Atherton 3
(La); Blackburn 19 (La); Blackley 1 (La); Bolton 1 (La); Bury 1 (La); Cadishead 8 (La); Chorlton
1 (La); Collyhurst 1 (La); Colne 3 (La); Conisbrough 2 (WRY); Crumpsall 1 (La); Droylsden
1 (La); Edgworth 4 (La); Failsworth 2 (La); Fallowfield 1 (La); Greenfield 1 (WRY); Harpurhey 1
(La); Hazel Grove 4 (Ch); Heywood 1 (La); Hyde 4 (Ch); Irlam 2 (La); Kinder 1 (De); Littleborough
11 (La); Longridge 10 (La); Manchester 1 (La); Middleton 1 (La); Miles Platting 1 (La); Milnrow
1 (La); Moston 1 (La); Nelson 5 (La); Oldham 1 (La); Openshaw 5 (La); Prestwich 1 (La);

Clough among respondents to the Boggart Census. In Figure 37, I have put, as a point of comparison, two other popular boggart sites. Firstly, there is Clegg Hall, home of Clegg Hall Boggart (by some accounts two murdered boys and according to others, their murderer), by far the most popular named boggart in 2019. Secondly, I have included all references to treacle mining, a pre-war comic folklore tradition associated with Sabden in Pendle.[782] It is sometimes said, although I suspect that this tradition came later, that *boggarts* mined the treacle reserves under the village; a distinction therefore needs to be made between treacle mining and boggart treacle miners. In the 1990s, boggart treacle miner dolls were sold (Figure 38); in 1996 and 1997, a cartoon about the treacle miners, *The Treacle People*, was broadcast nationally in the UK; and the treacle mines briefly became a tourist attraction (finally closed in 1998).[783]

It will be seen that Clegg Hall Boggart is known in a fairly circumscribed area around Rochdale and Littleborough: Clegg Hall stands almost halfway between these two communities. The boggart treacle miners had a far greater range; one suspects because of visits to the mines and the purchase of cuddly boggarts at the store there. It will be interesting to see whether memories of the boggart treacle miners survive. However, it will be seen that Boggart Hole Clough and its boggart belonged to a much greater area. Unsurprisingly, there are many references from Greater Manchester. However, memories and knowledge of the Clough stretch far beyond the conurbation, up to the west into the Fylde and, in the opposite direction, into the West Riding. Boggart Hole Clough is clearly a much better-known site than either Clegg Hall or the Sabden treacle mines.

And what boggarts were to be found in the Clough! Ceri Houlbrook has explored in a thesis, and subsequently in a number of talks and articles, the folklore of Boggart Hole Clough.[784] I have also, for this book, been able to bring to bear testimonies on the problem from the Boggart Census. What is striking about the folklore here is that it has evolved dramatically away from what we know of the folklore of the park in the early to mid nineteenth century. In the

Rastrick 2 (WRY); Rixton 1 (La); Rochdale 4 (La); Salford 2 (La); Smallbridge 2 (La); Southport 17 (La); Springhead 1 (WRY); Stockport 3 (Ch); Thornton-Cleveley 2 (La); Waterfood 4 (La); Whitefield 1 (La); Widnes 3 (La). Note in the case of multiple references in the same locality, I only included the first.

782. The earliest reference known to me for a treacle mine at Sabden is 1925, 'A Day's Ride', see also Simpson, 'Multi-purpose', 62; note that the subject became a matter of some dispute in a German prisoner-of-war camp in 1942 'Controversy'!

783. 'TV Treacle Mines': I'd be surprised to find any references to boggart treacle miners before the 1980s.

784. Houlbrook, 'The Suburban Boggart' (thesis).

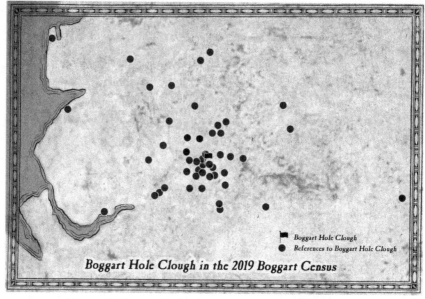

Figure 36: Boggart Hole Clough in the 2019 Boggart Census.

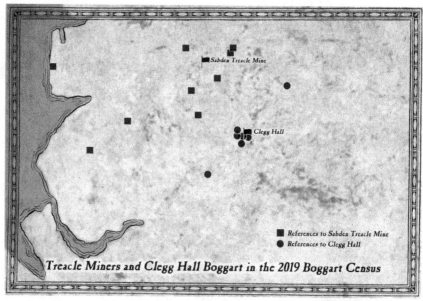

Figure 37: Treacle Miners and Clegg Hall Boggart in the 2019 Boggart Census.

early 1800s, there *seems* to have been a legend about a house spirit connected to a farm in the Clough. There are serious doubts because a Yorkshire story was applied to the traditions of the Clough for what are now obscure reasons.[785] Local folklore in the 2020s, however, is quite different, created by generations of children exploring the meadows and wild woods there. There are many references—not to *the* boggart—but to a tribe of boggarts: something that has absolutely no basis in any kind of Victorian tradition. Consider this man's memories of games in the Clough in the mid twentieth century:

> Obviously as kids it was more of a spooky folklore tale and as kids it was constantly exaggerated and added to in typical kids' fashion. I've lost count of how many of us kids had given an account of how each one of us had actually seen or had an encounter with one of these creatures. Amazingly once one kid had described this little black devil-like pixie creature lurking around the base of a dark hole in an ancient tree in the 'Clough', it was soon agreed by us all that these were indeed Boggarts because we all definitely had seen the same things.[786]

There are also references to a boggart who is buried in the Clough under a rock.[787] As we are primarily dealing with nineteenth-century traditions and their remains in this book, this is not the place to look at these stories for what I refer to in the next chapter as 'the New Boggart'. Ceri Houlbrook will, it is hoped, do so in ever more detail. However, I want to acknowledge these stories because they show goblin-boggarts (albeit not creatures that would have been recognized as such by Victorian Mancunians) in a vital contemporary folklore tradition. After pages in which we have discussed death and dislocation, here is something different.

I doubt very much that boggart-lore of any description would have survived in urban Greater Manchester without the park. If the Clough had been built over in the 1890s, say, Mancunian boggarts would have gone the way of Liverpudlian boggarts and the boggarts of Leeds and Bradford; or, more locally, John Higson's boggarts in nineteenth-century south Manchester.[788] But the park is still there and provides two important points of reference for those

---

785. See pp. 194–98 and Young, 'Boggart Hole Clough', 120–27.
786. BC, Collyhurst 3 (La).
787. See, e.g., BC, Moston 2 (La).
788. Think of Higson's boggarts from Droylsden and Gorton, see pp. 79–85.

growing up in the region. Firstly, it was a name that needed to be explained: 'The first time I heard the term "Boggart" was looking at the map of Blakeley [*sic*] near Middleton, Boggart Hole Clough'.[789] Secondly, it was a public space that was visited by children whose adventures both drew on and elaborated the new boggart traditions. These two factors, taken together, seem to have inoculated Manchester against the virus that wiped out urban boggart memories in so much of the Northwest.

Conclusion

This chapter has looked—with particular reference to the Boggart Census and the 1,100 respondents recorded there—at the death of the word 'boggart' in dialect and, in its traditional sense, in Standard English. The pages here offered a necessarily approximate attempt to show how, and on what timetable, 'boggart' disappeared from most of the Northwest and to hint at some of the reasons why. An important final question is the matter of whether a change in vocabulary meant a change in belief. Did the space that 'boggart' had previously filled disappear with the word, or was 'boggart' simply replaced by another term or terms? To attempt to make some sense of this problem we need to return to the word 'boggart' and the definition that I offered in earlier parts of the book (pp. 4–9). 'Boggart' in the nineteenth century had no specific connotations. It was, rather, a generic word, an umbrella term for a host of solitary and typically terrifying supernatural creatures which haunted the landscapes and the minds of those in Boggartdom. The very existence of that word evokes a galaxy of different entities: demons, ghosts, hobs, shape-changers, water monsters, and will o' the wisps.

It is fascinating that some respondents to the Boggart Census continue to give 'boggart' something like this sense in the twenty-first century. I was particularly struck by the way that Jenny Greenteeth and ghosts were occasionally described as 'boggarts'. 'My father used to tell us that Jinny Greenteeth, the Boggart of Fairfield Wells would come and get us if we didn't behave.'[790] This goes against modern folklore theory (popular and academic), but it is absolutely in line with the boggarts we meet in Victorian texts. Here we have, in fact, a remnant from an older way of looking at the supernatural and one that will, I suspect, disappear in the coming decades. Indeed, it is striking how respondents were often apologetic while giving this kind of antiquated

---

789. BC, Cadishead 8 (La).
790. BC, Audenshaw 1 (La). 'Jinny', note, is frequently used in Lancashire for Jenny Greenteeth.

interpretation, as if they knew that something was 'off': 'it may be a false memory but did mum once describe Jinny Greenteeth who lived down Antley back as a boggart?'[791]

Ultimately no word took the place of 'boggart': there is no convincing term in Standard English apart from perhaps (the related) 'bogie' and even that is playground banter, difficult to use in an adult context. Similar linguistic changes occurred over the rest of northern England as the equivalent terms 'dobbie' and 'boggle' disappeared (pp. 70–76). I would suggest that the loss of these words marked the end of a long-standing supernatural ecosystem: one in which the Victorians and perhaps the Elizabethans had dwelt. Over the space of two world wars, a supernatural folklore taxonomy 'devolved'.[792] What had previously been called a 'boggart' became a black dog, a ghost, or a goblin: the more specific but less charged Standard English terms. Supernatural descriptions were more exact, but lost some of the indeterminate horror that the term 'boggart' (and 'dobbie' and 'boggle') had provided; a shifting terror that could move from form to form, its ambiguity part of its power (see p. 103).

Not only did the general term cease to be necessary, some of the supernatural possibilities it had covered ceased to be credible—once something seems foolish it can no longer frighten—or remained so only among tiny minorities. Who could have written, in around 1920, that spirits might 'appear as ... some outlandish and invincible animal which would fairly have puzzled the most skilful zoologist to have named or classified', as Higson had in 1859?[793] Indeed, I would challenge anyone to find references to shape-changers in England after the First World War. The 'black dog' is the twentieth century's limp attempt to preserve this shape-changing 'horse, hound, hog, bear, fire, at every turn' for traditional British folklore.[794] Demons, too, have died away, save in charismatic Christian circles. Certainly,

---

791. BC, Accrington 8 (La), to which another family member replied: 'I remember Jinny Greenteeth but not the boggart bit'.

792. For devolution in folk taxonomies, Atran and Medin, *Native Mind*, 37–47. Here a generic word, 'boggart', is lost uncovering a series of subcategories.

793. Higson, *Droylsden*, 69.

794. Harte, 'Black Dog Studies', 5–7, note especially 7, 'by 1900 outré demons of this kind [shape-shifters] were not so common'. Just to put this in context, an English supernatural dog (*c.*1200), Stubbs, *Chronica*, IV, 123 appeared in the following way: A woman vomited two black toads, which became two black dogs, which became two asses ('Et exierunt ab ea duo buffones magni e nigri, qui statim conuersi sunt in immensos canes et nigerrimos, et paulo post conuersi sunt in asinos'), which on coming into contact with holy water, vanished into thin air. The black dog no longer has this range. Thanks to Davide Ermacora for the reference. The quotation in the main text is, of course, *A Midsummer Night's Dream* (3, 1). For the black dog more generally: Norman, *Black Dog*; Fanthorpe and Fanthorpe, *Padfoot*; Waldron and Reeve, *Shock*.

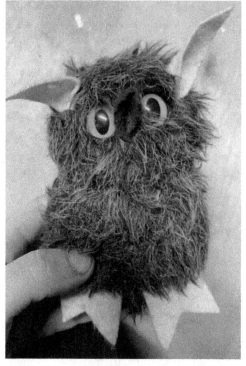

Figure 38: Treacle Mine Boggart.

there have been no recent reports of the Devil turning up to play football as he did at Crawshawbooth in the 1890s.[795] The marsh boggart, will o' the wisp, has had the worst fate of all and has been reduced to methane. Did these changes in the 'wiring' of belief make 'boggart' less useful as a word and so speed its decline? Or did the disappearance of 'boggart'—an ecumenical term—help whittle down the number of possible supernatural forms? I do not know. What is clear is that the traditional sense of 'boggart' was buried not just by the social avalanche that brought down dialect, but by the arrival of a new boggart in literature and popular culture, the subject of the next and final chapter.

---

795. 'Rossendale Boggart Tales' (1897).

CHAPTER EIGHT

The New Boggart

The Boggart in the Twenty-First Century

It is 6 September 2008 and in a glade in Boggart Hole Clough (Blackley) families are enjoying an open-air play. The protagonists of this work of woodland theatre are a Mr and Mrs Boggart, a curmudgeonly couple who dwell in the Clough and who catch birds and animals to eat. A surviving poster depicts Mr Boggart as an orc gone to seed: green skin, frizzy hair, beer belly, and a Neolithic axe in his hand.[796] Excitingly, the play is based on folklore in a local community (see pp. 183–88). In other cases, contemporary boggarts are based more on reading than on community traditions. Thirty miles to the east in Mytholmroyd, for instance, a boggart walk has been established. A local web page introduces potential visitors to a green, gobliny Bogley Wiggins (a boggart cycling champion with a flat cap) and (his paramour?) a green buxom boggart barmaid.[797] On the Pendle Sculpture Trail, twenty miles to the north-west, a magnificent goblinoid boggart stares out at passers-by from the undergrowth (Figure 39). Meanwhile, at Hawley Meadows in Hampshire, 200 and more miles to the south, a special boggart hike has been created. A leaflet, written for children, describes the battles between 'the boggart' and local nymphs: three illustrations of the boggart show a green-grey goblin-like humanoid.[798]

As at Hawley Meadows, those who most often come into contact with boggarts in the twenty-first century are children. At Stannington (Sheffield), a local school has the children in its care make boggarts from 'natural materials' and build 'boggart dens' for the boggarts to live in.[799] At Tees Heritage Park, children make

---

796. Houlbrook, 'The Suburban Boggart' (thesis), 66.

797. https://web.archive.org/web/20191225175032/http://www.discovermytholmroyd.info/visit-us/boggart-trail/ [accessed 19 May 2021].

798. http://documents.hants.gov.uk/countryside/storytrails/nymphsandboggart.pdf [accessed 7 January 2019].

799. http://www.stanningtoninfants.co.uk/files/forest-school-2h-week-4-pp.pdf [accessed 7 January 2019].

Figure 39: A boggart (pre-installation) for the Pendle Sculpture Trail, by Lee Nicholson and Victoria Morris (www.incredible-creations.com).

homemade dough: 'The ball of play dough becomes the [boggart's] body instead and items from the woodland are stuck to this to make legs/arms/wings etc.'[800] Back at Boggart Hole Clough, pupils are encouraged to scour the undergrowth looking for signs of boggarts. Afterwards at their school they are instructed to create boggarts.[801] In the Peak District National Park, children are told boggart stories to 'understand the importance of nature and wildlife, and the role we and the Boggarts play in looking after it'.[802] In Plymouth, a boggart hunt is held to children's delight.[803] At Clumber Walled Kitchen Garden, a joint project with Lancaster University has children work on a project called 'Boggarts': they are asked to create a group story containing boggart characters.[804] Lest anyone be

800. https://web.archive.org/web/20181221152615/http://teesheritagepark.org.uk/wp-content/uploads/2014/05/activity-7.pdf [accessed 19 May 2021].

801. Houlbrook, 'The Suburban Boggart' (thesis), 68–69.

802. https://www.peakdistrict.gov.uk/__data/assets/pdf_file/0005/691862/Boggarts-Teachers-notes.pdf [accessed 7 January 2019].

803. Collins and Hayes, 'Boggart hunt?' [accessed 9 January 2019].

804. https://static1.squarespace.com/static/5358c942e4b06021df9a0843/t/5979cf01be65943a4a93e827/1501155089238/July+%2717.pdf [accessed 7 January 2019].

surprised to see a university involved in boggart games, know that there is a well-regarded peer-reviewed chapter entitled: 'Playful Approaches to Outdoor Learning: Boggarts, Bears, and Bunny Rabbits'.[805]

Neo-pagans have also become familiar with boggarts in their quest for a new spirituality. Indeed, some of the children's games detailed previously very likely emerged ultimately from the work of Gordon MacLellan, a neo-pagan 'shaman', 'dancer and storyteller'. MacLellan pioneered boggart activities to connect not just children but adults to nature: boggarts, according to MacLellan, are 'spirits of nature' and 'people from the world of faerie'. One of his games is called 'the boggart dance' and involves 'a created parade with lots of stamping and sudden wary stillness'.[806] The idea that boggarts are part of natural processes—something at the very heart of contemporary fairy-lore[807]—is taken as a given by many in the neo-pagan community; 'the wood has other inhabitants too. British folk traditions speak of them as elves, dwarves, boggarts and so on—and collectively as the faery folk.'[808] These nature boggarts can take offence. One neo-pagan practitioner wrote, on a run of bad luck in a family, 'It might be something like a family feud with the local boggarts that his great-granddad had started by cutting down the boggarts' favourite tree without asking.'[809] Other neo-pagans associate boggarts with homes instead: 'Landwights are local nature spirits, and boggarts are house-dwelling spirits, while faeries might be of either type.'[810]

In the nineteenth century, 'boggart' was a generic word for solitary super-natural creatures; above all, for the undead. What we might call the 'new boggart' is goblin-like (green, dirty, found in groups) or sometimes fairy-like (small, winged, connected to nature). It is, in other words, far removed from the nightmare creatures of Victorian mill towns. Supernatural creatures change, of course. Medieval ghosts had chains, twenty-first-century ghosts rarely do: the headless ghost was perhaps an early modern innovation.[811] Medieval fairies did not have wings: the fairies of the twenty-first century are almost invariably drawn with wings.[812] But with boggarts we can speak of a revolution over the space of mere decades. In this final chapter, I look at the 'goblinification' of

805. Hayes.

806. Greenwood, *Nature*, 159–61.

807. Johnson, *Seeing Fairies*, passim.

808. Harvey, 'Boggarts', 157.

809. Kaldera, *Wyrdwalkers*, 246.

810. Davy, *Introduction*, 15.

811. Brown, 'Some Examples', 398–99; though see Brown, *The Fate*, 40–41.

812. Young, 'Wings'.

the boggart. How is it that 'boggart' has shifted from being a generic, sinister, and shadowy term, to a benevolent or mischievous nature-loving sprite?

Much is intangible, of course. However, there are four points at which the shift took place and which form the substance of this chapter. Firstly, the Irish writer, Thomas Crofton Croker, would write in 1828 what turned out to be the most popular boggart story in history: a boggart story about a house goblin. Secondly, in 1865, a mid-Victorian author, Juliana Horatia Ewing, created a children's tale—'The Brownies'—which included boggarts. This tale was absorbed into the Scout movement by Lord Baden-Powell and became part of the youth culture of hundreds of thousands of British and Commonwealth Brownies and Girl Guides. Thirdly, there was the failure of nineteenth-century Lancashire folklorists to communicate the boggart to a national and international audience. Fourthly, and finally, I will examine how the boggart has been portrayed in modern children's fiction and how it burst out from the Harry Potter universe in 1999.

P., Roby, Croker and 'The Pertinacious Cobold'

A key event in the triumph of the goblin-boggart took place at the Admiralty in London in December 1828 when a Lancashire man turned up there.[813] The visitor was John Roby (1793–1850), a banker with literary pretensions, who lived most of his life in Rochdale.[814] Roby was knocking on the door of Thomas Crofton Croker (1798–1854), who worked in the building. Croker had become famous in 1825 for one of the first works on British[815] and Irish folklore, *Fairy Legends and Traditions of the South of Ireland* (1825–1828), which was much read.[816] Croker and Roby may have already known each other as they were both friends of the early nineteenth-century editor William Jerdan (1782–1869),[817] or they may have met for the first time at Croker's workplace. In either case Roby was, at this meeting, able to wring from Croker a promise to contribute a story to a work that Roby was

---

813. We know of this meeting and something of the process by which Croker's story was written because of letters from Roby surviving at Cork Library, Croker Corr. 111: 125, 144, and 193. I want to thank Gerry Desmond of Cork library for helping me track down these long-missing documents. Young, ' What is a Boggart Hole?', 122–23.

814. Fishwick, 'Some Notes'.

815. The title is misleading. In volume II, and above all volume III, Croker recorded much British material.

816. Dorson, *Folklorists*, 44–52.

817. Jerdan, *Autobiography* IV, 332–33 and Matoff, *Conflicted Life*, 150–51 and 332–33.

Figure 40: Thomas Crofton Croker, the most influential of all boggart authors. Welsh Portrait Collection at the National Library of Wales.

preparing: *Traditions of Lancashire*.[818] Subsequent boggart history would depend on that promise.

Even if Roby had never met Thomas Crofton Croker, Croker would have had a place in the history of the boggart. In the first volume of *Fairy Legends*, Croker had included two versions from County Cork[819] of a tale that folklorists have termed 'The Pertinacious Cobold'.[820] The story is 'extremely rare in Ireland'.[821] I give here a British version from 1842 which has the great merit of being short:

---

818. Croker Corr. 111: 125: 'You may perhaps recollect at an unfortunate promise you made to me anent my *Traditions of Lancashire* to wit that you would write one of the tales. Perhaps you may call to mind too my annoying you at the admiralty one morning in December last, and that you said you would cast your eye over [illegible] book containing some of these tales and would jot down your remarks with corrections or information on the subject.' The letter is dated: 'Rochdale 28 February 1829'.

819. Croker, *Fairy Legends*, I, 149–68.

820. Taylor, 'Cobold'; F482.3. 1.1, 'Farmer is so bothered by brownie that he decides he must move to get rid of the annoyance'; Migratory Legend 7020 'Vain Attempt to Escape a Brownie/Nisse'. Kvideland and Sehmsdorf, *Scandinavian Folk Belief*, 246.

821. Almqvist, 'Irish Migratory Legends', 8, n. 20. Note that Baughman, *Type*, 230 and Briggs, *Folk-Tales*, 1B, 25, both wrongly claimed a Scottish story for Ireland: Sands, 'Ancient Superstitions in Tiree'.

In the days of yore, an honest farmer, who resided on the top of
the 'Clough,' was sorely annoyed by its unearthly tenant. Night
after night the sprite paid its unearthly visits. Tricks of all kinds
were played; sometimes the milk was churned, others it was
overset; the beds were stripped of their covering; the maids found
themselves in the morning either on the floor or with their heels
on the pillows; the children started in their sleep, their hair bris-
tled up, their eyeballs rolled, they woke and wept. The master of
the house tried every remedy, patience last of all; and when this
failed him, made up his mind to 'flit'. All was soon ready for the
removal; the waggons were loaded over night, only a few more
hours and they would be far enough from the goblin and his 'hole'.
The family for once contented themselves with straw beds. In the
morning they were surprised to find how comfortably they had
all slept, and now congratulated each other that if the Boggart saw
they were in earnest, he had made up his mind to part company
in a quiet, friendly manner. Breakfast was soon over, horses were
yoked, the carriages moved. 'Thank God,' said the farmer, 'we are
flitting at last.' 'Yes,' cried a voice (but too well known) from the
top of the first waggon, 'and I'm flitting wi ye.'[822]

'The Pertinacious Cobold' is well known in Germany and Denmark and
to a lesser extent in Britain. Indeed, one Yorkshire reader of *Fairy Legends*, who
signed themselves 'P.', wrote in excitement to Jerdan's periodical, *The Literary
Gazette*. P., it transpired, had been interested to read Croker's Irish version of
this tale for, 'Amongst the many traditional legends which its truly amusing
compiler has introduced is one which I considered belonged solely to the
neighbourhood of my native village.'[823] P. proceeds to tell the story of a
Yorkshire boggart terrorizing a house and the family trying to 'flit', the first
nineteenth-century boggart tale. P. does not mention where in the three
Ridings the story took place: the address given in *The Literary Gazette* is for
'Hendon', presumably Hendon in London.[824] Croker was intrigued by P.'s tale

---

822. 'A Determined Boggart' (1842).

823. P., 'Fairy Tales'.

824. Three important dialect words are used in P.'s essay: 'boggart', 'boggle' ('a Yorkshireism for a
shying horse') and 'laking' (playing). It might be possible to determine the parts of Yorkshire where
all of these words were used in the nineteenth century—particularly as 'boggart' and 'laking' seem
integral to the tale, but only 'boggart' would allow us to narrow down the area in question substantially.
For 'laking', a Yorkshire-wide word, see Orton and Wright, *Word Geography*, 94 [M45].

and included it in a later edition of the *Fairy Legends*.[825] P.'s story would also return in *Traditions of Lancashire*.

In 1829, the 'first series of two handsomely illustrated volumes [of *Traditions of Lancashire*] was sold in royal octavo with proofs and etchings for four pounds, four shillings ... and a second series, uniform with the first, was published in 1831'.[826] Both series were a great success despite their cost—a second edition of the first series was printed in 1829—and they were republished (in cheaper formats) over the next century.[827] Roby's tales were fictionalized local legends: the work 'faintly echoes the manner of Sir Walter Scott'[828] (who indeed approved of the *Traditions*);[829] and as Katharine Briggs recognized, 'the narratives have been so much adorned that it is almost impossible to find out what happened' in the folk traditions that they were based upon.[830] Roby did, however, give interesting introductions to each tale, with reflections on local lore. These introductions, rather than the stories, are the first works of Lancashire folklore writing.

In 1828/1829, Croker had made a promise to contribute a story and, plagued by Roby, who sent letters and representations, the Irishman made a curious choice. Pressed for time or lacking inspiration, he took P.'s story and crudely adapted it to a Lancashire setting: for example, changing a Yorkshire-sounding surname 'Gilbertson' to a Lancashire-sounding 'Cheetham' for the farmer-hero of the tale.[831] Entire paragraphs from P. were lifted from one tale to the other. The yarn, entitled confusingly, 'The Bar-Gaist or Boggart',[832] was then published with a woodcut of a goblin causing chaos in a kitchen (Figure 41).[833] What should we make of this 'adaptation'? Croker wrote in the introduction to the tale that it was 'a very worthy old lady who told me the story'.[834] Did he possibly know P.—whom Croker, in the *Fairy Legends*, refers to as a man?[835] Is it possible even that the 'worthy old lady' had given permission for Croker to use the tale? Or is Croker's tale 'a palpable

825. Second edition (1826), 142–46.

826. Dorson, *Folklorists*, 98.

827. Ibid., 98.

828. Sambrook, 'Roby'. Note that there is an enduring (and not credible) tradition that Roby did not write the *Traditions* himself. First reference, Bibliothecar. Chetham, 'Traditions' (1866) and Cognizance, 'Traditions' (1867); this re-emerges in the 1880s, Fishwick, 'Some Notes'.

829. Dorson, *Folklorists*, 98.

830. Briggs, 'Scepticism', 5.

831. *Traditions*, 295–301.

832. See pp. 29–30 for the barghest.

833. *Traditions*, II, 295–301.

834. II, 296.

835. In the second edition of the first volume (1826), iii–iv.

plagiarism'?[836] Most who have known of the similarity between the two tales have suspected the last.[837] Croker's version of P.'s tale would, in any case, become the single best-known boggart story and, as we shall see, was much reprinted and adapted in the years that followed. Roby wrote about boggarts elsewhere in his *Traditions*, although these proved far less influential than Croker's dubious production.[838]

'The Pertinacious Cobold' is often said to be ubiquitous in Britain: 'as common as daisies' according to one writer.[839] This is to make too much of a few indifferent sources. I know of thirteen geographically rooted pre-First World War references to 'The Pertinacious Cobold' from England and Wales.[840] Many of the thirteen tales referred to here were collected or written in, for our purposes, less than ideal circumstances. The single Welsh version was recorded by Wirt Sykes who had a poor reputation for sourcing his tales.[841] John Atkinson, who was based on the edge of Cleveland, stated categorically that he had never in his forty years in the region come across the tale—Atkinson had a keen interest in folklore.[842] Yet two of the thirteen occurrences cluster in precisely that area.[843] A Shropshire version of the tale, meanwhile, was carefully recorded, but it is rather different from the other British versions of the tale. 'Bogies' make their way to a new house where they are tricked into sitting by the fire and are then burnt to death.[844]

---

836. Hardwick, 'The north of England', 281. Beyond this the crucial question is whether Croker and Roby were imposing a tale on Boggart Hole Clough, or whether the tale type was told already of the Clough, Young, 'Boggart Hole Clough', 120–27.

837. Hardwick, 'The north of England'; Young, 'Boggart Hole Clough', 120–27.

838. Most notably in the tale 'Clegg Hall', Roby, *Traditions*, Second Series, II, 1–53.

839. 'Boggart Hole Clough' (1893); see also Briggs, *Folk-Tales*, B1, 25: 'This is a common tale in the British Isles'.

840. P., 'Fairy Tales' (somewhere in Yorkshire); Boggart Hole Clough (Blackley, La), Roby, *Traditions*, II, 295–301 (1829); Oldham (La), Butterworth, *Sketches* (1856), 28; Danby (Yorkshire) Phillips, *The Rivers*, 210–11 (1853), see also Walcott, *The east coast*, 238 (1861); Merionethshire, Sikes, *British Goblins*, 116–17 (1880); Baslow (De), 'The legends, legendary stories' (1883); Worthen (Shropshire), Burne, *Shropshire*, I, 45–49; Near York (Yorkshire), Jones, 'Finnish Folk-Lore', 402 (1884); Worsthorne, (La) Asten, 'Ghost' (1895); East Halton (Li), Duncan, 'Correspondence' (1897); Upleatham (Yorkshire), Blakeborough, *Wit*, 203–05 (1898); Cliviger, 'Barcroft Hall' (1902); Ormskirk (Lancashire), 'Queer Tales' (1910). I also include three Scottish references known to me: Sands, 'Ancient Superstitions in Tiree'; Campbell, *Superstitions*, 183; Bruford, 'Trolls', 119–20; note also that Phillips, *The Rivers*, 210 gives a Lowland reference (from Sir Walter Scott?) that I've been unable to trace.

841. Rhys, *Celtic Folklore*, I, 18: 'as to Mr. Sikes, I cannot discover whence his [version of a tale] has been derived, for he seems not to have been too anxious to leave anybody the means of testing his work, as one will find on verifying his references, when he gives any'.

842. Atkinson, *Forty Years*, 66–67.

843. Blakeborough, *Wit*, 203–05; Phillips, *The Rivers*, 210–11.

844. Burne, *Shropshire*, I, 45–49.

Figure 41: Croker's Boggart (Roby, *Traditions*, II, 295, 1829).

Even with these doubts and qualifiers we seem to have a tale that is associated with the north of England (see Figure 42). This is reinforced by the words of a series of nineteenth-century writers who commented on the tale more generally. Our oldest published version from Britain is P.'s, set in Yorkshire: it is not placed on the map, as we have no clue where in the three Ridings the story was set (see n. 824). At some point in 1846 or 1847 the archaeologist, J.J.A. Worsaae, told the Danish version of 'The Pertinacious Cobold' while visiting England and one of those present 'immediately expressed a lively surprise on hearing a legend related as Danish, and that, too, almost word for word which he had often heard in Lancashire in his youth'.[845] Thomas Turner Wilkinson commented in 1861 that the tale was 'common to both Lancashire and Yorkshire'.[846] Tennyson, meanwhile, put the story into verse in 1842 in his 'Walking to the Mail'.[847] Perhaps the tale came from his Lincolnshire childhood.[848]

---

845. *An Account*, 90.

846. Wilkinson, 'On the Popular Customs'; Harland and Wilkinson, *Lancashire Folk-Lore*, 45.

847. Probably written 1837/1838, published in 1842, Purton and Page, *Tennyson*, 326 text in Tennyson, *Works*, 67. As Tennyson gives no explanation as to its origin, I have not put this version on the map.

848. Collins, *Early Poems*, 168, n. 1, who suggests that Tennyson got the story from Croker.

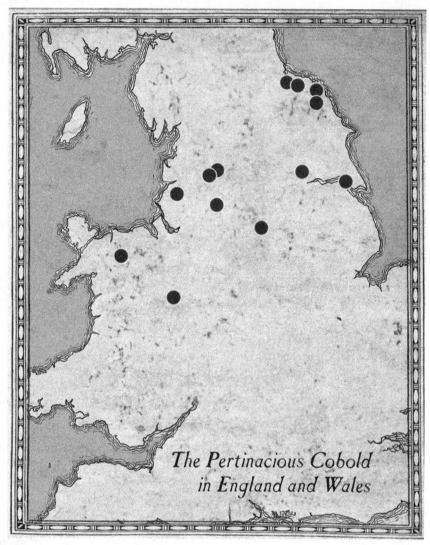

Figure 42: 'The Pertinacious Cobold' in England and Wales.

As one might expect with a story that stretches over such a wide territory, the name of the accompanying house spirit changes. In Tennyson's poem there is a 'jolly good ghost';[849] there is a 'spirit' in a version associated with Oldham.[850] Three of the Lancashire versions of the tale refer to a 'boggart':[851] the fourth

---

849. Tennyson, *Works*, 67.
850. Butterworth, *Sketches*, 28.
851. *Traditions*, II, 295–301; Asten, 'Ghost'; 'Barcroft Hall' (1902).

gives the troublesome sprite no name.[852] The reference from east Yorkshire is to 'Robin Red Cap'.[853] The two references from Cleveland, the reference from north Lincolnshire, and the tale from Derbyshire are all told about a 'hob'.[854] In Wales, meanwhile, we have the *bwbach*.[855]

At a national level, the tale came to be associated with boggarts. After all, British readers could now read a boggart version of the story in two influential works: Croker's *Fairy Legends*—which reprinted P.'s tale—and Roby's *Traditions*. From these it filtered down into folklore reference works. Thomas Keightley included the flitting boggart in his *Fairy Mythology*.[856] It was also picked up in Charles John Tibbits' *Folk-lore and Legends: English* in 1890.[857] Hardwick, in one of the most-read northern folklore works, repeated the boggart tale.[858] Then, decisively, the tale was adapted by the American children's writer and illustrator, Howard Pyle, and published in his extremely successful collection *Pepper & Salt* (1885). Farmer Cheetham/Gilbertson became Farmer Grigson and the story was bulked out with other bits of British folklore about household spirits.[859] Pyle also produced the only illustration known to me of the boggart leaving the farm during 'the departure' (Figure 43). Notice that, in many versions of the tale, the boggart or hob hides in a milk churn. Pyle has respected this small detail in his drawing.

'The Pertinacious Cobold' also appeared in ephemera. The version of the tale excerpted above (p. 196) is a digest of Croker's version from a Westmorland newspaper in 1842,[860] and there are many other examples from nineteenth-century newspapers and magazines. The story was amusing and short—an ideal filler for a Victorian or Edwardian editor. So *Ben Brierley's Magazine* gave the tale in 1881.[861] Tattersall Wilkinson published the Cobold in a Huddersfield review.[862] In 1854, it was included in an evangelical text on evil spirits by a Lancashire clergyman.[863] It then appeared in many Lancashire miscellanies and

852. 'Queer Tales' (1910).
853. Jones, 'Finnish Folk-Lore', 402.
854. Blakeborough, *Wit*, 203–05; Phillips, *The Rivers*, 210–11; Duncan, 'Correspondence'; 'The legends, legendary stories' (1883).
855. Sikes, *British Goblins*, 116–17.
856. 307–08
857. C.J.T., 170–80.
858. Hardwick, *Traditions*, 128–29—though see his later regrets in his article 'The north of England'; Harland and Wilkinson, *Lancashire Folk-lore*, 58.
859. 69–81.
860. 'A Determined Boggart' (1842).
861. 'A Shooting Boggart'.
862. Wilkinson, 'Boggart Ho' Clough'.
863. Hewlett, *Personal Recollections*, 19–24.

Figure 43: The Departure
(Pyle, *Pepper & Salt*, 71).

children's books.[864] In fact, there must be some concern that one or a number of the versions of 'The Pertinacious Cobold' listed above was actually filched from P. or Croker (or a derivative version), in much the same way that Croker had purloined the tale from P.[865]

The story continued to be popular in the twentieth century. W. Langley Roberts, for instance, included it in his *Legends and Folk-Lore of Lancashire* in 1931, with a goblin-like illustration (Figure 44).[866] We know that in 1935, a BBC radio programme was broadcast on 'the "True Story of the Boggart of Boggart-Hole-Clough" as recollected by one of his victims, Master Robert Cheetham'. Cheetham, it will be recalled, was the name of Croker's Lancashire farmer.[867] It is a great pity that this version does not survive. In 1948, Lewis Spence repeated the tale in his *Minor Traditions of British Mythology*. He noticed the common elements between P.'s and Croker's tale, but assumed (wrongly) that the story had gone from Croker (Lancashire) to P. (Yorkshire).[868] The story then appeared in the works of British

---

864. See, e.g., Girvin, *Round*, 68–69.
865. See, for instance, Atkinson, *Forty Years*, 66–67.
866. 90–96.
867. 'Today's Radio Programmes'.
868. *Minor*, 88–89, 165.

folklorist Katharine Briggs after the Second World War as *the* representative tale of boggarts, most importantly in her *Dictionary of Fairies* and in her *Dictionary of British Folk-Tales*.[869] In the same way that nineteenth-century villages had stock haunts,[870] so in folklore reference works entities have stock tales: the farmer tricks the bogie; the pixies work in a barn at night. 'The Pertinacious Cobold' is, for contemporary British readers, 'the Pertinacious Boggart'.

The importance of P.'s tale and Croker's adaptation in the goblinification of the boggart cannot be overstated. The connection of a house spirit with Boggart Hole Clough is perhaps the seed behind much of the modern goblin folklore of north Manchester (see pp. 183–88). But there were also national consequences. It is no accident that most versions of 'The Pertinacious Cobold' in Britain were originally ascribed to hobs (the classic English household spirit): see the tales from Derbyshire, from the Northeast, and from Lincolnshire.[871] As we have seen, only a tiny fraction of boggarts were 'brownies'. But because of the reach of this tale after *Traditions of Lancashire*, not least in folklore encyclopaedias, the boggart was to be defined as a house goblin, rather than a fearsome ghost or an inventive shape-changer. This was particularly the case for readers from outside of Boggartdom, who had no other source for information about boggarts. A generic term began to narrow to a specific one.

Boggart Meets Brownie

The next individual to influence the development of the boggart—and in much the same direction as Roby and Croker—was Juliana Horatia Ewing (1841–1885). Ewing grew up in a middle-class family (her father was a vicar) in Ecclesfield, in a part of Yorkshire where boggarts (or, as her working-class neighbours would have said, 'boggards'[872]) were well known.[873] In 1865, while she was still at Ecclesfield, Ewing published a story entitled 'The Brownies'.[874] The story has many traditional references and there is no question that Ewing knew British folklore well.[875] At the centre of 'The Brownies', though, is a

869. *Fairies*, 29–30; *Folk-Tales*, B1 24–25.

870. See p. 80 for this term.

871. See n. 840.

872. Ewing sometimes used dialect words: Jones, 'Dialect'.

873. Avery, *Mrs Ewing*; Jones, 'Ewing'.

874. 'The Brownies' (1865); *The Brownies*, 11–73 (1870).

875. Briggs, *Fairies in Tradition*, 234–35; Briggs, 'Folklore in Nineteenth-Century English Literature', 93; Sumpter, *Victorian Press*, 46–47.

Figure 44: The Boggart in Roberts (*Legends*, 91).

long untraditional discussion between a small boy, Tommy Trout, and an owl.
The owl sets out the conceit that will then dominate the rest of the story.
Are young children, specifically here Tommy and his brother and sister, brownies
or boggarts? Forget the Victorian commonplace that children should be seen
and not heard; the owl's point is, rather, that parasitic children ('they live
entirely upon other people') should make themselves useful around the house
and avoid sloth:

> The Brownies, or, as they are sometimes called, the Small Folk,
> the Little People, or the Good People, are a race of tiny beings
> who domesticate themselves in a house of which some grown-up
> human being pays the rent and taxes. They are like small editions
> of men and women, they are too small and fragile for heavy work;
> they have not the strength of a man, but are a thousand times more
> fresh and nimble. They can run and jump, and roll and tumble,
> with marvellous agility and endurance, and of many of the aches
> and pains which men and women groan under, they do not even
> know the names. They have no trade or profession, and as they
> live entirely upon other people, they know nothing of domestic
> cares; in fact, they know very little upon any subject, though they
> are often intelligent and highly inquisitive. They love dainties, play,
> and mischief. They are apt to be greatly beloved, and are themselves

capriciously affectionate. They are little people, and can only do little things. When they are idle and mischievous, they are called Boggarts, and are a curse to the house they live in. When they are useful and considerate, they are Brownies, and are a much-coveted blessing. Sometimes the Blessed Brownies will take up their abode with some worthy couple, cheer them with their romps and merry laughter, tidy the house, find things that have been lost, and take little troubles out of hands full of great anxieties.[876]

The tension between boggart and brownie stands at the very heart of the tale. The Trout children must help their parents and leave their boggarty ways behind them. They, of course, succeed and inspire other children to greater efforts.

'The Brownies' had a long life. It was reprinted in a book of Ewing's short stories by the Society for Promoting Christian Knowledge, *The Brownies and Other Tales* (1870). It then continued to be published after her death in 1885. A beautifully made edition was published in Britain in 1910, for example, and again in 1920 by George Bell; a rather cheaper American edition was published in 1946 (Charles Scribner). J.M. Dent later published its own in 1954. Some of these were still being reprinted in the 1980s. Several online versions of 'The Brownies' can be found; searched for, perhaps, by those who had thrilled at the story in the 1930s, the 1940s, and the 1950s.[877] 'The Brownies' clearly had narrative power, as it was even collected as an oral folktale in late twentieth-century Florida! 'This tale is so alien to the southern tradition that it is likely derived from a printed source.'[878]

The story's extraordinarily long life depended, though, not only on the intrinsic merit of 'The Brownies' but also on the fact that the story was known to Lord Baden-Powell (1857–1941). Ewing's tale was, as it happens, the inspiration behind his name for younger Girl Guides, 'the Brownies', who had previously been called—and to the disgust of members—'the Rosebuds'.[879] Baden-Powell included an adapted version of Ewing's story in his first hand-book for the Brownies in 1918.[880] The story then remained in the Brownie's handbook through many editions and only started to drop out of fashion in the 1960s. As a 'founding text' of the movement it has also been introduced

---

876. *The Brownies*, 44–45.
877. See, e.g., https://www.shortkidstories.com/story/brownies/ [accessed 10 May 2020].
878. Burrison, *Storytellers*, 60–62; note, 354.
879. Hampton, *Girl Guides*, 22.
880. Baden-Powell, *Girl Guiding*, 7–9.

Figure 45: The Brownie aka
the good Boggart (Ewing,
The Brownies, frontispiece).

into many different Brownie activities and 'spin-offs'. Baden-Powell expected,
for instance, Brownies to clap and thereby 'slay boggarts' in the Grand Salute.[881]

In the mid 1920s, F. O. Nash published a novel, *Some Brownies and a Boggart*
about the moral struggles of a young Guide: Nellie 'began to have an uneasy
feeling that she had behaved ... more like a Boggart than a Brownie'.[882] There
were the inevitable doggerel verses:

> At each Good Turn a Brownie did,
> An ugly Boggart ran and hid;
> Come then Brownies staunch and true
> We've no room for Boggart – shoo!
> Only those who have been good
> May play in our Enchanted Wood.[883]

---

881. Hampton, *Girl Guides*, 24.
882. *Some Brownies*, 36.
883. Harting, 'Brownie Piper'.

And, of course, there were the boggart-brownie sports. In one game, skipping-ropes were whirled under jumping Brownies. If the skipping-rope clipped a Brownie then the boggarts had caught her.[884] In the 'Snake Game', boggarts and Brownies had to tie knots to win.[885] In an elaborate version of tig (tag), the 'boggarty boggart' chased brownies who dared to come too close.[886] Boggarts and brownies continued to be employed by the movement after the war. The British Library, for example, has a 1956 play based on Ewing's story, printed for Kent Girl Guides.[887] The goblin-boggart was a vivid part of the childhood of hundreds of thousands of English-speaking women.

The Goblinification of Boggarts in Folklore Writing

Folklorists and folklore writers also influenced the boggart's evolution, particularly in the Northwest. Indeed, in the same period that Ewing was active, a number of Lancashire or Lancashire-based writers were taking up the challenge of writing boggart-lore: Bowker, Hardwick, Harland, and Wilkinson to name the most important. Looking back, we can see that from 1850 to about 1880 was the most exciting generation for Lancashire folklore, one that coincides with the greatest popularity of English dialect literature.[888] It is difficult to think of any other English county that had such a strong folklore headwind in the nineteenth century: perhaps here alone we can talk of a county *tradition* of folklore writing.[889]

Partly as a result of this ebullience, in the nineteenth century, boggarts became as Lancastrian as red roses, hotpot, and cotton looms. It was possible, indeed, to write sentences like the following: 'well may [the population] be excused for believing in the Yorkshire padfoot and the Lancashire boggarts'; 'No one can reside a year in Lancashire without hearing of its "boggarts"'; or even, 'Boggarts are the private concern of Lancashire and nowhere else do they exist under that name.'[890] In fact, with very few exceptions, boggarts *only* appear in Lancashire folklore writing in the nineteenth and very early twentieth

---

884. 'Brownie's Revel'.

885. 'The Snake'.

886. 'Two Brownie Games'.

887. General Reference Collection 12838.t.1. I have not established whether Brown Owl and Tawny Owl (Brownie leaders) were names inspired by Ewing's story.

888. Vicinus, *Muse*, 185: 'The outstanding period of dialect was 1860–85, a time of consolidation and rediscovery of working-class values and traditions by literary men'. This overlap is not, of course, coincidental.

889. See further pp. 12–13.

890. An Old Native, 'Reminiscences' (1863); Grindon, *Lancashire*, 187–88; Morton, *Boggarts*, 9.

centuries. The boggarts of Yorkshire, Cheshire, Derbyshire, Staffordshire, and Nottinghamshire were almost entirely lost to sight.[891] In Lincolnshire alone would boggarts nudge their way into folklore collections, in a modest way, in the interwar years.[892]

This uneven coverage had an effect on how boggarts came to be imagined. Folklorists from other regions, particularly those who might be called the 'national' folklorists, with the ambition of writing British-wide folklore, only learnt of boggarts from three places: from Lancashire folklore classics; from the Pertinacious Boggart in national collections; and perhaps by reading Ewing to their children. And for Lancashire they only had a limited range of publications: Roby, Bowker, Hardwick, Harland, and Wilkinson produced the canonical works of Lancashire folklore.[893] Unfortunately, the canonical Lancashire folklorists did not always give a good overview of boggart-lore: our folklore 'archives' for Lancashire, such as they are, do not reflect Lancashire folklore on this point.[894]

Take Hardwick, for example. The Preston author wrote a long chapter on Lancashire boggarts and fairies.[895] But he actually mentions only four established boggarts: the boggart of Syke Lumb Farm and the boggart of Boggart Hole Clough, both, in his version, household spirits.[896] He also included Bannister Hall Doll (a shape-changer) and the Grislehurst Boggart (an outdoor boggart).[897] At no point does he refer to these boggarts as being undead: the Bannister Hall Doll was, we know from elsewhere, said to be the spirit of a murdered girl (see p. 55); the Grislehurst Boggart may have been a ghost. A London-based folklorist, relying on Hardwick (and the other widely read Lancashire writers) would have read little or nothing of undead boggarts.

In fact, the single most important factor determining how boggart-lore was transmitted in folklore writing was the relative indifference to the undead. Nineteenth-century folklorists, like botanists, were interested in the rarest,

---

891. With some very few exceptions, e.g., Hole, *Traditions*, 144–65.

892. Rudkin, *Lincolnshire Folklore*, 34–38; 'Black Dog', 116–17. There were, note, Lincolnshire boggarts in late nineteenth-century folklore, but these were normally mentioned only in passing: e.g. Balfour, 'Legends', see also pp. 67–68.

893. Messier but often more interesting authors like Higson, see pp. 79–84, who appeared in newspapers and publications with only local circulation, were lost to view.

894. By 'archives' here, I refer to the canonical books that go to make up Lancashire folklore. For more on how we are prisoners of the biases of nineteenth-century collectors, Beyer, 'Are Folklorists?', 37.

895. *Traditions*, 124–42.

896. Ibid., 127–30.

897. Ibid., 130–32; note that Bannister Hall Doll is not named but can be identified, see p. 55.

most prestigious 'flowers', not the garden greenhouse ghost. Fairy-lore was certainly much more likely to appear in folklore collections than the fairies' ghostly cousins. This bias can be seen in the Lancashire writers and their boggart writing. Harland and Wilkinson described Puck as 'the Lancashire Boggart'.[898] Hardwick likewise wrote: '"Boggart," by some writers is regarded as the Lancashire cognomen for "Puck" or "Robin Goodfellow"'; a position Hardwick evidently shared.[899] Yet, while Puck could be described as a shape-changer, he has nothing to do with the ghosts, death-warners, and demons that go to make up the majority of traditional boggarts. Once more we see a generic term being sharpened to a specific goblin-like definition.

By the Second World War, the boggart had taken on a goblin-like identity not only among the general reading public, but also among folklorists (when they troubled with the boggart at all). As noted in the Introduction, from 1901 to 2000, *Folklore*, Britain's chief journal for popular traditions, had just thirty-one references to 'boggart' (p. 13). Of those thirty-one references, *only one* (dated 1903) was stated to involve the undead.[900] Yet as we have seen, the proportions would, if anything, be reversed in traditional tales from Boggartdom: there the undead dominated. This misunderstanding is also found in Lewis Spence's summary of the boggart from 1948: 'A good deal of confusion appears to exist concerning the significance of the spirit known as the boggart. By some writers, the boggart is regarded as a species of brownie ... *Occasionally* [my italics] the boggart appears as the ghost of a deceased man.'[901] When nineteenth-century dialect guides and glossaries defined 'boggart' they frequently used the word 'ghost' (see p. 6): when postwar folklore guides did this, they were far more likely to use the word 'goblin' or 'brownie' or 'fairy'.[902]

---

898. *Lancashire Folk-lore*, 16.

899. *Traditions*, 124.

900. Addy, 'Death'. Other references referred to legends that *arguably* involved the undead, but this was not an aspect brought out by the respective authors.

901. *Minor*, 88–89. See also Hole, *English Folklore*, 151 (1944) and the influential, Burne, *Shropshire*, I, 45 for 1883.

902. A selection: Howat, *Ghosts and Legends*, 106, boggart 'a goblin' (note, on the same page, boggle 'a goblin often found in wetlands'); Moorey, *Bible*, 386, 'Boggart: A poltergeist-type brownie'; Turner-Bishop, 'Sites', 95, 'One of the most common types of feeorin is the boggart, an often mischievous, even malevolent, house brownie'; Morton, *Boggarts*, 11 'The world is full of fairies and if anyone tells you it isn't, don't you believe them. There are fairies everywhere no matter whether they are called Leprechauns, Pixies, Elves, Parisees, or Tattie-Bogles. There are also the Little People of the hills like Puck, together with Trolls and Whimsies; and there are Boggarts'; Billingsley, *Folk Tales from Calderdale*,19, 'In the Calder valley, the most common "faerie" denizen is the boggart, and stories and rumours of them abound'; 22, 'Boggarts are a variety of the

This tendency to elevate the goblin-boggart can be tracked in the various fairy encyclopaedias and glossaries that have been published since the 1970s. Let us take, as an example, not just the boggart, but also the boggle and the dobbie. As we have seen, these terms have the same meaning (see pp. 70–76). They are generic words used in different regions for ambivalent solitary bogies. Yet, in the writings of one of Britain's most important postwar folklorists, Katharine Briggs, they are by no means the same thing. In her *Dictionary of Fairies*, Briggs writes that the boggart is a 'mischievous Brownie, almost exactly like a poltergeist in his habits'.[903] In fact, Briggs, for many years a Girl Guide leader, repeatedly states in her writings that a boggart is a brownie gone bad; she has been one of the principal channels through which Ewing's boggart-brownie jumped from fiction to folklore writing.[904] The boggart's cousins, the bogles, are 'evil demons'.[905] The dobbie, meanwhile, is a 'friendly name for a Hobgoblin in Yorkshire and Lancashire'.[906] Note again the absence of the undead.

The same exercise can be repeated in modern folklore guides, both printed and digital. In Ronan Coughlan's *Handbook of Fairies*, a boggart is a 'kind of homesprite', a 'bogle' is a 'being, ill-defined and evil, black in colour', and a 'dobie' is a 'being in West Yorkshire belief who will jump up behind a horseman

---

so-called "little people" … Boggarts seem to resemble Brownies … What we might refer to as a ghost or a poltergeist was frequently lumped in with boggarts.'

903. *Dictionary*, 29.

904. In 1957, in 'The English Fairies', Briggs warned: 'You must beware of offending your brownie or he may turn into a boggart and then woe betide you!'. In *Fairies in Tradition and Literature*, 33: 'The Brownie had turned into a Boggart, as has often happened before.' The brownie-boggart appears in the *Dictionary of Fairies*, 46: 'It was indeed very easy to offend a brownie, and either drive him away or turn him from a brownie to a BOGGART'. It is there in her massive reference work: *A Dictionary of British Folk-Tales*, IB, 23: 'The mildest form of [bogies] are boggarts, which are brownies gone bad.' The monster even appears in a title of an article published in the year of her death, 1980: 'Brownie into Boggart', which featured in a *festschrift* for American-Hungarian folklorist, Linda Dégh. It could be argued that Briggs used 'brownie' and 'boggart', as classes of household spirits; not as traditional bogeys from respectively, Scotland and Lancashire. The brownie, in the relevant passages, was the good household spirit. The boggart was, for Briggs, a naughty household spirit. That this was, in fact, Briggs's strategy can be seen clearly where she discussed one good-to-bad spirit tale. This tale 'strongly suggests', wrote Briggs, 'Some Late Accounts of the Fairies', 513 'the story of Brownie turned Boggart which is told by Rhys in *Celtic Folk-Lore*'. Rhys, *Celtic Folk-lore*, II, 593–96 does not use the words 'brownie' or 'boggart' in the story: he uses a single Welsh term (*bwca*)—see Bronner, *Practice*, 94, whose claim for a long phallic nose depends on this reference. Briggs is employing, then, at least here, the two words, as typological terms. But Briggs herself, in some of her works, often in the same paragraph, refers to the brownies and boggarts as both types and as locally rooted folklore beings, e.g. *Dictionary of Fairies*, 45–49.

905. *Dictionary*, 32.

906. Ibid., 103; note Briggs has a separate entry for 'Dobie' 'One type of Brownie'.

and garrote him'.[907] On Wikipedia, the most popular worldwide source for folklore, a boggart is 'either a household spirit or a malevolent *genius loci* inhabiting fields, marshes or other topographical features'.[908] A 'bogle' is 'a Northumbrian and Scots term for a ghost or folkloric being … They are reputed to live for the simple purpose of perplexing mankind, rather than seriously harming or serving them.'[909] Dobbie, meanwhile, 'is another term for hobgoblin in Lancashire and Yorkshire … especially one that is a relentless prankster'.[910] The dead here only creep into the Wikipedia definition for 'bogle'.

So strong has been the drive to order British supernatural creatures in the last two generations, that dialectal differences have been unknowingly turned into folklore differences. This is not to say that all definitions for boggarts and their kin are incorrect. Wikipedia's editors did a reasonable job with the first part of their definition for 'bogle'. Consider, too, Jacqueline Simpson and Steve Roud's excellent definition for boggart in the *Dictionary of English Folklore*: 'In the dialects of northern counties, "boggart" was a general term for any supernatural being which frightened people, whether indoors or out, without specifying whether it is ghost, malicious fairy, or minor demon.'[911] As we turn now to twentieth-century fiction we shall see that these are minority voices. For most writers (and readers) the boggart had become a goblin.

Twentieth-Century Fictional Boggarts and *Harry Potter*

The first fictional boggarts of the twentieth century appear in the theatre. We know that in 1909, a short performance was given at the Tivoli in Manchester, entitled *The Dance of the Boggarts of Boggart Hole*.[912] In 1913, in the same city, a play by Frank Rose entitled the *Whispering Well* was performed; it had some success and was later enjoyed in London, New York, and Chicago.[913] Rose's piece was subtitled 'a Lancashire fairy play' and included a chorus of boggarts who tempted the hero and his wife to their doom. Note, in both cases, the way boggarts work (or dance) together in a group, something typical of the goblin-boggart rather than the traditional solitary boggart. In fact, *The Dance*

---

907. *Handbook*, 21, 39. The dobbie reference depends upon Willan, 'A List' 144. See further Smith, 'Dobbies'.
908. https://en.wikipedia.org/wiki/Boggart [accessed 9 January 2019].
909. https://en.wikipedia.org/wiki/Bogle [accessed 9 January 2019].
910. https://en.wikipedia.org/wiki/Hobgoblin [accessed 9 January 2019].
911. Simpson and Roud, *Dictionary*, 29.
912. 'Theatres and Music Halls'.
913. Young, 'Boggart Plays', 93–95.

is the first hint of a new goblin-boggart, or better, a new goblin-boggart tribe living in the Clough, something which would become commonplace in the later twentieth-century folklore of north Manchester (see pp. 183–88). In the very early 1970s, a short comic piece entitled *The Boggart* by Henry Livings appeared on the stage. A traveller, Sam Pongo, outwitted a boggart on a Lancashire moor.[914] This dramatic sketch, which was adapted from a Japanese play, is, ironically, much more in line with traditional boggart-lore than the Lancashire productions of Rose and the Tivoli.

Boggarts also appeared in children's and fantasy fiction, at least in the postwar period. We might start with what could reasonably be called 'fantasy-folklore writing': authors offering their own fictional constructs as folklore. Take *All About Boggarts* told, in 1956 by H.F. Morton for one Gabrielle Cook, then a small girl. Morton adapted a series of Lancashire boggarts, weaving non-traditional but charming tales around his goblin-boggarts. These stories survived for the best part of forty years in Gabrielle's loft space, only being published in a limited edition in the early 1990s. In 1970, Ruth Tongue wrote a short tale entitled 'The Boggart in Top Attic', which supposedly originated in Lancashire.[915] The story is unlike any other in north-western tradition and was presumably invented by Tongue herself.[916] A third work of fantasy-folklore was Arthur Griffiths' *Lancashire Folklore*, which creates a goblin-boggart saga, from strands of medieval and Victorian supernatural lore and some very suspect philology. It was published by Leigh Local History Society in 1993 (although it seems to have been written a generation before) and often adopts a pseudo-historical tone.[917]

Morton, Tongue, and Griffith wrote little-read works. However, a number of more successful fantasy writers were ready to go further in emancipating the boggart from tradition. The first was Jean Fritz who published *Magic to Burn* in New York in 1964. Two American children on holiday in England meet a boggart, Blaze, who then returns with them to the USA. Blaze is some four inches high—comparisons are made to a leprechaun. He is mischievous and he wants to go home. British author William Mayne had a semi-traditional boggart in his *Earthfasts*, a postwar children's classic (1969): 'Boggarts are slightly touchy house spirits, with a taste for milk and other little gifts, and

914. 'Three Pongo Plays'; Gale, *British Humorists*, II, 684–90.
915. *Forgotten Folk-Tales*, 176–77.
916. For Tongue's unfortunate storytelling habits: Harte, 'Tongue'. Tongue's boggart tale has started to percolate through analyses of boggart- and supernatural-lore: Hartmann, 'The Black Dog', 46.
917. A very rare book, but happily available online: https://leigh.life/index.php?page=wiki&id=leighlife:lancfolk [accessed 20 October 2018].

they don't greatly care for cats and dogs.'[918] Mayne returned to the boggart later in his life in his Hob Stories for younger children (with delightful illustrations by Patrick Benson).[919]

In 1988, Martin Riley's *Tales from the Edge of the World* (which appeared on the BBC story programme *Jackanory*) included boggarts. The boggarts are very much goblins: accompanying illustrations show small humanoids dressed in rags. They are described as being dirty, and they live, rather confusingly, in a boggle hole.[920] In 1993, Susan Cooper, one of the most important British fantasy writers of the later twentieth century, published a novel entitled *The Boggart* about a Gaelic-speaking Scottish boggart who decamps with a family to Toronto (in a computer) and causes chaos there. Cooper would write a further two books with the boggart as a hero: in 1998, the *Boggart and the [Loch Ness] Monster*; and in 2018, *The Boggart Fights Back*. Again, the author knows modern folklore writing on boggarts. She even acknowledges Katharine Briggs in her afterword to the second volume, and introduces the boggart-brownie as folklore fact in the story there.[921]

However, the apotheosis of the boggart in fantasy fiction came—there is no question—in 1999. In that year, J.K. Rowling published her third Harry Potter novel: *The Prisoner of Azkaban*. *The Prisoner* was not, as we have seen, the first work of children's fiction to feature the boggart, but it was unquestionably the bestselling to do so. In Rowling's book, the boggart is described as 'a shape-shifting creature that feeds on its victim's emotions and assumes the shape of the victim's worse fears'.[922] Rowling's boggart is arguably the closest twentieth-century fiction comes to the nineteenth-century boggart: there is at least a sense of fear and horrid potential. Rowling's model tended not to be copied in subsequent works. But she had given the word 'boggart' immense prestige by including it in the *Harry Potter* universe, one of the most successful fantasy series in history.

After decades of relative obscurity, the boggart naturally basked in this new-found fame. He appeared, of course, in the movie of *The Prisoner*: it was the boggart's first outing on the big screen, and the episode is brilliantly filmed (2004).[923] Guides to the Potter world include references to the boggart.[924]

---

918. *Earthfasts*, 90.
919. *Red Book*, 'Hob and Boggart', unnumbered.
920. 64.
921. Cooper, *Boggart and the Monster*, 7.
922. Beahm, *Fact*, 12–13.
923. 40:25 secs.
924. Beahm, *Fact*, 12; Colbert, *Worlds*, 47–48.

There have been efforts among scholars to make sense of Rowling's boggart in folklore terms.[925] As Rowling used the boggart for her own ends, so have scholars. One example must stand for many: Emma Norman's 2012 essay, 'International Boggarts: Carl Schmitt, Harry Potter, and the Transfiguration of Identity and Violence'. Crucially, there has also been a notable uptick in boggarts appearing in fiction. One work of boggart fiction, in my possession, was sold with a sticker on its front cover: 'The Boggarts, as featured in *Harry Potter and the Prisoner of Azkaban*'.[926] Rowling opened the way to other authors who were more likely to fall back on the boggart as goblin than create, as she had done, their own original bogie.

Of these more recent works the most successful has been Tony DiTerlizzi and Holly Black's *The Spiderwick Chronicles*, the first volume of which was published in 2003.[927] One of the main characters is Thimbletack the Brownie, and in the Spiderwick universe, brownies turn into boggarts. They turn back after being fed honey.[928] *The Spiderwick Chronicles* have also been made into a film (2008). Another bestselling author who includes boggarts in his fiction is Joseph Delaney, resident at Stalmine, in the heart of what had been nineteenth-century Boggartdom. In *The Spook's Sacrifice*, for instance (2009), a sudden boggart attack ends with a maenad prisoner having all her blood sucked out of her.[929] 'Lancashire', writes Delaney on his webpage, 'is the home of real boggarts rather than the shape-shifting variety invented by J.K. Rowling. Lancashire boggarts are more like poltergeists.'[930]

Boggarts are also much loved by minor fantasy authors. In 2006, Roger Wood published *The Boggarts of Boggart Hole Clough*. As the name implies, we have a tribe of boggarts: 'with the help of Granddad and his mate Arnold—a computer wizard—[the children] rescue the boggart chief who has been kidnapped by a band of rival boggarts'.[931] In *Mayhem in Bath* by Sandra Heath we find: 'Slowly [Polly] entered, and then halted in dismay as she saw the furious boggart-brownie whose tail was now twirling so fast it was a blur.'[932] In Juliet McKenna's take on British folk monsters, 'Boggarts are vermin. They look like gargoyles that fell off a church and landed hard, face down … They

---

925. Hartmann, 'The Black Dog', 45–47; Cockrell, 'Password', 24.

926. Mills, *Boggarts*.

927. DiTerlizzi and Black.

928. Note this is common in modern fantasy fiction and has presumably come, via Briggs' writing, e.g. Ninness, *Macabre*, 90–98.

929. Delaney, *The Spook's Sacrifice*, 7–10.

930. https://josephdelaneyauthor.com/author-info/my-biography/ [accessed 16 January 2020].

931. Book blurb.

932. Heath, *Mayhem*, read in pageless electronic version.

constantly squabble among themselves, biting and scratching.'[933] However, the book that perhaps best sums up the change in the boggart from 1800 to 2000 is *Boggarts of Britain* by Frank Mills. There we see how far the goblinification of boggarts has progressed:

> [Boggarts] are always dressed in brown with little smudges of green and some reports say they can be as small as fifty centimetres high while others say they are more than twice as tall. Because Boggarts are so small, people think they are weak but this is not so. Inside their small bodies there is a tremendous amount of special energy which allows them to perform tasks with such speed and accuracy that it has all the appearance of magic. They are not spiteful or dangerous and they never mean to hurt anyone deliberately; but they do have a great sense of fun which, sometimes, leads them into serious mischief and it is at these times that some people say they dislike them. However, all the reports say that Boggarts are always bright and cheerful and that they love singing and dancing.[934]

Only in one part of Britain does community folklore have boggarts anything like this, that is the environs of Boggart Hole Clough in north Manchester (see pp. 183–88). For the rest of the English-speaking world, this is literary folklore or, to use a 2015 term, the 'folkloresque'.[935]

What would a Victorian 'Lancashire lad' have made of Mills' description? Boggart believer or boggart sceptic, he surely would have been astounded. Since the 1920s, there has been a complete revolution in boggart-lore. None of this should be taken as a criticism of those who have pushed the relevant changes along. As far as I am concerned the men, women and children responsible are, to paraphrase James Joyce, 'forging the conscience of their country in the smithy of their soul'. This is so whether they make millions from novels, or scrape to cover their costs with self-published books on Amazon or, for that matter, sculpt boggarts from leaves and play dough in walled gardens. Nor should the earlier analysis be taken as a criticism of the 'new boggart' with its gobliny ways. Supernatural creatures and human ideas about them very properly have a life of their own. However, let us at least acknowledge that the goblin-boggart of the early 2000s bears no resemblance to the generic

---

933. McKenna, *Heir*, read in pageless electronic version.
934. 11.
935. Foster and Tolbert, *Folkloresque*.

boggart of the 1800s. It might also be worth acknowledging that folklore writers—who ideally record rather than invent tradition—have been more important in creating this new boggart than all our boggart teachers, novelists, and scriptwriters put together.

Conclusion

Holden Rag is among the best known of the Burnley boggarts. A shape-changer, the Rag appeared, when it chose to confuse or terrify humans, either as a piece of cloth blown by the wind, or as a black dog.[936] At some point in the 1960s or 1970s, local historian Roger Frost went for a walk up Holden Clough and, while 'It might seem strange to admit this ...', he glimpsed the Rag. In fact, just as he arrived in the Clough, Frost ran into a turning, amorphous shape: 'I couldn't believe my eyes, for there in front of me was Holden Rag curling and twisting in the breeze! For a moment all rationality disappeared as the legend seemed to come alive before me.' But, no, the historian came back to his senses. This was not a visitation from the Rag, only a 'small detachment of the early morning mist', which 'was gradually vapourising as it was rising in the Clough before me'. The 'boggart' faded before his eyes.[937]

I have often, while writing this book, thought of Frost's encounter with Holden Rag. That vapourizing cloud of mist is as good an epitaph as any for the traditional boggarts that used to guard Boggartdom, the borders of which I outlined in Chapters 2 and 3: much of the West Riding, Lancashire, the Peak District, north Cheshire, parts of the Midlands, and Lincolnshire. These traditional boggarts are not yet entirely gone. There are, as we saw in Chapter 7, some Victorian boggarts that persist today in Clitheroe, New Mills, and Longridge. But their dominion began to die away in the 1920s and there is little time remaining to the hold-outs. Only rarely, in the twenty-first century, do our uncanny survivors relive their 'boisterous years' when they lurked in dells and abandoned houses and listened for anxious human footsteps to draw near. They are the last red squirrels among the grey.

But if the traditional boggart is 'gradually vapourizing', then there is the consolation that it has left behind it a great deal of evidence—evidence that can be exploited using an interdisciplinary approach drawing on folklore and

---

936. Young, 'Holden' for our many sources.
937. Frost, *A Lancashire Township*, 175.

on historical, dialect, and place-name studies. I have presented sentences and patterns, sentiments and impressions from the hundreds of thousands of words written about boggarts in the nineteenth and early twentieth centuries. Studying the boggart (a generic label) is not, as I suggested in Chapter 1, the equivalent of studying a species. It is, rather, a question of studying an ecosystem: the solitary supernatural spooks and monsters of much of northern England. In examining the boggart's place in the landscape, in tales, in poems, in the theatre, in children's rituals, and in flaps, hunts, and crowds, I have tried to sketch out that ecosystem and to give some sense of the way that humans navigated its dangers (e.g. nocturnal walks) and enjoyed its pleasures (e.g. fireside stories).

Sometimes while researching that ecosystem, I temporarily deluded myself— usually late at night or very early in the morning—that in writing about the ecology of Boggartdom I was uncovering folklore laws with wider applications. It is certainly true that the way boggart stories were transmitted (Chapter 5) resembled the ways that, for instance, pixie beliefs were passed on in nineteenth-century Cornwall and Devon. Likewise, elements of social boggartry (Chapter 6) can be found in other regions in the 1800s, although the northern Scottish flap depended on a mermaid and the Kentish flap on a ghost. It may also be true that the boggart's place in the landscape (Chapter 4) resembles structures that are to be found in Angus and Buckinghamshire (and perhaps further afield). But none of this can be assumed. In studying local data, the important thing is to find small stable truths, not large uncertain ones. It is premature generalization that led folklore writers to create, against the grain of tradition, the goblin-boggart (Chapter 8).

The aspect of this work that is, I would argue, worth replicating is the push for data collection, which made it possible.[938] While my first interest in this book has been the boggart and the ecosystem that this word repre-sents, I have also become fascinated by the potential for new explorations of Victorian supernatural beliefs. Prior to about 2000, historians and folk-lorists were limited to reading books and periodicals and, to a limited extent, searching in archives. In 2022, with 'the digital dividend', it is also possible to employ newspapers, broadsides, and other forms of ephemera; to use archives more efficiently; and there is, as I argue in Chapter 7, the possibility

---

938. While finishing this book I read Waters, *Cursed Britain*, on witchcraft, the best example to date of a historian writing supernatural history with these new sources. The author gives (ibid., 93), for instance, some sense of his data pool: 'The 462 newspaper reports about outbreaks of witchcraft in Britain between 1860 and 1899.'

of gathering recollections for a period that is, just, within living memory. The shift in methods of data collection and research might not matter for historians taking readings from the gilded barometer of high culture. But for those studying a half-hidden part of the 1800s, such as ghost- or fairy-lore, here is a *revolutionary* change. The long-closed door to the nineteenth-century supernatural is creaking ajar. Much that has been forgotten or obscure will soon be open to systematic study.

Appendix: Boggart A–Z

The following is a glossary of the different meanings of 'boggart', and asso-ciated locutions as they were used in the nineteenth and early twentieth centuries.[939] There has already, note, been one attempt to chart the use of 'boggart' in dialect. In 1898, Joseph Wright published the first volume of his *Dialect Dictionary* and Wright included the *vox* 'Boggart', to which he dedicated some 900 words. The entry had six sections. These were (i) 'an apparition, ghost, hobgoblin'; 'an object of terror'; (ii) 'fright, terror, in phr[ase], to take (the) boggart'; (iii) 'a coward, a timid person'; (iv) 'a scarecrow'; (v) a series of compounds, namely 'boggart-barns', 'boggart-feart', 'boggart-flower', 'boggart-freetened', 'boggart-hole', 'boggart-muck', 'boggart-neet', 'boggart-posy', 'boggart-tales'; (vi), meanwhile, was 'to take fright; to frighten'. Wright then gave two additional, separate senses for boggart: 'the common duckweed'; and 'the dried moisture of the nostrils'.[940] Wright's work for the *Dialect Dictionary* was, as we saw, in Chapter 3 (pp. 57–61), meticulous. However, in some cases, Wright missed meanings. And in some cases, meanings of words or phrases were wider than he had imag-ined. In other cases, Wright was perhaps even wrong. The following pages offer an alphabetical list of words and phrases often with reference to Wright's entry. The *voces* are offered in alphabetical order and in each *vox* I have tried to give examples, and if possible, some sense of where a word or phrase was used within Boggartdom. I have also sought similar expres-sions about other supernatural beings from neighbouring regions. It would, in fact, be possible to fill an entire volume with supernatural words, locu-tions and sayings relating to the bogies of the English-speaking parts of Britain. I have omitted from this list boggart meaning badger or a Christmas

---

939. An earlier version of this Appendix was published in Young, 'Wright'.
940. *Dialect Dictionary*, I. For the erroneous idea that duckweed was called 'boggart' see p. 234. Wright had further references to boggarts, under other *voces*, where the word 'boggart' appeared in compounds: e.g. 'Flay-Boggart' under 'Flay', II, 392. He also included some interesting additions in his supplement published in his sixth and final volume in 1905, VI, 37.

turkey or the dying white dot on old television sets, as these seem entirely isolated.[941] Clearly if anyone can provide other references, I would revise that opinion.

'As ill as Clegg Hall boggart': this referred to the tradition that the man who had possession of the Hall murdered the rightful heirs of Clegg Hall by drowning them in the moat, the heirs becoming the boggart. According to Fishwick, 'ill' here was 'used in the sense of "as difficult to get rid of"'.[942]

'Black Boggart': Wright makes no reference to a 'black boggart'.[943] Yet a number of nineteenth-century sources contain this expression, particularly as a name for child-scaring monsters. A woman stealing shoes in Liverpool in 1863, for example, 'threatened to fetch the "black boggart" to [a courageous boy] because he refused to give her his boots'.[944] We also learn that '"T' black boggard" was spoken of as if one personage or thing' in Wakefield in the 1860s.[945] A late nineteenth-century Burnley account tells of a man who had escaped from a chimney being mistaken for a boggart: the 'incoherent midnight visitor was either a burglar, a boggart, or something else equally "uncanny" or dangerous'.[946] Ainsworth, the novelist had a character with a face 'as black as a boggart'.[947] During the mid nineteenth century, it was, meanwhile, 'a common practice of parents when their little ones were naughty to tell them there was a black boggard up the chimney,' in Pudsey.[948] Given all this, it will come as no surprise that 'as black as a boggard'[949] was a Leeds simile in the nineteenth century and that boggarts, in that city, were said to be 'of a sable complexion'.[950] In parts of the north 'the Black Man' remained the child scarer of choice as late as the 1950s.[951] An account in the Boggart Census, meanwhile, from Warrington, reports, for the 1950s: 'There was often thick fog in winter

---

941. Hewlett, 'Badgers'; BC, Lytham 2 (La); BC, Bradford 7 (WRY).

942. Fishwick, *History*, 354.

943. Wright certainly knew how 'black' was combined with bogie words in English: e.g. I, 284. For black bogies see also, Cooper, 'Lexical reflections', 81.

944. 'Child Stealing'.

945. Banks, *A List*, 8.

946. Kerr, 'Sheepstealers', (1894). A common *topos*, Palmer, 'Demon', 106: ''Tis a boggart – a thief – or the Devil instead!'

947. Ainsworth, *Lancashire*, 8.

948. Lawson, *Letters*, 51.

949. Robinson, *The Dialect*, 407.

950. Ibid., 254.

951. Orton *et al.*, *Atlas*, L64.

(before the Clean Air Act) and we were warned that a "black man" would get us in the smog. Unfortunately, this led to white children being afraid of the very few people of colour around at the time.'[952] For another postwar memory: 'Growing up in the fifties in Middleton near Rochdale ... When out in the village on dark autumn nights, older women would frighten us young lads with tales of "The Black Boggart".'[953]

'Blash-Boggart': Wright drew on Nodal and Milner's definition of blash-boggart: 'a fire-goblin, or flash-goblin; that is, a goblin that flashes and disappears. It is more commonly used figuratively, and is applied to persons who are fiery, wild, or strange in appearance, either in dress or person'.[954] Nodal and Milner do not give an instance of the first meaning: though boggarts did sometimes disappear in a flash of fire.[955] But their second figurative meaning is worth discussing. In the example that Nodal and Milner offer, the easiest reading is someone who is scruffy: 'When it geet toaurd Setturday, he wur some dirty an tatter't—a gradely blash-boggart! Aw use't to think he slept among th' coals or else on a shelf somewheer.'[956] Two other examples I have found of the term blash-boggart involve a Lancashire 'character', Bodle, who was habitually covered in soot.[957] In this light, the Middle English term a slotir-bugge or dirty person is interesting.[958] Blash-boggart should be connected to the many twentieth-century references to scruffy or filthy boggarts, see 'Boggart (Scruffy)'.

'Boggart (Coward)': Wright claims that, in North Yorkshire, 'boggart' could mean: 'A coward, a timid person'. His only evidence for this comes from an 1876 Whitby glossary, where 'boggart' is 'a coward, one easily scared'.[959] The author of the glossary had not included this definition in an earlier dialect list that he wrote, which suggests that, if this sense existed, it was rare.[960] There are some instances of supernatural names being used to describe negative characteristics in people: e.g. the idea that a stupid or slow person is a 'dobie'

---

952. BC, Warrington 18 (La).
953. BC, Middleton 8 (La).
954. Nodal and Milner, *A Glossary*, 42; Wright, *Dialect Dictionary*, I, 290.
955. Wilkinson, 'Local Folklore', 5.
956. Nodal and Milner, *A Glossary*, p. 42 (Waugh).
957. Waugh, *Sketches*, 19; Robertson, *Rochdale*, 59, when Bodle falls down a chimney.
958. *Middle English Dictionary*, B.5, 1212; Sylvester, 'Naming', 283.
959. Robinson, *A Glossary*, 22.
960. An Inhabitant, *A Glossary*, 17.

in the Scottish borders.[961] 'Boggle', not 'boggart' was the typical word for a supernatural creature in the Whitby area, but as we have seen in Chapter 2, there are reasons for thinking that 'boggart' might have been used just to the north (see pp. 66–67). Is it possible that Robinson (or an informant) had got confused with the well-established idea that a boggart creates fear ('boggart-feart' etc.)?[962] Or perhaps here the word 'boggart' crossed to humans from jumpy 'boggarty' horses?[963]

'Boggart (Exaggerated Fear)': Several early sources use 'boggart' to mean an exaggerated or invented fear, such as 'be not afraide of fraybuggardes vvhich lye in the vvay, feare the euerlasting fire, fear the serpēt vvhich hath that deadly sting';[964] '[i]t is not as men saye, to wit, Hell is but a boggarde to scarre children onelie.'[965] This continues into the nineteenth century, for instance with 'the boggart of Romanism';[966] or 'We had been frightened with a great many boggarts and hobgoblins by Mr. Disraeli';[967] or an interesting 1892 instance from sports (reminiscent of 'bogie team'): 'We all know that the Trinity forwards are strong; but there is a tendency to make boggarts of 'em. They are not invincible, and if the Leeds men set their teeth to-day, [the Trinity forwards] won't have things all their own way.'[968] For a possible late example of this: 'I grew up in Glazebrook in the 1960s. My Mum would use the phrase of people who see boggarts where there aren't any, i.e. people who see a problem when there isn't one.'[969]

'Boggart (Nickname)': There are many references to men nicknamed 'boggart', some of which may give us folklore insights.[970] For 1903, we read that '[t]he [Boggart] house [on the outskirts of Manchester] was inhabited by a poor man of the Hampson family, whose nickname was "Boggart John"'.[971] Here the explanation for the nickname is straightforward—John lived in a

---

961. Henderson, *Notes*, 247.
962. Note that Robinson was not originally from the Whitby area, though he lived there for many years until his death in 1882, 'Local Authors'.
963. Egerton and Wilbraham, *A Glossary*, 25.
964. Foxe (1563), *Actes and Monuments*, V, 1116.
965. Rollock, *Lectures*, 132.
966. 'The Religious World and Work'.
967. 'Mr. Potter' (1868).
968. Penanink, 'Sports'.
969. BC, Rixton-with-Glazebrook 1 (Ch).
970. For the folklore of nicknames see Pinto-Abecasis, 'Towards'.
971. Crofton, *Stretford*, III, 74.

haunted house—and it can be paralleled in a 1697 text where a man, living at a 'Boggard House' (Whalley, Lancs), was known as 'Boggard Fletcher'.[972] A man from Burnley named Edmondson was called 'Sandygate Boggart' by his neighbours because he had, for a time, masqueraded as a boggart in that part of the town. In fact, he had been sent to prison for eighteen months for his crimes.[973] 'Boggart John', meanwhile, was so called in a story from 1895 because 'he always looked so black and so cross he frightened us'.[974] Compare this with a late article (1932) from Nelson discussing nicknames: 'Owd Boggart were a chimney sweep.'[975] The black boggart again? Might we even connect this to a man named 'Boggard-Muck' in Rochdale (although for 'Boggard Muck' see also pp. 234–35)?[976] Edwin Waugh, meanwhile, described a fictional Boggart Bill: 'I've yerd say that her faither use't to tell fortin, an' he reckon't to rule planets, an' sich like. He went bi th' name o' Boggart Bill,—for he wur seldom sin i'th dayleet; but he use't to wander about a good deeol bi hissel' i'th neet-time.'[977] There are then more mysterious references. An 1848 pamphlet published in Bradford was entitled *Boggard Jim an' his Mate, fro' Wibsa Slack wi' their awd Tales*. Is Jim a 'Boggard' because he is associated with spooky tales?[978] There was a Boggart John Young in late nineteenth-century Kentucky (USA), who was celebrated for his supernatural stories.[979] A 'Mr. James Whitehead (better known as "Owd Boggart")' is reported as living in Ashton-under-Lyne in 1868: but no explanation is given for this name.[980] The nickname boggart is, to judge by the Boggart Census, still used in the 2020s:[981] 'boggart' has also been applied to the inhabitants of Haslingden as a collective nickname.[982] Note that other supernatural nicknames emerged in the north-west of England. In Westmorland we have an example of a dobbie

---

972. Taylor, *Surey Demoniack*, 53–54.

973. E.C., 'Sandygate Boggart' (1915). An Irish maid who pretended to be a ghost in 1855, was subsequently known as the 'Seed-Hill Ghost' (Huddersfield), 'Levies on the Publicans'; note that this might be a translation from dialect as the phrase 'Seed-Hill Boggard' was also used, 'The Model Lodging-House'.

974. 'The Third Time'.

975. Bates, 'Arm Chair'.

976. Robertson, *Rochdale*, 376.

977. Waugh, *Tufts*, 282.

978. Smyth, *Boggard Jim* (*non vidi*, recorded in 'Bibliography of Bradford and Neighbourhood', 14).

979. Olson, *Still*, 239. For two possible boggart toponyms in the US: Woodyard and Young, 'Three Notes', 65 (Boggart Road): and, far more convincingly 'Boggard Hole Pool on Little Kanawha river, above Grantsville', briefly referenced in *Bulletin of the American Association of Petroleum Geologists* 4 (1920), 28.

980. 'Presentation', 6.

981. BC, Halsall 2 (La); Milnrow 6 (La); Todmorden 9 (WRY).

982. Dobson, *Lancashire*, 36–37; BC, Blackburn 25 (La).

nickname for a man, 'Dobby Danson', who was believed to be accompanied by a ghost in his day-to-day life.[983] In late nineteenth-century Clitheroe, meanwhile, there was a weaver called 'Jenny Greenteeth': no explanation is given as to what she had done to deserve this name.[984]

'Boggart (Oppressions)': Wright reported that boggart could be 'an object of terror': he largely limits himself to the supernatural, but there is an equally strong tradition of 'boggart' as a non-supernatural oppression.[985] 'Boggart can mean anything that is awkward or difficult to handle' in the words of one modern respondent.[986] In a 'Lankisher Encylopædia', 1894, we learn that 'apparition' 'is a fancy name for a boggart, a race as hes quite deed eawt— barrin' thad sort as come debt-collectin'.[987] Consider, too, this from 1891: 'Th' owd style o' boggart's gooan eawt o' date lung sin'; them 'at used to be dresti' white; boggarts as we hevneaw-a-days is dresti' black, an come reawnd a-collectin' brass for th' Deoth list, doctor's bills, coyl bilis [sic], an' things o' thad sort.'[988] Or this from 1933: 'The worst boggart we ever see is the devil who comes for the rent.'[989] These should be linked with the following sentence from Edwin Waugh: 'Naw; we never see'n no boggarts neaw; nobbut when th' brade-fleigh's (bread-rack) empty!'[990] There is certainly the idea in Lancashire dialect that a boggart can be something that is repugnant. A phrase noted by Wright, for example: 'A mon's a boggart when he's poor'.[991] We also have references to school inspectors and even a cane used in a Burnley school as 'boggarts'.[992]

'Boggart (Scarecrow)': In Britain, and indeed further afield, scarecrows were frequently named after supernatural creatures; and scarecrows sometimes became supernatural creatures.[993] Wright included some twenty instances in

983. Pearson, *Letters*, 35.

984. 'The Last of His Race' (1908), see also BC Prestwich 7 (La).

985. Whittingham, *A Brieff Discours*, 160: 'Hereoff will all theis waightie discommodities growe that they two (ye mustevnderstande) maie not be in so great authoritie with all men nor be such buggarddes to the pooreyff they maye not beare the bagge alone'.

986. BC, Stockport 10 (Ch).

987. Tum O' Dick O' Bobs, 'A Lankisher Encylopædia' (2 June 1894).

988. 'Dictionary of the Lancashire Dialect'.

989. 'New Lamps'.

990. Waugh, *Sketches*, 79.

991. Tum O' Dick O' Bobs, 'A Lankisher Encylopædia' (27 October 1894).

992. Kerr, 'Summer Rambles'; 'Who & What Was Tom Healey?'.

993. BC, Leyland 9 (La): '1960s in Lostock Hall not far from Leyland. "Boggarts" were prowling about after dark in the fields … Worst of all were the "Crow Boggarts" the supreme of all scary things.'

his dictionary of what might be called the supernatural scarecrow.[994] There is perhaps an easy association between a boggart scaring people and a scarecrow frightening birds. One Lancashire dialect story has a 'noted scarecrow builder' who had 'a reputation as a constructor of those hideous guardians of the orchard and cornfield' deputed to make a boggart (in the sense of bogie) to scare a local gamekeeper. 'Wod'll freeten a crow 'll freeten a keeper', comments one of his friends.[995] Wright acknowledged that scarecrows were often called 'boggarts' in Cheshire:[996] another source tells us that 'pay-boggart' was also used in that county with that sense.[997] According to Wright, in Lancashire, a 'corn boggart' and a 'crow-boggart' were the favoured terms.[998] Note that 'corn-boggart', in Lancashire dialect, seems to have been associated with ugliness (perhaps particularly in women). Three examples from the writing of Edwin Waugh: 'I'll tell yo what, Matty; hoo'd [she'd] mak a rare corn-boggart!';[999] 'If I're a lad I should as soon think o' gettin' wed to a corn-boggart as sich a trollops!';[1000] 'Thou darn't show thi face i'th dayleet. I'd stop theer if I're thee, for thou'rt likker a corn-boggart than a Christian. I wish thou could see thisel'! … Thou'rt feaw enough to breighk ony seemin'-glass i'th world!'.[1001] See also 'foul as a corn-boggart' and 'should soon as think as getting wed to a corn-boggart' in Wilkinson's *Thesaurus* (unreferenced).[1002] From the Boggart Census, we have similar meanings, 'My mum is from Adlington … and she used to talk about some men that used to hang around in the park area that her mother used to tell her and her sisters to stay away from and she used to call them "Crow Boggarts". I assumed they maybe worked in the pits or coal mines so that's why they were black as crows'; and 'We used to call each other crow boggarts and just looked it up and it's a scarecrow

---

994. Barley-buggle I, 166; Bo-boy I, 315; Bo-Cow I, 315; Bo-Crukes I, 315; Boakie I, 316; Boggart I, 326; Boggybo I, 327; Bogle I, 328; Boggleboe I, 328; Bubbock I, 424; Bucca I, 424; Buccaboo I, 425; Bug VI, 50; Bugahag, VI, 50; Bugalug, VI, 50; Bull-Beggar I, 436; Cauk I 544; Dead Man II, 41; Doolie II, 123; and Gally-baggar, II, 546. For British and Irish scarecrows and the supernatural, Haining, *Scarecrow*, 56–62 (valuable particularly for the comments of Jacqueline Simpson in her correspondence with the author, 59–61).

995. MacManus and Hull, *Tales*, https://minorvictorianwriters.org.uk/hull/b_tales.htm [accessed 11 February 2020].

996. *Dialect Dictionary*, I, 326.

997. Yarwood, 'Novel', 195.

998. *Dialect Dictionary*, I, 732 and I, 816.

999. Waugh, *The Chimney*, 20.

1000. Waugh, *Besom Ben*, 351.

1001. Waugh, *The Chimney*, 93: to a drunk husband who refuses to come home.

1002. 540.

to scare the crows as much as the boggarts scare humans.'[1003] Wright has no boggart scarecrows for Lincolnshire but Sims-Kimbrey claims that 'The man following the plough was a hoss-boggard or a plough-boggard.' Was this, originally, a comparison to a scarecrow in Lincolnshire fields?[1004] Wright also included, in his *Dictionary*, two curious southern references to boggart scarecrows. Firstly, one of his correspondents, the Reverend Hamilton Kingsford, resident at Stoulton in Worcestershire, reported that 'boggart' was used for scarecrows there.[1005] Here we have evidence for boggart some eighty miles to the south of the most southerly Staffordshire boggarts. Wright then included in his supplement (collected in the sixth and final volume of the dictionary) a further reference to 'boggart' as scarecrow from another correspondent: one 'K.M.G.' in Wiltshire.[1006] We know that the boggart scarecrow can survive without reference to a supernatural boggart. In fact, our earliest reference to 'boggart' in Coverdale is suggestive of this. Coverdale uses 'bugge' for a bogie and 'fray-boggarde' for a scarecrow (see pp. 36–37). It is also true that dialect in Wiltshire and Worcestershire received notably less coverage than, say, Yorkshire or Lancashire: although they were by no means as neglected as some of the Home Counties.[1007] But the complete lack of any other evidence for these names and their distance from Boggartdom might call into question these southern scarecrow boggarts. Had perhaps a 'bug' word been assimilated to boggart by a collector—much as Wright did with 'bawker' for Devon?[1008] We know that in Wiltshire a scarecrow could be called a 'gally-bagger'.[1009]

'Boggart (scruffy)': 'My mother used to tell me I looked as though a boggart had been after me whenever I looked particularly dishevelled, a frequent event';[1010] '[b]oth my parents were from Wigan, and used the word "boggart"

1003. BC, Euxton 10 (La); Warrington 16 (La).

1004. *Wodds*, 33. I can imagine the erect ploughman appearing like a scarecrow.

1005. *Dialect Dictionary*, I, 326. Kingsford was not a dialect speaker. He was from a Kentish family. He had studied at Oxford and he had worked in Somerset, Hereford and Gloucester early in his career in the Church. But he was vicar of Stoulton for the best part of fifty years, from 1867 (aged 35) to 1913 and he will not have heard (I think) 'boggart' in the other places that he had lived, 'Ecclesiastical' (1914).

1006. *Dialect Dictionary*, VI, 327. I have been unable to identify 'K.M.G.'.

1007. Wright, *The Life*, II, 358: 'Professor Wright states ... that his helpers are most numerous and most enthusiastic in the North of England and in the West'; see also II, 383 Praxmarer, 'Wright's *EDD*', 68: the two counties were middle-ranking in terms of coverage.

1008. *Dialect Dictionary*, I, 326.

1009. Jones and Dillon, *Dialect*, 62: 'gally' is scary; and with 'baggar' one recalls bull-beggar and related forms, see n. 107. Wright, *Dialect Dictionary*, II, 546 has 'gally-beggar' for Hampshire.

1010. BC, Rossendale 6 (La).

if my brother and I were dirty';[1011] '[g]rowing up in Skem when I was a kid if my mum or dad called me a "boggart" it meant I was a scruffy sod after being on the moss all day';[1012] a boys's father and grandmother always 'came out with this word when I was growing up and they didn't like the way I looked: "Tha favvers [resembles] a Boggart!"';[1013] '[s]imilarly if we were a bit scruffy he would say "eeh, tha looks like a reet boggart"';[1014] and 'I regularly call my husband a "boggart", especially when he's just woken up'.[1015] There is sometimes, too, the sense that someone with an outlandish appearance was a boggart: 'My dad used the word if he saw someone dressed a bit too creatively. He would say: "flaming hell! She looks a right boggart on that!"'[1016] 'My father who was born in 1918 used to say when we were watching the TV during the 1960s about singers with excessive eye makeup: "She looks a boggart."'[1017] See 'Blash-Boggart' (p. 222).

'Boggart (uncanny or mysterious)': The word 'boggart' can be applied as an adjective to spooky or uncanny phenomena: see 'Boggart Field' (p. 230), Boggart House and Boggart Lane (pp. 90–97).[1018] Apart from the landscape we have references to 'boggart rooms',[1019] 'boggart painting',[1020] 'boggart forms' (literary: shadows seen at night),[1021] and a 'boggartly' tapestry.[1022] Boggart can also have the sense of something unknown: 'My dad has used the word "boggart" for as long as I can remember when hearing or seeing something he couldn't identify.'[1023] Or consider this: 'My husband and I are keen walkers so when walking over Holcombe Moor and seeing walkers in the distance we refer to them as "boggarts" and I thought I just made it up, but reading this made me think maybe it came from my childhood.'[1024]

1011. BC, Wigan 2 (La).
1012. BC, Skelmersdale 6 (La).
1013. BC, Cadishead 7 (La).
1014. BC, Saddleworth 2 (WRY).
1015. BC, Hayfield 5 (De).
1016. BC, Bardsley 1 (La).
1017. BC, Littleborough 17 (La).
1018. Malham-Dembleby, *Original Tales*, 157 where 'boggard' is taken as an adjective: 'eerie, ghostly, devilish'.
1019. Tilley, *Old Halls*, I, 164.
1020. Bobbin, *Tim*, 308.
1021. Swain, *Dramatic*, 122, 'thy brain/Is full of boggart shapes and nervous fears'.
1022. 'Bishop Bardsley's Connection'.
1023. BC, Leyland 16 (La); see also Chorley 1 (La).
1024. BC, Haslingden 1 (La).

'Boggart Bell': A recorded interview with Rosemond Fishwick of Kirkham, born in 1904, recalls the 'boggart bell' at Kirkham, in the Fylde in the years before the First World War.[1025] Rosemond remembers that every night, in the winter months, a bell would ring at 8 pm: once on the first of the month, twice on the second, etc. Her mother used to tell Rosemond that as 'soon as you hear that bell you run home or the boggarts'll be after you': and, at 8 pm, Rosemond remembers 'we'd run like mad'. Rosemond connected the bell to a Kirkham Roundhead ghost. 'Taggy bell' in Penrith apparently had similar connotations: 'a simple appeal to the terrors of children against the personification of "the power that walketh in the darkness"'.[1026] This is all reminiscent of a late nine-teenth-century reference to 'boggart time' from Lancashire, which seems to have meant midnight.[1027] On the subject of boggarts and time, there is one 1920 claim that in the Peak District, boggarts lived behind clocks. 'In some of the old farmhouses, which have been in the same family for generations, the clock, usually the grandfather type, is never removed from its place, for behind it is supposed to dwell the "Family Boggart" and, were it disturbed, it might bring trouble to the household. Some tenants believe that the ghosts of their deceased ancestors harbour themselves behind the clock.'[1028]

'Boggart Chair': Wright does not list boggart chairs, but Kai Roberts has given a detailed study of two Calderdale houses, both of which, it was claimed, had this unusual item of furniture in the garden.[1029] In one case, the boggart chair was a fragment of a medieval font, and it has now been restored to a local church. There is, though, an unnoticed boggart chair at Colne, over the border in Lancashire. Here we have an 1842 tithe record of a 'Boggart Chair Field', presumably a field in which the boggart chair sat: then, in 1881, a reference to 'two cottages ... Netherheys, in Boggart-chair, Barrowford-road'.[1030] (These are almost certainly the same Boggart Chair.) Now what was a boggart chair? There are several instances from Britain and Ireland of

---

1025. Oral History Recordings: Rosemond Fishwick (1996.0012), Lancashire archives. The date for the recording is given as: 17 June 1905 (is this her date of birth?), which clearly cannot be right. Rosemond sounds like she is in her seventies or eighties. The recording perhaps dates to the 1970s: there is a reference to inflation! The relevant boggart bell passage starts at about 10 minutes 40 seconds.

1026. Powley, 'The Curfew Bell', 132.

1027. H. 'Catholic Soiree'.

1028. 'Family Ghosts'.

1029. Roberts, 'Don't Boggart', 21–23.

1030. This is just to the north of Vivary Way. 1848 OSLa 48 has Netherheys but no prominently marked stone. The immediate area has been built over but there are fields just to the north of Netherheys. Perhaps the Boggart Chair is still to be found there?

supernatural beings having rock seats.[1031] I would guess that 'boggart chairs' were unusual seat-shaped stones. Thanks to Alan Cleaver, I learn of a 'Boggle Resting Place' at St Bees in Cumberland: a plinth sticking out from the wall of a sixteenth- or seventeenth-century house (Nursery Cottage, Main Street), three to four yards up the gable wall.[1032]

'Boggart Cups': Archaeologist John J. Reid claimed in 1884, that cups with 'grotesque faces' were called, in the north '"boggle" or "boggart" (goblin) drinking cups'.[1033] Note, in this light, the following interesting reference from the Potteries: 'The term [boggart] is applied slightingly to the commonest kinds of earthenware chimney ornaments.'[1034]

'Boggart Field': There are twenty-six boggart field-type place-names.[1035] It is possible that some of these toponyms were given because a scarecrow stood in or near the named land, see 'Boggart (Scarecrow)'. Cavill prefers, instead, another explanation for boggart fields: 'The name is likely to be applied to land which is secluded and/or overgrown, or which contains physical hazards of some kind; one of the latter might have been the Yorkshire boggart-flower, or dog's mercury'.[1036] When asked in the Boggart Census, one man who was born in the 1920s stated: '"Nothing will ever grow except grass in any boggart field." I asked if he was talking specifically about the boggart field at Gristlehurst. "No—any boggart field", he said. But he didn't know of any other, but knew this was a fact.'[1037]

'Boggart-Haunted': 'Coffin Bridge' in Cheshire '*enjoys* ... the unhappy reputation of being boggart-haunted'.[1038] 'Boggart-haunted' also appears in nineteenth-century Lancashire writing: 'boggart-haunted hamlet';[1039] 'whatever

---

1031. See, e.g., Lysaght, *Banshee*, 126.
1032. This phrase comes from Donald Brownrigg, a lifelong native of the village. In Jopling, 'Well if you believe that ...'. Builders working on the house were reported as saying that the plinth was for witches to land upon.
1033. 'Notice of Two Vessels', 35.
1034. 'Staffordshire Dialect and Folk-lore' (1877).
1035. See BN.
1036. Cavill, *Field-Names*, 37. In an email, Paul Cavill, 23 January 2020, adds that the adoption of a place-name based on scarecrows 'is a natural semantic development, I guess, but the hesitation that I have about adopting it would be that scarecrows are likely to be transient: no reason why that should prevent a name being given, but perhaps a slight reason for it not enduring'.
1037. Heywood 3 (La). The 'I' here is Lynda Taylor who kindly collected this interview on my behalf.
1038. Burgess, *Cheshire*, 119.
1039. Waugh, *Sketches*, 210.

have aw done to be boggart-haunted so?' (for a person rather than a place);[1040] a mine is 'boggart-haunted, as all neighbouring folk know';[1041] and '[t]here is scarcely a village in the whole of Lancashire which does not boast of its boggart-haunted clough'.[1042]

'Boggart Hole': Wright described a 'Boggart Hole' as 'a haunted hollow; a mythical place of terror invented with the idea of frightening children into good behaviour'. 'Hole' was certainly used, in Lancashire and Yorkshire dialect to describe a closed claustrophobic space in buildings or the countryside: Wright himself worked, for some time, in 't' slave 'oil' at Saltaire Mill.[1043] A better formulation might be that 'a boggart hole is a boggart lair': a BBC radio play from 1931 was entitled: *the Boggart Who Had No Hole*.[1044] Quite where the lair is to be found changes through the Northern and Midland counties: see pp. 98–102. In the North Riding, a boggart hole was a cave or pot; in Lancashire it was usually a clough.[1045] There is a pool (in Barton, Lancs) described as a—this is not a proper name—'boggart hole': skeletons had apparently been found there.[1046] Boggart holes also appeared in buildings typically as small rooms (under the stairs or in the loft, see pp. 103–104). However, they sometimes had a slightly different sense. Our first published boggart story in 1825 includes the following section: we are at a farm at an undisclosed location in Yorkshire. 'One day the farmer's youngest boy was playing with the shoe-horn, and, as children will do, he stuck the horn into this knot-hole. Whether this aperture had been formed by the Boggart as a peep-hole to watch the motions of the family, I cannot pretend to say; some thought it was, for it was designated the Boggart's hole.'[1047] This story which came from somewhere in Yorkshire was later adapted by Thomas Crofton Croker in a story published by John Roby.[1048] In both versions the boggart would shoot the horn out of the hole: 'the horn darted out with velocity, and struck the poor child over the head'.[1049] This should be connected to the 'awfbore' or 'elfhole' from the north-east. That acute observer of north-eastern folklore, John Atkinson wrote:

1040. Axon, 'Gallowsfield Ghost'.
1041. Gilchrist, 'Black'.
1042. Baron, 'Lancashire Boggarts'.
1043. Wright, *The Life*, I 30.
1044. 'North Regional', 4.
1045. Young, 'What is a Boggart Hole?', 75–86.
1046. Logan, 'Historic Barton', 3.
1047. P., 'Fairy Tales', 252–53.
1048. Roby, *Traditions*, II, 287–381, see further below.
1049. P., 'Fairy Tales', 252–53.

[the Hob] was not of those who resent, with a sort of pettish, or even spiteful, malice, the possibly unintended interference with elfish prerogative implied in stopping up an 'awfbore' or hole in deal-boarding occasioned by the dropping out of a shrunken knot, and which displayed itself in the way of forcibly ejecting the intended stopping, in the form of a sharply driven pellet, into the face, or directly on to the nose, of the offender.[1050]

Compare this to an early nineteenth-century Scottish source: 'If you were to look through an elf-bore in wood, where a thorter knot has been taken out, you may see the elf-bull butting with the strongest bull in the herd.'[1051] The idea of a hole in wood being used by a boggart might be an isolated motif, but a tale published in *Once a Week* from 1874 has 'boggart holes' in a wooden cradle.

I noticed three or four smooth round holes pierced completely through the wood, looking exactly as if at one time it had served as a butt for pistol practice. So puzzled was I as to how they could have come there, that at last I drew the attention of my hostess to the phenomenon. 'Aye,' said she, 'those are Boggart holes.'[1052]

Apparently, the boggart had shot them into the cradle with a thunderbolt, while the cradle was being brought home! Perhaps holes in timber or wood could be referred to as 'boggart holes', then? I am reminded of Allen's writing on how house spirits liked 'corners of old houses least frequented'; and left and entered homes through small holes and cracks.[1053] Compare with, for Lincolnshire, 'boggle-'oles': 'openings high in the walls of barns for ventilation and, by implication ... for ghosts!'[1054]

'Boggart Hunt': In 1869, in Carnforth, a reading was given entitled 't' Boggart Hunt'.[1055] This work is unfortunately lost. But the expression 'boggart

---

1050. Atkinson, *Forty Years*, 66.

1051. Jamieson and Johnstone, *Dictionary*, III, 366. Note that according to Kirk, Walsh, *Secret Commonwealth*, 45, one way to have second sight was 'to look thus back through a Hole where was a Knot of Fir'.

1052. Quick, 'Two Nights', 304–05: the boggart holes are explained on page 305. The author seems to be well acquainted with Yorkshire lore.

1053. 'Influence' (1936), 906–07.

1054. Sims-Kimbrey, *Wodds*, 33; Elder (ed.), *Word Books*, 68 has 'bogie hole', 'a place where bogies are supposed to live'.

1055. 'Carnforth Readings', 5.

hunt' appears elsewhere, suggesting that it was an established term. One 1852 newspaper, for example, describes 'boggart hunters', and a newspaper in 1881 has instead 'boggart hunting' as its title.[1056] Both refer to crowds attempting to capture a local ghost; it must be remembered that this was a period in which ghosts were often revealed to be miscreants with white sheets over their heads.[1057] Edwin Waugh used the expression 'boggart hunt' with a different sense: 'An' th' woint went whistlin' an' yeawlin' reawnd that heawse as if o'th witches between theer an' th' big end o'Pendle had bin frozen eawt o' their holes, an' wurridin' reawnd upo' th' stonn, like a boggart-hunt i' th air.'[1058] There is also a comment in the Boggart Census: 'I remember the phrase "Hunt the Boggitt" used in my childhood. Not sure but I think it may have been related to asking for trouble.'[1059] These boggart hunts might be usefully related to Harold Speight's bizarre claim, made in 1898: 'In the Town's Book at Yeadon, it is worth noting, there are entries of sums paid for "boggard-catching." They appear to have been so troublesome in that locality as to have rendered necessary a call upon the public purse for their suppression.'[1060] The 'Town's Book' is not to be found in the West Yorkshire archives. Fortunately, Slater includes a page from the Churchwarden's Book for 1723 (this was apparently the origin of Speight's boggart hunting).[1061] Here the expenses include one shilling for 'getting the Boggard': Slater commented facetiously: 'The knowledge and wisdom that succeeding ages has brought to us emboldens us 19th century people to dispense with boggard getters.'[1062] I wonder if 'boggard' here does not refer to a fake local ghost, or just possibly a new toilet? Alternatively, there is a late and somewhat suspect reference to a badger being called a boggart...[1063] Note that boggart hunts definitely feature in contemporary boggart-lore.[1064]

'Boggart in the Throat': A memory from the 1950s: 'Oh and some boy at my infant school would say he had a boggart in his throat not a frog in his throat.'[1065]

1056. 'Extraordinary Superstition at Blackley', 7; 'Boggart' Hunting'.
1057. Middleton, *Spirits*, passim and pp. 149–52.
1058. Waugh, *Tufts*, 34.
1059. BC, Woodhouse 1 (WRY).
1060. Speight, *Chronicles*, 268.
1061. *Guiselely*, 156.
1062. Ibid., 156.
1063. Hewlett, 'Badgers'.
1064. BC, London 1 (Oth); Mirfield 1 (WRY); Shaw 1 (La).
1065. BC, Rawtenstall 5 (La).

'Boggart Meat': Wright failed to turn up this expression, which meant in (at least some parts of) Lancashire, ferns (presumably bracken). Consider these two comments, the first from 1863 (Bury): 'Ten years ago nothing was cared about [ferns]. They were called "boggart meat" (and were [sic] so still in some places), and were considered rather repulsive than otherwise.'[1066] The second writer, Henry Kerr, writing in a Burnley newspaper, connects, in 1893, 'boggart meat' and the idea that fern seed have magical qualities: 'the yet popular name for the common fern is "boggart meat," or "meyt" in the vernacular folk-speech'.[1067] Are the magical qualities of ferns the reason for the connection with boggarts, or can it be concluded that some boggarts dwelt in the woods where ferns would be found? While on matters botanical, it is also worth noting here that Wright claims (depending on the *Dictionary of English Plants*) that, in Yorkshire, a 'boggart-flower' or 'boggart-posy' is *Mercurialis perennis*, dog's mercury.[1068] Dog's mercury is a poisonous green plant with dull, unremarkable flowers. It carpets woodlands across much of the UK.[1069] It was also associated with snakes in folklore, perhaps underlining its poisonous nature.[1070] There is a solitary 1945 reference to 'boggard blossom' from the Colne area 'ever with us along the sides of the railway tracks', which must be another unidentified plant.[1071] There is no evidence, meanwhile, that common duck-weed, *Lemna minor* was called 'boggart' (*pace* many authors), although it was unquestionably associated, in some parts of the north and Midlands with Jenny Greenteeth.[1072]

'Boggart Muck': Boggart muck (owl pellets) was included by Wright who took his definition from Holland's *Cheshire Glossary of 1886*: 'the undigested portions of food cast up by owls'.[1073] Wright suggests that 'boggart muck' was

---

1066. 'Elements'. Roy Vickery, pers. comm., 30 September 2018, points out how strange it is to refer to ferns as being 'repulsive'.
1067. Kerr, 'Typical "Chips": No. 1', 3.
1068. I, 326.
1069. For more on this plant, particularly its poisonous properties, Jefferson and Kirby, 'Boggarts'.
1070. Britten and Holland, *A Dictionary*, 593.
1071. Maria, 'A Woman's Point of View': the article is under a 'Colne and District topics' rubrick. Blossom seen from a train can hardly be *Mercurialis perennis*.
1072. The error starts with Wright, *Dialect Dictionary*, II, 326 and continues, e.g. Vickery, *Folk*, 220 in 2019. It seems to have originated in a misreading of Britten, 'Boggarts': 'We are much indebted to MR. W. DAVIES for "laying" this "boggart" [i.e. Jenny Greenteeth]. He does not mention that this name is still in use; so he may like to know that at Birmingham the common duckweed (Lemna minor) is so called', which can only mean that the duckweed is called Jenny Greenteeth. For confirmation of 'Jenny' see Britten, *A Dictionary*, 878.
1073. Holland, *A Glossary*, 407.

restricted to Cheshire. Some late evidence suggests that the phrase was also used in Lincolnshire.[1074] As to meaning, there seems to be no question that these were owl pellets at least in some parts of Britain: 'the small bones, no doubt, [were] supposed to be remains of creatures devoured by boggarts'.[1075] In 1910, Edward Barber went considerably further while writing about Cheshire: 'The name of "Boggarts muck" is given to owl pellets, the idea being that the small bones therein are those of fairies eaten by boggarts'![1076] A 1940 Cheshire newspaper has the following consideration: 'When beetles have been generously included in the menu, the [owl] scuds shine, all iridescent, with such beauty that the country folk call them boggart's scuds. For they believe that fairies [i.e. boggarts?], and not owls, have thrown them up.'[1077] There is also this comment from 1898 connecting church owls to boggarts: 'This curious term doubtless originated from the fact that pellets are sometimes found in church towers and churchyards, and the mysterious hootings and screechings heard at night in these places give colour to the notion that boggarts (ghosts) are engaged upon their unhallowed feast!'[1078] In the nineteenth century, Boggard-Muck appeared as a Rochdale nickname.[1079] One late Lancashire source also has 'boggard muck' as an alternative name for toffee;[1080] and 'boggart muck' meant hedgehog droppings according to one respondent from the Fylde who grew up in the 1950s.[1081] Consider, too, the following unexplained sentence in Saddleworth writer, Ammon Wrigley: 'Awm noan feart o' boggart muck'.[1082] Could it mean, 'I'm not afraid of owl pellets'? It seems unlikely.

'Boggart Neet': Wright noted that 'Boggart Neet' was St Mark's Eve (24 April) 'when ghosts are said to "walk"'.[1083] Note, however, that there is an early twentieth-century play by Frederic Moorman, in Yorkshire dialect, entitled *An*

1074. Sims-Kimbrey, *Wodds*, 33: 'Boggard Muck', note that Sims-Kimbrey suggests that 'boggard' can sometimes mean 'owl', presumably a false deduction from this word.
1075. Coward, *Fauna*, I, 274.
1076. Barber, *Memorials*, 255; from which presumably Stephens, *The Boom*, 131–32.
1077. 'See How …' (1940). Is it possible that this is a misremembering of Barber, *Memorials*, 255?
1078. Adams, 'A Plea', 450. For more owl-boggart confusion in churches: 'A Boggart in a Church' and The Deeside Owl, 'A Hoot' (1889): see motif J1782.1, 'Robber or dog in church thought to be ghost'.
1079. Robertson, *Rochdale*, 376.
1080. http://www.briercliffesociety.co.uk/talkback/viewtopic.php?f=25&t=860&hilit, a poem about postwar Lancashire? [accessed 4 January 2019].
1081. BC, Freckleton 1 (La).
1082. Wrigley, *Old Lancashire Words*, 9 (an example not a saying).
1083. For our most extensive description: Easther and Lees, *A Glossary*, 13.

All Souls' Night Dream, in which Hallowe'en (31 October) is given the name 'Boggard Neet'.[1084]

'Boggart-Owned': In an 1891 American article on dialect words and phrases from the English Lake District there is the following sentence: 'if you are "'boggart-owned" you are destined or fated to be given over to some evil spirit'.[1085] I have been unable to find any other example or even a supernatural parallel in 'owned' from any English regional dialect.

'Boggart-Ridden': In the *Black Knight*, Manchester author, William Axon claims, after giving a long catalogue of supernatural monsters that haunted the countryside near Lees, that 'th' entoire world must ha bin boggart ridden'.[1086] The only other instance of this expression I have been able to find is in a Lancashire short story from 1956: 'The one day owd Stump th' bellman towd him there war a labourer wanted at Hacking's quarry[,] an off he went like he war boggart-ridden.'[1087] There are several other examples of 'ridden' compounded with supernatural creatures from Britain: e.g. pixy-ridden and hag-ridden.[1088] In this wider range of words, three meanings can be found: to be overcome with nightmares, to be attacked while sleeping by a supernatural creature (specifically hag-ridden);[1089] for a horse to be ridden at night by a supernatural creature and found sweating in its stable in the morning;[1090] for we might imagine by extension with the reference to horses, an area or person haunted or possessed by the supernatural.[1091] The two instances from Lancashire fit neatly into this spectrum.

'Boggart Seer': An 1856 source introduces us to these northern mystics: 'J.W. used to see fearin' on the new road betwixt East-end and Droylsden toll-bar; he was the last of the bona fide boggart seers.'[1092] 'Boggart seer' here should be compared to the use of 'ghost-seer' in the same region and period.[1093]

1084. *Plays of the Ridings*, 27–42.
1085. 'Dialect in England's Lake District'.
1086. 54.
1087. Miller, 'Job'.
1088. Edwards, *Hobgoblin and Sweet Puck*, 159.
1089. Hufford, *The Terror*.
1090. Whittle, 'Festivities', 304.
1091. Bourke, *Burning*, 66.
1092. [Higson], 'Droylsden Customs', 4, see also Higson, *Droylsden*, 69. Fearin' are 'fearful things': see p. 8.
1093. 'The Moss Lane Spectre' (1861); Snowden, *Tales*, 120.

'Boggart Stones': Wright claimed that 'boggart stones', were 'white quartz nodules found in gravel'. He goes on to note that '[w]hen rubbed together these are supposed to emit a brimstone-like odour'.[1094] His one source for this relates to Rochdale and Rossendale.[1095] Rubbing quartz stones together produces a dim luminous light, which would add to their 'haunted' quality.[1096] We have, meanwhile, two instances from the South Pennines of another type of boggart stone. One on Widdop Moor above Hebden Bridge (divided into Upper and Lower Boggart Stones); and the other on the moors above Saddleworth. Both are a group of prominent, naturally situated rocks, that are easily visible on the barren moorland.[1097] But why were they so called? Was it that the boggarts were supposed to sit on the stones (compare with 'Boggart Chair' pp. 229–30)?[1098] Or was it that boggarts had been turned into stones, as in other British legends?[1099] T.T. Wilkinson wrote unhelpfully in 1865 (of the Widdop Stones): '[t]he Boggart Stones need no explanation'.[1100] Note that 'boggart stone' seems never to have meant stones with a hole, used against the supernatural and sometimes called 'witch stones' or, in the Northwest, a 'dobbie stone'.[1101]

'Boggart Wood': Wright mentions, in his supplement, 'Boggart Wood' as a 'sarcastic' Lancashire word for a handloom from an informant.[1102] I know of several references, most from the writing of Benjamin Brierley, but I cannot explain the moniker unless there is the traditional association between 'various mechanical devices' and the devil.[1103] 'I've a better job i'view than keawerin between two lumps o' boggart wood';[1104] 'It's getting welly time for t'make a start, but I connot face yon lumps o' Boggart Wood this mornin';[1105] '"Boggart-wood, Ab," Sammy said, as he looked at th' owd worm-etten bits o' timber'—spindles in an American museum;[1106]

1094. II, p. 326.
1095. Cunliffe, *A Glossary*, 21.
1096. Robbins, *Fluorescent Minerals*, 1–5. For more on quartz and folklore, see Thompson, 'Clocha Geala/Clocha Uaisle'.
1097. OSY 214 (1851); OSY 271 (1854).
1098. For the social boggart, n. 693.
1099. See, e.g. Hunt, *Popular Romances*, 177–79.
1100. Wilkinson, 'On the Druidical Rock Basins', 6–7.
1101. Taylor, *The Old Manorial*, 231.
1102. VI, 37 (in the supplementary section).
1103. Scott, 'Bogus and His Crew', 170–71.
1104. Brierley, *Ben Brierley's Works*, 289.
1105. Birchall, 'Owd Butty's Lump o' Gowd'.
1106. Brierley, *Yankeeland*, 146.

'a loom's made o' boggart wood, an' 'll stond foire [stand fire] as lung as owd Juddie's safe'.[1107]

'Boggartin": In one Edwin Waugh short story two drunks decide to dress up as ghosts in sheets and scare passers-by: 'Let's have a go at boggartin'.'[1108] Compare this to the Boggart Census: 'On 4 Nov (mischief night) the teenagers went Boggarting which involved rolling up a newspaper and pushing it up the roof drainage down pipe and setting fire to it which made a loud moaning noise.'[1109] Consider, too, from the nineteenth century, 'play the boggart': 'It appears that the old lady, who is upwards of sixty years of age, took it into her head, whimsically enough, to play the boggart, and with that intent actually left her house for the purpose of interrupting a young woman, who had just before departed on an errand to a public house at the bridge.'[1110] The joker broke her leg while jumping into a ditch from which she wanted to surprise her friend.

'Don't Bogart that Joint': Sometimes offered up as a boggart expression, this, in fact, comes from postwar American counterculture and was said to anyone 'hogging' a marijuana cigarette. Humphrey Bogart was often filmed with a cigarette held lovingly in his hand.[1111]

'Everybody had a boggart i' their cubbort': This is presumably 'a skeleton in their cupboard'. Brierley writes that there was 'never a truer sayin'.[1112]

'Fause as a Boggart': Wright did not include this under 'Boggart', although he did include the expression elsewhere in his *Dictionary*.[1113] It is worth repeating here as readers might misinterpret the saying to be 'As false as a boggart'. It really means 'As cunning as a boggart'.[1114] Consider this sentence

---

1107. Brierley, *Ab-o'th'-Yate' Sketches*, I, 157, see also Brierley, 'Ab-O' Th'-Yate' (31 July 1869); Brierley, 'Ab-O' Th'-Yate' (7 August 1869); Brierley, *Ben Brierley's Works*, 244.

1108. Waugh, *Tufts*, 46.

1109. BC, Bentham (La), 4. Compare to Colne 3 (La): 'Wheer ar ta boggartin' off to?'; Rossendale 1 (La) 'when two dogs are chasing each other; they are said to be "boggarting around"'.

1110. 'Singular Frolic', *The Preston Chronicle and Lancashire Advertiser* (17 January 1857), 3.

1111. Hendrickson, *QPB*, 212. Thanks to Niall O' Donnell for help with this reference.

1112. Brierley, *Ab-o'th'-Yate's Dictionary*, 203.

1113. III, p. 291.

1114. See, e.g., Wilkinson and Tattersall, *Memories*, 61; picked up in John Billingsley, *Folk Tales from Calderdale*, 21. For the closeness of 'false' and 'cunning' in some dialects, Wright, *Dialect Dictionary*, II, p. 291.

of Waugh's in 'Ramble from Bury to Rochdale': 'He'll be as fause as a boggart, or elze he'd never ha' bin i' that shop as lung as he has bin, not he. There's moor in his yed nor a smo'-tooth comb con fotch eawt.'[1115] Here, instead, are two memories from the Boggart Census: 'My grandma was born in Ashton in the 1900s and she used to say to us "he/she is as faus as a boggart", faus meaning false, and the saying used to mean that someone was being nice to you but that they were up to no good';[1116] 'I grew up in Droylsden in 1940s/1950s. If I was trying a fast one on my Mother she would say "you're as farce [sic] as a boggart". Still don't know what she meant.'[1117] Why were boggarts said to be cunning? We have little evidence of this in boggart-lore unless we think of the battle of wits between families and house boggarts: or perhaps this relates to their mischievous side, see 'to Make Boggarts'. Note the poorly attested expression: 'As fause as a Pendle Witch'.[1118]

'Hello, Mr Boggart': A boggart 'also resides at the Devil's Elbow [and] as you come up the brew from Whalley to Read, you have to say "hello, Mr Boggart" as you travel the tight bend or you're in for trouble'.[1119] Compare this with folklore from Boggart Hole Clough which 'says the local boggart is buried under that stone, and if you don't say "hello" when you pass he will jump up from below and grab you … with dire consequences'.[1120] Might this be a twentieth-century innovation?

'If they were born in [Mankinholes] they believed in boggards': This phrase is only attested in one source: Mankinholes is a hamlet above Hebden Bridge.[1121] Why were Mankinholes folk believers? Perhaps because the village had a number of haunted places (as did most most villages), or perhaps the inference was that Mankinholes was somewhat behind the times (isolated and high up on the valley side).

1115. Waugh, *Sketches*, 32.

1116. BC, Ashton-Under-Lyne 4 (La).

1117. BC, Droylsden 4 (La).

1118. Wright, *Rustic*, 211–12.

1119. BC, Pendle 2 (La).

1120. BC, Moston 2 (La); possibly also Oldham 8: 'To this day, whenever I walk down by Chamber Hall Close (where the sadly demolished medieval hall once stood) I say "Hi" to the sleeping boggart!'.

1121. 'Astrology and Boggards' (1916).

'In an' aght like Fearnla boggard': Wright gives this expression but with no explanation; as does, Wilkinson.[1122] Wright may have had no idea of its meaning and I have not been able to check the original source.[1123] A Haworth informant in the Boggart Census gives the solution: 'as children, if we were running in and out of the house a lot, my grandmother would say "ee!, you're in and out like Butterfield Boggart!" And despite asking around I've never been able to find out who "Butterfield Boggart" was!'[1124] Compare: 'Up and Down Like a Boggart' (p. 246).

'Marsh Boggart': In *Comlyn Alibi*, a novel serialized in newspapers by Norfolk author, Headon Hill, in 1916 (1917 in book form), there is a reference to a 'marsh boggart' (in Cornwall!): '"There's more to it than that, Master Toney," she said. "There's talk in Comlyn village that you were seen down here on the day of the murder. I've done my level best to track the rumour, but t'wasn't any good. It appears to have just blazed up and died out again, like a marsh boggart."'[1125] This does not sound very promising, but 'marsh boggart' is found in the Boggart Census: 'My Wigan grandparents … mentioned boggarts … when they chastised us for cheekiness: "tha'r a boggart!" and even "tha'r a marsh boggart!".[1126] In 1868, a Salford delegate at an Oddfellows Congress said that enrolment was 'a mere boggart to frighten us'.[1127] In 1897, Ughtred Kay-Shuttleworth told a public meeting at Colne that foreign competition was 'not a mere boggart conjured up to frighten weak and silly folk'.[1128] 'Mere' is ambiguous in both these cases: does it mean 'mere' (marsh) or 'mere' (simply)? I would be inclined for the second meaning. However, in his 1860 novel, *Scarsdale*, James Kay-Shuttleworth (the father of Ughtred) has one of his characters talk of the 'mere boggart': 'The Jack O'Lanthron was among the reeds again last night, and some of my neighbours are sore fleyed. They callen it the Mere Boggart.'[1129] The 'mere boggart' is evidently a will o'the

---

1122. II, p. 326, Wright gives this reference: '*Brighouse News* (July 20, 1889)'; Wilkinson, *Thesaurus*, 540.

1123. John Widdowson (pers. comm. 7 March 2019) points out to me the north-western phrase 'in and out like a dog at a fair', 'meaning frequently going in and out (of a house etc.)'.

1124. BC, Haworth 1 (WRY).

1125. Hill, 'Comlyn': the newspaper serialization. Note also Sutcliffe, 'Nick o' Desperates' (1911) a serialized novel set in a very 'picturesque' version of Lancashire: 'Boggarty Marsh lay close beside them now; the gnomes had lit corpse-candles in the rain'.

1126. BC, Aspull 1 (La); see also Oldham 10 (La).

1127. 'Burnley Meeting'.

1128. 'Sir Ughtred Kay-Shuttleworth at Colne', compare with the wording in 'Sir U. Kay-Shuttleworth'.

1129. Kay-Shuttleworth, *Scarsdale*, II, 267–68.

wisp and, as it transpires, the locals in Kay-Shuttleworth's novel fear that it will bring illness in its wake. Note that 'mere' as a 'pool' or 'pond' seems to be restricted, in dialect, to Staffordshire and Derbyshire.[1130]

'Tek Thi Boggarts': 'Grandma used to use this word [boggart], if she wanted you to get out of her way, "tek thi boggerts!" she would say! This was a Lancashire saying.'[1131] The memory dates back to a 1950s childhood.

'There's been Boggarts in here': There is a good deal of twentieth-century evidence for the idea that boggarts caused domestic confusion. 'If anything went missing around our house, or anything unexplained happened', 'There's been Boggarts in here' was exclaimed by the respondent's mother.[1132] 'We had boggarts in Accy in Lancs. So my dad said if owt went wrong.'[1133] 'My dad said boggarts did it when string always got knotted, jerseys all inside out, also newspapers stuck together.'[1134] '[W]hen my nan couldn't find something she claimed it must have been the boggarts.'[1135] 'I remember my mother talking about boggarts, as in, "the boggarts must have taken it", if she had lost something and couldn't find it.'[1136] 'Grew up in Irlam in 1960s. If anything mysteriously disappeared in the house my mum used to say that the boggart had taken it.'[1137] 'My grandparents in Tarleton definitely used the word "boggart" in the 1980s when I was a child—e.g. If the door blew open slightly when no one was there—they would blame the boggart.'[1138] The only nineteenth-century equivalent I can find are the naughty tricks of some household boggarts,[1139] and a poetic fragment describing a long day at work:

> It's just as if the boggarts coom
> To set things all awry;
> Aw conna get 'em lookin' reet,
> Hewever mich aw try.[1140]

1130. Upton *et al.*, *Survey*, 258; thanks to John Widdowson for this point.
1131. BC, Wigan 4 (La).
1132. BC, Warrington 16 (La).
1133. BC, Accrington 2 (La).
1134. BC, Accrington 6 (La).
1135. BC, Euxton 1 (La).
1136. BC, Lydgate 1 (La).
1137. BC, Irlam 4 (La).
1138. BC, Tarleton 1 (La).
1139. See p. 196.
1140. Bealey, *Field flowers*, 37.

Note that there is also the idea that boggarts can cause confusion outside: chickens won't lay eggs; hunters won't catch rabbits.[1141]

'There's no bigger boggart than yourself': This saying came from the Fylde and was recorded in the Boggart Census.[1142] It is presumably connected with 'to be a boggart' and 'boggart (oppression)' and was said in the spirit of casting out beams before pointing to motes (Matthew 7, 1–5). Compare to 'You're no better than Newhall Boggart' (see pp. 245–46).

'Think Every Bush a Boggart': This phrase, denoting unreasonable fears, see also 'Boggart (Exaggerated Fear)', appeared in the seventeenth century in two sources (one from Lancashire and one probably from Yorkshire).[1143] I have found no later examples.

'To Be a Boggart to Someone': This expression was passed over by Wright but appears in two late nineteenth-century newspaper pieces and means 'to be repugnant'. In 1861, a man loitering in the street in Lancaster turned on a police constable with fury and his comments were later repeated in court: 'I think I'm a boggart in this country. It is only spite you have against me. I never did you any harm in my life, Mr. Allison [the policeman]. It's a boggart I am to you, and I can neither stir nor stand right for you; I never did you any harm.'[1144] A report from 1877 is equally interesting. A woman from the Preston area has seen her engagement with a man disregarded and takes the matter to court. Her *quondam* fiancé described the downward spiral in the relationship. 'At the agricultural show at Croston, on the 9th of August, he purposely avoided the plaintiff, and on the following day he received a letter from her saying she was sorry she had spoiled his pleasure, and that she did not know she was a "boggart" to him.'[1145] 'Boggart' could certainly be an insult. Consider the words of one son to his father, just hours before he committed patricide: 'Thou old foul-faced rogue, I always told thee thou was a fool and a boggard.'[1146] See also this modern memory: 'Apparently my Grandma used this term [boggart] on an Aunt,

1141. BC, Hooley Hill 1 (La); Hyde 2 (Ch).
1142. BC, Preesall 4 (La).
1143. Ray, *A Collection*, 232; Webster, *The displaying*, 60. Wilkinson, *Thesaurus*, 540, dates it, unreferenced, to '1534'. This is almost certainly a mistake: his words are precisely those of Ray.
1144. 'Loitering In The Street'.
1145. 'Extraordinary Breach of Promise'.
1146. 'York Assizes' (1805).

who she didn't like very much, and when she came up to visit, my Grandma would say "uh boggart's back".' [1147]

'To Come Again Like X Boggart': There are a number of references in our sources to men and women returning like either Clegg Hall Boggart (from near Rochdale) or Towneley Boggart (from Burnley). [1148] 'Come again', note, is typically used to refer to the dead periodically haunting an area: 'Jinny Chorlton, of Gatley, used "to come again," until they pulled her old house down.' [1149] The logic here is certainly that many boggarts are said to return at intervals of, say, seven years or ninety-nine years. There is probably also a sense that the person returning is not entirely welcome: 'turning up like a bad penny', is perhaps the closest modern expression.

'To Favour a Boggart's Nest': 'I was born 1969 and my dad often referred to anything that was a mess as it "fathered [sic] a boggerts nest", i.e. it resembles a boggart's nest.' [1150] There is an early reference to a Barghest nest. [1151]

'To Flay a Boggart Out of the Ground': Lahee gives 'enew to flay a buggart eawt o'th' greawnd', to cause extreme fear to someone who is not normally easily affected. [1152] Note that there are several descriptions from the north-west of boggarts, conversely, sinking into the ground: 'th' figure went reet through th' ground—I never see sich a thing i' my life—reet into th' ground it went'. [1153] Compare: 'My husband still says it when he sees anything ugly: "Who'd frighten a boggart"; and "for eze enif ta freetan a boggard ta death"'. [1154]

'To Lay a Boggart': 'Laying a boggart' refers to the rituals of clergy or of those knowledgeable in magic to trap the spirit in a box or under a tree or in water: [1155] for example, 'By prayer and supplication at the confluence of two streams near Rowley—at Netherwood Bridge, and at the Water Meetings, a little lower down the stream, the boggart was successfully laid.' [1156] Rituals were occasionally involved:

1147. BC, Accrington 10 (La).
1148. Wright, *Rustic*, 192; Oldbuck, 'Hapton Tower', 3 (7 in Bib).
1149. Moss, *Folk-lore*, 135.
1150. BC, Eccleston 1 (La).
1151. Carr, *Horae*.
1152. Lahee, *Betty*, 6.
1153. Francis, 'Tales', 123.
1154. BC, Blackburn 36 (La); Treddlehoyle, *The Bairnsla Foaks Annual*, 14.
1155. Westwood and Simpson, *Lore of the Land*, 398 and Young, *Exorcism*, 59–64.
1156. Heaton, 'Stray Notes'.

'Three men must receive three silver coins each, and at midnight with torches they must take the skin and fleece of the sheep to the clough, and bury them under the tree on which the magpie was seen to rest.'[1157] Sometimes the laying is associated with a rhyme or jingle: 'For this purpose the combined power of priest and parson was brought into operation; the ghost was "laid" under the bridge, near the hall, with the injunction that it had to remain quiet 'so long as the water flowed down the hills, and the ivy remained green'; or "Whilst ivy climbs and holly is green / Clayton Hall boggart shall no more be seen."'[1158] The boggart will often win a concession whereby it can occasionally visit the world again.[1159] The Lumb Boggart, for instance, was laid in a pond in the form of a fish, but on Christmas eve, 'the ghost should assume the form of a white ousel, and fly to Lumbly pool'.[1160] Note this associated phrase from 1899 Blackburn: it will 'be a hard thing to lay. It's like th' Owd House Boggart.'[1161]

'To Make a Boggart Stare': I have only found one example of this phrase, from 1897: 'according to what she saw of herself in the glass, would "make a Boggard stare"'.[1162] Notice the inverted commas suggesting that this was a well-known expression.

'To Make Boggarts': A reference to 'making boggarts' appears in a disturbing newspaper report from 1867. Two girls are passing through the countryside near Lancaster when one of them, a thirteen-year-old, is sexually abused by a man. Prior to the abuse, a passer-by describes how '[t]he girls were larkish and making boggarts, and were very forward': although one of the girls denied being so, 'I was not larking on the road. I was not pretending to make boggarts.'[1163] What is 'making boggarts'? A reference from Blackburn in the Boggart Census might give the answer: 'My mum used to say "stop making Bogarts" meaning stop making a fuss. She is in her eighties and from Blackburn. I've just asked her about it, she says boggarts meaning "trouble". However, she probably picked up the phrase from my dad's mum who came from Rotherham, Yorkshire originally.'[1164]

1157. Royd, 'The Abbot's Knowl'.
1158. Atticus, *Our Country Churches*, 437; Baron, 'Lancashire Boggarts'.
1159. Harland and Wilkinson, *Lancashire Folk-lore*, 44.
1160. Evans, *Bradwell*, 44–45.
1161. Tuft, 'Bits'.
1162. Tirebuck, 'Meg o' the Scarlet Foot'.
1163. 'County Petit Sessions'.
1164. BC, Blackburn 2 (La).

'To Take (the) Boggart': Wright gave an excellent entry on this phrase for horses bolting after a scare.[1165] What Wright did not realize (or perhaps more likely what he chose not to record) was that the expression could easily be applied to more modern forms of 'bolting'. We have from 1869 a newspaper report about a velocipede (i.e. a bicycle) taking boggart with an inexperienced rider on a downhill stretch of the road between Bacup and Todmorden.[1166] In 1883, a runner is described who 'now and again "takes the boggart"'.[1167] In 1900 a man near Burnley caused much hilarity seeing (for the first time) a car speeding down a hill. He screamed out, as he jumped behind a hedge, 'Hey up, chaps, there's a carriage off at boggart beawt [without] horse. Get o'er that wall eawt o' th' road.'[1168] We have a reference, meanwhile, from 1916 to a catastrophe in a Whitworth factory where a fly wheel exploded killing two and maiming several other workers. 'To the 250 operatives in the shed, the first they knew that something was wrong was when the machinery speeded up to a terrific pace—"set off at boggart".'[1169] The expression continued to be used in the late twentieth century. 'If the cat started racing round the walls or the washing machine was dancing about the kitchen floor, the verdict would be "It's took boggarts!"'[1170] Or there is this marvellous example: 'I was working in Hyde in the 1970s and when I reported a broken roller towel in the gents a local woman said "it's tekken boggarts" which she said meant it was broken.'[1171]

'You look like a boggart, have you got a haunting job on?': This sentence appeared in the Boggart Census. It was said 'if we were sick and looking a bit pale'.[1172] Compare with a pre-war Rochdale man who 'often referenced boggarts when describing someone who looked pale and sickly'.[1173]

'You're no better than Newhall Boggart': 'my earliest memory of hearing the word "boggart" was as a small child (late 1950s or early 1960s) from both my grandma and a great aunt, who would raise their eyebrows if I misbehaved/ spoke out of turn/etc. and say, "You're no better than Newhall Boggart."

1165. I, 326.
1166. 'A Velocipede Taking "Boggart"'.
1167. 'The final …'.
1168. Stott, 'Off at Boggart'.
1169. 'Fly Wheel Bursts'. For other industrial examples of this type McEwen, 'Runnin". Thanks to Alan McEwen of www.sledgehammerengineeringpress.co.uk for providing me with this article.
1170. BC, Hazel Grove 1 (Ch).
1171. BC, Droylsden 10 (La).
1172. BC, New Mills, 18 (De).
1173. BC, Rochdale 3 (La).

However there was never any explanation of who or what this was.'[1174] An 1866 article sheds a little light on the subject: 'In the days of our grandfathers before gas-lights were introduced, the darksome nights occasioned many lonely localities to be considered the habitation of ghosts and boggarts, one of the most noted, in this neighbourhood, being a boggart, at New Hall, an old mansion that once stood in New Hall-lane, to which it gave its name. Many are the stories told by old Preston people of the freaks of this supposed unearthly visitant.'[1175] Compare to 'There's no bigger boggart than yourself'.

'Up and Down Like a Boggart': 'My father used to say to me, "sit still you're up and down like a Boggat" so that must be what they (Boggats) do.'[1176] 'I remember my mum used the word [boggart] when someone was dashing about or restless—"He's up and down like a boggart!"'[1177] 'Up and down like a boggart! Often said in our house if you couldn't keep still or was in and out a lot, or used when referring to someone when wondering what they were up to. He's been up and down like a boggart all day.'[1178] This sense of fidgeting took on other forms too: '"Boggart" was used a lot by mum mostly telling me to sit down cos I'm like a bloody boggart';[1179] if one respondent were 'fidgeting grandmother would say "Sit still! You're like a bouncing boggart"';[1180] '[i]f I was fidgety, my great aunt who lived with us would tell me to sit still "thou art like a boggart".'[1181] Compare 'In an' aght like Fearnla boggard' (see p. 240).

'Weavers go into boggarts or donkeys': A mysterious sentence, given as a commonplace in 1915: 'Oh [weavers] never dee, they goo into boggarts or donkeys!' The boggart presumably relates to weavers becoming ghosts, but the role of the donkeys is unclear. 'So, you see, if by any chance we get to the seaside we are reminded of our work when we see the donkeys, thinking it will come our turn some day.'[1182]

1174. BC, Southport 13 (La).
1175. 'Another New Hall Boggart'.
1176. BC, Slaithwaite 1 (WRY).
1177. BC, New Mills 5 (De).
1178. BC, New Mills 15 (De).
1179. BC, New Mills 8 (De).
1180. BC, Whitefield 3 (La).
1181. BC, Ashton-Under-Lyne 3 (La).
1182. A Woollen Weaver, 'The Wages', 4.

Bibliography

'A Balloon Mistaken for a Boggart', *The Preston Chronicle and Lancashire Advertiser* (22 Feb 1873), 5.

'A Boggart at Littlemoss', *Ashton Weekly Reporter* (6 Sep 1856), 3.

'A Boggart in a Church', *Cheshire Observer* (10 Feb 1883), 4.

'A Child Frightened to Death by "Boggarts"', *The Dundee Courier and Argus* (9 Feb 1871), 4.

'A Day's Ride', *Todmorden Advertiser* (2 Oct 1925), 8.

'A Determined Boggart', *Kendal Mercury* (14 May 1842), 1.

'A Determined Housebreaker', *Leeds Intelligencer* (12 Aug 1854), 7.

'A Freehold Dairy Farm', *Leeds Mercury* (16 Apr 1904), 2.

'A Ghost!', *Bolton Chronicle* (24 Oct 1835), 3.

'A "Ghost" at Bolton', *Lancashire Evening Post* (13 Jan 1887), 4.

'A Ghost at Egton', *Burnley Advertiser* (23 Jan 1864), 3.

'A Ghost in Rusland', *Kendal Mercury* (25 Nov 1854), 8.

'A Ghost in 1852', *Kendal Mercury* (30 Oct 1852), 8.

'A Ghost Story', *Sheffield Independent* (26 Jan 1839), 6.

'A Ghost Story', *Glossop Record* (9 Dec 1865), 4.

'A Ghost Story', *Ashton Weekly Reporter* (3 Jul 1869), 2.

'A Hunt for Brownies', *Sunderland Daily Echo* (20 May 1909), 5.

A.L., *Forty Years Ago: A Sketch of Yorkshire Life and Poems* (Huddersfield: Woodhead, 1869).

A Liberal, 'Canvassers and Canvassed', *Kendal Mercury* (6 Feb 1880), 8.

'A Literary Celebrity', *West Sussex County Times* (25 Dec 1926), 5.

'A Minister's Masquerade', *Western Morning News* (19 Sep 1927), 4.

A Parish Apprentice, 'Some Passages of the Life of a Parish Prentice', *Stephens Monthly Magazine* (Apr 1840), 73–80.

A Prestonian, 'Preston More than Forty Years Ago', *Preston Chronicle* (2 Oct 1852), 6.

'A Ride from Keswick to Penrith on the "Orton Ghost"', *Kendal Mercury* (22 Sep 1849), 4.

'A St Helen's Ghost Story', *Cheshire Observer* (29 Aug 1885), 2.

'A Shooting Boggart', *Ben Brierley's Journal* 3 (1881), 65.

'A Suspended Rule: Christmas Eve', *Sussex Agricultural Express* (23 Dec 1893), 6.

'A Tale of the Cuddy Beck Boggle', *Cumberland & Westmorland Herald* (14 Jun 1902), 3.

'A Troublesome Ghost', *Manchester Courier and Lancashire General Advertiser* (10 Sep 1881), 11.

A True Volunteer, 'The "Boggart" at Whaley', *Glossop Record* (25 Feb 1860), 4.

'A Tuberculous Cow', *Manchester Courier* (5 Dec 1896), 9.

'A Twin Brother of the Newtown Boggle', *Cumberland Pacquet, and Ware's Whitehaven Advertiser* (13 Apr 1893), 4.

'A Velocipede Taking "Boggart"', *Ashton Weekly Reporter* (1 May 1869), 2.

A Villager, 'A Boggart at Worsthorne', *Burnley Express and Advertiser* (26 May 1883), 7.

A.W., *The Westmorland Dialect, in three familiar dialogues: in which an attempt is made to illustrate the provincial idiom* (Kendal: Ashburner, 1790).

'A Westmoreland Ghost Story', *Bradford Observer* (17 May 1849), 7.

A Woollen Weaver, 'The Wages of Woollen Weavers', *Rochdale Observer* (24 Mar 1915), 4.

Adams, Lionel E., 'A Plea for Owls', *The Zoologist* 2 (1898), 449–51.

Addison, Joseph, *The Works of the Right Honourable Joseph Addison* (London: T. Cadell, 1811), 6 vols.

Addy, Sidney, *A Glossary of words used in the neighbourhood of Sheffield, including a selection of local names, and some notices of folklore, games and customs* (London: Trübner and Co 1888).

———— 'Death and the Herb Thyme', *Folklore* 14, (1903), 179–80.

Ahier, Philip, *The Legends and Traditions of Huddersfield and its District* (Huddersfield: Advertiser, 1940–1945), 2 vols.

Ainsworth, William Harrison, *The Lancashire Witches: A Romance of Pendle Forest* (London: Routledge, 1878).

Aker-Whitt, 'The Dunkenhalgh Boggart', *Blackburn Standard* (21 Dec 1889), 3.

'Alarming Accident at Bolton Theatre Royal', *Manchester Courier and Lancashire General Advertiser* (25 Feb 1880), 5.

'Alleged Game Trespass', *Barnet Press* (13 Oct 1883), 6.

Allen, Hope Emily, 'Influence of Superstition on Vocabulary: Two Related Examples', *PMLA* 50 (1935), 1033–46. https://doi.org/10.2307/458106.

———— 'The Influence of Superstition on Vocabulary', *PMLA* 51 (1936), 904–20. https://doi.org/10.2307/458074.

Allies, Jabez, *The British, Roman, and Saxon antiquities and folklore of Worcestershire* (London: John Russell, 1856).

Almqvist, Bo, 'Irish Migratory Legends on the Supernatural: Sources, Studies and Problems', *Béaloideas* 59 (1991), 1–43. https://doi.org/10.2307/20522374.

Altick, Richard D., *The English Common Reader: A Social History of the Mass Reading Public, 1800–1900* (Columbus: Ohio State University Press, 1998).

'An Alleged Dangerous Crossing', *Nottingham Evening Post* (6 Mar 1899), 2.

An Enthusiast, 'Catching a Salmon', *Preston Chronicle and Lancashire Advertiser* (15 Oct 1853), 3.

An Inhabitant [F.K. Robinson], *A Glossary of Yorkshire Words and Phrases: Collected in Whitby and the Neighbourhood* (London: John Russell Smith, 1855).

An Old Native, 'Reminiscences of Ashton and Stalybridge', *Ashton Weekly Reporter* (29 Aug 1863), 3.

'Ancient Coin', *Kendal Mercury* (18 Mar 1848), 2.

Anderson C., 'There are no Boggarts Now', *Burnley Express* (15 Feb 1902), 3.

Andrews, Elizabeth, *Ulster Folklore* (London: Elliot, 1913).

Andrews, William 'Yorkshire Folk Lore', *The Yorkshire Magazine* 1 (1871–1872), 204–05.

———— (ed.), *North Country Poets* (London: Simpkin, 1888).

'Another New Hall Boggart', *Preston Chronicle* (27 Jan 1866), 5.

ANTIQUARIAN, 'Boggart Renown', *Preston Chronicle* (26 Aug 1871), 6.

'Assault Upon a Child', *The Preston Chronicle and Lancashire Advertiser* (24 Dec 1858), 6.

Asten, J.H., 'Ghost', *Burnley Express* (9 Feb 1895), 2.

'Astrology and Boggards', *Todmorden & District News* (31 Mar 1916), 8.

Atkinson, J.C., *A Glossary of the Cleveland Dialect* (London: John Russell Smith, 1868).

———— *Forty Years in a Moorland Parish: Reminiscences and Researches in Danby in Cleveland* (London: Macmillan, 1891).

Atran, Scott and Douglas L. Medin, *The Native Mind and the Cultural Construction of Nature* (Cambridge MA: MIT Press, 2008). https://doi.org/10.7551/mitpress/7683.001.0001.

'Attempt at Murder and Suicide', *Lancaster Gazette* (19 Apr 1828), 3.

Atticus [A. Hewitson], *Our Country Churches & Chapels: Antiquarian, Historical, Ecclesiastical and Critical Sketches* (London: Simpkin, Marshall and Co., 1872).

Avery, Gillian, *Mrs Ewing* (New York: Walck, 1964).

Axon, William E.A., *Black Knight of Ashton* (Manchester: John Heywood, n.d.).

———— 'The Gallowsfield Ghost', *Ashton Weekly Reporter* (27 May 1865), 6.

———— *Echoes of Old Lancashire* (London: William Andrews & Co., 1899).

Back O' Birket, 'Sir', *Cumberland & Westmorland Herald* (13 Feb 1892), 7.

Baden-Powell of Gilwell, Lord, *Girl Guiding: A Handbook for Brownies, Guides, Rangers and Guiders* (London: Pearson, 1938).

Baildon, W.P., and F.J. Baildon, *Baildon and the Baildons: A History of a Yorkshire Manor and Family* (Bradford: St Catherine Press: 1912–1927), 3 vols.

Bale, John, *Yet a course at the Romyshe foxe A dysclosynge or openynge of the Manne of synne, co[n]tayned in the late declaratyon of the Popes olde faythe made by Edmonde Boner bysshopp of London. wherby wyllyam Tolwyn was than newlye professed at paules crosse openlye into Antichristes Romyshe relygyon agayne by a newe solempne othe of obedyence, notwythsta[n]dynge the othe made to hys prynce afore to the contrarye. An alphabetycall dyrectorye or table also in the ende thereof* (N.p.: n.p., 1543).

———— *Illustrium Maioris Britanniae scriptorum* ([1548]).

Balfour, M.C., 'Legends of the Lincolnshire Cars, II' *Folklore* 2 (1891), 257–83. https://doi.org/10.1080/0015587X.1891.9720066.

Bamford, Samuel, *The Dialect of South Lancashire; or, Tim Bobbin's Tummus and Meary* (London: Smith, 1854).

———— *Homely Rhymes, Poems, and Reminiscences* (London: Simpkin, 1864).

———— *Passages in the life of a radical, and Early days,* (London: T. Fisher Unwin, 1905), 2 vols.

Bane, Theresa, *Encyclopedia of Fairies in World Folklore and Mythology* (Jackson: McFarland and Co., 2013).

Banks, William Stott, *A List of Provincial Words in Use at Wakefield in Yorkshire* (London: J. Russell Smith, 1865).

Bann, Jennifer, 'Ghostly Hands and Ghostly Agency: The Changing Figure of the Nineteenth-Century Specter', *Victorian Studies* 51 (2009), 663–85. https://doi.org/10.2979/vic.2009.51.4.663.

Barber, Edward, *Memorials of Old Cheshire* (London: G. Allen, 1910).

'Barcroft Hall', *Burnley Express* (1 Feb 1902), 7.

Bardsley, Charles, *Chronicles of the Town & Church of Ulverston* (Ulverston: James Atkinson, 1885).

Baring-Gould, S., *Yorkshire Oddities: Incidents and Strange Events* (London: Methuen, 1890).

———— *Margery of Quether, and Other Stories* (London: Methuen, 1891).

Barlow, T. Worthington, *The Cheshire and Lancashire Historical Collector* (Manchester: Bell, 1853).

Barnes, Wally, *Ghosts, Mysteries and Legends of Old Warrington* (Wigan: Owl Books, 1990).

Baron, Joseph, 'Lancashire Boggarts', *The Blackburn Weekly Standard and Express* (14 July 1894), 2.

Barrett, Frank, 'The Black Spider', *Walsall Observer* (24 Jan 1914), 2.

Barrow, L., *Independent Spirits: Spiritualism and the English Plebeians, 1850–1910* (London: Routledge & Kegan Paul Books, 1986).

Barrowclough, David A. and John Hallam, 'The Devil's Footprints and Other Folklore: Local Legend and Archaeological Evidence in Lancashire', *Folklore* 119 (2008), 93–102. https://doi.org/10.1080/00155870701806233.

Bartholomew, Robert with Bob Rickard, *Mass Hysteria in Schools* (Jefferson: McFarland, 2014).

Bartley, Paula, *Emmeline Pankhurst* (London: Routledge, 2002).

Basso, Keith H., *Wisdom Sits in Places: Landscape and Language Among the Western Apache* (Albuquerque: University of New Mexico Press, 1996).

Bates, Joe, 'From the Old Arm Chair', *Nelson Leader* (23 Sep 1932), 9.

Bath, Jo and John Newton, '"Sensible Proof of Spirits": Ghost Belief during the Later Seventeenth Century', *Folklore* 117 (2006), 1–14. https://doi.org/10.1080/00155870500479851.

Baughman, Ernest, *Type and Motif Index of the Folktales of England and North America* (The Hague: Mouton, 1966). https://doi.org/10.1515/9783111402772.

Beahm, George, *Fact, Fiction and Folklore in Harry Potter's World* (Charlottesville, VA: Hampton Roads, 2005).

Beal, Joan C., *An Introduction to Regional Englishes* (Edinburgh: Edinburgh University Press, 2010).

Bealey, Richard Rome, *Field Flowers and City Chimes; Poems* (London: Simplin & Marshall, 1866).

Beatty, Bernard, 'Determining Unknown Modes of Being: A Map of Byron's Ghosts and Spirits', *Byron's Ghosts: The Spectral, the Spiritual and the Supernatural* (Liverpool: Liverpool University Press, 2013), 30–47. https://doi.org/10.5949/liverpool/9781846319709.003.0002.

Beaven, Brad, *Leisure, Citizenship and Working-class Men in Britain, 1850–1945* (Manchester: Manchester University Press, 2005).

Beccaria, Gian Luigi, *I nomi del mondo. Santi, demoni, folletti e le parole perdute* (Turin: Einaudi, 1995).

Beilby, J.T., 'Boggarts: A Sketch', *Burnley Express* (13 Jan 1940), 11.

Belfour, John, 'The Life of Mr John Ray', *A Complete Collection of English Proverbs*, edited by John Ray and John Belfour (London: George Cowie and Co, 1813), ii-xii.

Bell, Karl, *The Legend of Spring-Heeled Jack* (Woodbridge: Boydell & Brewer, 2012).

———— *The Magical Imagination: Magic and Modernity in Urban England 1780–1914* (Cambridge: CUP, 2012).

——— 'Phantasmal Cities: The Construction and Function of Haunted Landscapes in Victorian English Cities', *Haunted Landscapes: Super-Nature and the Environment*, edited by Ruth Heholt and Niamh Downing (London: Rowman, 2016), 95–110.

Bennell, John, 'Great Missenden', *Records of Buckinghamshire* 17 (1965), 416.

Bennett, Gillian, *Traditions of Belief* (London: Pelican, 1988).

——— *Alas, Poor Ghost! Traditions of Belief in Story and Discourse* (Logan: Utah State University Press, 1999).

——— *Bodies: Sex, Violence, Disease and Death in Contemporary Legend* (Jackson: University of Mississippi, 2005).

Betteridge, Tom, 'Saunders, Lawrence', *Oxford Dictionary of National Biography* (Oxford: OUP, 2019) [accessed 21 Mar 2019].

Beville, Maria, *The Unnameable Monster in Literature and Film* (London: Routledge, 2014). https://doi.org/10.4324/9780203496916.

Beyer, Jürgen, 'Are Folklorists Studying the Tales of the Folk?', *Folklore* 122 (2011), 35–54. https://doi.org/10.1080/0015587X.2011.537132.

'Bibliography of Bradford and Neighbourhood', *Bradford Antiquary* 1 (1895), 9–14.

Bibliothecar. Chetham, 'Roby's *Traditions of Lancashire*', *Notes and Queries* 10 (1866, 3rd), 450. https://doi.org/10.1093/nq/s3-X.258.450c.

Bill-o'-Jacks [William Baron] 'Bits i' Broad Lanky: Th' Pell Mell Boggart', *Blackburn Standard* (20 Aug 1887), 2.

Billingsley, John, *Folk Tales from Calderdale: Place legends and lore from the Calder Valley* (Mytholmroyd: Northern Earth, 2007).

——— *West Yorkshire Folk Tales* (Stroud: History Press, 2010).

Billington, William *Pendle Hill* (Blackburn: The Times, 1876).

Binnall, Peter B.G., 'A Brownie Legend from Lincolnshire', *Folklore* 51 (1940), 219–22. https://doi.org/10.1080/0015587X.1940.9718236.

Birchall, James, 'Owd Butty's Lump o' Gowd', *Blackburn Standard* (12 Jul 1879), 2.

Bird, S., Elizabeth 'Playing with Fear: Interpreting the Adolescent Legend Trip', *Western Folklore* 53 (1994), 191–209. https://doi.org/10.2307/1499808.

Bisagni, Jacopo, 'Leprechaun: a new etymology', *Cambrian Medieval Celtic Studies* 64 (2012), 47–84.

'Bishop Bardsley's Connection with Burnley Grammar School', *Burnley Express* (3 Sep 1887), 8.

Blake, N.F., *Non-standard Language in English Literature* (London: André Deutsch, 1981).

Blakeborough, Richard, *Wit, character, folklore & customs of the North Riding of*

Yorkshire; with a glossary of over 4,000 words and idioms now in use (London: Henry Frowde, 1898).

Bland, John Salkeld, *The vale of Lyvennet, its picturesque peeps and legendary lore* (Kendal: Wilson, 1910).

de Blécourt, Willem, *Termen van toverij* (Nijmegen: SUN, 1990).

'Board of Surveyors', *Bradford Observer* (18 Apr 1850), 6.

'Board of Trade', *Manchester Courier* (21 Nov 1896), 11.

Bobbin, Tim, *The Lancashire Dialect or the Adventures and Misfortunes of a Lancashire Clown* (London: Hodgson, n.d. late 18C?).

——— *The Works of Tim Bobbin, Esq. in Prose and Verse* (Rochdale: Westall, 1819).

'Boggart', *Glossop Record* (4 Feb 1860), 3.

'Boggart Hole Clough and Its Ghost', *Manchester Times* (27 Oct 1893), 5.

'Boggart House Farm', *Preston Chronicle* (1 Nov 1879), 6.

'"Boggart" Hunting at Tyldesley', *The Manchester Evening News* (19 Sep 1881), 2.

'Bolton Le Sands: Something about Ghosts', *Lancaster Gazette* (15 Oct 1870), 8.

Bonhomme, Julien, 'The dangers of anonymity: Witchcraft, rumor, and modernity in Africa', *Hau: Journal of Ethnographic Theory* 2 (2012), 205–33. https://doi.org/10.14318/hau2.2.012.

Booth, Thomas, 'A Ramble Through a Lancashire Vale', *Burnley Express and Advertiser* (26 May 1883), 6.

——— 'A Morning Ramble into the Pennine Range', *Burnley Express* (19 Jul 1884), 6.

Borghi, Guido, 'Großindogermania o Grande Indoeuropa pluricontinentale e multimillenaria come modello per la preistoria linguistica dello spazio indomediterraneo', *Quaderni di Semantica* 27 (2006), 51–134.

Bottrell, William, *Traditions and Hearthside Stories of West Cornwall* (Penzance: W. Cornish, 1870).

Bourke, Angela, *The Burning of Bridget Cleary: A True Story* (London: Penguin, 2011).

Bowker, James, *The Goblin Tales of Lancashire* (London: W. Swan Sonnenschein & Co., n.d. [1883]).

Boyle, Thomas, *Black Swines in the Sewers of Hampstead* (New York: Viking, 1989).

Braccini, Mauro and Giovanna Princi Braccini, 'Maschera e masca: "macchia". Parole e cosa dall'antico folclore', *Studi Medievali* 49 (2008), 589–655.

Bradbury, Joseph, *Saddleworth Sketches* (Oldham: Hirst and Rennie, 1871).

Bradford, Anne, *Haunted Pubs and Hotels in and around Worcestershire* (Redditch: Hunt End Books, 2013).

Bridges, Thomas, *Homer Travestie: Being a new translation of the four first books of the Iliad. By Cotton, Junior. To which is prefix'd, some small account of the author* (London: R. Marriner 1762).

Brierley, Benjamin, *Bunk Ho or A Lancashire Merry Christmas* (Manchester: Abel Heywood and Son, 1860).

———— 'Ab-O' Th'-Yate on his Feel Loss o' Speed', *Ashton Weekly Reporter* (31 Jul 1869), 7.

———— 'Ab-O' Th'-Yate on his Feel Loss o' Speed', *Ashton Weekly Reporter* (7 Aug 1869), 3.

———— *Ab-o'th'-Yate's Dictionary; Or, Walmsley Fowt Skoomester: Put T'gether by Th' Help O' Fause Juddie* (Manchester: A. Heywood & Son, 1881).

———— *Ben Brierley's Works: Tales and Sketches of Lancashire life* (Manchester: Heywood, 1884).

———— *Popular Edition of Tales and Sketches of Lancashire Life: Marlocks of Merriton and Red Windows Hall* (Manchester: Abel Heywood and Son, 1884).

———— *Nights with Ben Brierley being a selection of Lancashire readings and recitations from the works of Ben Brierley adapted for schools and social gatherings* (Manchester: Abel Heywood and Son, 1885).

———— *'Ab-o'th'-Yate' in Yankeeland* (Manchester: Abel Hey, 1885).

———— *'Ab-o'th'-Yate' Sketches and Other Short Stories* (Oldham: Clegg, 1899), 3 vols.

———— *Lancashire Wit and Humour* (Oldham: Clegg, 1892).

Briggs, John, *The Remains of John Briggs: Containing Letters from the Lakes; Westmorland as it was; Theological essays; Tales; Remarks on the Newtonian theory of light; and Fugitive pieces* (Kirkby Lonsdale: Arthur Foster, 1825).

Briggs, K.M., 'The English Fairies', *Folklore* 68 (1957), 270–87. https://doi.org/10.1080/0015587X.1957.9717577.

———— *The Anatomy of Puck: An Examination of Fairy Beliefs among Shakespeare's Contemporaries and Successors* (London: Routledge, 1959).

———— 'Some Late Accounts of the Fairies', *Folklore* 72 (1961), 509–19.

———— *The Fairies in Tradition and Literature* (New York: Routledge, 2002 [1967]).

———— *A Dictionary of British Folk-Tales: Part B Folk Legends* (London: Routledge and Kegan, 1971), 4 vols.

———— 'The Necessity of Scepticism', *Journal of the Folklore Institute* 9 (1972), 5–9. https://doi.org/10.2307/3814017.

———— 'Folklore in Nineteenth-Century English Literature', *Folklore* 83 (1972), 194–209. https://doi.org/10.1080/0015587X.1972.9716469.

———— *A Dictionary of Fairies* (London: Routledge, 2003 [1976]).

———— 'Brownie into Boggart', *Folklore on Two Continents*, edited by N. Burtakoff, and C. Lindahl (Bloomington, IN: Trickster Press, 1980), 79–85.

Britten, James, 'Boggarts, Feorin, "Jenny Greenteeth"', *Notes and Queries* 5 (1870), 28. https://doi.org/10.1093/nq/s4–V.115.287c.

Britten, James and Robert Holland, *A Dictionary of English Plant-Names* (London: Trübner and Co., 1886). https://doi.org/10.5962/bhl.title.127470.

Broadhurst, Paul and Hamish Miller, *The Sun and the Serpent* (Launceston: Mythos, 2006).

Brogden, J. Ellett, *Provincial Words and Expressions Current in Lincolnshire* (London: Robert Hardwicke, 1866).

Bronner, Simon J., *The Practice of Folklore: Essays toward a Theory of Tradition* (Jackson: University of Mississippi Press, 2019). https://doi.org/10.14325/mississippi/9781496822628.001.0001.

Brown, Cecil H. *et al.*, 'Some general principles of biological and non-biological folk classification', *American Ethnologist* 3 (1976), 73–85. https://doi.org/10.1525/ae.1976.3.1.02a00050.

Brown, Charles D., 'The Ancient Parish of West Kirby', *Transactions of the Historic Society of Lancashire and Cheshire* 37 (1888), 29–66.

Brown, Lucy, *Victorian News and Newspapers* (Oxford: Clarendon Press, 1985).

Brown, Theo, 'The Black Dog', *Folklore* 69 (1958), 175–92. https://doi.org/10.1080/0015587X.1958.9717142.

———— 'Some Examples of Post-Reformation Folklore in Devon', *Folklore* 72 (1961), 388–99. https://doi.org/10.1080/0015587X.1961.9717281.

———— *The Fate of the Dead* (Ipswich: Brewer, 1979).

'Brownie's Revel', *Buckingham Advertiser* (19 Jul 1947), 6.

Bruford, Alan, 'Trolls, Hillfolk, Finns and Picts: The Identity of the Good Neighbours in Orkney and Shetland', *The Good People: New Fairylore Essays*, edited by Peter Narváez (Lexington: University Press of Kentucky, 1997), 116–41.

Brushfield, T., 'Reminiscences of Ashford-in-the-Water, Sixty Years Ago', *The Reliquary* 6 (1865–1866), 12–16.

'Building and Sanitary Committee', *Burnley Gazette* (29 Oct 1881), 7.

Burgess, W.V., *Cheshire Village Stories* (London: Sherratt, 1906).

'Burglary', *Sheffield Independent* (6 Sep 1851), 5.

Burne, Charlotte Sophia, *Shropshire Folk-Lore: A Sheaf of Gleanings* (London: Trübner, 1883–1886), 3 vols. https://doi.org/10.1080/17442524.1885.10602785.

'Burnley Meeting of Oddfellows', *Burnley Gazette* (6 Jun 1868), 2.

Burns, Robert, *The Poetical and Prose Works of Robert Burns* (London: Charles Daly, 1855).

Burrison, John A., *Storytellers: Folktales and Legends from the South* (Athens: Brown Thrasher Books, 1991).

Burt, Edward, *Letters from a Gentleman in the North of Scotland to his Friend in London; … likewise an account of the Highlands, with the customs and manners of the Highlanders. To which is added, a letter relating to the military ways among the mountains, begun in the year 1726* (London: Oggle, Duncan and Co., 1822), 2 vols.

Butterworth, Edwin, *Historical Sketches of Oldham* (Oldham: John Hirst, 1856).

C.J.T. [Charles John Tibbits], *Folk-lore and Legends: English* (London: W.W. Gibbings, 1890).

Caciola, Nancy, *Afterlives: the Return of the Dead in the Middle Ages* (Ithaca: Cornell University Press, 2016). https://doi.org/10.7591/cornell/9781501702617.001.0001.

Cameron, K., J. Field and J. Insley, *The Place-Names of Lincolnshire* (Cambridge: CUP, 1985–2010), 7 vols.

Campbell, John Gregorson *Superstitions of the Highlands and Islands of Scotland* (J. Maclehose & Sons: Glasgow).

Campbell, John L. and Trevor H. Hall, *Strange Things: The Story of Fr Allan McDonald, Ada Goodrich Freer, and the Society for Psychical Research's Enquiry into Highland Second Sight* (Edinburgh: Birlinn, 2006 [1968]).

Caldecott, R., *The Three Jovial Huntsmen* (London: Warne, ND).

'Carlisle in the Olden Times', *Carlisle Journal* (26 Feb 1864), 6.

'Carnforth Readings', *Lancaster Gazette* (4 Dec 1869), 5.

Carr, James, *Annals and Stories of Colne and Neighbourhood* (Colne: Thomas Duerden, 1878).

Carr, William, *Horæ momenta cravenæ, or, The Craven dialect, exemplified in two dialogues, between farmer Giles and his neighbour Bridget. To which is annexed a copious glossary* (London: Hurst and Robinson, 1824).

——— *The Dialect of Craven, in the West-Riding of the County of York* (London: W. Crofts, 1828).

Cavill, Paul, *A New Dictionary of English Field-Names* (Nottingham: English Place-Name Society, 2018).

Century Dictionary (New York: Century, 1889–1891), 10 vols.

Chambers, Paul, *The Cock Lane Ghost: Murder, Sex & Haunting in Dr Johnson's London: Murder, Sex and Haunting in Dr. Johnson's London* (Stroud: History Press, 2006).

Charles, Richard, 'Interesting Local Notes', *Burnley Gazette* (19 Jun 1875), 8.

'Child Stealing at St Helen's', *Liverpool Mercury* (22 Oct 1863), 7.

Chip, 'Cuttock Clough Boggart', *Blackburn Standard* (24 Sep 1887), 2.

——— 'Smelt Mill Boggart', *Blackburn Standard* (4 Feb 1888), 2.

'Churchyard Stories', *Leeds Times* (4 Aug 1877), 2.

Clarke, Allen *Windmill Land: Rambles in a Rural Old-Fashioned Lancashire Countryside, with Chat about its History and Romance* (London: W. Foulsham, 1933).

Clarke, David, 'Unmasking Spring-heeled Jack: a case study of a 19th century ghost', *Contemporary Legend* 9 (2006), 28–53.

Clarke, Stephen, *Clitheroe in its Coaching and Railway Days* (Blackpool: Landy 1989 [1897–1900]).

Clay, John, *Prison Chaplain: A Memoir of the Rev. John Clay, with Selections from his Reports and Correspondence and a Sketch of Prison Discipline in England* (Cambridge: Macmillan, 1861).

Clayton, John A., *The Boy Witchfinder of Pendle Forest: The Other Pendle Witch Trial of 1634* (Hockley: Barrowford Press, 2012).

Clegg, James, *Extracts from the Diary and Autobiography of the Rev. James Clegg, nonconformist minister and doctor of medicine, A.D. 1679 to 1755* (Buxton: C.F. Wardley, 1899).

Clegg, John Trafford, *The Works of John Trafford Clegg: Stories, Sketches, and Rhymes in the Rochdale Dialect* (Rochdale: James Clegg, 1895).

Coatman, John 'Lancashire Dialect', *Manchester Review* 5 (1948–1950), 118–26.

Cockrell, Amanda, 'Harry Potter and the Secret Password: Finding Our Way in the Magical Genre', *The Ivory Tower and Harry Potter: Perspectives on a Literary Phenomenon*, edited by Lana A. Whited (Columbia: University of Missouri Press, 2002), 15–26.

Cockrell, Dale, *Demons of Disorder: Early Blackface Minstrels and Their World* (Cambridge: Cambridge University Press, 1997).

Cognizance, 'Roby's *Traditions of Lancashire*', *Notes and Queries* 11 (1867, 3rd), 24. https://doi.org/10.1093/nq/s3–XI.262.24f.

Colbert, David, *The Magical Worlds of Harry Potter: A Treasury of Myths, Legends, and Fascinating Facts* (New York: Berkley Books, 2008).

Cole, R.E.G., *A Glossary of Words Used in South-west Lincolnshire (Wapentake of Graffoe)* (London: Trübner, 1886).

Collins, Di and Tracy Hayes, 'A playful approach: want to go on a Boggart hunt?' (2017), http://insight.cumbria.ac.uk/id/eprint/3107/ [accessed 9 Jan 2019, abstract].

Collins, John Churton, edited by *The Early Poems of Alfred, Lord Tennyson* (London: Methuen, 1901).

Colls, Robert, *Identity of England* (Oxford: Oxford University Press, 2002). https://doi.org/10.1093/acprof:oso/9780199245192.001.0001.

'Commitment of a Ghost to the Tread-Mill', *Leeds Times* (25 Jan 1834), 3.

'Concert at Catforth', *Preston Chronicle* (3 Nov 1877), 5.

Contini, Michel, 'Les désignations de l'épouvantail en domaine gallo-roman',

Langues et cultures de France et d'ailleurs. Hommage à Jean-Baptiste Martin, edited by Fréchet Claudine (Lyon, PUL, 2007), 281–305.

'Controversy Over Sabden Treacle Mines', *Burnley Express* (24 Dec 1942), 7.

'Conviction of Two Boatmen for Rape', *Wolverhampton Chronicle and Staffordshire Advertiser* (16 Aug 1843), 4.

Cooke, M.A.L. 'Richard Surflet, Translator and Practitioner in Physic', *Medical History* 25 (1981), 41–56. https://doi.org/10.1017/S0025727300034098.

Cookson, R., *Goosnargh, Past and Present* (Preston: H. Oakey, 1888).

Cooper, Brian, 'Lexical reflections inspired by Slavonic **bogŭ*: English *bogey* from a Slavonic root?', *Transactions of the Philological Society* 103 (2005), 73–97. https://doi.org/10.1111/j.1467–968X.2004.00145.x.

Cooper, Susan *The Boggart* (London: McElderry Books 2018).

———— *The Boggart and the Monster* (London: McElderry Books 2018).

———— *The Boggart Fights Back* (London: McElderry Books 2018).

'Copyhold Premises', *Morning Advertiser* (1 Oct 1831), 4.

Corfe, Isabel, 'Sensation and Song: Street Ballad Consumption in Nineteenth-Century England', *Media and Print Culture Consumption in Nineteenth-Century Britain*, edited by Paul Raphael Rooney and Anna Gasperini (London: Palgrave and Macmillan, 2016), 131–45. https://doi.org/10.1057/978–1–137–58761–9_8.

Cornish, C.J. 'Roman and Druid Bridges', *Country Life* 9 (1901), 810–12.

Cornwell, David and Sandy Hobbs, 'Hunting the Monster with Iron Teeth', *Perspectives on Contemporary Legend* 3 (1988), 115–37.

Correll, Timothy Corrigan, 'Believers, Sceptics, and Charlatans: Evidential Rhetoric, the Fairies, and Fairy Healers in Irish Oral Narrative and Belief', *Folklore* 116 (2005), 1–18. https://doi.org/10.1080/0015587052000337680.

Coughlan, Ronan, *Handbook of Fairies* (Milverton: Capall Bann, 1998).

'County Petit Sessions: Indecent Assault', *Lancaster Gazette* (2 Mar 1867), 8.

Coupe, Frank, 'A Spook', *Lancashire Evening Post* (6 May 1953), 5.

Coward, T.A. (ed.), *The Vertebrate Fauna of Cheshire and Liverpool Bay* (London: Witherby and Co., 1910), 2 vols. https://doi.org/10.5962/bhl.title.48659.

Cowdell, Paul, 'Ghosts and their Relationship with the Age of a City', *Folklore* 125 (2014), 80–91. https://doi.org/10.1080/0015587X.2013.853516.

Cowper, Henry Swainson, *Hawkshead (The Northernmost Parish of Lancashire): Its History, Archaeology, Industries, Folklore, Dialect etc., etc.* (London: Bemrose & Sons 1899).

Crofton, H.T., *A History of the Ancient Chapel of Stretford in Manchester Parish* (Manchester: Chetham Society, 1899–1903), 3 vols.

———— *A history of Newton chapelry in the ancient parish of Manchester* (Manchester: Chetham Society, 1904–1905).

Croker, Thomas Crofton, *Fairy Legends and Traditions of the South of Ireland* (London: John Murray, 1825–1828), 3 vols.

Crossley, James, (ed.), *Potts' Discovery of Witches In the County of Lancaster* (Manchester: Chetham Society, 1845).

'Crowds stop in the street and stare up at the sky as mesmerising 'giant white ball' UFOs are seen floating above Mexico City', *Mail Online* (19 Dec 2017).

[Cudworth, William], 'Round About Bradford', *Bradford Observer* (23 Dec 1875), 7.

Cudworth, William, *Round about Bradford: A Series of Sketches* (Bradford: Thomas Brear, 1876).

———— *Rambles Round Horton: Historical, Topographical and Descriptive* (Bradford: T. Brear and Co., 1886).

Cunliffe, Henry, *A Glossary of Rochdale-with-Rossendale Words and Phrases* (London: J. Heywood, 1986).

D.S., 'Depledge', *Notes and Queries* 12 (1867, 3rd), 129. https://doi.org/10.1093/nq/s3-XII.294.129b.

Daisy, 'Green Head House', *Burnley Express and Advertiser* (26 Oct 1895), 3.

Dal Negro, Silvia, *The Decay of a Language: The Case of a German Dialect in the Italian Alps* (Bern: Peter Lang, 2004).

Darlington, Thomas, *The Folk-speech of South Cheshire* (London: Trübner, 1887).

Dash, Mike, 'Spring-heeled Jack: To Victorian Bugaboo from Suburban Ghost', *Fortean Studies* 3 (1996), 7–125.

Davies, John, 'The Celtic Element in the Dialectic Words of the Counties of Northampton and Leicester', *Archaeologia Cambrensis* 2 (1885), 1–182.

Davies, Owen, 'Methodism, the Clergy, and the Popular Belief in Witchcraft and Magic', *History* 82 (1997), 252–65. https://doi.org/10.1111/1468-229X.00036.

———— *The Haunted: A Social History of Ghosts* (London: Palgrave Macmillan, 2007).

Davis, Henry H., *The Fancies of a Dreamer* (London: Simpkin, 1842).

Davitt, Jacqueline, *Witches and Ghosts of Pendle and the Ribble Valley* (Stroud: History Press, 2008).

Davy, Barbara Jane, *Introduction to Pagan Studies* (Lanham: Altamira, 2007).

Dawson, Henry, 'Spire-Holly's Sprite', *Glossop Reporter* (3 Mar 1860), 4.

Dawson, James Jn, 'Th' Club Neet', *Ashton Weekly Reporter* (4 Feb 1865), 7.

Day, Abby, 'Everyday Ghosts: A Matter of Believing in Belonging', *The Ashgate Research Companion to Paranormal Cultures*, edited by Olu Jenzen and Sally R. Munt (London: Ashgate, 2016), 149–58.

'Death of a Girl from Fright', *Ashton Weekly Reporter* (11 Feb 1871), 4.

'Death of Mr John Gornall', *Preston Chronicle* (16 Mar 1867), 5.

'Death of Mr John Higson of Lees', *Ashton Weekly Reporter* (16 Dec 1871), 8.

'Debating Societies: Belief in Boggarts', *The Preston Chronicle and Lancashire Advertiser* (24 Jan 1857), 4.

Dégh, Linda 'Conduit Theory/Multiconduit Theory', *Folklore: An Encyclopedia of Beliefs, Customs, Tales, Music, and Art*, edited by Thomas Green (Santa Barbara: ABC-Clio, 1997), 142–44.

Delaney, Joseph, *The Spook's Sacrifice* (London: Random House, 2009).

Delargy, James H., 'The Gaelic Story-Teller with some notes on Gaelic Folk-Tales', *The Proceedings of the British Academy* 31 (1945), 177–221.

Derksen, Rick, *Etymological Dictionary of the Slavic Inherited Lexicon* (Leiden: Brill, 2008).

'Desperate Attempt at Suicide', *Todmorden Advertiser* (16 Aug 1907), 2.

Devereux, Paul, *Spirit Roads: An Exploration of Otherworldly Routes* (London: Collins and Brown, 2007 [2003]).

Devlin, Judith, *The Superstitious Mind: French Peasants and the Supernatural in the Nineteenth Century* (New Haven: Yale, 1987).

Dewsbury, Stephen, 'Vanishing Cheshire dialect words', *Languages in Contact 2010* (Wrocław: Wrocław Publishing, 2010), edited by Zdzisław Wąsik, 61–80.

'Dialect in England's Lake District,' *The Buffalo Commercial* (30 Apr 1891), 5.

Dickins, Bruce, 'Yorkshire Hobs', *Transaction of the Yorkshire Dialect Society* 7 (1942), 9–23.

Dickinson, William, *Cumbriana: Fragments of Cumbrian Life* (London: Whittaker, 1876).

Dickinson, Joseph, 'Appendix: The Flora of Liverpool' [separate pagination], *Proceedings of the Literary and Philosophical Society of Liverpool* 6 (1849–1851), 1–166.

'Dictionary of the Lancashire Dialect', *Manchester Courier* (21 Mar 1891), 2.

'Died', *Manchester Courier* (8 Nov 1828), 3.

Ditchfield, P.H., 'Lancashire Legends', *Memorials of Old Lancashire*, edited by Henry Fishwick and P.H. Ditchfield, (London: Bemrose, 1909), 2 vols, I, 90–106.

DiTerlizzi, Tony and Holly Black, *The Field Guide (Spiderwick Chronicle)* (New York: Simon & Schuster, 2003).

Dobson, Bob, *Lancashire Nicknames and Sayings* (Clapham: Dalesman 1973).

Dobson, William, *Rambles by the Ribble* (Preston: W. and J. Dobson, 1883).

Dodgson, John McNeal, 'Review: Linguistic Atlas', *Geographical Journal* 145 (1979), 151–52. https://doi.org/10.2307/633131.

Doroszewska, Julia, 'The Liminal Space: Suburbs as a Demonic Domain in Classical Literature', *Preternature* 6 (2017), 1–30. https://doi.org/10.5325/preternature.6.1.0001.

Dorson, Richard, *The British Folklorists* (London: Routledge, 1968).

Dragan Radu, *La représentation de l'espace de la société traditionelle: les mondes renversés* (Paris: L'Harmattan, 1999).

Dragstra, Henk, '"Bull-Begger": An Early Modern Scare-Word', *Airy Nothings: Imagining the Otherworld of Faerie from the Middle Ages to the Age of Reason*, edited by Karin E. Olsen and Jan R. Veenstra (Leiden: Brill, 2014), 171–93. https://doi.org/10.1163/9789004258235_010.

'Droylsden Customs & Superstitions in Bygone Days', *Ashton Weekly Reporter* (21 Jul 1855), 4.

Drury, Nevill, *The Dictionary of the Esoteric* (Delhi: Motilal Banarsidass, 2004).

Duncan, Leland L., 'Correspondence', *Folklore* 8 (1897), 69. https://doi.org/10.1080/0015587X.1897.9720412.

Dundes, Alan, *Folklore Matters* (Knoxville: University of Tennessee Press, 1989).

———— *Meaning of Folklore: The Analytical Essays of Alan Dundes* (Logan: Utah State University Press, 2007).

Durkin, Philip 'The *English Dialect Dictionary* and the *Oxford English Dictionary*: A continuing relationship between two dictionaries', *Joseph Wright's English Dialect Dictionary and Beyond*, edited by Manfred Markus, Clive Upton, and Reinhard Heuberger (Frankfurt: Peter Lang, 2010), 201–18.

Dyer, Samuel, *Dialect of the West Riding of Yorkshire: A Short History of Leeds and Other Towns* (Brighouse: John Hartley, 1891).

E.C., 'Sandygate Boggart', *Burnley News* (8 May 1915), 3.

E.R.B., 'The Southport of Sixty Years Ago', *Transactions of the Historic Society of Lancashire and Cheshire* 64 (1919), 131–45.

Easther, Alfred and Thomas Lees, *A Glossary of the Dialect of Almondbury and Huddersfield* (London: Trübner and Co., 1883).

Eberly, S., 'Fairies and the Folklore of Disability: Changeling, Hybrids, and the Solitary Fairy', *The Good People*, edited by Peter Narváez (Lexington 1997), 227–50.

'Ecclesiastical', *Gloucestershire Chronicle* (31 Jan 1914), 3.

Edwards, Gillian, *Hobgoblin and Sweet Puck: Fairy Names and Natures* (London: Geoffrey Bles, 1974).

Egerton, Leigh and Roger Wilbraham, *A Glossary of words used in the dialect of Cheshire* (Chester: Minshull and Hughes, 1877).

Elbourne, Roger, *Music and Tradition in Early Industrial Lancashire, 1780–1840* (London: Folklore Society, 1980).

Elder, Eileen, *The Peacock Lincolnshire Word Books, 1884–1920* (Scunthorpe: Scunthorpe Museum Society, 1997).

'Elements of Botanical Society', *Bury Times* (3 Jan 1863), 4.

'Elf lobby blocks Iceland road project', *Guardian* (22 Dec 2013).

Ella, Colin, 'The Old River Don', *Lincolnshire Poacher* (Summer 2015), 56–58.

Elliot, William Hume, *The Country and Church of the Cheeryble Brothers* (Selkirk: G. Lewis and Son, 1893).

Elos, 'The 'Boggart' at Whaley', *Glossop Record* (18 Feb 1860), 4.

Elton, Charles, *Origins of English History* (London: Bernard Quaritch, 1882).

English, E.D., 'Boggart House', *Shipley Times* (30 May 1945), 14.

'Entertainment at St. Andrew's School', *Wigan Observer and District Advertiser* (15 Nov 1884), 5.

'Entertainment at the Baptist School', *Bury Times* (30 Nov 1867), 5.

'Eruptions of Pendle', *Burnley Gazette* (16 Aug 1905), 3.

'Estate in Thornton', *Leeds Mercury* (24 Jul 1841), 2.

ETA, 'Traditions and Superstitions of the Olden Times, Legends of Lowther and Hawswater', *Kendal Mercury* (26 Dec 1857), 3–4.

Evans, A.L., *Lost Lancashire: The Story of Lancashire Beyond the Sands* (Kendal: Cicerone Press, 1991).

Evans, Seth, *Bradwell, Ancient and Modern: History of the Parish and Incidents in the Hope Valley & District: being collections and recollections in a Peakland village* (Bradwell: Privately Printed, 1912).

Ewing, Juliana, 'The Brownies: A Fairy Story', *Monthly Packet* 30 (1865), 658–701.

———— *The Brownies and Other Tales* (London: SPCK, 1870).

'Extraordinary Breach of Promise', *The Manchester Courier and Lancashire General Advertiser* (9 Aug 1877), 6.

'Extraordinary Case', *Preston Chronicle* (21 Jul 1832), 3.

'Extraordinary Superstition at Blackley', *Manchester Courier and Lancashire General Advertiser* (6 Nov 1852), 7.

'Eyam, Stoney Middleton, Calver and District', *Derbyshire Times and Chesterfield Herald* (11 Jul 1903), 6.

Eyre, Kathleen, *Lancashire Ghosts* (Keighley: Dalesman, 1977).

F.B. 'Letters', *Burnley Express* (27 Apr 1946), 5.

Faber, George, *An Inquiry into the History and Theology of the Ancient Vallenses and Albigenses: as exhibiting, agreeably to the promises, the perpetuity of the sincere church of Christ* (London: R.B. Seeley, 1838).

'Fairy Superstition and the Present Age', *Chester Chronicle* (23 Apr 1859), 8.

Falconer, William, 'Plant Galls of the Huddersfield District', *The Naturalist* 808 (1924), 151–56.

'Family Ghosts Which Are Respected in Derbyshire', *Nottingham Journal* (14 Jun 1920), 6.

Fanthorpe, Patricia and Lionel Fanthorpe, *Padfoot: A Supernatural History* (N.P.: King's England Press, 2015).

'Fatal Result of an Accident at Darwen', *Lancashire Evening Post* (28 Oct 1889), 3.

Fedler, Fred, *Media Hoaxes* (Ames: Iowa State University, 1989).

Ferguson, Robert, *The Dialect of Cumberland* (London: Williams and Norgate, 1873).

Field, John, *English Field Names: A Dictionary* (Newton Abbot: David and Charles, 1972).

Fieldhouse, Harry, *Old Bradford* (Bradford: P. Lund, 1889).

Fischer, Andreas, 'Non olet: Euphemisms we live by', *New Perspectives on English Historical Linguistics*, edited by Christian Kay, Carole Hough, and Irené Wotherspoon (Amsterdam: John Benjamins, 2002), 2 vols, II, 91–107.

Fishwick, Henry, *The History of the Parish of Rochdale* (Rochdale: J. Clegg, 1889).
———— 'Some Notes on the Author of *The Traditions of Lancashire*', *Rochdale Observer* (2 May 1914), 4.

Fizzwig, Oliver, 'From Glossop to Disley and Thereabouts', *Glossop Record* (15 Dec 1866), 2–3.

Flom, George T., 'The Etymology of Big-bug', *Modern Language Notes* 17 (1902), 61–62. https://doi.org/10.2307/2917647.

'Fly Wheel Bursts', *Rochdale Observer* (19 Feb 1916), 7.

'Folklore', *Ashton Weekly Reporter* (26 Sep 1857), 4.

Forbes, Hamish, *Meaning and Identity in a Greek Landscape* (Cambridge: Cambridge University Press, 2007). https://doi.org/10.1017/CBO9780511720284.

Ford, Edward, George Hodson, *A history of Enfield in the County of Middlesex; including its royal and ancient manors, the chase, and the Duchy of Lancaster, with notices of its worthies, and its natural history, etc.* (Enfield: Enfield Press, 1873).

Forster, Rev. B., 'Dear Sir', *Illustrations of the Literary History of the Eighteenth Century*, edited by John Nichols (London: Nichols and Son, 1817–1831), 6 vols, V, 308–09.

Foster, Michael Dylan and Jeffrey A. Tolbert (eds), *The Folkloresque: Reframing Folklore in a Popular Culture World* (Colorado: University Press of Colorado, 2015). https://doi.org/10.7330/9781607324188.

Foxe, John, *Actes and Monuments of these latter and perilous days, touching matters of the Church, wherein are comprehended and described the great persecutions and* *horrible troubles that have been wrought and practised by the Romish prelates, specially in this realm of England and Scotland, from the year of our Lord 1000 unto the time now present; gathered and collected according to the true copies and writings certificatory, as well of the parties themselves that suffered, as also out of the bishops' registers, which were the doers thereof* (London: John Day, 1563).

Franceschetto, Gisla, *I capitelli di Cittadella e Camposampiero: Indagine sul sacro nell'alto Padovano* (Rome: TeI, 1972).

Francis, M.E., 'Old Folks' Tales', *The National Review* 26 (1895), 121–28.

Frater, Jamie, *Listverse.com's Ultimate Book of Bizarre Lists: Fascinating Facts and Shocking Trivia* (Berkeley: Ulysses Press, 2010).

Fritz, Jean, *Magic To Burn* (New York: Cowart-McCann, 1964).

Frog, 'Revisiting the Historical-Geographic Method(s)', *Retrospective Methods Network* 7 (2013), 18–34.

Frost, Roger, *A Lancashire Township: The History of Briercliffe-with Extwistle* (Briercliffe: Rieve Edge Press, 1982).

Gale, Steven H., *Encyclopedia of British Humorists: Geoffrey Chaucer to John Cleese* (London: Garland, 1996), 2 vols.

Garnett, Richard, *The Philological Essays of the Late Rev. Richard Garnett, of the British Museum* (London: Williams and Norgate, 1859).

Gaskill, Malcolm, *Crime and Mentalities in Early Modern England* (Cambridge: Cambridge University Press, 2000). https://doi.org/10.1017/CCOL0521572754.

Gaster, Moses, *Greeko-Slavonic: Ilchester lectures on Greeko-Slavonic literature and its relation to the folk-lore of Europe during the Middle Ages* (London: Trübner and Co., 1887).

'General News', *Shields Daily Gazette* (29 Aug 1871), 2.

'"Ghost" in Three-Cornered Hat at Barnoldswick', *Burnley News* (26 Sep 1928), 8.

'Ghost Legend', *Lancashire Evening Post* (30 Apr 1953), 7.

'Ghost Rumours at Burnley', *Burnley Express* (3 Jan 1903), 8.

'Ghost Stories', *Burnley Express and Advertiser* (30 Mar 1895), 3.

'Ghost Story', *Lancaster Gazette* (25 Jan 1851), 5.

'Ghostly Hounds at Horton', *Folk-lore Journal* 4 (1886), 265–67. https://doi.org/10.1080/17442524.1886.10602822.

Gibson, A., Craig 'Ancient Customs and Superstitions in Cumberland', *Transactions of the Historic Society of Lancashire and Cheshire* 10 (1858), 97–110.

Gibson, Thomas, *Legends and Historical Notes of North Westmoreland* (London: Unwin Brothers, 1887).

Gilchrist, Murray, 'Black Sir William', *Supplement to the Manchester Courier* (11 Feb 1905), 4.

Girvin, Brenda, *Round Fairyland with Alice* (London: Wells, Gardner and Co.).

Goodare, Julian, *The European Witch-Hunt* (London: Routledge, 2016). https:// doi.org/10.4324/9781315560458.

Goodman, Matthew, *The Sun and the Moon: The Remarkable True Account of Hoaxers, Showmen, Dueling Journalists and Lunar Man-Bats in Nineteenth-Century* (New York: Basic Books, 2008).

Gordon, Avery, *Ghostly Matters: Haunting and the Sociological Imagination* (Minneapolis: University of Minnesota Press, 2008).

Greenwood, Susan, *The Nature of Magic: An Anthropology of Consciousness* (Oxford: Berg, 2005).

Grenier, Paola and Karen Wright, 'Social Capital in Britain: Exploring the Hall Paradox', *Policy Studies* 27 (2006), 27–53. https://doi.org/ 10.1080/01442870500499900.

de Grey, Thomas, *The Compleat Horseman and Expert Ferrier in Two Bookes. The first, shewing the best manner of breeding good horses, with their choyce, nature, riding and dyeting ... The second, directing the most exact and approved manner how to know and cure all maladies and diseases in horses* (London: Thomas Harper, 1639).

Griffiths, Arthur, *Lancashire Folklore* (Leigh: Leigh Local History Society, 1993).

Griffiths, Trevor, *The Lancashire Working Classes, c.1880–1930* (Oxford: Clarendon, 2001). https://doi.org/10.1093/acprof:oso/9780199247387.001.0001.

Grigson, Geoffrey, *Freedom of the Parish* (London: Anthony Mott, 1982).

Grindon, Leo H., *Country Rambles, and Manchester Walks and Wild Flowers: being rural wanderings in Cheshire, Lancashire, Derbyshire, & Yorkshire* (Manchester: Palmer & Howe, 1882). https://doi.org/10.5962/bhl.title.24831.

———— *Lancashire; Brief Historical and Descriptive Notes* (London: Seeley, 1892).

'Gringley', *Stamford Mercury* (4 Aug 1854), 2.

Gruffydd, W.J., *Folklore and Myth in the Mabinogion* (Cardiff: University of Wales Press, 1958).

Gunn, William, *Select Works of Robert Rollock* (Edinburgh: Woodrow Society, 1849), 2 vols.

Gunnell, Terry, 'The Power in the Place: Icelandic Álagablettir Legends in a Comparative Context', *Storied and Supernatural Places: Studies in Spatial and Social Dimensions of Folklore and Sagas*, edited by Ülo Valk and Daniel Sävborg (Helsinki: SKS, 2018), 27–41.

Guppy, H. Miles, 'Coverdale and the English Bible', *Bulletin of the John Rylands Library* 19 (1935), 300–28. https://doi.org/10.7227/BJRL.19.2.2.

Gutch, E. and Mabel Peacock, *Examples of Printed Folk-lore Concerning the North Riding of Yorkshire, York & the Ainsty* (London: Nutt, 1901).

H. [Higson, John], 'To and Through Didsbury', *Ashton Weekly Reporter* (25 Oct 1856), 4.

———— 'Reminiscences of Droylsden and the Neighbourhood', *Ashton Weekly Reporter* (26 Jun 1858), 4.

———— 'A Tramp in Derbyshire', *Ashton Weekly Reporter* (9 Nov 1867), 2.

H., *Lines on the Green Lane Boggert* (n.d.).

H., 'Catholic Soiree at Newton', *The Lamp* 1 (1856), 107.

H.H., 'Some Lancashire Boggart Tales', *Burnley Express and Advertiser* (30 Dec 1899), 3.

H.S., 'The Stone Shackled Ghost of Dilworth', *Lancashire Evening Post* (12 Oct 1932), 4.

Hafstein, V., 'Biological metaphors in folklore theory: an essay in the history of ideas', *Arv* (2001), 7–32.

Haigh, Walter, *A New Glossary of the Dialect of the Huddersfield District* (Oxford: Oxford University Press, 1928).

Haining, Peter, *The Scarecrow: Fact and Fable* (London: Robert Hale, 1988).

Hall, Alan, *The Story of Bradford* (Stroud: History Press, 2013).

Hall, Alaric, 'Getting Shot of Elves: Healing, Witchcraft and Fairies in the Scottish Witchcraft Trials', *Folklore* 116 (2005), 19–36. https://doi.org/10.1 080/0015587052000337699.

———— 'Are There Any Elves in Anglo-Saxon Place-names?', *Nomina* 26 (2006), 61–80.

———— *Elves in Anglo-Saxon England* (Woodbridge: Boydell, 2007).

Hall, Peter, 'Social Capital in Britain', *British Journal of Political Science* 29 (1999), 417–61. https://doi.org/10.1017/S0007123499000204.

Hall, Robert G., *Voices of the People: Democracy and Chartist Political Identity, 1830–1870* (Monmouth: Merlin, 2007).

Hamer, Sarah Selina, 'Ab' O' Ned's "Witchins"', *The Manchester Weekly Times* (12 Dec 1890), 3.

Hampson, R.T., *Medii aevi kalendarium: or, Dates, charters, and customs of the Middle Ages: with kalendars from the tenth to the fifteenth century, and an alphabetical digest of obsolete names of days, forming a glossary of the dates of the Middle Ages, with tables and other aids for ascertaining dates* (London: Henry Kent, 1841), 2 vols.

Hampton, Janie, *How the Girl Guides Won the War* (London: Harper Press, 2011).

Hand, Wayland D., *Boundaries, Portals, and Other Magical Spots in Folklore* (London: Folklore Society, 1983).

Handley, Sasha, *Visions of the Unseen World: Ghost Beliefs and Ghost Stories in Eighteenth-Century England* (London: Pickering and Chatto, 2007).

Hanks, Patrick, Richard Coates and Peter McClure, *The Oxford Dictionary of*

Family Names in Britain and Ireland (Oxford: OUP, 2016), 3 vols. https://doi. org/10.1093/acref/9780199677764.001.0001.

'Happy Old Age', *Yorkshire Evening Post* (12 Dec 1935), 12.

Hardcastle, C.D., 'The story that the ...', *Leeds Mercury* (21 Mar 1891), 24.

Hardwick, Charles, 'Ancient British Remains at Over Darwen', *Transactions of the Historic Society of Lancashire and Cheshire* 6 (1866), 273–78.

——— 'Boggarts', *Supplement to the Manchester Weekly Times* (29 Apr 1871), 134.

——— *Traditions, Superstitions and Folklore (Chiefly Lancashire and the North of England)* (Manchester: Ireland & Co., 1872).

——— 'The north of England domestic or "flitting" boggart: its Scandinavian origins', *Manchester Literary Club Papers* 6 (1880), 278–83.

Hardy, Thomas, *The Life and Death of the Mayor of Casterbridge* (Peterborough: Broadview, 1997).

Harland, John and Thomas Turner Wilkinson, *Lancashire Folk-lore: Illustrative of the Superstitious Beliefs and Practices, Local Customs and Usages of the People of the County Palatine* (London: Frederick Warne & Co., 1867).

——— *Lancashire Legends, Traditions, Pageants, Sports &c* (London: George Routledge and Sons, 1873).

Harland, John, *A Glossary of Words used in Swaledale, Yorkshire* (London: Trübner and Co., 1873).

Harris, Jessie and Julie Neely, 'Southern Illinois Phantoms and Bogies', *Midwest Folklore* 1 (1951), 171–78.

Harris, Marc, *Folklore and the Fantastic in Nineteenth-Century British Fiction* (Farnham: Ashgate, 2008).

Harrison, Richard D., 'Taylor, Zachary (1653–1705)', *Oxford Dictionary of National Biography* (Oxford: Oxford University Press, 2004) [accessed 21 Aug 2018].

Harte, Jeremy, 'Haunted Lanes', *The Ley Hunter* 121 (1994), 1–7.

——— 'Ruth Tongue: the story teller', *3rd Stone* 41 (2001), 16–21.

——— *Explore Fairy Traditions* (Loughborough: Explore Books, 2004).

——— 'Black Dog Studies', *Explore Phantom Black Dogs*, edited by Bob Trubshaw (Loughborough: Explore Books, 2005), 5–20.

——— 'Subversive or What? Fairies and Rebellion', *Gramarye* 11 (2017), 7–16.

——— 'Dorset: Fairy Barrows and Cunning Folk', *Magical Folk*, edited by Simon Young and Ceri Houlbrook (London: Gibson Square, 2018), 65–78.

——— 'From Ogre to Woodlouse: A Journey Through Names', *Gramarye* 14 (2018), 33–38.

——— 'Names and Tales: On Folklore and Place Names', *Folklore* 130 (2019), 373–94. https://doi.org/10.1080/0015587X.2019.1618071.

Harting, M.W.G., 'Brownie Piper', *Milngravie and Bearsden Herald* (30 Nov 1934) 2.

Hartmann, Laura, 'The Black Dog and the Boggart: Fantastic Beasts in Joanne K. Rowling's *Harry Potter and the Prisoner of Azkaban* and Where to Find Them in Mythology and Traditional Folklore', *'Harry – yer a wizard': Exploring J.K. Rowling's Harry Potter Universe*, edited by Marion Gymnich, Hanne Birk, and Denise Burkhard (Baden-Baden: Tectum Verlag, 2017), 41–50.

Harvey, Graham, 'Boggarts and Books: Towards an Appreciation of Pagan Spirituality', *Beyond New Age: Exploring Alternative Spirituality*, edited by Steven Sutcliffe and Marion Bowman (Edinburgh: Edinburgh University Press, 2000), 155–68.

Harvey, William, *Scottish Chapbook Literature* (Paisley: Gardner, 1903).

Haslam, David, *Ghosts and Legends of Nottinghamshire* (Newbury: Countryside Books, 1996).

Haslam, Michael, 'Rock-solid Boggarts in a Ring', *Northern Earth* 115 (2008), 20–23.

Haworth, D. *et al.*, *Cheshire Village Memories* (Tilston Court: the Federation, 1952–1961) 2 vols.

Hayes, Jarrod, *Queer Roots for the Diaspora: Ghosts in the Family Tree* (Ann Arbor: University of Michigan, 2016). https://doi.org/10.3998/mpub.8781040.

Hayes, Tracy, 'Playful Approaches to Outdoor Learning: Boggarts, Bears, and Bunny Rabbits', *Play and Recreation, Health and Wellbeing*, edited by Bethan Evans, John Horton, and Tracey Skelton (London: Springer, 2016), 156–70. https://doi.org/10.1007/978–981–4585–51–4_12.

'Hayfield', *Glossop-dale Chronicle* (4 Dec 1869), 3.

Haylock , Charlie and Barrie Appleby, *In a Manner of Speaking: The Story of Spoken English* (Stroud: Amberley, 2017).

Heanley, R.M., 'The Vikings: Traces of Their Folklore in Marshland', *Saga Book of the Viking Club* 3 (1901–1903), 35–62.

Heath, Robert, 'Epigram', *Clarastella: Together with Poems Occasional, Elegies, Epigrams, Satyrs* (London: Humph. Moseley, 1650).

Heath, Sandra, *Mayhem in Bath* (N.P.: Belgrave House, 2010).

Heathcote, C., 'A History and Gazetteer of the Mines in the Liberty of Peak Forest, Derbyshire: 1605–1878', *Mining History* 14 (2001), 1–28..

Heaton, James, 'Stray Notes by the Wayside: The Environs of Burnley', *Burnley Advertiser* (13 Feb 1869), 3.

Heesen, Anke te, *The Newspaper Clipping: A Modern Paper Object* (Manchester: Manchester University Press, 2014).

Heide, Eldar and Karen Bek-Pedersen (eds), *New Focus on Retrospective Methods:*

Resuming Methodological Discussions: Case Studies from Northern Europe (Helsinki: FFC, 2014).

Henderson, Lizanne, *Witchcraft and Folk Belief in the Age of Enlightenment Scotland, 1670–1740* (London: Palgrave Macmillan, 2016). https://doi.org/10.1057/9781137313249.

Henderson, William, *Notes on the Folk-Lore of the Northern Counties of England and the Borders* (London: W. Satchell, 1879).

Hendrickson, Robert, *QPB Encyclopedia of Word and Phrase Origins* (New York: Facts, 1998).

Hengsuwan, Manasikarn and Amara Prasithrathsint, 'A Folk Taxonomy of Terms for Ghosts and Spirits in Thai', *Manusya* 17 (2014), 29–49. https://doi.org/10.1163/26659077–01702003.

Henricks, Thomas S., *Disputed Pleasures: Sport and Society in Preindustrial England* (New York: Greenwood Press, 1991).

Henry, P.L., 'The Goblin group', *Études Celtiques* 8 (1958–1959), 404–16. https://doi.org/10.3406/ecelt.1959.1321.

Hepburn, James, *A Book of Scattered Leaves: Poetry of Poverty in Broadside Ballads of Nineteenth-Century England* (Lewisburg: Bucknell University Press, 2000–2002), 2 vols.

Hewitt, Martin, *The Dawn of the Cheap Press in Victorian Britain: The End of the 'Taxes on Knowledge', 1849–1869* (London: Bloomsbury Academic, 2014).

Hewitt, Martin and Robert Poole (eds), *The Diaries of Samuel Bamford* (New York: St Martin's Press, 2000).

Hewlett, E.H., 'Boggarts and Badgers', *Spectator* 129 (1923), 208.

Hewlett, Edgar, *Personal Recollections of the Little Tew Ghost reviewed in connection with the Lancashire Bogie* (London: Aylott, 1854).

Higham, N.J., *A Frontier Landscape: The North West in the Middle Ages* (Oxford: Windgather, 2004).

[Higson, John], 'Droylsden Customs & Superstitions in Bygone Days', *Ashton Weekly Reporter* (21 Jul 1855), 4.

Higson, John, *The Gorton Historical Recorder* (Droylsden: Privately printed, 1852?).
———— 'Droylsden Customs & Superstitions in Bygone Days', *Ashton Weekly Reporter* (26 Jul 1856), 4.
———— *Historical and Descriptive Notices of Droylsden: Past and Present* (Manchester: Beresford & Souther, 1859).
———— 'Boggarts and Feorin', *Notes and Queries* 4 (1869, 4th), 508–09. https://doi.org/10.1093/nq/s4-IV.102.508.
———— 'Boggarts, Feorin, etc.', *Notes and Queries* 5 (1870, 4th), 156–57. https://doi.org/10.1093/nq/s4-VI.138.156f.

———— 'Walton-le-Dale Folk Lore', *Notes and Queries* 6 (1870, 4th), 211. https://doi.org/10.1093/nq/s4–VI.141.211b.

———— 'Five Days' Walks and Drives in North Lancashire', *Preston Herald* (10 Feb 1872), 7.

———— 'The Boggart of Gorton Chapelyord', *Ballads and Songs of Lancashire: Ancient and Modern*, edited by John Harland (London: George Routledge and Sons 1875), 536–39.

———— *South Manchester Supernatural: The Ghosts, Fairies and Boggarts of Victorian Gorton, Lees, Newton and Saddleworth* (N.P.: Pwca Ghost, Witch and Fairy Pamphlets, 2020).

Hill, Headon, 'The Comlyn Alibi', *Coventry Evening Telegraph* (13 Sep 1916), 4.

Hindley, Charles, *Curiosities of Street Literature: Comprising 'Cocks', Or 'Catchpennies'* (London: Reeves, 1871).

Hobbs, Andrew, *A Fleet Street in Every Town: The Provincial Press in England, 1855–1900* (Cambridge: Open Book Publishers, 2018). https://doi.org/10.11647/OBP.0152.

Hocking, Silas K., *Real Grit* (London: Frederick Warne and Co., 1900).

Hodgson, Mrs, 'On some Surviving Fairies', *Transactions of the Cumberland and Westmorland Antiquarian and Archaeological Society* 1 (1901), 116–18.

Hole, Christina, *Traditions and Customs of Cheshire* (Wakefield: S.R. Publisher, 1970 [1937]).

———— *English Folklore* (London: Batsford, 1945).

Holland, Robert, *A Glossary of Words used in the County of Chester* (London: Trübner and Co., 1886).

Hoole, Charles, *An Easy Entrance to the Latin Tongue* (London: William Dugard, 1649).

Hopkins, R. Thurston, *Ghosts Over England* (London: Meridian Books, 1953).

Houlbrook, Ceri, 'The Suburban Boggart: Folklore's survival, revival, and recontextualisation in an urban, post-industrial Environment' (unpublished undergraduate thesis, The University of Manchester, 2011).

———— 'The Suburban Boggart: Folklore of an inner-city park' *Gramarye* 11 (2017), 19–32.

Houlding, Henry, 'Local Glimpses: Rhymes and Dreams', *Burnley Literary and Scientific Club* 10 (1892), 65–72.

Howat, Polly, *Ghosts and Legends of Lincolnshire and the Fen Country* (Newbury: Countryside Books, 1992).

Howcroft, A.J., *Tales of a Pennine People* (Oldham: Lee, 1923).

Howells, William, *Cambrian Superstitions* (Tipton: T. Danks, 1831).

Hoy, Albert Lyon, 'An Etymological Glossary of the East Yorkshire Dialect' (unpublished doctoral thesis, Michigan School of Agriculture and Applied Science, 1952).

Hrobat, Katja, 'Conceptualization of Space Through Folklore: On the Mythical and Ritual Significance of Community Limits', *Archaeological Imaginations of Religion*, edited by Thomas Meier (Budapest: Archaeolingua Alapítvány, 2014), 359–82.

———— '"Emplaced" Tradition: The Continuity of Folk Tradition in the Landscape', *Traditiones* 41 (2012), 41–52. https://doi.org/10.3986/Traditio2012410203.

Hudson, Martyn, *Ghosts, Landscapes and Social Memory* (London: Routledge, 2018). https://doi.org/10.4324/9781315306674.

Hufford, David J., *The Terror That Comes in the Night: An Experience-Centred Study of Supernatural Assault Traditions* (Philadelphia: University of Pennsylvania, 1982).

Hughes, Helen MacGill, *News and the Human Interest Story* (New York: Greenwood Press, 1968).

Hughes, T. McKenny, 'Acoustic Vases in Churches Traced Back to the Theatres and Oracles of Greece', *Cambridge Antiquarian Society* 67 (1915), 63–90.

'Hull Esperanto Society', *Hull Daily Mail* (26 Apr 1909), 6.

Huloet, Richard, *Huloets dictionarie newelye corrected, amended, set in order and enlarged, vvith many names of men, tovvnes, beastes, foules, fishes, trees, shrubbes, herbes, fruites, places, instrumentes &c. And in eche place fit phrases, gathered out of the best Latin authors. Also the Frenche therevnto annexed, by vvhich you may finde the Latin or Frenche, of anye English woorde you will. By Iohn Higgins late student in Oxeforde.* (London: 'in aedibus Thomae Marshij', 1572).

Hunt, Robert, *Popular Romances of the West of England or the Drolls, Traditions and Superstitions of Old Cornwall* (London: Chatto and Windus, 1908).

Hunter, Joseph, *The Hallamshire Glossary* (London: W. Pickering, 1829).   .

Hunter, Michael, 'New light on the "Drummer of Tedworth": conflicting narratives of witchcraft in Restoration England', *Historical Research* 78 (2005), 311–53. https://doi.org/10.1111/j.1468–2281.2005.00226.x.

———— *The Decline of Magic: Britain in the Enlightenment* (New Have: Yale University Press, 2020).

Hutton, Ronald, *The Triumph of the Moon* (Oxford: Oxford University Press, 1999). https://doi.org/10.1093/acprof:oso/9780198207443.001.0001.

'Idle Quiz', *Shipley Times* (9 May 1945), 10.

'In parliament ...', *Stamford Mercury* (23 Nov 1860), 6.

'In Sunny Silverdale', *Burnley Express* (28 Jul 1928), 11.

'In these enlightened days', *Northern Daily Telegraph* (11 Aug 1904), 2.

'**Ingleton as a summer resort**', *Leeds Mercury* (30 Mar 1885), 3.

J.A., 'The Ghosts of Delamere Forest', *Cheshire Observer* (6 Mar 1915), 4.

Jackson, Bruce, *Fieldwork* (Urbana: University of Illinois, 1987).

Jackson, W., 'The Curwens of Workington Hall and Kindred Families', *Transactions of the Cumberland and Westmorland Antiquarian and Archaeological Society* 5 (1881), 181–232.

Jakobsson, Ármann, 'The Taxonomy of the Non-Existent: Some Medieval Icelandic Concepts of the Paranormal', *Fabula* 54 (2013), 199–213. https://doi.org/10.1515/fabula-2013-0018.

———— *The Troll Inside You: Paranormal Activity in the Medieval North* (Punctum Books, 2017).

James, Maureen, *Lincolnshire Folk Tales* (Stroud: History Press, 2013).

James, Ron M., *The Folklore of Cornwall: The Oral Tradition of a Celtic Nation* (Exeter: University of Exeter Press, 2019).

Jamieson, John and John Johnstone, *A Dictionary of the Scottish Language* (Edinburgh: William Tait, 1846), 4 vols.

'**Jaunts for Half Holidays**', *Northampton Mercury* (12 Jul 1912), 9.

Jefferson, Richard and Keith Kirby, 'Boggarts, ants and poison: The shady natural history of Dog's Mercury', *British Wildlife* 22 (2011), 241–45.

Jerdan, William, *Autobiography of William Jerdan, with his literary, political, and social reminiscences and correspondence during the last fifty years* (London: Arthur Hall, 1852–1853), 4 vols.

Jewel, John, *The Works of John Jewel* (Oxford: OUP, 1848), 8 vols.

Johnson, Marjorie, *Seeing Fairies: From the Lost Archives of the Fairy Investigation Society, Authentic Reports of Fairies in Modern Times* (San Antonio: Anomalist Publishing, 2014).

Johnson, Samuel, *A Dictionary of the English language: in which the words are deduced from their originals, and illustrated in their different significations by examples from the best writers: to which are prefixed, a history of the language, and an English grammar* (London: Rivington, 1785 [1755]), 2 vols.

Jones, Aled Gruffydd, *Powers of the Press: Newspapers, Power and the Public in Nineteenth-Century England* (London: Routledge 2016).

Jones, Malcolm and Patrick Dillon, *Dialect in Wiltshire* (Wiltshire County Council, 1987).

Jones, Melvyn, 'Juliana Ewing, Children's Writer and Ecclesfield's Countryside', *Aspects of Sheffield: Discovering Local History*, edited by Melvyn Jones (Barnsley: Wharncliffe, 1999), 2 vols, II, 112–30.

———— 'West Riding Dialect in the Stories of Juliana Ewing, Victorian Children's Writer', *Transactions of the Yorkshire Dialect Society* 19 (1999), 29–38.

Jones, W. Henry, 'Finnish Folk-Lore', *Notes and Queries* 10 (1884), 401–04. https://doi.org/10.1093/nq/s6–X.256.401.

Jopling, Bob, 'Well if you believe that …', *St Bees News* (July–August 2017), 15.

Josephson-Storm, Jason, *The Myth of Disenchantment: Magic Modernity and the Birth of the Human Sciences* (Chicago: University of Chicago Press, 2017). https://doi.org/10.7208/chicago/9780226403533.001.0001.

Joyce, Patrick, *Visions of the People: Industrial England and the Question of Class, 1848–1914* (Cambridge: CUP, 1991). https://doi.org/10.1017/CBO9780511560651.

Kaldera, Raven *Wyrdwalkers: Techniques of Northern Tradition Shamanism* (Hubbardston: Asphodel Press, 2007).

Karl, Jason and Adele Yeomans, *Preston's Haunted Heritage* (Lancaster: Palatine Books, 2012).

Kay-Shuttleworth, James Phillips, *Scarsdale; or, Life on the Lancashire and Yorkshire border, thirty years ago* (London: Smith, Elder, 1860), 3 vols.

Keightley, Thomas, *The Fairy Mythology: Illustrative of the Romance and Superstition of Various Countries* (London: H.G. Bohn, 1850).

'Kendal Natural History and Scientific Society', *Kendal Mercury* (13 Mar 1841), 4.

Kenrick, Eddie, 'Tramps in Ribbleland: The Sabden Valley', *Burnley Express* (14 Jun 1930), 10.

Kerr, Henry, 'Summer Rambles in and around Cliviger Valley: 2', *Burnley Express* (30 Jul 1892), 7.

———— 'Marriage and Morals in the Sixteenth Century', *Burnley Express and Advertiser* (31 Dec 1892), 7.

———— 'Typical "Chips" of Lancashire Boggart Lore: No. 1 [*sic* actually No. 2]', *Burnley Express* (6 Jan 1894), 2.

———— 'Sheepstealers, Highwaymen and Burglars in Cliviger early in the present century', *Burnley Express* (10 Feb 1894), 2.

Kirk, Edward, 'A Nook of North Lancashire', *Lancashire Advertiser* (30 Sep 1876), 3.

———— 'The Folk of a North Lancashire Nook', *Manchester Literary Club* 3 (1877), 102–14.

Kirk, James, 'Rollock, Robert (1555–1599)', *Oxford Dictionary of National Biography* (Oxford: Oxford University Press, 2004) [accessed 9 Dec 2015].

Kirkby, Bryham, *Lakeland Words; a collection of dialect words and phrases as used in Cumberland and Westmorland, with illustrative sentences in the North Westmorland dialect* (Kendal: T. Wilson, 1898).

Kreilkamp, Ivan, *Voice and the Victorian Storyteller* (Cambridge: CUP, 2005). https://doi.org/10.1017/CBO9780511484865.

Kvideland, Reimund and Henning K. Sehmsdorf (eds), *Scandinavian Folk Belief and Legend* (Minneapolis: London 1988).

Lahee, Margaret R., *Betty o' Yep's Laughable Tale of Jinny Cropper at th' Halton Feast* (London: J. Heywood, 1865).

———— *Trot Coffie's Boggart: A Lancashire Ghost Story*, (Manchester: John Heywood, 1882).

'Lancashire and Yorkshire Railway', *Bradford Observer* (22 Nov 1860), 7.

Landy, Joshua and Michael Saler, *The Re-Enchantment of the World: Secular Magic in a Rational Age* (Stanford, CA: SUP, 2009). https://doi.org/10.11126/stanford/9780804752992.001.0001.

Langdale, Thomas, *A Topographical Dictionary of Yorkshire* (Northallerton: J. Langdale, 1822).

Langshaw, Arthur, 'It Raineth Every Day', *Clitheroe Advertiser* (26 Sep 1952), 6.

Larrington, Carolyne, *The Land of the Green Man* (London: I.B.Tauris, 2017).

Larsen, Marianne A., *The Making and Shaping of the Victorian Teacher: A Comparative New Cultural History* (Basingstoke: Palgrave Macmillan, 2011).

'Latest Freak', *Todmorden and District News* (12 Jul 1907), 5.

Latham, Minor White, *The Elizabethan Fairies: The Fairies of Folklore and the Fairies of Shakespeare* (New York: Columbia University Press, 1930).

Laughton, Benjamin, 'Letters to the Editor', *Lincolnshire Life* 2 (1962), 40.

du Laurens, André, *Discours de la conservation de la veuë : des maladies melancoliques: des catarrhes, & de la vieillesse* (Theodore Samson, 1598 [1594]).

———— *A discourse of the preseruation of the sight: of melancholike diseases; of rheumes, and of old age. Composed by M. Andreas Laurentius, ordinarie phisition to the King, and publike professor of phisicke in the Vniuersitie of Mompelier. Translated out of French into English, according to the last edition, by Richard Surphlet, practitioner in phisicke* (London: Felix Kingston, 1599).

Lawson, Joseph, *Letters to the young on progress in Pudsey during the last sixty years* (Stanningley: J.W. Lawson, 1887).

Lawson, Richard, *A History of Flixton, Urmston, and Davyhulme. Eleven illustrations* (Urmston: Richard Lawson, 1898).

Leach, Maria (ed.), *Funk and Wagnalls Standard Dictionary of Folklore Mythology and Legend* (London: Harper and Row, 1984).

Lee, Alan J., *The Origins of the Popular Press in England: 1855–1914* (London: Crom, 1976).

Leese, Philip R., *The Kidsgrove Boggart and the Black Dog* (Stafford: Staffordshire Libraries, 1989).

'**Legends of Worsthorn**', *Burnley Advertiser* (17 Jan 1880), 8.

Leighton, Robert, 'To the Editor of the "*Spiritual Magazine*"', *Spiritual Magazine* 6 (1865), 335–36.

'**Levies on the Publicans**', *Leeds Mercury* (12 May 1855), 7.

Levins, Peter, *Manipulus Vocabulorum: A Dictionary of England and Latin Words Arranged in the Alphabetical Order of the Last Syllables* (Westminster: Camden Society, 1867).

Lincoln, Bruce, *Apples and Oranges: Explorations In, On and With Comparison* (Chicago: University of Chicago Press, 2018). https://doi.org/10.7208/chicago/9780226564104.001.0001.

'**Lincolnshire Legends and Folk-Lore**', *Lincolnshire Standard* (21 Oct 1933), 4.

Linton, Elizabeth, *The Lake Country* (London: Smith, Elder, 1864).

'**Literary Notices**', *Preston Chronicle* (20 Apr 1867), 4.

Litt, William, 'Henry and Mary: A Local Tale', *Whitehaven News* (21 Jul 1859), 4.

Lloyd, Amy J., 'Education, Literacy and the Reading Public', *British Library Newspapers* (Detroit: Gale, 2007).

'**Local Authors & Other Worthies**', *Whitby Gazette* (25 Jun 1887), 6.

'**Local Law Case**', *Manchester Courier* (11 Mar 1881), 8.

'**Local Police Courts**', *Lancaster Gazette* (15 Dec 1880), 2.

'**Local Superstitions**', *Carlisle Patriot* (26 Feb 1886), 6.

Löfstedt, Torsten, 'How to Define Supernatural Beings', *Studies in Folklore and Popular Religion* 1 (1996), 107–12.

Lofthouse, Jessica, *North-Country Folklore: in Lancashire, Cumbria and the Pennine Dales* (London: Robert Hale, 1976).

Logan, S.F., 'Historic Barton', *Lancashire Evening Post* (12 Feb 1942), 3.

'**Loitering In The Street**', *The Lancaster Gazette Supplement* (2 Nov 1861), 1.

Longbotham, A.T., 'Lambert House, Elland', *Halifax Antiquarian Society* 33 (1933), 48–70c.

'**Longnor: New Postal Arrangements**', *Derbyshire Times* (7 Nov 1874), 8.

Lonsdale, Henry, *A Biographical Sketch of the Late William Blamire, Esquire of the Oaks and Thackwood Nook* (London: Routledge, 1862).

Loveday, Ray, *Hikey Sprites: The Twilight of a Norfolk Tradition* (Norwich: Swallowtail Print, 2014).

Lupton, Rev. J.H., *Wakefield Worthies or Biographical Sketches of Men of Note* (London: Hamilton, 1864).

Lysaght, Patricia, *The Banshee: The Irish Supernatural Death Messenger* (Dublin: O'Brien Press, 1996 [1986]).

McCandlish, A 'Back O' Th' Hill Boggart', *Burnley Express* (4 May 1895), 2.

McClenon, James, *Wondrous Events: Foundations of Religious Beliefs* (Philadelphia:

University of Pennsylvania Press, 1994). https://doi.org/10.9783/9781512 804201.

McCoog, Thomas M., 'Radford [alias Tanfield], John (*c.*1562–1630)', *Oxford Dictionary of National Biography* [accessed 11 Jun 2018].

McEvoy, Emma, *Gothic Tourism* (London: Palgrave, 2018).

McEwen, Alan, 'Runnin' t'Boggart', *Old Glory* (2013), 56–60.

McFarlane, Robert, *Landmarks* (London: Hamish Hamilton, 2015).

MacGregor, Alasdair Alpin, *The Ghost Book: Strange Hauntings in Britain* (London: Robert Hale Ltd, 1955).

McKay, James, *The Evolution of East Lancashire Boggarts* (Digitally published 2016 [1888]), https://www.academia.edu/28026366/McKay_The_Evolution_of_East_Lancashire_Boggarts [accessed 10 May 2021].

McKenna, Juliet, *The Green Man's Heir* (Trowbridge: Wizard Tower Press, 2018).

MacManus, C. and George Hull, *Tales from the Ribble Valley* (Blackburn: Toulmin and Sons, 1914).

Maddox, Jessica, 'Of Internet born: idolatry, the Slender Man meme, and the feminization of digital spaces', *Feminist Media Studies* 2 (2017), 235–48. https://doi.org/10.1080/14680777.2017.1300179.

Malham-Dembleby, John, *Original tales and ballads in the Yorkshire dialect, known also as Inglis, the language of the Angles, and the Northumbrian dialect: spoken to-day in Yorkshire, and in early times from South Yorkshire to Aberdeen* (London: The Walter Scott Publishing Co., 1912).

Marcombe, David, 'Whittingham, William (d. 1579)', *Oxford Dictionary of National Biography* (Oxford: Oxford University Press, 2004) [accessed 21 Aug 2018].

Maria, Matilda, 'A Woman's Point of View', *Barnoldswick and Earby Times* (1 Jun 1945), 4.

Markham, Geruase, *Cauelarice, or The English horseman contayning all the arte of horse-manship, as much as is necessary for any man to vnderstand, whether he be horse-breeder, horse-ryder, horse-hunter, horse-runner, horse-ambler, horse-farrier, horse-keeper, coachman, smith, or sadler. Together, with the discouery of the subtill trade or mistery of horse-coursers, & an explanatio [sic] of the excellency of a horses vnderstading [sic], or how to teach them to doe trickes like Bankes his curtall: and that horses may be made to drawe drie-foot like a hound. Secrets before vnpublished, & now carefully set down for the profit of this whole nation* (London: Edward Allde and W. Jaggard, 1607).

Markus, Manfred, 'The Genesis of Joseph Wright's *English Dialect Dictionary*', *Joseph Wright's* English Dialect Dictionary *and Beyond*, edited by Manfred Markus, Clive Upton, Reinhard Heuberger (Frankfurt: Peter Lang, 2010), 11–19.

Marr, Andrew, *The Making of Modern Britain* (London: Pan Books, 2010).

Marshall, Peter, *Mother Leakey and the Bishop: A Ghost Story* (Oxford: Oxford University Press, 2007).

Master Quiz, 'Hugh Hobble, the Absent Man', *Kendal Mercury* (19 Nov 1842), 4.

Mather, Marshall, *Lancashire Idylls* (London: Frederick Warne and Co., 1898).

Matoff, Susan, *Conflicted Life: William Jerdan, 1782–1869, London Editor, Author & Critic* (Eastbourne: Sussex Academic Press, 2011).

Mayhew, Henry, *London Labour and the London Poor* (London: Office, 1851), 4 vols.

Mayne, William, *Earthfasts* (London: Hodder, 1995 [1966]).

———— *The Red Book of Hob Stories* (London: Walkers, 1984).

'Melancholy Suicide', *Preston Chronicle* (10 Jun 1848), 4.

'Members Talk', *Shipley Times* (9 Oct 1957), 3.

Menefee, Samuel, '"Watch the Wall, My Darling": Shadowplays, Supernatural Enemies and the Folk World of the Smuggler', in *Supernatural Enemies*, edited by Hilda Ellis Davidson and Anna Chaudhri (Durham: Carolina Academic Press, 2001), 119–33.

Melville, James, *The Autobiography and Diary of Mr. James Melvill, with a Continuation of the Diary* (Edinburgh: Wodrow Society, 1842).

Metcalfe, John, *The Bunderley Boggard and Other Plays* (London: Cranton, 1919).

Meuli, Karl, *Schweizer Masken. Mit einer Einleitung über schweizerische Maskenbräuche und Maskenschnitzer* (Zürich: Atlantis, 1943).

Middle English Dictionary edited by H. Kurath *et al.*, (Ann Arbor: University of Michigan Press, 1954–).

Middleton, Jacob, *Spirits of an Industrial Age: Ghost Impersonation, Spring-heeled Jack, and Victorian Society* (N.P.: Create Space, 2014).

Middleton, Thomas, *Annals of Hyde and district: containing historical reminiscences of Denton, Haughton, Dukinfield, Mottram, Longdendale, Bredbury, Marple, and the neighbouring townships* (Manchester: Cartwright and Rattray, 1899).

———— *Legends of Longdendale; being a series of tales founded upon the folk-lore of Longdendale Valley and its neighbourhood* (Hyde: Clarendon Press, 1906).

'Mill Haunted by the Screaming Lady', *Blackburn Standard* (7 Sep 1889), 6.

Millar, Robert McColl, William Barras and Lisa Marie Bonnici, *Lexical Variation and Attrition in the Scottish Fishing Communities* (Edinburgh: Edinburgh University Press, 2014).

Miller, George C., 'Boggart of Platt's Farm', *Lancashire Evening Post* (30 Jun 1956), 6.

———— 'A Quarryman's Job for Jonty', *Lancashire Evening Post* (2 Mar 1957), 3.

Mills, Frank, *Boggarts of Britain* (Harpenden: Oldcastle, 2000).

Milner, George, *Country Pleasures: The Chronicle of a Year Chiefly in a Garden* (Boston: Robert Brothers, 1881).

Milton, John, *The English Poems of John Milton* (Ware: Wordsworth, 2004).

Moorey, Teresa, *The Fairy Bible* (London: Sterling, 2008).

Moorhouse, Sydney, *Holiday Lancashire* (London: Robert Hale, 1955).

Moorman, Frederic, *Plays of the Ridings* (London: Elkin Mathews, 1919).

'More Wyke Wonders', *Leeds Mercury* (11 Jun 1909), 3.

Morgan, Marjorie, *National Identities and Travel in Victorian Britain* (New York: Palgrave Macmillan, 2001). https://doi.org/10.1057/9780230512153.

[Morris, J.P.] *T' Lebby Beck Dobby: A Sketch in the Furness Dialect* (Carlisle: George Cowards, 1867).

Morris, James P., *A Glossary of the Words and Phrases of Furness (North Lancashire)* (London: J. Russell Smith, 1869).

Morton, H.F., *All About Boggarts* (York: Skewbalk Press, 1993).

Moss, Fletcher, *Folk-lore, Old Customs and Tales of My Neighbours* (Didsbury: privately printed, 1898).

'Mr. Potter at Cutgate', *Rochdale Observer* (14 Nov 1868), 7.

'Mysterious Death of a Child', *Manchester Courier* (26 Feb 1887), 14.

N.N. *The Lancashire Levite Rebuked: Or, a Vindication of the Dissenters from Popery, Superstition, Ignorance and Knavery, unjustly Charged on they by Mr. Zachary Taylor in his Book Entitled the Surey Impostor in a Letter to Himself* (London: Warwick Lane, 1698).

Nash, F.O.H., *Some Brownies and a Boggart* (London: Sheldon Press, n.d. [1925?]).

'Naturalists foxed by pictures of Bogart', *Independent* (1 Apr 1988), 5.

'New Lamps for Old', *Clitheroe Advertiser* (13 Jan 1933), 3.

New Lights from the World of Darkness or the Midnight Messenger with Solemn Signals from the World of Spirits (London: Maiden, 1800).

'New Year's Day', *Huddersfield Chronicle* (2 Jan 1864), 1.

Newman, L.F. and E.M. Wilson, 'Folklore Survivals in the Southern "Lake Counties" and in Essex: A Comparison and Contrast', *Folklore* 63 (1952), 91–104. https://doi.org/10.1080/0015587X.1952.9718106.

Newstead, G. Coulthard, *Gleanings towards the annals of Aughton, near Ormskirk* (Liverpool: C. & H. Ratcliffe, 1893).

'Nichol Forest Ghost Story', *Carlisle Journal* (12 Jul 1845).

Ninness, James, *Macabre Rising: Tales of Man, Myth and Monster* (self-published, 2012).

Nodal, John Howard and George Milner, *A Glossary of the Lancashire Dialect* (Manchester: Alexander Ireland and Co. 1875).

Nordstrom, John, *Stained with Blood: A One-Hundred Year History of the English Bible* (Bloomington: Westbow 2014).

Norfolk lists from the reformation to the present time; comprising lists of lord lieutenants, baronets, high sheriffs, and members of Parliament, of the county of Norfolk; bishops, deans, chancellors, archdeacons, prebendaries, members of Parliament, mayors, sheriffs, recorders, & stewards, of the city of Norwich; members of Parliament and mayors of the boroughs of Yarmouth, Lynn, Thetford, and Castle Rising; also a list of persons connected with the county, of whom engraved portraits have been published, and a descriptive list of tradesmens' tokens & provincial halfpennies issued in the county of Norfolk (Norwich: Matchett and Co., 1837).

Norman, Emma R., 'International Boggarts: Carl Schmitt, Harry Potter, and the Transfiguration of Identity and Violence', *Politics and Polity* 40 (2012), 403–23. https://doi.org/10.1111/j.1747–1346.2012.00357.x.

Norman, Mark, *Black Dog Folklore* (Woodbury: Llewellyn Publications, 2020).

North, Frank, 'More about Place Names', *Leeds Mercury* (5 Apr 1939), 4.

Northall, G.F., *English Folk-rhymes; a collection of traditional verses relating to places and persons, customs, superstitions, etc.* (London: K. Paul, 1892).

'North Regional', *Nottingham Evening Post* (18 Jul 1931), 4.

'Northern hunts', *Lancashire Evening Post* (19 Nov 1906), 19.

North-Westerner, 'The Way of the North West', *Lancashire Evening Post* (22 Sep 1932), 4.

———— 'The Way of the North West', *Lancashire Evening Post* (10 Jan 1933), 4.

'Not a Case for the Psychical Research Society', *Lancashire Evening Post* (23 Dec 1902), 5.

'Notes and Comments', *Burnley Express and Advertiser* (10 Jan 1903), 7.

'Notice of Two Vessels of Grey Stoneware', *Proceedings of the Society of Antiquaries of Scotland* 19 (1884), 34–38.

Ó Giolláin, Diarmuid, 'Myth and History: Exotic Foreigners in Folk-belief', *Temenos* 23 (1987), 59–80. https://doi.org/10.33356/temenos.6170.

Obelkevich, James, *Religion and Rural Society: South Lindsey, 1825–1875* (Oxford: Clarendon Press, 1976).

Oesterdiekhoff, Georg W., 'Why Premodern Humans Believed in the Divine Status of Their Parents and Ancestors? Psychology Illuminates the Foundations of Ancestor Worship', *Anthropos* 110 (2015), 582–89. https://doi.org/10.5771/0257–9774–2015–2–582.

Old Yew Tree, 'A Day in Cheshire', *Ashton Weekly Reporter* (17 Jul 1869), 7.

Oldbuck, Jonathan, 'Hapton Tower', *Burnley Express* (30 Nov 1895), 3.

Oldham, 'Answers to Correspondents', *Rochdale Observer* (31 Jan 1914), 7.

Olson, Ted, *James Still in Interviews, Oral Histories and Memoirs* (Jefferson: McFarland, 2009).

'On Sale', *Rochdale Observer* (20 Mar 1915), 3.

'Original Poetry. Scallow Beck Boggle', *Cumberland Pacquet, and Ware's Whitehaven Advertiser* (15 Jan 1861), 7.

Ormerod, Frank, *The Cock Hall Boggart and Other Stories* (Manchester: Express Printing Co., 1926).

Ormerod, Rev. T., 'The Psychology of Belief, in Reference to Illusions and Hallucinations', *Burnley Literary and Scientific Club Transactions* 23 (1905), 18–22.

Orton, H., *Survey of English Dialects: Introduction* (Leeds: E.J. Arnold, 1962).

Orton, Harold and Wilfrid J. Halliday *Survey of English Dialects (B), The Basic Material: The Six Northern Counties and the Isle of Man* (Leeds: Arnold and Son, 1962).

Orton, Harold, Stewart Sanderson and John Widdowson, *The Linguistic Atlas of England* (London: Croom Helm, 1977).

Orton, Harold and Nathalia Wright, *A Word Geography of England* (London: Seminar Press, 1974).

Ostling, Michael and Richard Forest, 'Goblins, owles, and sprites', *Religion* 44 (2014), 547–72. https://doi.org/10.1080/0048721X.2014.886631.

Owen, Hywel Wyn, *The Place-names of East Flintshire* (Cardiff: University of Wales Press, 1994).

P., 'Fairy Tales', *The Literary Gazette* 430 (1825), 252–53.

Palmer, F.F., 'The Demon Bird or the Legend of Gertrude Gray', *Illuminated Magazine* 1 (1843), 105–08.

Parker, James, *Illustrated Rambles from Hipperholme to Tong* (Bradford: Lund, 1904).

Parkinson, Thomas, *Yorkshire Legends and Traditions* (London: E. Stock, 1888).

Partridge, Eric, *A Dictionary of Slang and Unconventional English* (London: Routledge, 1984).

Payne, James *The Clyffards of Clyffe* (London: Hurst and Blackett, 1866), 3 vols.

Peacock, Edward, *A Glossary of Words Used in the Wapentakes of Manley and Corringham, Lincolnshire* (London: English Dialect Society, 1877).

Peacock, Mabel, *Tales and Rhymes in the Lindsey Folk-Speech* (London: George Bell, 1886).

———— 'Th' Man an' th' Boggard', *Northamptonshire Notes and Queries* 2 (1888), 99–100.

———— 'The Horse in Relation to Water-Lore', *Antiquary* 33 (1897), 72–76.

———— *Folklore and Legends of Lincolnshire* (N.P., 2010) [work digitized by Gillian Bennett, available from Folklore Society].

Peacock, Robert Backhouse and J.C. Atkinson, *A Glossary of the Dialect of the Hundred of Lonsdale, North and South of the Sands in the County of Lancaster* (London: Asher and Co.,1869).

Pearson, Mike, *'In Comes I': Performance, Memory and Landscape* (Exeter: University of Exeter Press, 2006).

Pearson, William, *Letters, Papers and Journals* (London: Victoria Press, 1863). https://doi.org/10.5962/bhl.title.128550.

Pease, Howard, *Border Ghost Stories* (London: E. Macdonald, 1919).

Pechenick, Eitan Adam, Christopher M. Danforth and Peter Sheridan Dodds, 'Characterizing the Google Books Corpus: Strong Limits to Inferences of Socio-Cultural and Linguistic Evolution', *PLoS ONE* 10 (2015), 1–24. https://doi.org/10.1371/journal.pone.0137041.

Pegge, Samuel, 'Derbicisms', edited by Walter Skeat, *Nine Specimens of English Dialects* (Oxford: Frowde, 1896) 1–138.

Penanink, 'Sports and Pastimes: Penanink's Notebook', *Leeds Times* (16 Apr 1892), 3.

Perez, Domino Renee, *There Was a Woman: La Llorona from Folklore to Popular Culture* (Austin: University of Texas Press, 2008).

Phantom, 'Calverley Forty Years Ago', *Bradford Observer* (28 Mar 1874), 7.

Phillips, John, *The Rivers, Mountains, and Sea-coast of Yorkshire* (London: John Murray, 1853).

del Pilar Blanco, María, *Ghost-Watching American Modernity* (New York: Fordham University Press, 2012). https://doi.org/10.2307/j.ctt13x0d1w.

Pinto-Abecasis, Nina, 'Towards the Inclusion of Nicknames in the Genres of Folklore: The Case of the Former Jewish Community of Tetuan, Morocco', *Folklore* 122 (2011), 135–54. https://doi.org/10.1080/0015587X.2011.570520.

Playfere, Thomas, *A Most Excellent and Heauenly Sermon vpon the 23. chapter of the Gospell by Saint Luke* (London: A. Wise, 1595).

'Playing Pitch and Toss', *Bolton Evening News* (10 Sep 1903), 3.

'Pollution of the Ribble', *Manchester Courier* (9 Jul 1880), 8.

Potter, Louisa, *Lancashire memories* (London: Macmillan and Co., 1879).

Powley, Miss, 'The Curfew Bell', *Transactions of the Cumberland and Westmorland Antiquarian and Archaeological Society* 3 (1878), 127–33.

Praxmarer, Christoph, 'Joseph Wright's *EDD* and the geographical distribution of dialects: A visual approach', *Joseph Wright's* English Dialect Dictionary *and Beyond*, edited by Manfred Markus, Clive Upton, and Reinhard Heuberger (Frankfurt: Peter Lang, 2010), 61–73.

'Presentation to a Colliery Manager at Waterloo', *Ashton Weekly Reporter* (5 Sep 1868), 6.

'**Preston**', *Lancashire Evening Post* (1 Jul 1892), 3.

Preston, Kathleen, *Cumbria: Lore & Legend* (Kendal: Preston, 1979).

Price, William Frederick, 'Notes on Some of the Places, Traditions, and Folk-Lore of the Douglas Valley', *Transactions of the Historic Society of Lancashire and Cheshire* 51 (1899), 181–220.

Proctor, Rev. W.G., 'The Manor of Rufford and the Ancient Family of the Heskeths' *Transactions of the Historic Society of Lancashire and Cheshire* 59 (1907), 93–118.

Profili, Olga, 'Les désignations de l'épouvantail dans les parlers roman d'Italie', *Espaces romans* (Grenoble: Ellug, 1988) 2 vols, II, 402–27.

Pryme, George, *Autobiographic recollections of George Pryme, Esq. M.A., sometime fellow of Trinity College, Professor of political economy in the University of Cambridge, and M.P. for the borough* (Cambridge: Deighton and Bell, 1870).

'**Public Meetings of Rate Payers on Municipal Affairs**', *Bradford Observer* (7 Dec 1843), 6–7.

Puhvel, Martin, *The Crossroads in Folklore and Myth* (New York: Peter Lang, 1989).

Purton, Valerie and Norman Page, *The Palgrave Literary Dictionary of Tennyson* (London: Palgrave Macmillan, 2010). https://doi.org/10.1057/9780230244948.

Pyle, Howard, *Pepper & Salt; or, Seasoning for Young Folk* (New York: Harper and Brothers, 1886).

'**Queer Tales: Legends of Ormskirk**', *Aberdeen Evening Express* (16 Sep 1910), 4.

[**Quick, Jerrod?**], 'Two Nights in the Country', *Once A Week* 13 (1874), 301–05.

R.P.C., 'Bawker', *Report and Transaction of the Devonshire Association* 25 (1893), 183.

Raahauge, Kirsten Marie, 'Ghosts, Troubles, Difficulties, and Challenges: Narratives about Unexplainable Phenomena in Contemporary Denmark', *Folklore: Electronic Journal of Folklore* 65 (2016), 89–110. https://doi.org/10.7592/FEJF2016.65.raahauge.

Radford, John, *A Directorie Teaching the Way to the Truth in a Briefe and Plaine Discourse Against the Heresies of this Time. Where Vnto is Added, a Short Treatise Against Adiaphorists, Neuters, and Such as Say They May be Saued in Any Sect Or Religion, and Would Make of Many Diuers Sects One Church* (1605).

Rambler, 'Out and About Chester', *Cheshire Observer* (13 Mar 1886), 2.

———— 'Out and About Chester', *Cheshire Observer* (5 Feb 1887), 2.

———— 'Out and About Chester', *Cheshire Observer* (4 June 1887), 2.

Ray, John, *A Collection of English Proverbs digested into a convenient method for the* *speedy finding [of] any one upon occasion: with short annotations: whereunto are added local proverbs with their explications, old proverbial rhythmes, less known or exotick proverbial sentences, and Scottish proverbs* (Cambridge: John Hayes, 1670 and a second edition in 1678).

Rayner, S., *The History and Antiquities of Pudsey* (London: Longmans, Green and Co., 1887).

Rea, Alice, *The Beckside Boggle and Other Lake Side Stories* (London: T. Fisher Unwin, 1886).

'Readers', *Lancashire Evening Post* (1 Apr 1954), 10.

Redding, Cyrus, *The Pictorial History of the County of Lancaster with One Hundred and Seventy Illustrations and a Map* (London: George Routledge, 1844).

Redmonds, George, *Names and History: People, Places and Things* (London: Hambledon 2004).

———— *A Dictionary of Yorkshire Surnames* (Donington: Paul Watkins Publishing, 2015).

Rees, Gareth, 'The Monsters of Hackney and Walthamstow Marshes: The Haunting of East London's Lower Lea Valley by Prehistoric Ghosts', *The Ashgate Research Companion to Paranormal Cultures*, edited by Olu Jenzen and Sally R. Munt (London: Ashgate, 2016), 391–403.

Reppion, John (ed.), *Spirits of Place* (Brisbane: Daily Grail, 2016).

'Review: The Clitheroe District', *Folklore* 34 (1923), 98. https://doi.org/1 0.1080/0015587X.1923.9720255.

Rhys, John, *Celtic Folklore: Welsh and Manx* (Oxford: Clarendon Press, 1901), 2 vols.

Richardson, John, *Cummerland Talk: Being Short Tales and Rhymes in the Dialect of that County: Together with a Few Miscellaneous Pieces in Verse* (London: J.R. Smith, 1871).

Rider, Catherine, Magic and Religion in Medieval England (London: Reaktion, 2012).

Rieti, Barbara, 'Newfoundland Fairy Traditions: A Study in Narrative and Belief' (unpublished doctoral thesis, Memorial University, St Johns, 1990).

Riley, E., *Juvenile Tales for Boys and Girls: Designed to Amuse, Instruct, and Entertain those who are in the Morning of Life* (Halifax: William Milner, 1849).

Riley, Martin, *Tales from the Edge of the World* (London: BBC Books, 1988).

Robbins, Manuel A., *The Collector's Book of Fluorescent Minerals* (New York: Springer Science, 1983). https://doi.org/10.1007/978–1–4757–4792–8.

Roberts, Kai, *Haunted Huddersfield* (Stroud: History Press, 2012).

———— *The Folklore of Yorkshire* (Stroud: History Press, 2013).

———— 'Don't Boggart That Joint', *Northern Earth* 137 (2014), 21–23.

———— *Haunted Halifax and District* (Stroud: History Press, 2014).

Roberts, W. Langley, *Legends and Folk-Lore of Lancashire* (Collins, n.d. [1931?]).

Robertson, William, *Rochdale and the Vale of Whitworth: Its Moorlands, Favourite Nooks, and Scenery* (Rochdale: the author, 1897).

Robinson, C. Clough, *The Dialect of Leeds and its Neighbourhood, illustrated by conversations and tales of common life, etc. To which are added a copious glossary; notices of the various antiquities, manners, and customs, and general folk-lore of the district* (London: J.R. Smith, 1862).

———— *A Glossary of Words pertaining to the dialect of mid-Yorkshire; with others peculiar to lower Nidderdale. To which is prefixed on Outline grammar of the mid-Yorkshire dialect* (London: Trübner, 1876).

Robinson, F.K., *A Glossary of Words Used in the Neighbourhood of Whitby* (London: Trübner, 1876).

Robson, Catherine, *Heart Beats: Everyday Life and the Memorized Poem* (Princeton: Princeton University Press, 2012). https://doi.org/10.23943/princ eton/9780691119366.001.0001.

[Roby, Elizabeth], *The Legendary and Poetical Remains of John Roby with a Sketch of His Literary Life and Character* (London: Longman, 1854).

Roby, John, *Traditions of Lancashire* (London: Longman, 1829), 2 vols [First Series].

———— *Traditions of Lancashire, second series* (London: Spottiswoode, 1831), 2 vols.

———— *Lancashire Legends: Selected from Roby's* Traditions of Lancashire (London: Constable and Co., 1911).

Rockwood, Camilla (ed.), *Brewer's Dictionary of Phrase and Fable* (London: Chambers, 2009).

Roeder, Charles, 'Some Moston Folklore', *Transactions of the Lancashire and Cheshire Antiquarian Society* 25 (1907), 65–78.

Rollock, Robert, *Lectures, vpon the history of the Passion, Resurrection, and Ascension of our Lord Iesus Christ Beginning at the eighteenth chapter of the Gospell, according to S. Iohn, and from the 16 verse of the 19 chapter thereof, containing a perfect harmonie of all the foure Euangelists, for the better vnderstanding of all the circumstances of the Lords death, and Resurrection. Preached by that reuerend and faithfull seruant of God, Mr. Robert Rollocke, sometime minister of the Euangell of Iesus Christ, and rector of the Colledge of Edinburgh* (Edinburgh: Andro Hart, 1616).

———— *Fiue and twentie lectures, vpon the last sermon and conference of our Lord Iesus Christ, with his disciples immediately before his Passion contained in the fourteenth, fifteenth, and sixteenth chapters of the Gospel of Sainct Iohn. As also vpon that most excellent prayer, contained in the seuenteenth chap. of the same Gospel. Preached by the reuerend and faythfull seruant of God, M. Robert Rollok, minister of the Kirke (and rector of the Colledge) of Edinburgh* (Edinburgh: Andro Hart, 1619).

'**Romantic Suicide in Bolton**', *Bolton Chronicle* (27 Jun 1863).

Roper, Jonathan, 'Folk Disbelief', *Storied and Supernatural Places*, edited by Ülo Valk and Daniel Sävborg (Helsinki: Finnish Literature Society, 2018), 223–36.

Rose, Carol, *Spirits, Fairies, Gnomes and Goblins: An Encyclopedia of the Little People* (Oxford: ABC-Clio, 1998).

'**Rossendale Boggart Tales**', *Burnley Express and Advertiser* (28 Aug 1897), 3.

'**Round about Bradford**', *Bradford Observer* (23 Dec 1875), 7.

Routh, John, *Illustrated Rambles in Swaledale and Neighbourhood* (Reeth: G. Peacock, 1880).

Rowling, J.K., *The Prisoner of Azkaban* (London: Bloomsbury, 1999).

[**Royd**, James] 'The Abbot's Knowl', *Rochdale Pilot* (13 March 1858), 3.

Ruano-García, Javier, *Early Modern Northern English Lexis: A Literary Corpus-based Study* (Bern: Peter Lan, 2010).

Rudkin, Ethel H., *Lincolnshire Folklore* (Wakefield: E.P. Publishing, 1936).

———— 'The Black Dog', *Folklore* 49 (1938), 111–31. https://doi.org/10.1080/0015587X.1938.9718739.

Russell, Dave, *Looking North: Northern England and the National Imagination* (Manchester: Manchester University Press, 2004).

'**S Bend Collision**', *Lancashire Evening Post* (3 Jan 1935), 7.

Sambrook, James, 'Roby, John (1793–1850)', *Oxford Dictionary of National Biography* (online version 2004) [accessed 3 Sep 2018].

Sanderson, S.F., 'Towards an Atlas of British Folk Culture', *Folklore* 82 (1971), 89–98. https://doi.org/10.1080/0015587X.1971.9716715.

———— 'Folklore Material in the English Dialect Survey', *Folklore* 83 (1972) 89–100. https://doi.org/10.1080/0015587X.1972.9716459.

Sands, J. "Ancient Superstitions in Tiree, *Folk-Lore Journal* 1 (1883), 167–168.

Sandy Banks, 'Sandy Banks's Criticism of Hayfield's Bird's Eye View', *Glossop Record* (4 Nov 1865), 2.

Sartin, Stephen, *The People and Places of Historic Preston* (Preston: Carnegie Press, 1988).

Sayers, William, 'Puck and the Bogymen as Reflexes of Indo-European Conceptions of Fear and Flight', *Tradition Today* 8 (2019), 52–56.

Schmid, Monika S., *Language Attrition* (Cambridge: Cambridge University Press, 2011).

'**Scotforth township meeting**', *Lancaster Gazette* (30 Mar 1889), 7.

Scott, Charles P.G., 'The Devil and His Imps: An Etymological Inquisition', *Transactions of the American Philological Association* 26 (1895), 79–146. https://doi.org/10.2307/2935696.

———— 'Bogus and His Crew', *Transactions of the American Philological Association* 42 (1911), 157–74. https://doi.org/10.2307/282580.

Scott, Maggie, 'Scots Word of the Season: Bogle', *Bottle Imp* 20 (2016), https://www.thebottleimp.org.uk/2016/12/scots-word-of-the-season-bogle/.

Search, John, 'Natland Dobies', *Kendal Mercury* (25 May 1867), 4.

Sebo, Erin, 'Does OE Puca have an Irish Origin?', *Studia Neophilogica* 89 (2017), 167–75. https://doi.org/10.1080/00393274.2017.1314773.

'See How They Fly', *Chester Chronicle* (23 Mar 1940), 2.

Semple, Sarah, *Perceptions of the Prehistoric in Anglo-Saxon England: Religion, Ritual and Rulership in the Landscape* (Oxford: Oxford University Press, 2013). https://doi.org/10.1093/acprof:oso/9780199683109.001.0001.

'Serious accident to a coachman', *Lancaster Gazette* (6 Jun 1891), 5.

Serjeantson, Mary S., 'The Vocabulary of Folklore in Old and Middle English', *Folklore* 47 (1936), 42–73. https://doi.org/10.1080/0015587X.1936.9718626.

Shadwell, Thomas, *The Lancashire Witches and Tegue O Divelly the Irish priest: A Comedy* (London: Knapton, 1736).

Sharpe, James, 'In Search of the English Sabbat: Popular Conceptions of Witches' Meetings in Early Modern England', *Journal of Early Modern Studies* 2 (2013), 161–83.

Shaw, Giles, (ed.), *Local Notes and Gleanings: Oldham and Neighbourhood in Bygone Times* (Manchester: R.H. Sutton, 1887).

Shaw, Thomas, *Recent Poems, on Rural and Other Miscellaneous Subjects* (Huddersfield: J. Lancashire, 1824).

Shuttleworth, James Phillips Kay, *Scarsdale; or, Life on the Lancashire and Yorkshire border Thirty Years Ago* (London: Smith, Elder and Co., 1860), 3 vols.

Sikes, Wirt, *British Goblins: Welsh folk-lore, fairy mythology, legends and traditions* (London: Sampson, 1880).

'Silverdale and Fairy Steps', *Lancashire Evening Post* (8 Jun 1933), 9.

Silkstone Valley Walks: Silkstone Common to Falthwaite (Barnsley: Barnsley Metropolitan Borough, undated).

Simmelbauer, Andrea, *The Dialect of Northumberland: A Lexical Investigation* (Heidelberg: Winter, 2000).

Simpson, Jacqueline, *British Dragons* (London: Wordsworth, 1980).

———— 'Multi-purpose Treacle Mines in Sussex and Surrey', *Lore and Language* 3 (1982), 61–73.

———— 'God's visible judgements: the Christian dimension of landscape legends',

Landscape History 8 (1986), 53–58. https://doi.org/10.1080/01433768.1986. 10594397.

———— 'On the Ambiguity of Elves', *Folklore* 122 (2011), 76–83. https://doi. org/10.1080/0015587X.2011.537133.

Simpson, Jacqueline, and Steve Roud, *A Dictionary of English Folklore* (Oxford: Oxford University Press, 2000).

Sims-Kimbrey, J.M., *Wodds and Doggerybaw: A Lincolnshire Dialect Dictionary* (Boston: Richard Kay, 1995).

Sims-Williams, Patrick, 'The visionary Celt: the construction of an "ethnic preconception"', *Cambridge Medieval Celtic Studies* 11 (1986), 71–96.

'Singular Frolic', *The Preston Chronicle and Lancashire Advertiser* (17 Jan 1857), 3.

'Sir U. Kay-Shuttleworth', *Burnley Gazette* (6 Nov 1897), 4.

'Sir Ughtred Kay-Shuttleworth at Colne', *Manchester Courier and Lancashire General Advertiser* (4 Nov 1897), 6.

Skeat, Walter W., *English Dialects from the Eighth Century to the Present Day* (Cambridge: Cambridge University Press, 1912).

Slagle, Judith Bailey, 'Thomas Shadwell', *The Encyclopedia of British Literature: 1660–1789*, edited by Gary Day and Jack Lynch (Chichester: Wiley Blackwell, 2015) 3 vols, I, 1114–18. https://doi.org/10.1002/9781118607268.wbebl282.

Slater, Philemon, *History of the Ancient Parish of Guiseley: With Introductory Chapters on the Antiquities of the District* (London: Hamilton, Adams 1880).

Smajic, Srdjan, *Ghost-Seers, Detectives, and Spiritualists: Theories of Vision in Victorian Literature and Science* (Cambridge: CUP, 2013).

Smidchens, Guntis, 'Urban Folklore', *Folklore: An Encyclopedia of Beliefs, Customs, Tales, Music, and Art* (Santa Barbara: ABC-Clio, 1997), edited by Thomas Green, 817–23.

Smith, A.H., *The Place-Names of the West Riding of Yorkshire* (Cambridge: CUP, 1961–1963), 8 vols.

Smith, Andrew, *The Ghost Story 1840–1920: A Cultural History* (Manchester: Manchester University Press, 2012).

Smith, John B., 'The Devil of Croyden Hill: Kinship, Fiction, Fact, Tradition', *Folklore* 116 (2005), 66–74. https://doi.org/10.1080/0015587052000337725.

———— 'Robert Willan's Dobbies and Their Kin', *Tradition Today* 4 (2014), 1–12.

———— 'Killing the Devil', *Tradition Today* 8 (2019), 58–62.

Smith, William, *Old Yorkshire* (London: Longmans, Green 1881).

Smyth, John Denholme, *Boggard Jim an' his Mate, fro' Wibsa Slack wi' their awd Tales, Readings and Sangs* (Bradford, 1848).

Snowden, Keighley, *Tales of the Yorkshire Wolds* (London: Sampson, Low, Marston & Co., 1893).

'Some of Sir Humphrey de Trafford's Sporting Dogs', *Illustrated Sporting and Dramatic News* (19 Mar 1898), 22.

Speight, H., *The Craven and North West Yorkshire Highlands* (London: E. Stock, 1892).

———— *Chronicles and stories of old Bingley. A full account of the history, antiquities, natural productions, scenery, customs and folklore of the ancient town and parish of Bingley, in the West Riding of Yorkshire* (London: Elliot Stock, 1898).

Spence, Lewis, *The Minor Traditions of British Mythology* (London: Rider, 1948).

———— *The Fairy Tradition in Britain* (London: Rider, 1948).

Spencer, Ken, *Tattersall Wilkinson: A Very Remarkable Man* (N.P.: Briercliffe Society, 1987).

Spooner, Barbara 'The Haunted Style', *Folklore* 79 (1968), 135–39. https://doi.org/10.1080/0015587X.1968.9716586.

'Staffordshire Dialect and Folk-lore', *Staffordshire Advertiser* (10 Nov 1877), 8.

Stead, I.M., J.B. Bourke, and Don R. Brothwell, *Lindow Man: The Body in the Bog* (London: British Museum Publications, n.d. [1986]).

Steadman, Lyle B., Craig T. Palmer and Christopher F. Tilley, 'The Universality of Ancestor Worship', *Ethnology* 35 (1996), 63–76. https://doi.org/10.2307/3774025.

Steggle, Matthew, 'Markham, Gervase (1568?–1637)', *Oxford Dictionary of National Biography* (Oxford: Oxford University Press, 2004) [accessed 21 Aug 2018].

Stephens, Roger, *The Boom of the Bitterbump: The Folk-history of Cheshire Wildlife* (Chester: Gordon Emery, 2003).

Sternberg, Thomas, *The Dialect and Folk-lore of Northamptonshire* (London: John Russell, 1851).

Stockdale, James, *Annales Caermoelenses, Or Annals of Cartmel: or, Annals of Cartmel* (Ulverston: Kitchin, 1872).

[Story, Alfred, T.], 'Legends and Stories of Northamptonshire', *Northampton Mercury* (24 May 1879), 8.

Story, Alfred, *Historical legends of Northamptonshire* (Northampton: John Taylor, 1883).

Stott, M.H., 'Off at Boggart', *Burnley Express* (12 May 1900), 2.

Stubbs, W., *Chronica magistri Rogeri de Houedene* (London: Longman, 1868–1871), 4 vols.

Sugden, John, *Slaithwaite Notes of the Past and Present* (Manchester: Heywood 1905).

Sullivan, Jeremiah, *Cumberland and Westmorland, ancient & modern* (London: Whittaker and Co., 1857).

Sumpter, Caroline, *The Victorian Press and the Fairy Tale* (London: Palgrave, 2008). https://doi.org/10.1057/9780230227644.

'Superstition in the Fylde: Whitegate-Lane Boggart', *The Preston Chronicle and Lancashire Advertiser* (2 May 1857), 5.

Sutcliffe, Halliwell, 'Nick o' Desperates', *Lincolnshire Chronicle* (15 Dec 1911), 6.

Sutcliffe, T., 'A Tour in Midgley', *Halifax Antiquarian Society* 28 (1928), 113–57.

Swain, Charles, *Dramatic Chapter: Poems and Songs* (London: Longman, 1850).

Sweeney, P., 'The Dumber Boggert' (Merrin: D. Alexe, ND) [one-page bill].

Sydney, William Connor, *The Early Days of the Nineteenth Century* (London: George Redway 1898), 2 vols.

'Syllabus', *Burnley Literary and Scientific Club Transactions* 6 (1888), 9–10.

Sylvester, Louise, 'Naming and Avoiding Objects of Terror: A Case Study', *Placing Middle English in Context*, edited by Irma Taavitsainen, Terttu Nevalainen, Paivi Pahta, and Matti Rissanen (Berlin: de Gruyter, 2000), 277–92.

T.H.H., 'Letter: Village Superstitions', *The Spectator* (25 Jan 1902), 33.

Tangherlini, Timothy R., 'Legendary Performances: Folklore, Repertoire and Mapping', *Ethnologia Europea* 40 (2010), 103–15. https://doi.org/10.16995/ee.1072.

Taylor, Archer, 'The Pertinacious Cobold', *The Journal of English and Germanic Philology* 31 (1932), 1–9.

Taylor, Henry, *The Ancient Crosses and Holy Wells of Lancashire* (Manchester: Sherratt and Hughes, 1906).

Taylor, Michael Waistell, *The Old Manorial Halls of Westmorland & Cumberland* (Kendal: T. Wilson, 1892).

Taylor, Zachary, *The Surey Impostor: being an answer to a late fanatical pamphlet, entituled The Surey Demoniack* (London: John Jones, 1697).

'Ten Hours Factory Bill', *Poor Man's Guardian* (13 Jun 1835), 4.

Tennyson, Alfred, *The Complete Poetical Works* (Boston: Osgood, 1877).

The Beauties of all the magazines selected. For the year 1762, 1763, 1764 (London: T. Waller, 1762–1764), 3 vols.

The Black Non-Conformist, Discover'd in More Naked Truth (London: Larkin, 1682).

'The Boggart!!' (Bradford: H. Wardman, printer [1832]).

'The Borrowdale Road Boggle', *West Cumberland Times* (2 Mar 1895), 3.

'The Burnley Antiquary', *Burnley Advertiser* (17 Jan 1880), 8.

'The Capture of the Ghost', *Huddersfield and Holmfirth Examiner* (31 March 1855), 4.

'The Copp Boggart', *Preston Chronicle*, (21 Dec 1872), 3.

'The Cruel and Wanton Folly ...', *Sheffield Independent* (17 Nov 1887), 5.

The Deeside Owl, 'A Hoot from the Deeside Owl: Hoot! Hoot!! Hoot!!!: to the editor of the Cheshire Observer', *Cheshire Observer* (17 Feb 1883), 2.

The Diarist, 'Men and Affairs', *Boston Guardian* (23 Nov 1938), 10.

'The Dungley Boggart', *Blackburn Standard* (21 May 1892), 5.

'The Eagle and Child Story', *Stonehaven Journal* (12 May 1904), 3.

'The Earthquake', *Liverpool Mercury* (24 Mar 1843), 93.

'The final ...', *Athletic News* (2 May 1883), 4.

'The following placard ...', *The British Labourer's Protector* 12 (1832), 89–90.

'The "Freetown Pie"'————**Witchcraft Revived'**, *Bury Times* (6 Dec 1862), 2.

'The Garstang Ghost', *Illustrated Police News* (17 Sep 1881), 1 (illustration) and 4.

'The Ghost of John Parkinson's Farewell', *Preston Chronicle* (29 May 1880), 6.

'The Last of His Race', *Clitheroe Advertiser and Times* (7 Feb 1908), 2.

'The Late John Higson', *The Ashton Weekly Reporter, and Stalybridge and Dukinfield Chronicle* (30 Dec 1871), 8.

'The Late Mr Howard Pease of Otterburn', *The Scotsman* (2 Feb 1928), 6.

'The legends, legendary stories, and traditions of Derbyshire: Hob-i'th'————**Hurst at Baslow Moor and Other Places'**, *Derbyshire Courier* (28 Apr 1883), 6.

'The Liberal Candidates at Little Leigh', *Nantwich Guardian* (10 Apri 1880), 2.

'The Midnight Robbers Being Reminiscences of Stalybridge and Mottram', *Ashton Weekly Reporter* (30 Jan 1869), 7.

'The Miner and the Ghost', *Nottinghamshire Guardian* (31 Dec 1887), 8.

'The Model Lodging-House and a Benighted Son of Bacchus', *Huddersfield Examiner* (7 Apr 1855), 5.

'The Moss Lane Spectre', *Manchester Times* (26 Jan 1861), 5.

'The New Railway to Facit', *Rochdale Observer* (22 Oct 1870), 7.

'The Orton Dobbie', *Westmorland Gazette* (5 May 1849), 2.

'The Peel Family: its rise and fortunes: Bury Eighty Years Ago', *Supplement to Manchester Examiner and Times*, (2 Nov 1850), 3.

'The Religious World and Work', *Blackburn Standard* (28 Sep 1895), 2.

'The St. Bees Boggle', *Cumberland Pacquet, and Ware's Whitehaven Advertiser* (9 Jul 1844), 3.

'The Seed-Hill Ghost', *Leeds Times* (24 Mar 1855), 5.

'The Snake', *Milngavie and Bearsden Herald* (27 Jan 1933), 2.

'The Spaw "Boggart"', *Bolton Chronicle* (19 Jan 1839), 3.

'The Spital Estate', *Derbyshire Times and Chesterfield Herald* (4 Jun 1932), 3.

'The Starling Bridge Boggart', *Blackburn Standard* (2 Jun 1894), 3.

'The Sweetclough Boggart Caught at Last', *Burnley Advertiser* (12 Jul 1862), 2.

'The Third Time of Asking', *Sacramento Daily Record-Union* (24 Aug 1895), 6.

'The Town Centre ...', *Rochdale Observer* (5 Feb 1941), 2.

The Victorian history of the county of Lancashire (N.p.: n.p. 1906–1914), 8 vols.

The Village Atlas: The Growth of Manchester, Lancashire and North Cheshire, 1840–1912 (Edmonton: Alderman Press, 1989).

'The Westmoreland Boggle', *Carlisle Journal* (25 May 1849), 2.

'Theatres and Music Halls', *Manchester Courier* (16 Jan 1909), 10.

Thomas, Keith, *Religion and the Decline of Magic* (London: Penguin, 1971).

Thomassen, Bjørn, *Liminality and the Modern: Living Through the In-Between* (Farnham: Ashgate, 2014).

Thompson, Tok, 'Clocha Geala/Clocha Uaisle: White Quartz in Irish Tradition', *Béaloideas* 73 (2005), 111–33.

Thornber, William, *The History of Blackpool and its Neighbourhood* (Nelson: 1985, Galava [reprint of the 1837 original]).

'Three Pongo Plays', *Birmingham Daily Post* (30 Nov 1970), 25.

Threshfield and Low Baildon Walk (Baildon: Baildon Local History Society, 2016).

Tilley, Joseph, *The Old Halls, Manors and Families of Derbyshire* (London: Simpkin, 1892–1899), 3 vols.

Timson, John, 'The Evolution of boggart', *Verbatim* 20 (1994), 10–11.

Tirebuck, William Edwards, 'Meg o' the Scarlet Foot', *Lancashire Evening Post* (4 Aug 1897), 4.

'To Be Lett', *Leeds Intelligencer* (25 Jan 1796), 1.

'To Correspondents', *Kendal Mercury* (21 Apr 1866), 2.

'To the Editor of the Bradford Observer', *Bradford Observer* (1 Jun 1837), 7.

'Today's Radio Programmes', *Sunderland Daily Echo* (23 Jul 1935), 6.

Tongue, Ruth L., *Forgotten Folk-Tales of the English Counties* (London: Routledge and Kegan Paul, 1970).

'Towneley Hall', *Burnley Express* (18 January 1902), 7.

Traice, Elizabeth C., 'The Little Velvet Shoe: A Ghost Story', *Leamington Spa Courier* (24 Jun 1904), 7.

Treddlehoyle, Tom, *The Bairnsla Foaks Annual and Pogmoor Olmenack for 1843* (Barnsley: John Ray, 1843).

Trovesi, Andrea, 'La famiglia di parole da base [bog] "dio" nelle lingue slave (con particolare riguardo alle esclamazioni)', *Mosty mostite: Studi in onore di Marcello Garzaniti*, edited by Alberto Alberti, Maria Chiara Ferro, and Francesca Romoli (Firenze: Firenze University Press, 2016), 217–27.

Tuft, Tansy, 'Bits o' Owd Lanky', *Blackburn Standard* (12 Aug 1899), 8.

Tum O' Dick O' Bobs, 'A Lankisher Encylopædia', *Blackburn Standard* (2 Jun 1894), 2.

———— 'A Lankisher Encylopædia', *Blackburn Standard* (27 Oct 1894), 8.

Turner, John Horsfall, 'Fragments of Local History: No 10, Place Names', *Brighouse News* (Apr 1869) [undated clipping without page or number, recorded http://www.yorkshireindexers.info/wiki/index.php?title=Brighouse_Place_Names, accessed 8 Jan 2020].

Turner, R.C., 'Boggarts, Bogles and Sir Gawain and the Green Knight: Lindow Man and the Oral Tradition', *Lindow Man: The Body in the Bog*, edited by I.M. Stead, J.B. Bourke, and Don R. Brothwell (London: British Museum Publications, 1986), 170–76.

Turner-Bishop, Aidan, '*Fairy* and *Boggart* Sites in Lancashire,' *Lancashire's Sacred Landscape*, (Stroud: History Press, 2010), 94–107.

'TV Treacle Mines closed by vandals ... and Teletubbies', *Lancashire Telegraph* (20 Mar 1998).

Twemlow, Francis Randle, *Twemlows, their Wives and their Homes from Original Records* (Wolverhampton: Whitehead Brothers, 1910).

'Two Brownie Games', *Kirkintilloch Herald* (18 Feb 1931), 2.

'Under the title', *Derbyshire Courier* (16 Nov 1867), 4.

'Up and Down the Country: Ranscliff', *Staffordshire Sentinel and Commercial and General Advertiser* (6 Dec 1879), 7.

Upton, Clive Dave Parry and J.D.A. Widdowson, *Survey of English Dialects: The Dictionary and Grammar* (New York: Routledge, 1994).

Vae Victis, Joseph, 'Rejected by His Brethren, A.D. 1901', *Cumberland & Westmorland Herald* (20 Apr 1901), 5.

Valk, Ülo, 'Ontological Liminality of Ghosts: The Case of a Haunted Hospital' *Storied and Supernatural Places*, edited by Ülo Valk and Daniel Sävborg (Helsinki: Finnish Literature Society, 2018), 93–112.

Varii, 'Fairy Pipes', *The Monthly Chronicle of North-country Lore and Legend* (1889), 561–62.

Vasilev, Georgi, *Heresy and the English Reformation: Bogomil-Cathar Influence on Wycliffe, Langdale, Tyndale and Milton* (Jefferson, NC: McFarland and Co., 2008).

Verney, Frances Parthenope, *Stone Edge* (London: Smith Elder, 1868).

Vicinus, Martha, *The Industrial Muse* (London: Croom Helm, 1974).

Vickery, Roy, *Vickery's Folk Flora* (London: Weidenfeld and Nicolson, 2019).

Vincent, David, *Literacy and Popular Culture: England 1750–1914* (Cambridge: Cambridge University Press, 1989). https://doi.org/10.1017/CBO9780511 560880.

Vollam, J.T., 'In Evil Days: A Story of the Cotton Famine', *Burnley Express* (16 Sep 1891), 4.

W.D. 'Recollections', *Cumberland Pacquet* (18 Sep 1827), 4.

Walcott, Mackenzie, *The East Coast of England from the Thames to the Tweed* (London: Stanford, 1861).

Waldron, David and Christopher Reeve, *Shock: The Black Dog of Bungay* (N.P.: Hidden Publishing, 2010).

Waldron, David and Sharn Waldron, 'Playing the Ghost: Ghost Hoaxing and Supernaturalism in Late Nineteenth-Century Victoria, Australia', *Folklore* 127 (2016), 71–90. https://doi.org/10.1080/0015587X.2015.1121622.

Walker, Barbara G., *The Woman's Encyclopedia of Myths and Secrets* (San Francisco: Harper and Row, 1983).

Walsh, Brian, *The Secret Commonwealth and the Fairy Belief Complex* (N.P.: Xlibris 2002).

Walsh, Marcus, 'Something Old, Something New, Something Borrowed, Something Blue: Christopher Smart and the Lexis of the Peculiar', *The Yearbook of English Studies* 28 (1998), 144–62. https://doi.org/10.2307/3508762.

Walsham, Alexandra, 'The Reformation and "The Disenchantment of the World" Reassessed', *The Historical Journal* 51 (2008), 497–528. https://doi.org/10.1017/S0018246X08006808.

——— *The Reformation of the Landscape: Religion and Identity, and Memory in Early Modern Britain and Ireland* (Oxford: Oxford University Press, 2011).

Ward, John, *Moston Characters at Play* (Manchester: Barber, 1905).

Ward, Nathaniel, *The Simple Cobler of Aggawam in America* (London: John Dever, 1647).

Warner, Marina, *No Go the Bogeyman: Scaring, Lulling and Making Mock* (London: Chatto and Windus, 1998).

Warren, Melanie, *Lancashire Folk: Ghostly Legends and Folklore from Ancient to Modern* (Atglen: Schiffer Publishing 2015).

'Was it a Ghost They Saw?', *Cumberland Pacquet* (22 Jun 1893), 3.

Wasson, Valentina Pavlovna and R. Gordon Wasson, *Mushrooms, Russia and History* (New York: Pantheon Books, 1957), 2 vols.

Waters, Thomas, 'Belief in Witchcraft in Oxfordshire and Warwickshire, c.1860–1900: The Evidence of the Newspaper Archive', *Midland History* 34 (2009), 98–116. https://doi.org/10.1179/175638109X406640.

———— 'They seem to have all died out: witches and witchcraft in Lark Rise to Candleford and the English countryside, c.1830–1930', *Historical Research* 87 (2014), 134–53. https://doi.org/10.1111/1468–2281.12023.

———— 'Magic and the British Middle Classes, 1750–1900', *Journal of British Studies* 54 (2015), 632–53. https://doi.org/10.1017/jbr.2015.56.

————*Cursed Britain: A History of Witchcraft and Black Magic in Modern Times* (New Haven, CT: Yale, 2019).

Watson, Nigel, 'The Case of the Liverpool Leprechauns', *Magonia* (1985), republished http://magoniamagazine.blogspot.com/2013/11/the-case-of-liverpool-leprechauns.html [accessed 1 Jan 2019].

Waugh, Edwin *Sketches of Lancashire Life and Localities* (London: Whittaker, 1855).

———— *Tufts of Heather* (Manchester: Heywood, 1881).

———— *The Chimney Corner* (Manchester: Heywood, 1890).

———— *Poems and Songs* (London: Heywood, 1893).

———— *Besom Ben Stories* (Manchester: Heywood, 1900).

Way, Albert, *Promptorium parvulorum sive clericorum, dictionarius anglo-latinus princeps* (London: Camden Society, 1843), 3 vols.

Webster, John, *The displaying of supposed witchcraft wherein is affirmed that there are many sorts of deceivers and impostors and divers persons under a passive delusion of melancholy and fancy, but that there is a corporeal league made betwixt the Devil and the witch ... is utterly denied and disproved: wherein also is handled, the existence of angels and spirits, the truth of apparitions, the nature of astral and sydereal spirits, the force of charms, and philters, with other abstruse matters* (London: J.M., 1677).

Wedgwood, Hensleigh, 'On English Etymologies', *Transactions of the Philological Society* 5 (1851), 31–39. https://doi.org/10.1111/j.1467–968X.1851.tb00138.x.

Weeks, Self 'Haunted Houses: Some Clitheroe Legends', *Burnley Express and Advertiser* (9 Jun 1900), 2.

———— 'Haunted Houses: Some Clitheroe Legends', *Burnley News* (25 May 1918), 7.

Weld, John, *A History of Leagram: The Park and Manor* (Manchester: Chetham Society, 1913).

Wentworth, Peter, *The History and Annals of Blackley and Neighbourhood* (Middleton: J. Bagot, 1892).

Wentz, W.Y. Evans, *The Fairy-Faith in Celtic Countries* (Oxford: Oxford University Press, 1911).

'Wesleyan Missionary Society', *North Devon Journal* (14 May 1863), 5.

West, Thomas, *A Guide to the Lakes* (Kendal: William Pennington, 1812 [1778]).

Westaway, Jonathan and Richard D. Harrison, '"The Surey Demoniack":

Defining Protestantism in 1690s Lancashire', *Unity and Diversity in the Church*, edited by R. Swanson (Oxford: Blackwell, 1996), 263–82. https://doi.org/10.1017/S042420840001545X.

Westwood, Jennifer, *Albion: A Guide to Legendary Britain* (London: Grafton, 1992 [1985]).

Westwood, Jennifer and Jacqueline Simpson, *The Lore of the Land* (London: Penguin, 2005).

'Wheatley Lane', *Burnley Express* (28 July 1897), 3.

Whitaker, Thomas, *An History of the Original Parish of Whalley, and Honor of Clitheroe* (London: Nichols, Son and Bentley, 1818).

———— *An History of Richmondshire, in the North riding of the county of York: together with those parts of the Everwicschire of Domesday which form the wapentakes of Lonsdale, Ewecross, and Westmoreland* (London: Longman, 1823), 2 vols.

White, Walter, *A Month in Yorkshire* (London: Chapman and Hall, 1861).

Whitehall, John, *The Leviathan found out, or, The answer to Mr. Hobbes's Leviathan in that which my Lord of Clarendon hath past over* (London: A. Godbid, 1679).

Whitehead, Anthony, *Legends of Westmorland and Other Poems With Notes* (Penrith: R. Scott, 1896).

Whittingham, William, *A Brieff Discours off the Troubles begonne at Franckford in Germany Anno Domini 1554 Abowte the booke off off* [sic] *common prayer and ceremonies, and continued by the Englishe men theyre* (1575).

Whittle, Mrs James, 'Festivities and Superstitions of Devonshire', *Bentley's Miscellany* 21 (1847), 301–10.

'Who & What Was Tom Healey?', *Burnley Advertiser* (1 Jul 1871), 3.

Widdowson, John, 'The Bogeyman: Some Preliminary Observations on Frightening Figures', *Folklore* 82 (1971), 99–115. https://doi.org/10.1080/0015587X.1971.9716716.

———— 'Aspects of Traditional Verbal Control, Threats and Threatening Figures in Newfoundland Folklore' (unpublished doctoral thesis, Memorial University, St Johns, 1972).

Wiegelmann, Günter and Joan L. Cotter, 'The *Atlas der deutschen Volkskunde* and the Geographical Research Method', *Journal of the Folklore Institute* 5 (1968), 187–97. https://doi.org/10.2307/3814210.

Wigfull, Chas. S., 'Alton Addenda', *Derbyshire Advertiser* (6 May 1927), 31.

Wilbraham, Roger, *An Attempt at a Glossary of Some Words Used in Cheshire* (London: Bulmer, 1820).

Wildhaber, Robert, 'Folk Atlas Mapping', *Folklore and Folklife: An Introduction*, ed. Richard Dorson (Chicago: University of Chicago Press, 1972), 479–96.

Wilkinson, P.R., *Thesaurus of Traditional English Metaphors (Second Edition)* (London: Routledge, 2009 [2002]).

Wilkinson, T.T., 'On the Popular Customs and Superstitions of Lancashire: Part 2', *Transactions of the Historic Society of Lancashire and Cheshire* 12 (1859–1860), 85–98.

———— 'On the Druidical Rock Basins in the Neighbourhood of Burnley', *Transactions of the Historic Society of Lancashire and Cheshire* 5 (1865), 1–12.

———— 'Ancient Mansions Near Burnley; their history and owners', *Burnley Gazette* (1 Mar 1873), 6.

———— 'Boggart Ho' Clough', *Huddersfield College Magazine* 2 (1874), 170–71.

———— 'On the Lancashire Dialect: More Especially as Relating to the Blackburn Hundred', *Burnley Literary and Scientific Club* 1 (1874–1881), 56–60.

Wilkinson, Tattersall, 'The Barcroft Boggart', *Burnley Express* (16 Apr 1887), 10.

———— 'Folk lore of the District: Some Interesting Tales of Superstition', *Burnley Express* (27 Feb 1895), 3.

———— 'Local Folklore', *The Halifax Antiquarian Society* (1904), 2–9.

———— 'A Christmas Tale: A Legend of By-Gone Days', *Burnley Gazette* (22 Dec 1906), 7.

Wilkinson, Tattersall and J.F. Tattersall, *Memories of Hurstwood, Burnley, Lancashire. With tales and traditions of the neighbourhood* (Burnley: J. & A. Lupton, 1889).

Willan, Robert, 'A List of Ancient Words at Present Used in the Mountainous District of the West Riding of Yorkshire', *Archaeologia or Miscellaneous Tracts Relating to Antiquity, Society of Antiquaries of London* 17 (1814), 135–67. https://doi.org/10.1017/S0261340900017707.

Williams, Noel, 'The Semantics of the Word Fairy: Making Meaning Out of Thin Air', *The Good People: New Fairylore Essays*, edited by Peter Narváez (Lexington: University Press of Kentucky, 1997), 457–78.

Williams, S.C., *Religious Belief and Popular Culture in Southwark, c.1880–1939* (Oxford: Oxford University Press, 1999). https://doi.org/10.1093/acprof:oso/9780198207696.001.0001.

Wilson, John F., *Lighting the Town: A Study of the Management in the North West Gas Industry, 1805–1880* (London: PCP Publishing, 1991).

Wilson, W., 'Thirlmere and Its Associations', *Transactions of the Cumberland Association for the Advancement of Literature and Science* 9 (1883–1884), 53–82.

Winberry, John J., 'The Elusive Elf: Some Thoughts on the Nature and Origin of the Irish Leprechaun', *Folklore* 87 (1976), 63–75.

Winterbottom, Vera, *The Devil in Lancashire* (Stockport: Cloister Press 1962).

Wiseman, A.G., 'A Local Boggart Tale', *Burnley News* (24 Oct 1914), 3.

'Woman burned as a witch in Peruvian rainforest, prosecutor says', *Guardian* (28 Sep 2016).

Wong, Tessa and Saira Asher, 'Malaysia school shuts after "mass hysteria" outbreak', *https://www.bbc.com/news/world-asia-36069636* (19 Apr 2016) [accessed 10 May 2021].

Wood, Andy, 'Spectral Lordship, popular memory and the boggart of Towneley Hall', *Popular Culture and Political Agency in Early Modern England and Ireland*, edited by Michael J. Braddick and Phil Withington (Woodbridge: Boydell, 2017), 109–22.

Wood, Anthony A., *Athenae Oxonienses: an Exact History of all the Writers and Bishops who have had their Education in the University of Oxford* (London: F.C. Rivington and Co.., 1813–1820), 4 vols.

Wood, Roger, *The Boggarts of Boggart Hole Clough* (N.P.: Author House, 2006).

Woodyard, Chris and Simon Young, 'Three Notes and a Handlist of North American Fairies', *Supernatural Studies* 6 (2019), 56–85.

Worsaae, J.J.A., *An Account of the Danes and Norwegians in England, Scotland, and Ireland* (London: John Murray, 1852). https://doi.org/10.1093/nq/s1-V.129.369d.

Wright, Elizabeth Mary, *Rustic Speech and Folk-lore* (Oxford: Oxford University Press, 1918).

———— *The life of Joseph Wright* (London: Oxford University Press, 1932), 2 vols.

Wright, Joseph, *A grammar of the dialect of Windhill, in the West Riding of Yorkshire* (London: Trübner, 1892).

———— (ed.), *The English Dialect Dictionary, being the complete vocabulary of all dialect words still in use, or known to have been in use during the last two hundred years; founded on the publications of the English Dialect Society and on a large amount of material never before printed* (Oxford: Oxford University Press, 1898–1905), 6 vols.

'Wrightington Cycle Tragedy', *Lancashire Evening Post* (25 Feb 1941), 5.

Wrigley, Ammon, *Saddleworth Superstitions and Folk Customs* (Oldham: W.E. Clegg Printer and Bookseller, 1909).

———— *The Wind Among the Heather* (Huddersfield, Alfred Jubb & Son, 1916).

———— *Old Lancashire Words and Folk Sayings* (Stalybridge: Geo. Whittaker and Sons, 1940).

X, Miss [A. Goodrich Freer], *Essays in Psychical Research* (London: George Redway, 1899).

Yarwood, John, 'A Novel Swarm-Catcher', *The British Bee Journal* 27 (1899), 194–95.

Yeats, W.B., *Irish Fairy and Folk Tales* (London: Walter Scott, 1893).

'York Assizes', *Lancaster Gazette* (30 Mar 1805), 4.

'Yorkshire Dialects', *Yorkshire Folk-lore Journal* 1 (1888), 12–16.

Young, Francis, *A History of Anglican Exorcism: Deliverance and Demonology in Church Ritual* (London: I.B.Tauris, 2018). https://doi.org/10.5040/978135 0985056.

Young, Simon, 'Fairies and Railways: A Nineteenth-Century Topos and its Origins', *Notes and Queries* 59 (2012), 401–03. https://doi.org/10.1093/notesj/gjs095.

————— 'Some Notes on Irish Fairy Changelings in Nineteenth-Century Newspapers', *Béascna* 8 (2013), 34–47.

————— 'Boggart Hole Clough: Sources, Publics and Bogies', *Transactions of the Antiquarian Society for Lancashire and Cheshire* 109 (2013), 115–44.

————— 'The Lancashire Boggart Plays: A Lost Local Theatre Tradition?' *Transactions of the Historic Society of Lancashire and Cheshire* 163 (2014), 93–110. https://doi.org/10.3828/transactions.163.8.

————— '"To sound cheerily in other ears when we are no more": Edward Slater and the Burnley Part Song Union', *Retrospective* 32 (2014), 17–27.

————— 'What is a Boggart Hole?' *Nomina* 37 (2014), 73–107.

————— 'Boggart Dialect Literature and a Handlist of Boggart Works', *Tradition Today* 5 (2016), 1–19.

————— 'In Search of England's Fairy Trees: The Fair Oak of Bowland', *Northern Earth* 147 (2016), 16–21.

————— '*Shantooe Jest*: A Forgotten Nineteenth-Century Fairy Saga', *Supernatural Studies* 3 (2016), 9–22.

————— 'What are Feorin?', *Yorkshire Dialect Society* 23 (2017), 55–61. https://doi.org/10.1144/pygs2015–364.

————— 'In Search of Holden Rag', *Retrospective* 35 (2017), 3–10.

————— 'Joseph Wright meets the Boggart', *Folk Life* 56 (2018), 1–13. https://doi.org/10.1080/04308778.2018.1446400.

————— 'And a Historical Folklore Survey? A Reply to John Widdowson's "New Beginnings"', *Folklore* 129 (2018), 181–91. https://doi.org/10.1080/0015 587X.2018.1441948.

————— 'Boggart Origins in Dialect and Folklore', *Transactions of the Yorkshire Dialect Society* 23(2018), 2–34.

————— 'When Did Fairies Get Wings?', *The Paranormal and Popular Culture: A Postmodern Religious Landscape*, edited by Darryl Caterine and John W. Morehead (London: Routledge, 2019), 253–74. https://doi.org/10.4324/9781315184661–20.

———— 'In Search of Jenny Greenteeth', *Gramayre* 16 (2019), 24–38.

———— 'The Fairy Placenames of Cumbria', *Tradition Today* 8 (2019), 41–51.

———— 'Public Bogies and Supernatural Landscapes in the North West of England in the Nineteenth Century', *Time and Mind* 13 (2020), 1–26.

———— *The Boggart Sourcebook: Texts and Memories for the Study of the British Supernatural* (Exeter: Exeter University Press, 2021). https://doi.org/10.47788/QXUA4856

Zender, Matthias *et al.*, *Der Atlas der deutschen Volkskunde* (Marburg: N-G. Elwert Verlag, 1959–1982), 2 vols.

Index

CPSIA information can be obtained
at www.ICGtesting.com
Printed in the USA
LVHW102319041122
732396LV00003B/5